REVIEWS FOR THE EMPIRES OF DUST TRILOGY

'Fierce, gripping fantasy, exquisitely written; bitter, funny and heart-rending by turns' Adrian Tchaikovsky, Clarke Award Winner, *Children of Time*

'A dynamic new voice' Scott Lynch

'Gripping ... definitely one to read and prize' *Publishers Weekly* starred review

'A masterwork of dark fantasy' *Nightmarish Conjurings*

'One of the most exciting authors not only in grimdark but in fantasy ... Eclipses almost everything else I've read this year' *Grimdark Magazine*

'Literary Game of Thrones' *Sunday Times*

'Dazzling. Howls like early Moorcock, converses like the best of Le Guin' *Daily Mail*

'Weaves a spell that will consume you' *Barnes and Noble*

'Stunning ... Epic' *Starburst Magazine*

'Immense depth and breadth ... the best voice in the genre' *Three Crows Magazine*

'All hail the queen of grimdark fantasy!' Michael R Fletcher

'Grim, gritty and fast paced, with great battle scenes! Anna Smith Spark is one to watch' Andy Remic

'Marked by intense, action-packed battle scenes, this grimdark epic fantasy is the escape you need right now' *Kirkus Review*

'Gritty and glorious!' Miles Cameron

'On a par with R Scott Bakker' *Grimdark Alliance*
'Brilliantly powerful ... enthralling' *Run Along the Shelves*

'The master strokes of a poet who is completely comfortable in her craft ... Joe Abercrombie, Scott Lynch and Mark Lawrence make way because the Queen of grimdark is ready to lead the charge in a new wave of dark fantasy fiction' *Fantasy Faction*

'One of the most unique writing styles I've ever read, and it is an absolute pleasure to read' *Superstar Drifter*

'Flowing like molten bronze ... it carries all before it' *Fantasy Hive*

A WOMAN OF
THE SWORD

ANNA SMITH SPARK

Text Copyright 2023 Anna Smith Spark
Cover 2023 © Stas Borodin

Editorial Team: Francesca T Barbini & Shona Kinsella

First published by Luna Press Publishing, Edinburgh, 2023
All rights reserved.

A CIP catalogue record is available from the British Library
www.lunapresspublishing.com

ISBN-13: 978-1-915556-06-6

*For all the mothers who got through
the last few years.*

Contents

Part One

The Soldier

One

'Lidae!'

The voice is so desperate. She lashes out with long fingers, takes a man down, rushes at him to hack him down dead. Panic in the voice calling her. Delin. Poor innocent thing. A man comes at her at a run, almost throws himself into her sword. Useless, she thinks, the way he's coming at her, but he's young, she sees it in his boy's bright eyes as she takes him down, she sees him see her as she kills him and he's startled. Delin's voice calls urgently.

'Lidae! Lidae!'

She says, although he can't hear her, 'I'm coming, Delin.' These poor sweet boys. All a fun game, they think, playing. *'Let's fight!' they shout at each other. 'Hit me, come on! You a coward or something?'* She says, 'Hold on, I'm coming, Delin.' She can look for a moment, the battle ebbs just here just now, it's strange, she thinks, when she looks back at all the battles she's fought in, the way killing flows and ebbs. A lump of flesh that might be Delin is down half-way to dying, trying to ward off blows of enemy weight. He was crying last night, in the ranks, his eyes beneath his bronze helmet were sore and red. He sees her.

'Lidae! Help me! Please!'

'I'm coming, I'm coming, Delin.' They want so much out of her, these poor young soldier boys. *'You're like a mother to them, Lidae,'* Eralene the only other woman in the squad says. *'You should make them learn the hard way.'*

But Eralene is so young. And the men—the boys—they're so young.

But the killing had ebbed here, like water ebbs on shingle, the enemy is fighting other soldiers in their army, men she does not know. She runs in three steps over to Delin's crouching body, kills the man bent killing over him. Delin stumbles to his feet, bloody, coughing. She pulls his arm to get him up quicker, because at any moment the fighting will begin hard again over them.

'Thank you, Lidae,' Delin whispers. His voice is dry and cracked, his tongue is dust in his bloody mouth. He's back crying. Poor boy, she thinks.

She shrugs. 'It's nothing.' In the brief pause she takes out her waterskin, goes to drink. She gives it to Delin, first, to drink.

Delin's eyes widen, he stares past her into the melee of the battlefield. Silver light in the sky behind him. Crowns him. He croaks out in terror: 'The enemy! They're coming again!'

She thinks, mocking him: this is a battlefield, remember, Delin? A pitched battle that I suspect we may be losing. The enemy ranks— traitors, betrayers, the enemy of all those who serve the true king. The enemy come at us and come at us, gold banners flying proud, for hours we grappled with them, our lines almost embracing, spears gripped teeth clenched we swayed together, knee to knee cheek to cheek. They broke us. Or we broke them. I can scarcely remember. So well matched we were, our lines and the enemy lines in gold, shining. All day we have fought until the black earth beneath us is stained red. The last of it now, knots of men slugging it out with their swords, spears long broken and abandoned, too cumbersome, the great ashwood spears, too unwieldy now to lift. An answering flash in the sky behind her, brighter, longer, almost blinding, a smell of hot metal, roasted meat. The enemy's banners are sunlit, glowing, and the battle for us I think will soon be lost.

'They're coming, Lidae!' Delin cries out again. Ten of them, maybe. Tall hard bronze men, eyes blazing. Gold badges that sing out their treachery to everything Lidae is. They come straight at Lidae and Delin. Red cloaks, red nodding horsehair plumes on their helmets. Veterans and masters of this last stage of the fighting.

A hard enemy voice roars, 'The leader there! Get him!'

She realises, as their swords reach for her, that 'him', 'the leader', the enemy means her, Lidae, a grey-haired middle-aged woman.

'Lidae!' Delin shrieks. She thinks: I told you, I warned you, Delin, we are losing. A great two-handed blade takes the boy down beneath it. His teeth gnaw the black earth the light hisses from his body cold silence claims him. She can think, briefly: oh poor sweet Delin. And anger: I saved his life, I gave him the last of my water, I killed three man to save him, but now he's dead. I'll be avenged on the man who killed him. The two-handed sword swings towards her, dripping blue fire. A huge man, all of bronze and iron. Spittle on his mouth, his lips are parted, panting. His cheeks are flushed. She is disgusted, after the boy's dying fear. But she knows, sees, as the enemy squares up to her, that she is also flushed, eager, panting. Her own excitement disgusts him.

Bronze eyes stare down at her. She stands in her enemy's shadow. Bronze weight between her and the sun. Bronze mouth smiling. He's killed the man beside her, young, strong, a bull-calf, muscles flexed. Kill this greying woman easy as breathing. The two-handed sword swings...

Crash. Music. Blue sparks, silver ripples, red light gleaming.

Their swords meet.

Briefly she can see herself, outside of herself, a shining weight of bronze, fine armour, sweating, dancing, so much blood on her sword, blood splashing her face. Triumphant. She can see it like a story, flow of her arms, her blade flowing, her feet twist in the dark earth this perfect moment. Blood hangs in the air before her. She was born, she thinks, to do this. She is so good at this. Her sword alive in her hand. She strikes out, iron clashes against iron, iron crashes against bronze. Sparks like the blacksmith's anvil. He is good at this also, and that makes her heart leap. The world is spinning around her in fire. She is more alive that she can imagine. She cannot think what she is doing in this bright moment, but she feels how fine everything is. She shouts in triumph. And he moves and she moves, their blades ring and ring. He is panting, and now he is gasping, grunting, because he is afraid she can kill him. His sword almost cuts her, she flinches, skips, her feet trample down on Delin's blood. Her sword almost cuts him.

She is so alive. She is. So. Damned. Good. At. This.

And the man is dead.

And another man is dead. And another man is dead.

'Lidae!'

The battle's fading now. Ebb tide of life and hope. A voice, shaky, uncertain still, shouts, 'Victory!' Another, pale, hesitant, calls out, 'Have we won?'

A shudder of disappointment, in her, in the voice calling: is that the end of it? We have to stop? Cease to be these great god-like powers of iron and bronze. She, Lidae, wipes sweat from her lips, looks around her hoping for more fighting. A struggle, there, look, where the sunlight falls, men pushing, scrabbling, someone goes down in a splash of red. Lidae runs towards it. Big glorious men still fighting. Gold badges. Enemies. Traitors. Throws herself at them. I'm so good at this. So alive. I don't want this moment to end.

And she, Lidae, thinks, hesitantly; those voices calling victory ...

they are not my companions' voices. She thinks, in great grief: we are indeed losing. All I am, all I can be, brilliant bright Lidae the soldier, but it's lost now, the enemy is claiming the battle as won. Traitors against everything I have fought for these ten long sweet years. Such grief. Fears, anxieties, other parts of her life, come back to her. If I am not a solder for the king… She hacks and swings at the enemy still fighting, she can hear at a distance her own voice scream at them. She presses forward, sword raised, smiling. Red light cast on her face. They cower before her. Fear her. She is the star that marks the coming of winter, brings the snowfall, death from cold and hunger in dark nights. She is the storm in the high mountains. She thinks: we are lost, my comrades are dead around me, but I, Lidae, I can still be a warrior. I will not cease from the fighting.

Behind her, distant somewhere, she can hear another young man's voice calling her name. It sounds familiar. Sweet, lisping. Rainwater and apple blossom and birdsong. Almost, almost, she turns her head to answer. 'We've lost,' the voice calls, grieving, and she wants to go to it. Comfort it. A voice she cares about far more than almost anything else.

Like a mother to them, Lidae.

She shakes her head, she is imagining it, she thinks. The woman that voice is calling is far away. And think of … Delin, she thinks, struggling in her mind to remember his name, poor young boy, I went to help him and a moment later he was dead. She drives herself harder into her enemies. She fights alone. Alone, undefeated, she, Lidae the soldier, will kill them.

A man swims in the blood before her. Gold badge. Gold sunlit banner. She nods at him. Beckons him. They approach to kill each other. His armour is battered, his sword is strong. His young man's eyes search her face, disgusted. She raises her blade at him. Traitor, betrayer, enemy of her army and her king. Her sword is hot in her hand, hungry. A growl of rage builds in her throat. If we've lost, if I am no longer a soldier in the true king's army … I think my heart will break. The gold badge shines for the enemy's victory. Revolting. She lunges forward to kill him. Spittle on her lips. The enemy is young, handsome in his armour, blood slicks across his fine-carved face. In defeat, even, the brief victory of killing him. He is looking at her, confused. She looks in confusion back at him.

Trumpets are blowing to mark the enemy victory. The enemy soldier before her lowers his sword, hesitant. His hair, his skin, his eyes, this young man, this enemy, traitor, lump of meat to hack down and kill—

'Mother,' the enemy soldier says.

Part Two

The Mother

Two

Lidae lay on her back in the pale morning and watched the may tree blossom dance in the wind. The dawn splendour had faded, a grey sunshine of spring with the sky a nothing colour, cloud-scudded; the wind had changed direction and the air smelled damp, a good smell of rich soil, of green shoots crushed against her body. Look to windward and the sky and the air were clear running right onto the horizon, green grass and green trees. The may tree was just coming into blossom, a sweet heavy stink of scent to it up close where the branches reach downwards, the flowers that seemed like smiling eyes in the green. On all the field bounds, great banks of whitelace-flower were foaming up. Beech mast from the previous autumn, fallen beech leaves faded from fire-red to old bronze. In a shaft of sunlight mayflies were dancing. A great high bank of roots and moss and wild garlic plants and violets, traced through with animal tracks like wading through a stream. Meadows so thick with buttercups the air seemed golden, the sky seemed bathed in gold. Before her, just visible as a mark in the green and a drift of hearth smoke, the little village of Salith Drylth, 'Bright Field', named for the buttercups and the may blossom, and her own little farmstead beyond that. Behind her, the sea stretched itself grey-silver, moving as the wind blows the young stems of a wheat field, murmuring, nodding, tracing out patterns, moving with the ripple of a child's limbs. On the shingle beach a fire burned. The smoke of her husband's funeral pyre rose grey into the light.

All night, long and bitter, she had sat by the pyre, watching the flames. The body was raised up on a stack of black rocks, the height of a man's waist: at high tide, in the night, the water had lapped at the wood of the pyre, making the flames flicker and hiss. In the dark the flames had gleamed in the water. The reflection of the fire had moved as the waves moved, as the sparks above it flew up. It had looked to her like the beating of great wings. She had stood with the sea breaking around her ankles, her dress wet and heavy around her legs, the smoke in her eyes; she had stood close enough to the fire that she felt the heat on her face although she had shivered with cold in the sea and the wind. The flames had leapt up high, dancing. The darkness, and her husband's life leaping up bright. She had seen a thousand funeral pyres burn but here she had felt a great new fear and wonder. A glorious, terrible thing.

The dawn had tamped down the light of the fire, the body had sunk down as grey ash and blackened bones. The gulls cried out overhead. The fire would soon burn itself to nothing. The tide went out, leaving a mound of black rocks on the shingle, the embers of the pyre smouldering, stinking.

A woman of almost forty, tall and strong like the fire. White-pale skin with the thick rough redness of a life spent out in the open. Dark hair, 'raven hair, black horse hair, black iron hair,' her husband had called it, black like the black rocks and the ash. She had hacked her hair short for mourning; when it grew back long she thought it would be mostly grey. The locks of her hair had burned up as soon as the pyre caught, scattered over her husband's dead hands. The smell of it had been filled with memory.

The white blossom danced and scattered. She was wet with salt and wet with dew. She got up slowly, looked down at the green fields, the meadows, the trees dancing. The leaves of the beech trees whispered, a blackbird sang, a skylark sang, the gulls screamed. She half turned to look at the beach behind her, then turned away. She walked down the slope of the fields shimmering. A boggy place, yellow mallow-flowers, crossing a stream so narrow she could step across, soft damp fetid mud sucking at her feet. A dragonfly, brilliant blue. Pushing through a bank of whitelace as high as her shoulders, pollen and petals dusting her, tasting the damp sweet scent. Spider webs dew-jewelled. Little green pale clear-winged flying things. Beneath the beech trees there were bluebells, crushed and trampled, staining the earth blue. A great beating of wings, panicked, as a woodpigeon in the trees started up in flight. A crow called out, very loudly; it made her jump even though she could see it. The peace of being alone in the waking world, her hands and her feet wet on the wet earth, listening, feeling. Bury her husband and bury the last of the old years, and live in peace.

'Lidae!'

Lidae sat down at the table in the house she and her husband had shared. Her husband's chair stood opposite her. She could almost see him.

'Lidae.'

One of the women from Salith village, Cythra, who had become perhaps her closest friend. Cythra's hair was grey-silver-golden and made Lidae think of dried grasses in the heat of late summer. Her eyes were green-grey as the sea. Her face and her hands were red and rough like Lidae's. Strong thick muscled arms, strong, broad hands, worn and scarred in different ways and the same ways to Lidae.

'It's done, then?' Cythra said. She poured a cup of milk; Lidae drank it without speaking. The cup was silver, a big heavy wine cup, decorated in enamel, yellow garlands around a scene of fighting birds. Cythra still looked confused at the cup. Had never seen such a thing, dreamed of such a thing. Her hands and Lidae's hands looked crude against the silverwork.

'Is it done then?' Cythra said again.

'I'll have to go back later,' Lidae said. 'Gather the ashes up.' She ran her fingers over the birds on the cup. 'I'll bury this with him.'

'Will you bring the children?'

She thought for a time. 'No.'

'They'll want to see their father buried, Lidae.'

'They saw him dead.' She closed her eyes. So tired. Her clothes were damp and vile, her hair smelled of the smoke that had burned her husband away. She rubbed her face and found it was smudged with ashes. She felt sick, frightened, started up again to scrub water over her face.

'I'll heat you some water,' said Cythra. 'Have something to eat first, Lidae, then a wash, before you do anything.' She fetched bread and soft white cheese and a jar of honey, began to heat the big iron kettle for washing and for tea. Caring, like a mother caring for children. Although she was barely older than Lidae.

'I can do that myself. I'm fine, it's fine, Cythra.' Years and years and years, she had done everything herself, and before that and after that if something was done for her it was done by a campslave ordered and cowering.

'Not today,' Cythra said. 'Let me do it.'

And that was nice, not having to do it. Carrying water, heating water … slave things. Cythra's arms creaked, lifting the big kettle.

'I forget every time, how heavy this is,' Cythra said. 'I'll need more water.'

'There's a crock by the door there,' Lidae said, pointing, her mouth full of bread.

'By the door? A wonder the boys haven't kicked it over.'

'I suppose so. Yes.' A stupid place, yes, she always knew that, and the boys had kicked it over before now, once broken a full crock. They'd never have left a crock of water lying around where someone could knock it over in camp, if a campservant did it she'd have been bawled half to pieces. Next time, when I set up house properly, definitely I'll put it somewhere better, Lidae thought.

The house was small, two rooms and a loft place, a barn for animals behind it; the sound of the cow and the calf they kept there moving against the thin wall. Lidae liked to go in there, breathe in the smell of the cow, warm and hay soft, even the smell of its dung. She like the sound of it now moving behind the wall. She went through into the sleeping place, the bed she and her husband had shared with its embroidered silk coverlet, red and real silver, water-stained and smoke-stained, a tear in it that she had mended with crude stitches in rough thread. Far too big for their bed. A chest stood at the foot of the bed, the wood pale gold, almost glowing, the colour of honey or of good butter, carved with a design of flowers and leaves and ripe apples through which hidden faces seemed to gaze. Lidae bent down before it, looked at it. Opened it. Inside the chest was a sword with a piece of red glass in the hilt like a ruby, a warrior's helmet made in fine bronze with a crest of horsehair dyed red. Her husband's eyes and her eyes had once met through the dark eye holes in the bronze. She carried it back into the main room where Cythra was fussing over the fire while the water heated in the cauldron.

The smell of hot metal stopped her, as the smell of her husband's body burning had stopped her. A hand striking her. A hot red wound seemed to open in her face. She had boiled water in the cauldron every day for eight years, it had been many years since the smell of metal had caught her like this. She clutched at the chair her husband had used to sit in, put her helmet down heavily on the table, tried to hear the sound of the cow and the calf moving on the other side of the wall behind her.

'Lidae?' said Cythra. 'Lidae?' The woman put her arms around her. And Lidae finally began to weep.

His face running with sweat, his eyes open and blind seeing nothing or seeing something so far off, she had known, always, she had known what he saw as he lay dying, somewhere far distant, she had wanted to see it again with him. He had cried out words that their children heard as nonsense. 'He is raging against his fever,' she had told them, and the lie had been heavy as stones in her mouth, and his words had sung in her head.

His beautiful yellow hair that had been one of the things she first liked about him; when he was ill she had had to cut it off him with a knife, she had a lock of it, a thick curl bright as buttercups, smelling of blood. His strong body, withering. In the last days he had lost control of his bladder and bowels, she had had to clean him, wipe the muck from him as she had to wipe the muck from their children, as he had had to wipe the muck from her when she had wrestled with her own body in childbirth. He whom she had nursed through fever once before when a wound was infected. He who had nursed her through the same. He had saved her life then, held her hand while she was screaming, he had watched while another man scraped pus from her, sewed up the wound in her thigh. She had realised then that he loved her and that she could trust him, and now he was dead.

'A scratch, nothing,' he had said, 'a scratch while cutting wood. When you think what you and I have seen…' His hand had swollen, the skin bruise-coloured like they had seen the sky once, before a great, vast storm. Rena the healer from the village had come with herbs and stones and bones and the rattle of walnut shells, muttered things over the swelling, and then suddenly she and he had both known. He who had been so strong, who had laughed off so many wounds, who had seen and done such things.

'I'll go and fetch the children,' said Cythra. 'They need to see him buried, Lidae, they need to say goodbye to him also.'

'They saw him before I burned him.' She thought: they saw him whole. They said goodbye then and it hurt them then, I saw them as they looked at him. I never want to see their faces like that again, never, that grief they had for him.

'Rena came and made a charm, Mummy, you asked her to come, and do it right, so how can this be happening?'

But she nodded slowly, too weak with her grief to argue.

'They should see him buried,' Cythra said again. She does not like it that I burned him, Lidae thought. And he died of sickness, I had no right to burn him. The people here are buried in the rich black earth beneath their houses, lie with their parents and their parents' parents before them. Part of the house, like the bed they were born and died in, like the cauldron and the tripod, the grindstone, the cow in the byre.

Taste the rot of his body every day as she trampled over him. She

washed her face and her hands, changed into dry clothes, went back
down to the shore. The tide was coming in, she would have to paddle
again, she knotted her dress up around her hips, walked out. The sea was
so cold it made her gasp.

The pyre had burned out, when she reached it; the sea had come
as high as her knees. The black stones beneath the water gleamed, the
wood of the pyre was thick ash, cold. Her husband's bones were charred
and half consumed. Pieces of his skull. The long bones of his legs. His
sword was blackened and damaged, the gold leaf on the hilt and the
cord for the handgrip burned away. She gathered up the remains in his
sealskin knapsack, hung the sword at her hip, waded back to the shore.
The seabirds wheeled far overhead and did not come near. Her hands
were crusted with his ashes, mixed with saltwater to make a black paste.
Tiny pebbles and seashells and strands of brilliant green seaweed crusted
themselves to her wet legs.

When she got back to the house Cythra had brought the children
back, they pushed up around her like little bull calves, hugging her with
their silken arms plump as fruit, thin and fragile as dry twigs. Their grief
for their father gone a moment in their happiness at their mother. And it
was an astonishing thing, still, that she should have these two children,
her own children. They pressed against her with the sand rubbing off her
legs onto them.

'You've been away a day and a night and this morning, little ones,
that's all.'

Pleasing: her husband went away for days, hunting, and they did not
wallow the same way in him.

Exhausting: a day and a night, little ones, that's all you've been away,
and that's the longest you've ever been away from me.

She hugged them back, tightly and fiercely. My loves. My small
things. They were finally old enough she could leave them with him and
be alone for a while, and now he was dead.

'But where's father?' the younger one, Samei, said brightly.

Lidae looked at Cythra. But what can I say? They saw him dead. They
saw their father dying and they saw him dead. And she thought: but I
have seen more death than I can remember, and I cannot understand,
truly, that he is dead. Even as I lit his pyre, she thought, I expected him
to be there beside me, '*Let me help you, Lidae,*' helping me heft his body
up onto the black stones and the wood.

A memory, then, very strong and clear, a child perhaps the same age
as Samei her youngest, clutching its dead mother's body, refusing to let

go of the body even as soldiers dragged it away, 'Mummy, Mummy, help me, they're taking her away.' Her own confusion, now the memories came, of seeing a comrade die, shouting and fierce beside her and then nothing. Of seeing a column march out and later they did not march back, then other men had their squad name and their duties like they'd never been.

'Your father's gone,' she said, her voice very weak. She stared stricken at Cythra. 'Your father's gone, remember Samei, smallest thing?'

Samei said, 'Why didn't you stop him?'

'Your father ... your father's dead, your father ... remember Samei?' I tried to stop him going, I tried to keep him. She sounded almost angry, and she saw the boys' faces crumple up. She stared over at Cythra in a panic. The boys were both about to start sobbing. Shrieking.

'Let's find something to eat, shall we?' said Cythra. Her hair shone like old dried apples in the dim of the house. 'Your mother's tired, look, she's had a hard few days. Let's get her something to eat.' Cythra took the boys by the hand, turned them towards the table. 'We'll make your mother a cup of tea, shall we? Let's see what we can find to eat, then.'

'Honey cakes!' said Samei.

'Clever thinking, Samei boy.'

The relief that they stopped crying, the pain that they stopped crying. Clever thinking, Cythra, you always know what to do. Lidae thought: Why can't I do it like that, easily, say the things that stop them crying rather than make them cry worse? Cythra the wise mother woman who knows what to do, how to comfort. Sometimes Samei would call Cythra 'mummy' without noticing, and Ryn had done the same, when he was little, didn't notice now to correct Samei.

I've stood on the battlefield while dragons fought in the sky above me. I've felt the heat of their fires overhead. I've stood in my line, unmoving while white mage fire runs over the bodies of the men next to me, burns them away to nothing. I've walked through a wall of dragon fire, my sword smoking and glowing, my face blazing with heat. I've stood my ground while the sky grows black with shadows, they came down on me with claws and great bloodied teeth and I held the line, hacked away pointlessly at them. But Cythra the wise woman ... she knows what to do.

Lidae sat down at the table. Closed her eyes for a moment. So the house was filled with bustle, Cythra and the children putting together more food, oatcakes, honey, smoked fish, Ryn dropping the oil jar and crying that Samei had pushed him, suddenly seeming briefly younger than his brother, Samei almost dropping the meal crock because Ryn said he had pushed, Samei somehow almost cutting his fingers with a knife being helpful and bringing it. All their fear and grief about their father, Lidae's grief, Cythra's grief for them, coming out as they cooked and ate. Lidae ate a great deal of fish and oatcakes and honey, her mouth tasting dry and sour, to please them.

'Why are you eating like that?' Ryn said suddenly.

'Like what? What do you mean? I'm just eating.'

'No, you're not.' Ryn curled his fingers an odd way, holding an oatcake that dripped honey onto his sleeve. Lidae looked at her own hand. She put the piece of fish down carefully. 'I was just holding my hand funny. I don't know. Never mind.' She said, with a harshness that frightened her, 'Stop holding your hand like that, Ryn. And you, Samei. Stop it. Stop it!'

'Hold it this way,' Acol says, kindly, helpful, the first evening she joins them. 'See, tips of your fingers, curl your hand ... no, no, like this, see? Hold it like this, right, and you won't get blood on it like you have there. No, no, like this, see?'

'It's not really something I've needed to think about before,' Lidae says, embarrassed somehow. 'How not to get someone's blood on your food when you're eating.'

'There's a trick to it, Lidae, girl,' Acol says. 'You'll learn. We all had to.'

'You'll learn quickly,' Maerc says.

'I was just doing what you were doing,' Ryn said, glaring. 'You've made Samei cry.'

'Have some more milk, Samei,' said Cythra, looking at Lidae. Samei was so on edge that he dropped the cup, milk poured everywhere, they had to run around cleaning it up, changing his shirt, the meal had to be cleared away, everything put right, Samei was crying and Lidae stroked his hair and he cried more.

'It's just milk,' she shouted, helpless, because he wouldn't stop crying and because Ryn was starting to glare at him.

'Stupid baby,' Ryn muttered.

'Don't be silly, little man,' Cythra said soft and firm and Samei stopped crying, 'look, help Aunty Cythra clean it up, see how easy it is? And you can help too, Ryn,' and the boys did.

And then there were things to attend to, the cow, the chickens, grain for the doves, she almost tripped over Ryn's spinning top lying on the floor in the doorway, Samei was shouting because he'd had a poo and wanted her to wipe him even though he was four years old, 'You are a silly little man, Samei, you can do it yourself, there now, you see?' Cythra said, but he couldn't since his father couldn't get out of bed himself to shit, and Cythra knew that even when Lidae had been about to shout at him. And then the cow needed milking, Lidae needed to fetch more water, the boys started quarrelling again, she'd forgotten about Samei's shirt that hadn't been rinsed clean.

It all made her exhausted, trying to manage it. How do I manage it?

A little longer to hold on to the chaos of normal daily things.

At dusk they buried the sealskin bag containing her husband's bones. Just the three of them, Lidae and her sons. Cythra frowned before she left them, her kind eyes all crinkled up. Looked at the bag, looked at the earthen floor where the dead should be buried. Lidae led her children away from the house to a tangle of may blossom, the trees no higher than her head, very heavy with flowers. The scent of the may blossom had the sweet rot scent of death. She wore the ruined sword, carried the bag of ashes on her shoulder, carried in her hands a loaf of bread and a jug of milk and an arm ring of silver worked with stags and dragons and eagles fighting. She could not bring herself in the end to bury the silver cup alongside her husband's ashes.

Mine, she thought, looking at the cup. Mine. I won that, before I ever met him. So much pride I had, when I won that.

'Useless,' Acol says, 'not even that valuable.'

'But beautiful,' Maerc says.

Mine. The first thing I won. I will not give it to him.

She stopped beneath the may trees, knelt and dug a hole with her hands in the damp earth. The children squatted beside her, that little child squat with feet planted, knees bent. The sensuous, unconscious grace of them. Samei her youngest looked so scrawny plump squatting like that. That's why, she thought, that's why I love them, moments like that the way they are so perfect so unlike anything I could think is a real thing, but I somehow made them. The boys' faces were full of concentration, digging very solemnly, they understood that they were burying their father's bones, Lidae thought, even though they did not truly understand that he was dead. The earth felt good, smelled good. They were enjoying digging.

'That's enough.'

'No, deeper.'

She nodded at Ryn's child wisdom. 'Deeper.'

Ryn said, 'It has to be deep. Very deep.'

'We'll put stones on the top, small ones,' Lidae said. They dug deeper
and wider, a good deep hole under the may trees, a little rough trench.
Lidae put the sealskin bag containing her husband's bones into the hole,
with the sword next to it, and the arm ring.

*Shining piles of treasure, gold, silver, jewels, beautiful things. Piles and
piles and piles of things. When we had to cross the river Immias, do you
remember, gods, that was an awful night, the sky was burning brighter than
summer sunshine, the water was burning so hot it hurt us ... we must have
abandoned more wealth that night alone than most men have seen in their
lives, in their dreams, even ... Or that morning in Tuva, when we were
readying ourselves to cross the mountains, do you remember, the piles of it we
heaped up, abandoned, a mountain range itself in gold and jewels, do you
remember the jokes we made about it?*

*'We'll be as poor as hermits, when we're old, and we'll regret leaving it,'
Maerc says when we're in the mountains, that's a bad time, almost the worst,
'but right now,' Maerc says, 'I don't regret leaving it.'*

*'Six iron pennies for a jug of wine?' Maerc says much later on the other
side of the mountains in a city that has opened its gates wide to them, begged
and grovelled for them to come in, 'six in iron, gods and demons, I really do
regret it.'*

I should bury the cup with him, Lidae thought. The last of it, except
the bedcover and the chest, and I need those, but the cup I don't need,
I should give it to him.

*'Anything you want, you choose, Lidae girl,' Acol says. 'You earned it.
Proper star you were, wasn't she lads? Wasn't she?' They cheer, Acol claps her
on the shoulders: 'Lidae! Lidae!'*

It's too far to walk back to the house to get it now, she thought.

'This,' said Ryn, and dropped in a wooden ball he had had since he
was tiny, that he had slept for a while holding, *'ball, where ball?'* he used
to shout sometimes in the night waking up if it had rolled away from
him.

'This,' said Samei, echoing him, dropping in a little figure made of
cow-bone that their father had carved for him.

'Oh, my children, my small ones.' They think, she thought, they
think this is magic that will make him come back. And don't we all think
that? They'll regret it, she thought, later, later tonight I will come back,
dig their things up again, when they cry for them.

They scraped earth back over the hole, shoving it down. It took a
long time, the boys looked more and more tired, smudging earth on
their faces, it was full dark with only a thin moon, very dark beneath

the trees, they looked frightened. Burying their father's ashes: they were right, they ought to be frightened. But they had to do this. She thought of doing it herself, in the dark, alone with the bag with his ashes and his ruined sword, the last ghost things of him. Selfish, she thought then, to have brought them, made them do this. When the earth was sort of put back, a crude hump of soil with the strap of the bag still almost showing, they gave up, piled stones and sticks, Samei dragged up a big branch of may with leaves and faded flowers still thick on it. Lidae crumbled the bread, scattered it, poured out the milk. In the dark the liquid lay on the earth in a dark pool. She felt sick, a cold sweat on her back.

After a long time, Ryn said, 'I'm tired, Mummy. I'm cold.' And she saw that Samei was almost asleep, his eyes huge and blank, holding Ryn's hands. They got up stiffly and walked back to the house together, after a few steps Lidae picked up Samei in her arms, he fell asleep on her shoulder. They went into the house, she folded Samei into bed still covered in earth, Ryn got in beside him still covered in earth too. Lidae lay down in her own bed beneath the silk coverlet, still dirty with earth herself. Lay staring into the dark feeling the earth coating her skin. Ryn, she knew, somehow, was awake staring as she was. What does he think? Does he think it's my fault his father died? The bag was buried beneath the trees and their father would not come in. The bed felt huge, without him. Too huge to sleep in. She felt the bag there outside, as if it was a fire still burning.

A low smooth curving hillside, on the summit of the hill the bodies of the dead have been piled. Mound upon mound of them, dark against the sky. Beside them, a red banner is flying. An ashwood spear planted as a standard, holding aloft a bronze image of a horse's head. The crows and the flies buzz over them; great black ravens, the wisest of all birds; kites and buzzards; eagles, cursed creatures above all others, with their gold-tipped wings. A trumpet sounds, a man steps forward, his skin is fine bronze like his sword-blade, his armour is trimmed with gold, he is bare-headed and his golden curls are shining. He holds up a torch that burns with the stink of pitch, he thrusts it into the first of the pyres. The dead are heaped there together, their bodies run together, holding each other tight-bound in their comradeship. All their faces and their features rotted out of memory, one mass of them, together, dead. The golden-haired man thrusts the torch onto the pyre and the death-fire blazes up brilliant. The sun seems weak and faint beside it. The army stands with eyes raised to watch the fire. Their own wounds, these living soldiers carved and scarred with the words of their fighting, their own wounds ache. In silence, many of them are weeping.

The sun sinks towards the west and the shadows grow longer. The trumpet sounds, they sigh and murmur like children waking. Blink eyes that are red with tears and smoke. In the cold dawn the next morning they march out again to battle, going west, the sun is behind them hidden, they march past the battlefield where the bodies of their enemies lie in mounds uncountable and uncounted, stinking, rotted, soiled flesh dissolving back into the earth. Long years after, the bones of the enemy dead will lie here.

'Burn the dead,' Acol tells her. 'We always burn the dead, we make them glorious in the fire, and then they are gone.'

She woke in the dawn with the fear that he was there beside her, dying. A sound in the grey dark that she thought for a moment was his burned hands scratching at the door. She could see the bag with his ashes and the ruined sword, feel them out there in the grey dark beneath the may tree. Ryn whimpered in his sleep, thrashed about, he had never been a good sleeper, 'Mummy!' he shouted, still asleep, 'No!' Samei woke up then too with a wail, 'Ryn's shouting. Shouting.' Indignant.

She took them both into her own bed, made it smaller. They wriggled like puppies. The ashes and the sword were buried outside, she could feel them.

'Father!' Ryn shouted. 'Father! Mummy!'

'Hush. Hush.'

Samei said, 'Why aren't you sad, mummy?'

'I am sad. Very sad.'

Ryn shouted, 'Father! Mummy! Mummy!'

'Shush. Shush, little one, hush, it's all right, little one, little on, little one, little one.' He was crying, and just as he had cried when he was a tiny baby she could not make him stop.

Three

The new emptiness of the house. Every noise and they turned to the door, expecting him to come in. 'I won't come for a few days,' Cythra had said. 'It's best.' At Lidae's frightened face, she had said, 'You need to get used to it, Lidae.' It reminded Lidae of the day Ryn had been born, Rena the healer and Hana, Rena's daughter, and Cythra had been with her, washed the baby, washed her, changed the bed linen, seen the baby was feeding, then gone. And she and her husband had sat with the baby sleeping on her breast, alone, with everything forever changed around them. 'What do I do?' she had asked herself. 'I don't know what to do. How do I know what to do?' I know how to hold a sword. Not this. This does not feel easy and natural.

The boys helped her get breakfast, helped her clear it up, didn't drop or spill anything, until suddenly they were screaming at each other, really properly fighting, and she had to get down on her knees and separate them. They crushed into her, crying, almost smothering her in their bodies and their cries. 'Ryn ... Samei ... please...' It went on and on, endless, battering at her. How do I make them stop? How can I make them happy now? She was standing before a great city wall, alone, unarmed, how? It came to her that she had dreamed of that, last night. The cow was stamping around in the byre, knocking up against the wall, she needed to tend to it, and she went out relieved to have an excuse with the boys screaming and dragging around her. They got distracted then, of course, cheered up suddenly, ran off to play because Samei had found his second-best stick.

'I'm King Durith! The greatest king in Irlawe! I've raised the horse head! Look at me fight!'

'I'm Lord Temyr! The greatest warrior! The King's General! Look at me fight!'

'King Durith and Lord Temyr never fought with their breakfast smeared all over their face. No, don't wipe your face while you're holding the stick! Look out! Samei! Watch out with the stick, both of you! No!'

Running off playing, oblivious, delighting, almost hitting each other with the stick. Watch them, watch them forever, little bright figures in the landscape, running, jumping, so filled with life. But at last Lidae went back to the house, sat alone at the table looking at the empty chair. The little house felt huge.

She went to the chest by her bed, opened it, took out her sword and her helmet. She put them on the table, with the silver cup beside them. There had been five cups, and she had sold four of them and kept the one. '*You could have kept two, at least,*' her husband had once said.

Emmas. His name had been Emmas. He had had golden curls and bronze skin and amber eyes; it had been for his beauty that she had first noticed him. She groped for his face in her memory, a sudden fear that she could not picture him. A tall figure in a helmet and armour, a few ranks before her in the lines. A kind dark shape bending over the boys' bed in the night hushing them, letting her sleep. A sick man smelling and gasping in a fever, pushing her hands away from his forehead. 'Flash bastard,' Maerc muttering about him. She thought about going out and digging up his sword, so that she could look at it and remember that at least, him holding it, have it. I wish, she thought, I wish I hadn't burned it. Ruined it.

She put the sword and the helmet back in the chest and put the silver cup in beside them. An absurd thing to have in her small house to drink milk and beer from. I'll give it to Ryn, she thought, when he marries; his wife can be proud of it. And she shuddered with fear now at the thought of Ryn growing up, seeing him married, hanging around doting on his children.

This is all real, she thought. This life. Here in my little house with my children by the sea, a farmer woman living off her little patch of earth raising her children. Salith Drylth, 'Bright Field': we liked the name, it seemed a pretty, lucky name. When Emmas her husband had been alive, she thought, it had been a game that they were playing, they hadn't really been farmers and parents.

Look at these fields, the walls of her farmstead, the smell of cows and sheep.

She made bread the next morning. Took in great breaths of the warm bread smell, trying to think calm things. It was pleasant, pouring out flour and water, kneading the bread dough, watching grey spring rain come down waiting for the bread to bake. The children ate little scraps of dough and liked it. Then clearing out the byre, the smell of dirty straw there was pleasant also, and the calf butting up against her with its wet nose and big eyes, it reminded her of Samei or Samei reminded her of it; Ryn was good at the work, Samei wasn't, but Samei liked scattering the new straw afterwards and that too smelled good, felt good. The night again, again the boys came in with her. She lay awake a long time listening to them breathing. Samei snored. Ryn farted in his sleep. Towards dawn Samei woke crying for her. He didn't talk about this father, and neither did Ryn when he was woken by Samei. They all three lay pressed up together listening to the rain on the turf roof above them, none of them speaking.

The next morning after that she went off to hunt wild birds out in the high hills.

'Go,' Cythra said. 'I'll take care of the children. You need a bit of alone time, Lidae.'

And don't you, Cythra? You never have time alone. You never groan at playing with my children.

'I've things that need doing on the farm that will be good for them to learn,' Cythra said. 'I'd appreciate the boys' help, Lidae.'

Really? You're lying Cythra, aren't you? You must be. But time alone, without the children needing her, dragging at her, hands gripping her. Walking fast and free.

In the morning is the time to catch birds. Hear their song, the joy of it, let them sing out their hearts, fill the world with beauty before you catch them. The night's rain came rushing down from the highest peaks in streams cold as moonlight, the turf was wet under foot, rain gleamed jewelled on the grass blades, on the petals of flowers, moss green and shining wet as fish skin. The wheat in the fields was palest jewel-scattered green-silver. Purple saxifrage in spreading pools of colour, white anemones and white poppies and white laceflower; elderflower frothed like seafoam, sweet-calm-scented with a musk to it like a child's skin. Above, on the high crags inland, the snow would still linger, the sheer slopes with greying broken ice. Sea eagles flew there, their feathers and their talons and their beaks made of grey iron, so huge they could carry off a full-grown man. Cursed birds. But they were shy of men. A great sudden rush of starlings, lacing the sky; a curlew, soft white and brown as eggshell, calling with joyous yearning; a tern, calling in a clink of smooth dry round pebbles. The boys would be playing with Cythra's dogs and with Ayllis, Cythra's daughter, who saw them half as her playmates and half as her charges to care for and scold and laugh at as a mother would. The birdsong was what had made Lidae think of them.

She stopped to pick a spring of may blossom, wove it into the pin of her cloak. Scrabbled on up steep green slopes where the turf was springy, up grey rocks that rubbed at her hands and boots, up and up into the hills.

From the heights she could see the rooftops of her own village, Salith Drylth, and the village beyond it, Baerryn Geiamnei, 'Burned Field', where the plough sometimes turned up burned earth and human bones, and beyond that again the new stone walls of the town in the distance, Karke, dark against the bright line of the sea. The new road that led to the new gates was a bright muddy scar on the spring landscape. Black water cart ruts as deep as a man's knee. The walls were black stone from the cliffs near her own village, thicker than the span of a man's opened arms, the gates were oak braced in bronze. Beyond the walls would come the stink and roar of a thousand people, the clatter of tools beating stone on wood and stone on iron. A thousand houses and halls and storehouses now raised in Karke. Thick stone houses with domed roofs, narrow little windows turned away from the grey sea to look at each other. Low, windowless houses built of willow and turf and whale bones, with a hole in the roof for smoke. The Lord of Karke's new house, tall and grand. It had pillars outside it of imported marble.

Beyond the town, the sea. Beyond the sea, nothing. The sheen of the water stretching on and on. At the end of everything, the fishermen said, the sea and the sky blurred together into a cold mist, a boat could no longer sail, and after that no one knew. Lidae looked back at the town. She did not often go into the town. Too many memories. Voices, shouting. In the town her face would feel hot and sore, her hands sticky as if she hadn't washed them. She would have to go there more, now that Emmas was dead.

The sun was still high in the sky when her bag was full of bird corpses. 'You're too good at that,' Cythra's husband Devid would say, wonderingly, envious, whenever she brought back a full bag. 'But I suppose you would be,' he would say then, his voice harsh and suspicious.

'It's not the same thing,' Lidae would say back, but her eyes would be lowered.

The last time he said that, Cythra had said in Lidae's defence, 'You killed a pig last week, husband, and this winter we said we'd have to kill the roan cow, and you go birding, and you go fishing and sela hunting.'

'It's not the same,' Devid had said. He had walked off, calling the dogs to him.

'I'm sorry,' Cythra had said. 'You know,' she had said, after a moment's awkwardness, 'you know I don't think that about you, Lidae.'

'Yes,' Lidae had said. 'Thank you, Cythra.'

I should feel shame, she thought. I should feel far more shame than I do. '*You're a natural, Lidae. Like you were born to it,*' Acol used to say to her. '*Poet of the sword,*' Maerc had called her after one battle, only half joking.

I should feel such shame, she thought. Standing there now on the high hillside looking out at the town and the sea beyond that ran away north until the word ended, sea wind in her hair, alone and widowed, she thought, now perhaps I will.

I should go back now, she thought. Back to them. I can't leave them with Cythra too long.

She took the smallest of the bird corpses out of her bag, held it up to look at it. Soft brown feathers, grey at the breast and the throat, a yellow beak. She did not know what kind of bird it was or what its song was, if it sang. She had seen birds like it wheeling over the house in the evening. She looked up at the pale sky, thinking of it flying, and she saw, for a moment, in the north—she thought she saw a dark shape in the sky, a blot like a scratch on the light there. A bird, a little thing like this she held in her hands. A sea eagle, huge, fishing.

She had seen other things flying, once, dark shapes, flying against the light. She would not see such things again now in this place. A bird, an eagle, smaller and nearer than she imagined it, dreamed it. And it was gone. A scratch in the light. A speck in her eyes. A yearning. She shivered: now I will feel shame, she thought. I remember the fires, the terror, whole cities, I remember … But the memory of it is joyous, I look at the birds flying, and I remember, and I pretend I see it again.

She set the bird corpse down on the turf. Placed a circle of stones around it. Blood for the wild gods of the wild places, that walked here. Such things also she had seen. There were paths here across the high hills, Rena the healer said, where the dead walked. Blood for them.

She went back down to the low rich meadows by the seashore, to get her children, show them the success of her hunt. The empty house, dark, lifeless, loomed before her in her mind. She had seen a lot of empty houses. The empty, dead look of the windows, like dead eyes looking out mourning. At the foot of the hill Lidae raised her face to the north, but the sweep of the hills was between her and the northern horizon. She was glad of it.

The pretence of seeing it. Not seeing it. The longing.

Cythra said, 'He was the one … Emmas … He was the one who wanted to settle down here, wasn't he?'

How could she have seen that? But it is written in me all over, Lidae thought, for a woman like Cythra who knows these things. Her eyes, when Cythra asked it, had gone to the door of the sleeping room, and the yellow chest. Cythra only had to see her eyes move. She said, 'He wanted to settle somewhere. He didn't care where. Somewhere far from the places we'd fought. It was why he'd become a soldier at all, he said once. I'd not known him long then. We were celebrating a victory, a great feast, we were all drunk and boasting.'

A feast. The sack of a city, drunk on slaughter as much as looted spirits. But some things all soldiers knew could not did not need to be said. "I fight for glory!" "I fight because I am a man!" "I fight to make myself great!" He was as bad as all of us, swinging his sword and shouting. Later, we were alone somehow, in a little street where the houses had all been decorated with flowers, and he told me quietly that his family had been so poor his father had sold his little brother and sister as slaves, to save them from starving, he'd gone away to war when he was still a boy, to stop himself from starving, make enough to keep his parents from starving. All he dreamed of, he said, was to win enough loot to settle himself and then somewhere they could live. They had died, of course, both his parents. He didn't say how. But he dreamed of a house, and children who had food in their bellies, and the smell of new-baked bread...

Lidae and Cythra were sitting by the fire in Lidae's house, with the boys sleeping in the room next door, Cythra had come back with them after the hunting, because the boys were tired, she might as well help Lidae feed them and get them into bed, she said. Thank you, thank you, Cythra, Lidae had not been able to say in return. 'They've been so helpful all day, so sweet, both of them, it was a pleasure to have them.' The fire spat, badly made too quickly. Lidae stared into the fire. That night, in her memory, Emmas' face and armour had been gilded by the flames.

'I didn't love him. Never. Not then, not ever, I don't think. But he was handsome and the sound of his voice when spoke about it...'

'Good a reason as any,' said Cythra. 'I married Devid because he was the only man in the village the right age to marry.'

Lidae laughed. 'Oh, I didn't marry him them! It was five years later, when they disbanded a whole lot of us, offered us silver, horses or ships to take us east or north. He asked me, and I said no, and then I thought about it, and I said yes.

'It seemed like a change. They said, some of the veterans that had been with us a long time, they said the north was a good place. We took the coin we were offered, came north to Thalden with some of the King's own guards, Emmas heard the name 'Bright Field' somewhere and he said there were so many reasons it sounded a good place.'

She stopped. Why am I telling her all this? I've never told anyone this.

Who would there be to tell? she thought then. I could hardly tell Emmas this: 'I married you, husband mine, because my knees ache and my hands ache day and night and the wound on my thigh never properly healed and the wound on my shoulder hurts deep, and I thought, maybe, I might as well try a new thing in a new place because they were offering. That's why I married you, Emmas, bore your children, built this house with you, toiled tilling the earth with you—because my shoulder hurts and my knees hurt at night, because I thought it would make a change from soldiering, because I was thirty years old and thinking about being a woman and that meaning that I might bear children, which is a thing women often do. Because I didn't realise what it meant.'

Cythra shook her head and her hair shimmered. Silver-trimmed armour. Great pale shining beating wings.

'You must have been a solider since you were a girl?' said Cythra. In all the years Lidae had been here, Lidae thought, and she had finally been able to ask that.

'I—' Lidae's eyes moved again to the doorway, the chest with her helmet and her sword and the silver cup, the coverlet that she had ripped once from a great lord's bed in a white marble palace almost as big as the whole of Karke. 'I—' A noise outside, in the dark above them, a wild calling, mournful and bitter, like a thing baying in grief. Lidae started up, frightened, the dark shape that she had dreamed up on the hillside came terrible into her mind, crying and beating its wings.

Geese, coming back north for the summer. An arrowpoint of them flying over the house. They flew over the dead paths out in the hills, Rena the healer said of them. Harried the things that walked there. Warned them away, kept the people in the lowlands safe from them.

Lidae took a long breath, stared into the fire. Now, tonight, suddenly! Tell me the truth of it, all of it, the silent things that all the people of the village tried to imagine when they thought about her. 'I lived in Raena. A city,' she said, seeing Cythra look blank, 'a city in the south in Cen Elora. My father worked hauling stone for a mason. My mother raised me and my sisters. When I was sixteen the soldiers came to Raena, sacked it. My family died in the sack. When the soldiers marched out of Raena, I went with them. The next city we came to, I helped to sack it.'

A long silence from Cythra. You think I don't know that about you, Lidae.

'I'd want Ayllis to do the same,' Cythra said. 'If she had to.'

The geese came over the house, crying. Cythra pulled her shawl tighter around her, made a luck sign with her left hand, spat into the fire for luck.

'Devid wanted to be a soldier,' Cythra said. 'When he was young. Begged and begged his father. Once he ran away, I remember, got as far as Karke, although of course Karke was only another village then. His father threatened to break his right arm, to stop him going. The next summer he married me. He has three iron pieces in a box under our bed that he was saving to buy a sword with. He's never spent them.'

Cythra left soon afterwards, walking down the track in the dark back to her own house. Lidae lay down in the big bed beneath the looted coverlet, listening to the boys sleeping. They knew in their sleep she was there now, thrashed about and woke up and came in. The silence after Cythra had gone must have disturbed them.

That's why we fought, Lidae thought. Not for glory. The fighting was the game. Playing at soldiers. This is the real, good thing.

She felt afraid knowing that she was lying.

Four

The days grew very hot and sullen. Too hot for spring. Then it poured down with rain, trapping them in the house. Then it was too hot again. The boys fought constantly, bickering, sniping at each other, at her, once they fought with hands and feet so fiercely Lidae was frightened. But when they weren't fighting they clung together, holding hands as they had done when Samei was first walking; if Lidae scolded Samei for something Ryn would come running in, 'What's happening, what's wrong with Samei?' hugging his brother, glaring at Lidae.

'It's nothing, just your brother being foolish, everything's fine, Ryn.'

Ryn would glare at her, stare with narrowed eyes, a chill would creep across her. He hates me. He blames me. My son. What can I ever have done, what kind of mother can I be, that my child hates me like this? Cythra scolded her children, I heard her sometimes shout at them worse than I've ever done. The boys would go off together, looking back over their shoulders at her, 'Never mind, Samei, never mind her,' Ryn would whisper loud enough to hurt her.

'Ryn should be a general,' Emmas had said once, 'the way he understands battle tactics.'

That night Ryn got up after Samei had fallen asleep, came into Lidae sitting by the hearth too tired to go to bed, snuggled up close to her, his head in her shoulder. He didn't speak, but he stroked very gently at her cropped hair.

She thought of her own mother, exhausted, and she had stroked her hair like that. Remembered talking her mother's hands, holding them to her face. Breathing in the smell of her mother's hands, that she saw now was only the smell of dry raw cracked skin. Her own hands, she thought, smelled of cold metal.

'Rov,' Samei cried, panicked, the next morning. 'I can't find Rov.' His cow-bone doll, that was buried with Emmas its maker. 'This,' in his solemn lisping boy's voice as he dropped it in, she'd known then he'd regret it.

'Rov is out in the garden, Samei, remember? Out beneath the may tree, buried.' She knew it was the wrong thing to say, as she said it. But what else could she say?

'Dig him up!'

She felt sick thinking about it. The leather bag all slimy in the earth, the ashes wetting down to sludge. Cythra would have said, 'We'll look for him. Hope he turns up…' when he didn't turn up it would have been sad but… Emmas would have said 'I'll carve you another one little boy, don't fret.' Young Lidae would have said, 'I'll loot you another one.'

'He's… with daddy, remember, Samei? A burial gift. We can't dig him up.'

'Dig him up!' Ryn shouted, very suddenly.

'I can't dig it up, Ryn.' Gods, for a moment, she'd thought he meant… 'It's buried in the earth,' she said, she kept saying it, 'buried, buried,' like she was daring herself to say it to hurt them. Enjoying saying it to hurt them.

'Dig him up! Rov!'

'You gave him to daddy, remember? I can't dig it up.'

Ryn said, soldier-eyed, 'You should have stopped him.'

Her hand rose, to hit him. She didn't hit him.

The next day there was a hole in the earth beneath the may tree; they'd been digging there with sticks, not got deep enough and got frightened, she thought. She said nothing. They said nothing. Not the right place anyway, the wrong side of the tree. I should get it, she thought, dig it up. One man's ashes, in a bag … and the things I've done, she thought. Carrying bodies hacked and bloody, dragging them to the pyre. Looting a city, an enemy camp, and we… and I… the things we did, looting.

In Raena, at sixteen, lying hidden for hours, eyes screwed closed, blood-stink on her nose and mouth…

'I'll make you a new one,' she said. 'Please, Samei. Don't cry.' Her voice shook when she said please. Pleading, begging. I can't carve a doll out of a cow bone, out of anything, and they know it. The two boys stared back, unmoved.

She went out into the night after they were sleeping, with a candle, dug up the doll and Ryn's old wooden ball. *Ball! Ball! Where ball?* Sitting on the table the next morning when the boys got up. Two faces staring, amazed, arms hugging her. She thought, to Emmas, to Cythra, to herself: there, look.

We need to get out for a little. Do something. Lidae borrowed Rena's horse and cart, took the boys with her to Karke to sell soft brown bird feathers to be made into rich men's bedstuff, buy a bolt of linen for new summer tunics.

'Stop growing small ones!' Long bronze limbs, lanky as goats. Astonishing how tall they had got. Ryn would be eight this summer, in the winter at Sun Return Samei would be five. So she had spent eight years here in the north, married. Almost as long as she had spent fighting.

Sixteen years in Raena as a child. Ten years of fighting in the Army of Illyrith under Lord Brychan and King Durith. Eight years here in Salith Drylth as a wife and mother. They aren't babies any more. Kyrana in the village, the blacksmith's wife, her daughter was a baby, fussed over as young and special.

'Come on! Hey, hey!'

She had drifted off into dreaming and the cart was going too slowly. Ryn looked annoyed at it. She shook up the reins to get the horse moving. There were bleached driftwood sticks tied to the wheels of the cart, they rattled together as they creaked along. Luck charms, Rena said. The horse defecated as they creaked along and the boys shouted with amusement.

'Look at it, look, look, look!'

'Yes. Astonishing.' A horsefly buzzed around her face, she batted it off.

The track ran south-west inland through an elm wood, the trees reaching to form a green roof far overhead. The air felt close and heavy, as though a storm might come, with a lovely smell behind it of green things. Further on, they passed a clearing where trees were being felled, the track was deeply rutted and muddy even in the heat. A long tree trunk lay with chains wrapped around it, waiting to be hauled away. Soon afterwards they passed two men with woodsmen's axes, coming back along the road to their work.

'They make ships' backbones out of elm trees,' said Ryn. 'Do you think that tree will be made into a ship?'

'Possibly. How did you know that? I didn't know that about ships.'

'Ayllis told me,' said Ryn. 'She knows about ships.'

'Does she?'

'It will go sailing off into the south,' said Ryn, 'where the cities have houses made of solid gold.'

'Do they?'

'You've seen them!'

She said, 'I saw one city once that once upon a time had a palace with a golden roof and walls of solid bronze. But that city was destroyed by a demon. And you couldn't get there on a ship.'

The wet cart-ruts in the road were attracting more flies. One of them bit Samei, who yelled. There was a strong smell of wild garlic. Behind them came the thud of the woodsmen's axes. A magpie started cawing angrily about something.

Samei stopped yelling and sang instead very loudly: '*Summer is a coming in, Today we'll spend in mirth. Dappled, sparkling, dancing, sparkling, summer singing.*'

'*Singing, singing, singing,*' Lidae sang with him.

A cuckoo, another crow, a pigeon. The road ran through a stream that was thick with watercress and duckweed; there was a ford, easy to cross, but just further on the bank was steep suddenly, there were yellow irises and bull rushes, an explosion of white lace flowers that must be as tall as Ryn at least. After they crossed the stream the horse and the cartwheels left wet trails for a little on the beaten earth of the road.

'The best cartwheels,' Lidae said, 'are made of elm. The tree will be made into a cart to carry small boys in.'

The wood ended, the road turned sharply northwards, ran through green fields towards the long spit of land that was Karke Point. The horse toiled up a hill, there, on the other side of the hill, green fields ran down to the sea. The water looked grey as iron, heavy. The sky was dull, hot grey.

'Karke!' Ryn shouted, jumping up on the cart seat. 'Look! Karke!'

'*Look! There!*' *The captain pointing, smiling, and Acol and all of them cheer.*

'I saw it first,' shouted Samei.

'No, you didn't! Samei's lying!'

'Did!'

'Did not!'

'Did! Did, did, so did!'

'Gods and powers! I'd rather bring an army into a city than those two boys when they're quarrelling,' Emmas had said after their last visit.

'Babies ... Please ...' Weak. Exhausted.

Ryn seemed to think about fighting Samei or crying, if they'd been at home he would have done both, she thought, but they were travelling, doing something, he pulled himself together to take the high ground as older, pointed out the building that he said was the lord's house and shapes on the water that he said were ships with elm wood keels. Lidae nodded and smiled and agreed with him. Samei couldn't remember Karke and had no idea about ships and buildings, being four, so listened with admiration, occasionally saying, 'I saw them first!' The road dipped downhill, the town vanished, the road rose again, passed between the humped backs of twin hillocks, ran over a narrow stone bridge that was not pleasant to drive the cart on. The wooden walls rose in front of them, the timber scented new and clean. Above the town on the very tip of the headland there was a great mass of activity, a mass of men working and wooden posts; Lidae could not make them out individually but they moved in a drift like birds, a raw colour and a raw texture to the earth where they worked. They were up by the godstones on the point. The godstones looked smaller, lost, in the seething of the men. Lidae could almost hear the men's voices as they worked. Imagine them sweating and swearing and singing.

Lidae said, 'Karke. I saw it first this time.'

There was a shrine outside the gates, a lump of stone as tall as her shoulder that could almost be a human shape. The stone was deep cool brown, mottled through rust red. A pool of very clear water had formed around it, tinted red also. There was a garland of violets around what could be its neck. A spiral pattern had been carved into the stone where its face and its breasts might be, if it was a woman. Tracing round and round. It looked to Lidae like the pattern of skin.

Ryn and Samei said, 'What's that?'

'What do you think it is?'

'A lady,' said Ryn

'A bit of stone,' said Samei, and Lidae and Ryn both laughed at him.

The gates were open, a single guard wearing the black-and-green badge of the Lord of Karke standing watching people coming in and out, bored. He had an ashwood spear taller than he was, his helmet was bronze with a black horsehair crest that nodded as he moved his head. His eyes looking through the helmet were owl eyes, unblinking. The helmet looked absurd, worn without armour. The walls looked absurd, high strong walls, the gates gleaming with bronze, circled around a fishing town.

'He looks like a beast!' Samei cried out. 'He hasn't got a face!' The boy looked pale and frightened. Drew back roughly in the cart, stared at the guard.

'It's a helmet,' Ryn said. Trying to be all-knowing and bold, and his voice was frightened too.

Lidae had sworn her helmet for Ryn once when he was about Samei's

age. He had been terrified, screamed until she put it away. 'It's only
Mummy, it's only Mummy, look, look,' his father had to shout at him.
The guard now looked at them with distaste. The look of a man who did
not know about small children. Lidae tried to express apology with her
shoulders as they took the cart in through the gates.

The streets were wet mud ruts, sticking around the cart's wheels, slip
and filth of sewage and waste. A cart carrying willow withies was ahead
of them, forcing itself through the narrow streets. Its wheels slipped and
stuck in the filth. Lidae followed in its wake. The horse was nervous in
the bustle, A girl ran out in front of it whooping, and Lidae had to pull
hard on the reins. She cried out, Ryn cried out. The girl turned and gave
them a look, like the guard had done: country people, rustics.

'This is why we don't come to Karke,' Lidae said.

'It's the biggest city in the world,' said Samei, his eyes very wide. 'The
whole world can't be as big as this!'

Ryn said, 'It smells bad. Like the toilet pit.'

Lidae said, 'It's not even a city, Samei baby boy tiny one. King Durith
in Thalden lives in a palace as big as the whole of Karke, and Thalden
is not even a big city, compared to some. Lord Temyr the king's highest
ranking general, Lord Sabryyr, Lord Brychan ... all the great nobles,
they all live in palaces as big as this.' She said to Ryn, wrinkling her nose
at him, 'It does smell bad, doesn't it?'

Sweat and smoke and raw meat. They passed a butcher's stall where
the butcher in a blood-spattered leather apron was swinging his cleaver,
cutting up a cow carcass. A stink as the body was opened up. The sound
of a blade on raw meat. There was an inn near the marketplace, where
they could leave the cart and horse for one in iron, get some food. Only
now it turned out to be two in iron, and the floor in the horse yard
was vile. This, Lidae thought, is also why I don't come to Karke. They
sat under a cloth awning like a sail, eating, watching the bustle around
them; Samei, with utter predictability, dropped his bread in the mud.
Lidae drank beer, the boys drank milk that had been watered thin.

'What are they doing up there?' Ryn asked, pointing west to the
headland. The cliffs rose very sheer, the work at the top loomed over the
town dark against the light.

'Building,' said Lidae.

'Building what?'

She paused. 'A fortress.'

'A fortress for King Durith!' shouted Samei.

'It could be a palace,' said Ryn. 'With a golden roof like King Durith's palace in Thalden!'

'No. A fortress.'

'King Durith's palace doesn't have a golden roof, stupid,' Samei said.

'You said there were whole cities with solid gold houses, Samei, that's more stupid.'

'Will King Durith come and live here?'

'No, stupid, not if it's a fortress. Fortresses are for soldiers and fighting.'

'King Durith might want to live in Karke. Then we'd get to see him!'

Lidae said, 'I don't think King Durith even knows Karke exists. Now hush.'

'Karke's the biggest place in the world!' said Samei. 'How stupid is he?'

'Even stupider than you, Samei.'

Oh please. Not again. 'King Durith is very wise indeed, and so is Samei.' She tried so hard to smile at them.

'How do you know it's not a palace?' said Samei. 'I think it's a palace.'

The day was brightening, the clouds and the sky showing a pale water-blue. A shaft of sun brought out the gold in Samei's hair. He had fine downy hair like peach fur on his upper lip. A little moustache, at four, little silly baby man. Lidae looked away from the headland. 'I know.' She said sharply, 'Now hush.'

When they had eaten they took the sack of brown feathers to the marketplace. It was a horrible walk carrying the sack, which was very light but very large, being full of feathers, fat and cumbersome, and holding Samei and Ryn's hands both tight. The old ache in Lidae's shoulder and in her thigh started up. Samei cried and wanted to be carried; in the end Lidae had to carry him and the sack and hold Ryn's hand the last bit. All that way, hours in the cart, and now she was staggering under everything. The marketplace was beside the Lord of Karke's house, so he could keep watch over it. Lidae jostled through the people buying and selling, sweating and irritable under all the weight. A man barged past her, a pole slung over his shoulders slung with white geese carcasses. The end of the pole narrowly missed the side of her head. She felt hot and angry and weak and lost. One of the geese swung and hit Ryn in the face and would almost have been funny, almost, if Ryn hadn't shrieked, if the man hadn't turned, sworn violently at him.

A memory, very strong, very clear. Striding through a marketplace in a town far bigger and richer than Karke, the townspeople flowing before her, cowering out of her way, bowing their faces too afraid to look at her. Striding through a great city, one marketplace alone larger than the whole of Karke, streets paved in white marble, palaces of white marble and black onyx if not quite of solid gold. Great lords in crimson silk cowering, eyes averted.

Manal's stall was over in the furthest corner, naturally, past stalls heaped with bolts of embroidered cloth, jewellery, gold-hilted daggers, fine pottery that had been carried a thousand miles without breaking that the boys kept reaching for and the sack swung for, a returned soldier's swinging sword... Lidae dropped the sack of feathers down before Manal. Looked at him hopefully, panting. *If he says he has no need for them at the moment, I'll scream at him.*

Manal walked with a limp where he had been injured once trapping birds himself. Out on the high cliffs, scrambling over a boulder. Fallen. Three days Manal had been out there. 'I saw the sea eagles flying so close to me,' he had said of it afterwards, 'they spoke to each other in men's speech, but I was too far to hear what they said.' He walked very slowly now, Lidae could see the pain in his face just from him moving to greet her. He smiled at Lidae, thought Samei was Ryn, ruffled Samei's hair, was astonished at how big Ryn had grown. A long awkward silence when he asked how Emmas was.

'Four in iron,' Manal said when she showed him the feathers. He sucked in his lips, winked at Samei. 'No, they're good feathers, aren't they, young man? Keep a king's loyal soldier warm on a cold night. A bedcover for a general, Lord Sabryyr, Lord Brychan, one of those great ones. They complain about the cold on campaign all the time, the soldiers, always sending letters home asking for better coverlets, for all they must have a different woman every night to warm their beds... unlike you, I bet, young man, you never complain, I'm sure. Five in iron.'

'Five.' The coins clicked into Lidae's hand. *He's patronising and pitying me,* she thought. *The whole bag isn't worth four.* 'Thank you, Manal. Say thank you to Manal, Ryn, Samei,' Lidae said.

'Our feathers,' said Samei, 'our feathers making a coverlet for the king's soldiers! A king's general! Lord Sabryyr!'

A shout from across the square: 'Gather round, gather round!' Ryn pointed, wondering, at a group of people being led in surrounded by guards. A young woman, her hair bright golden; a woman around Lidae's age; a tall man, skin blue-white as the watered milk, a bruise spreading across his face. They were chained together, wore iron collars around their necks.

'Slaves,' Ryn said. He sounded shocked and frightened and fascinated.

The slaver's voice rose through the bustle of the market. 'All the way from Eralath, these slaves, fresh off the ship, look at them! A young woman, look at her, pretty thing, new to being a slave she is, not second-hand goods, new-broken. The soldier who took her said he's almost been minded to keep her and I can't blame him. Six in iron? Six in iron? Anyone? And the man here, not some beaten-down defeated old soldier, see him here, quality, he is, he can read and write, keep accounts: seven in iron? Anyone?'

'Come away,' Lidae said. Ryn was staring. Old enough to know what a slave was. 'Come on, Ryn.'

'Six in iron? Anyone? Five for the girl?'

'Five,' a voice called back. 'Let me have a look at her.' The girl stared out ahead, eyes raised to the sky not seeing not hearing. She had the face of a soldier having a wound searched. Maerc, when Acol had once taken a barbed arrowhead out of him. She was pretty, petal-white skin that had kept a glow to it, her hair very fine spun gold. Little and delicate, a fragile body, the stark hateful set of her face.

'Come away, Ryn. Samei. Come away.' Lidae pulled them into the market until there were stalls blocking their view of the slaves. Clay pots, goat skins, bolts of bright cloth. Lidae took a deep breath. The seller's voice carried behind them, 'And this woman here, all the way from Theme, a fine worker she is, cooking, spinning...' but now she could not see.

One stall was selling round fruit, pink-red, mottled golden, as large as Lidae's hand. Over the smoke and stink of the market, it smelled like the richest flower scent. Summer flowers, warm breeze, a woman's skin in the evening, a child's hair damp from rain... The sun sinking low in the evening over the sea, it looked like.

'Cimma fruit,' the stall holder called, seeing her looking. 'From far south, from Elora, at the end of the world. The land it comes from is desert, the earth is hot, dry yellow sand there, their children play outside naked, they can go for weeks before it rains. Think what that would feel like. Like the warmth of a fire on your skin. Sun fruit.'

The boys were looking at it with wide eyes. The stall holder was a woman, tall and dark with red glass beads in her hair; like Manal, she smiled at the boys, held a fruit out to them.

'Please, oh please, oh please, oh please.'

'Merchants brought it with the slaves there, traded a single box of these fruit for a whole narwhale tusk,' the woman went on. The beads in her hair danced and clicked. Like raindrops. 'Think of that! A whole narwhale tusk for a single box of sun fruit. That's how rare and fine it is. The great lords in Thalden, the king himself, it's a treat day for them, when they get to eat this fruit.'

'Please, please, please.' Ryn and Samei pressed round Lidae like a calf trying to suck from its mother. 'Please.'

'It smells better than it tastes,' said Lidae. 'And Elora is not the end of the world, or even the centre of it. And King Durith and Lord Sabryyr and the other great ones, they can eat all the cimma fruit they want, because they are in the south fighting, they could be fighting a battle now in the shade of cimma fruit trees.' She sighed. 'How much?'

'Two in iron,' the staff keeper said. 'A single box cost a narwhale tusk.'

'The man just gave you five in iron, I saw it,' Ryn said, delighted.

'One and we divide it in two.'

'But the man just gave you five in iron,' said Ryn. 'Not fair.'

'Three of those fruit,' said Lidae, 'would cost the same as that girl we saw. Stop it.'

'Samei will eat it all!' Ryn howled. 'Or drop it.'

'No, I won't! Ryn will eat it all. Hog it, like he always does.'

'Samei gets everything! He always gets everything! He's the hog!'

'Not. Not. Not. Hog!'

'Ryn… Samei… Please…'

'He'll drop it! I'm not sharing with him.'

'Three of those fruit cost the same as that girl's life, Ryn. Gods, I've seen soldiers in a sack acting with more dignity than this. That girl will never get to eat a single slice of cimma fruit in her life. Or meat, or honey cakes, or fresh bread. She'll have to—' She was shouting at the top of her voice: the stall holder looked at her, shocked. The two children's faces stared at her, frightened, Ryn almost in tears. Little things. Such little things.

'One each. Two of them, please, then.' She handed over four of the five coins she had worked for hunting birds out in the mountains all through the spring. 'You'd better eat it all, both of you.'

'It was an accident,' Samei said later, when they were looking all three of them at the mess on the floor.

'It was horrid anyway,' Ryn said.

And Lidae wanted to shout, and then she laughed and laughed until her eyes watered, and then she hugged and kissed Samei and hugged and kissed Ryn. And the floor probably needed cleaning anyway.

Five

They go in through the gates, pouring in, jostling, almost fighting. It's hot and sweet. 'You don't need to rush, plenty of time, plenty of time there!' Lord Temyr, shouting himself hoarse, unheeded, he wasn't Lord Temyr yet then just an officer with a clever sword and a good loud voice, 'They've surrendered, there's no need to rush, no need to rush,' Lord Temyr shouts after them. They've surrendered, gods, yes, surrendered, opened the gates, given in. So they pour in. Rush in. And the buildings are burning, the whole city is burning, and Maerc is shouting in a rage because the fires are coming too fast, the city is timber dried out in this damned heat and the fire is spreading too quickly, they won't be able to get anything good because the houses are burning up, walls of flame, streets of flame, it's like the city is in a flood of fire, living by the sea now she thinks of the fire as the tide breaking on rocks, drowning them. 'There's no rush, they've surrendered, no need to rush,' Lord Temyr is shouting. 'It's a rich city, enough for everyone.' They know it is, that's why they've been besieging it. But there's a shout, even as they're pushing their way through the gates behind their comrades, reckoning up the wealth they can make in their blood-red heads. 'Fire!' a voice is screaming, 'gods, fuckers, fire! Fire!' and the city is burning. 'Even the temple here is wood,' Maerc shouts in fury, 'gold and wood, and it's burning, look.' 'They fired it themselves,' says Emmas, 'I'll bet, to stop us getting it.' He's angry because he's been counting on this city to make him good coin to send back to his mother, Lidae thinks, starving and hungry, and all this wealth here lost. Gold and silver, melting. Bread snatched from his mother's mouth. He goes to grab a girl and in his anger it looks like he's going to kill her straight off. 'No, don't, you fool,' Maerc shouts roughly, 'don't kill any of them. She's the only thing we have here to make coin out of.' Maerc goes to take the woman and she lashes out at him with her nails, and he shouts. Lidae gets her, while Maerc is cursing. She's young and pretty, a rich man's daughter: even with the glut of slaves there'll be in the markets now, she'll be worth something.

The city burns for three days before the flames die down at last to ashes. The palaces and the temples and the wealth are all gone. Columns of slaves, filthy and stinking. Towers on the horizon calling them onwards. A rich city, the city ahead, someone says. Good things. We will make the sacrifice, raise up the luck horse, we will march out for it. Lidae whispers to herself, over and over, 'Better to do it than to suffer it. Better to do it than to suffer it. Better to do it.' The girl looks at her, spits in her face. The girl's eyes say she understands what Lidae means.

The young King Durith, strong and beautiful, who defeated a demon, who rides across the world with his banners shining. He was crowned king in Thalden, the city he had saved from ruin and made his own, he stood in a palace of gold and silver built for him in joy; the workmen sang, they said, as they built their king his house after the years of sorrow, for he was a good king. Crowned and robed all in gold and scarlet, he swore to be a good king. A just king. He led his armies out into the world where the people had forgotten their obedience to Illyrith. A time of war, of violence, all good government is overthrown, the fields are barren, the rivers poisoned, armies and warlords and warrior bands ranged across the world of Irlawe in fury, children have grown up knowing nothing but war and bloodshed. Women live in fear, staring at the horizon waiting for another warband to come down on them. Bear their assailants' children in shame and grief. Beggars, refugees, the poor, the starving, at the mercy of any man who can wield a sword. This, King Durith swore to his men, this horror he would end, he would make the world one empire of peace again, beneath a great strong king. He fought the warlords, the ravaging armies, brought them to kneel before him. Great rich cities, that had once paid homage to Illyrith the mighty: he took them by force, swept them clean; good laws, justice: these things he will bring them, their people will never need to live in fear again.

Slowly, slowly. A lifetime of fighting. In the south, where the earth is dry desert, he fights the false Queen of Eralath who is crowned in willow leaves and flowers; again and again he drives her armies fleeing across the desert wastes. In the east, the men of Arborn and the Immlane river gnaw at his armies, flock to the banner of a great magelord, claim vengeance and the power of old magics; he harries them, fights them, brings them peace in which to tend their fields, until the evil breaks out again. In the west, the old cities that were once each a kingdom rise up against him, each crowning themselves a warrior king; every city, in five fierce years, he besieges and brings to submission, but they will not accept his rule, challenge him and defy him again and again. His men spread out across the world in blood and ruin, to build a world of peace for him. Lidae, Acol, Maerc, Emmas, in fine armour, fine swords, fine strong spears, warm thick war cloaks, bronze helmets. They stand in their rows on the battlefield, faces proud, while their king makes his promises of hope and glory to them. They cheer him, rejoicing, fight with their hearts singing. That sad little girl in the dusty streets of Raena, a few days' bad luck away from begging … she is gone as if she had never been. She eats good meat and good bread now, drinks from a silver cup.

'When we have conquered the world,' the squad captain says, the king says, 'when we have conquered the world, when the war is over, when we have made peace, brought justice …' She has a sword with a lump of red glass in its hilt, like a ruby, and it winks and flashes as the squad captain speaks or the king speaks. She is the fiercest warrior in the squad, they all know it, she fights like a demon, Maerc says. She practices with the sword and spear while the men are resting sometimes. Drills herself, pushes herself. She has never lost a sword fight.

Six

And Lidae was dreaming of a city falling the next night, when it came. The red fires, but in the dream they're not fires but walls of red, columns of red coming down all over the city crushing things. And then they're people or huge trees, it's her own city, Raena, in the country of Cen Elora that is certainly not at the edge of the world and is certainly not a desert, and it's a city she's dreamed about before, since she was a child, or the idea that she's dreamed it before is part of the dream. And sometimes she's sacking the city and sometimes she's a victim of the sack and the army attacking her don't look like people, but she can't see what they look like.

And she woke, confused, and it came.

From off in the distance, very far off, a dog barked. A sharp angry warning. A noise, outside the house, the click of metal on something. The cow in the byre moved suddenly, a thud of its body, and it lowed. It was afraid for its calf.

Something is wrong, Lidae thought. Something— A memory out of the dream, the dark in their camp one night, out on the flank in the mountains ahead of the rest of the army, too much silence, a sound of metal catching, very distant, enemy swords coming suddenly down on them out of the dark, they couldn't see, they died, and they couldn't see. Maerc had died that night, the wound had been in his back, he had been sleeping.

The same silence. The same feeling.

Wake the boys get them up get them up.

'I hope he was dreaming of good things, a woman, something,' Acol had said of Maerc, and Acol had been weeping. They burned Maerc's body as if he'd died gloriously in battle. It had broken Acol's heart to think of Maerc dead without knowing, sweaty and foetid.

Get the boys up. Get away. Something terrible is coming. I cannot bear to think of them dying in their sleep. A sound of metal. The cow in the byer lowed and stamped. Something terrible is here now. I feel it.

Thieves, she thought. Thieves.

'Ryn. Samei.' She clamped her hands over their mouths, tried to wake them but keep them silent, the terror in their faces at her hands over them, her face pressed down to them. Lidae thought: they think I am killing them.

'Ryn. Samei. Keep silent. Get down under the bed.' She'd have thought it was Samei who'd have shouted, refused, flailed about. So young, too little to understand anything, but the fear in her voice made him dumb, he did as she ordered him mutely, too frightened of his mother's voice and her hands that he must think were trying to kill him. Ryn, older, understanding things were wrong, trying to fight her off, ask questions, protest that he had been sleeping. Noise: him pushing her away, speaking.

'Ryn! Samei! Get under the bed! Get under the bed!'

She opened the chest, there was no time to put on the helmet, she stood in her nightshift and drew her sword.

The blade gleamed in the dark. Hunger stirred and flickered in the metal. Bronze, the colour of the boys' skin. Polished rich bronze, burning.

In the hilt of the sword there was a red stone. Red glass. In the dark the red seemed to gleam. Ryn cried out. The sword felt so good in her hands. Samei whimpered like a beast. She thought: he thinks I will kill him.

She shifted her grip on the sword hilt. Stood still one pace back from the doorcurtain that divided the sleeping place off from the living place. All the last years falling away. She felt the sword whispering. Light seemed to run in rainbows up the blade. She could remember very clearly the first time she had used a sword to kill someone.

The sound of someone fumbling with the door, trying to shove it open. A voice said, 'It'll be barred. Just burn it.'

'Stay there,' she hissed to the children. 'Just stay there, don't move. Stay.'

The village was too far for help to come. A hill between the house and the village, Emmas had wanted that, because he'd wanted to be apart in silence, after years piled together in the army four to a tent. The dog barked again, furious. She thought: if there is anyone left alive in the village to come. She thought: but that's madness. This is thieves prowling around.

'Stay and be utterly silent. Ryn, keep Samei silent. You must.'

The dog barked, far off, and then the barking stopped.

'He said there was coin here. A widow, he said, with gold hoarded away.' The door was kicked open. They were going to burn us alive in here, Lidae thought. Cold night air through the door, making the doorcurtain tremble. Footsteps coming inside. On the other side of the wall the cow lowed suddenly and loudly and frantically. Cattle thieves. See? See?

The doorcurtain was ripped aside and a man stood before her, staring at her through a helmet. Dead cold blank eyes, the cold set of his teeth. The sword in his hand trembled. It knew, the bronze sword that he carried, it knew what she was. Lidae's sword came up took him. His throat, just at the point where the collarbones almost meet together, the red glass in the hilt of her sword smiling at her as the sword went in. The site of the soul, she had heard it said of that place in the throat. He made a noise as the sword took him. She had forgotten the sound of a man dying like this. The sword leapt and her heart leapt.

Others in the house, shouting, swearing. Dark shapes, running in. The sword in her hand cried out, leapt up. She thought they might curse, laugh at her, a woman in a nightgown with a bloody sword. Four of them, she thought, in the dark, shadowy shapeless big men. They did not look at their companion's body. They stopped, standing crowded in her house with blood on them, and they were afraid of her. In the dark, they saw her, and they saw something that frightened them.

Ryn broke out from under the bed, screaming. He was running towards them, the men with swords, the enemy, because the door was there behind them and he had to get out. He pushed past her, the only thing protecting him, ran mad towards the enemy to get out. They flinched, even, in the dark not seeing that he was only a child, just a dark shape rushing at them screaming. They seemed to come awake, then. One of them moved. Struck him.

In the dark she saw Ryn fall.

They turned on her. She turned on them.

Big man, close up, ripping at her, in the dark they had looked huge and he was huge, armed and furious. His anger at his fear of her. His rage that his companion was dead. In the dark it was impossible to see to know what he would be doing. Their swords met and met. The noise of the sword blows, his armour creaking, the noise of their breathing, and the smell of him up close, blood and smoke and muck and his sweat. She felt her sword bite home on him, the joy feeling of the blade cutting him. He got her, hard, came in at her, pushed her backwards. Her feet slipped on the blood of the one she had killed. His companions pushed through the doorway behind him. Swords all around her. Dark shapes that stink of killing. Her sword is raging at her for being weak. She thinks she gets one, through his armour. Her mouth tastes bloody. She wants to laugh. Her heart is beating so hard. She's... remembering. The joy of it, the first time she had a sword in her hand. Struggling, cursing, 'I can't do this, I don't know what I'm doing, that thing you do holding the sword, the way you move it, I don't understand,' then one day suddenly understanding it. Her body knowing it. 'Like you were born to it, Lidae. Gods! Thank all the gods you're on the same side as me!' She struck hard, quick, going under the man's guard, the memory: this is my place, fighting! They were crowded in the doorway, couldn't use their numbers. One of them went down, bloody. She was herself in pain somewhere. In the dark she felt and heard and smelled the death stroke. She drove herself at them, they were crammed in trying to get through the doorway, she used the doorway, the doorcurtain, she struck and swung at them, pain in her arm in her leg sweet pleasure because it's fight pain, battle pain, the wounds are our badge of triumph, Lidae, be proud of them! She felt her sword close with skin and muscle, felt the shock of wounding one of them deep.

A roar, from one of them. A sword smashed into her face and the pain blinded her. She fell.

'Now burn it.'

'No wait, wait ... look here!'

'Good. Now burn it. We need to get back.'

'Get her sword.'

Through the pain in the dark, she thought: no. No. Not my sword. She was still holding it.

'No time. Need to get back. Just fucking burn it.'

She thought: I remember saying these things.

'What about Julius? And Garet?'

'What about Julius? What about Garet?'

'Come on. Just come on.'

She thought: when they burn the house, they'll burn the bodies. So that's good. '*Just like they've been burned with the rest of our dead, see?*' Acol had said to her. '*Thing to be glad of.*'

She couldn't see properly. Just fire heat. She could smell it. Her house burning. Feel the heat on her, burning her. Someone will come, she thought. Acol. Maerc. I'm alive, they'll come.

Another sound, above the burning. Her head rang with pain. Hard to hear it. Something screaming. A horse, she thought. That's cavalry. A charge being taken down. Burned, she thought, breathing the smoke smell. The dragon burned them. I'd like to see the dragon again. Such a beautiful thing. So … we won, I suppose. The enemy's horses, screaming. We always win. No, that's a lie, we tell ourselves we always win. Screaming, howling, an animal trapped in the fire with her. Like when a city burned and the dogs howled.

She thought: Salith Drylth. My village. Burning.

She thought: child. Baby boy. Little boy. Crying. Can't make him stop.

She got up, stumbled, fell, got up. Go slowly. On her feet she was blind, and then it was just dark, and then she was blind. She touched her face and it was wet.

'Odd thing,' Acol says, 'but you don't feel your own blood.'

The wound on her face was too painful to feel. She thought: my house is burning. My children.

'Samei? Ryn? Ryn? Samei? Samei?'

In the flames now she could see. Ryn was lying on the floor, in the living place, thrown sideways. He's dead, she thought, he's dead dead dead. She screamed. She could see herself yelling at him and him crying when he hadn't liked the cimma fruit, 'What a waste, Ryn, oh, Ryn, what a waste, I told you.' All the dead she'd seen. He looked like all of them. She scrabbled beneath the bed for Samei. He was right at the back, it was impossible that he'd got so small to be squeezed in there. In the dark she couldn't see him, just a shadow, the firelight reflected in his eyes. 'Samei!' Lidae screamed. 'Samei. Get out. The house is burning. Get out. Get out. The house is burning,'

A noise like a horse being butchered. He was pushing back away from her, back into the wall. The wall would be burning. 'Samei!' Samei! Get out!' she screamed.

When he was born, he had stuck, 'Push, push!' Rena had shouted at her, 'come on, bairn, come on, push, come on, bairn.' 'I can't push,' she had screamed. 'I can't push.'

'Samei!' I'm dying, she thought, if I don't get him out of there, I'm dying I'll die here he'll die. 'Samei!'

He came out on his belly like a worm, in the flames his eyes were vast, his lips were drawn back showing all his teeth. He ran past her, gasping his dying noises, running in a crouch almost on all fours, out of the house into the dark. Lidae ran after him, staggering, she almost fell, smashed her shoulder and her hip against the doorframe through to the living place, she was blind and then the fires were too bright, and everything was golden and then she was blind again. 'Samei! Go to the village! Run! Run!' She wasn't sure she was speaking. She came to Ryn's body crumpled up and stretched out, his limbs all wrong. She couldn't go past him.

In her head, screaming: 'We burn the dead, the dead are gone to nothing.' 'I told you, you wouldn't like it, I told you, oh Ryn what a waste why don't you listen, when will you ever just listen to me, Ryn?'

Outside the house Samei was choking, howling.

Ryn's hand twitched.

Just the flames. The light moving. She could not go past him. His head moved. She saw him through the pain. His eyes were open, staring at her.

'Ryn! Ryn!' She got down, nothing hurt her, the fire was a glorious light by which she could see his face, his chest moving. His lips moving, trying to say something to her. She got him up, he was frail and light and so heavy, his hands seemed to beat against her, pushing her away, he made a noise like the noise Samei was making, a beast noise, terrified. Sheets of flame, the building was falling, it had burned so fast, so absurdly fast nothing could burn this fast it would take hours. She carried him out of the house through the fire. He was silent now. He struck at her.

Seven

When they came out of the house the sun was rising, and she was running into the dawn sun. She screamed, 'Samei! Ryn!' She fell down onto the ground, the grass was wet with dew, fragrant. All about her the birds were singing. Ryn screamed. Lidae clutched him. He struck her arms, pushed himself away from her. The whole side of his face was smashed and bloodied. Both of them all broken up. He ran a little way, wavering, sank down away from her with his arms wrapped around himself.

'We have to go to the village,' Lidae cried at him. 'Get help. Get your wound treated. You'll die. I'll die.' She thought: I don't know what to do.

The sky was pink and golden. The wind was blowing from the sea. In front of them, in the wet grass, there were buttercups bright as sunshine. White daisies. A fat black beetle. A spider's web. She could hear the sea, they were near the sea, the waves broke on the shingle, made the stones whisper. When Ryn was little he had liked her to make a shushing sound when he was crying like the waves moving the shingle. She raised her head a little and she could see the line of the water ahead of her, the green turf broke off suddenly and there beyond was light and thin distance that was pale sky or pale sea. Don't go near the cliff edge, Ryn, Samei. Promise. She didn't remember running so far to be near the cliff top. A gull cried out, she could see gulls circling, beyond the green line where the cliff ended in the sky and the sea. Somewhere far off there was a cockerel crowing.

'Where's Samei?' She was so confused. She remembered being in the sick tent, once, her leg all bashed, the man next to her had been wounded in the head, he was clean and bandaged but he didn't know where he was, shouted, nothing he said made sense, just a jumble of words, and he had screamed that the noise they made around him was so loud it hurt him. They killed him, in the end, because there was nothing they could do, all he did was scream in pain, rant senseless things. The buttercups nodded in the wind, hazy golden. There was a field to the west of the village so heavy with buttercups that the air above it was golden. At night, the flowers glowed. If Rena had told her it was magecraft, an ancient magician's blessing on them, Lidae would have believed it.

Ryn was sobbing. Lidae looked up. He had dragged himself back a little towards the house. She could see the house now, so much further away than she remembered running. It was almost all consumed by the fire, slumped, dregs and ash. The flames barely showed now it was day. Ryn had found Samei, the two of them were together holding each other, so tight together she couldn't see where their bodies were separate. Lidae stumbled back towards them.

'Ryn. Samei. Babies. My small ones.'

They both turned and looked at her. Samei's face was empty. Little blind baby thing, asleep with his eyes open. His lips were drawn back showing bleached white gums. His eyes were round. Ryn was wounded, bleeding, his face black with clotted blood. He could have lost his right eye, she thought.

'Ryn. Samei.'

Ryn said, 'Go away. Go away. Get away.' He screamed, 'Mummy. Mummy.'

'Ryn—'

'Get away!' he screamed. He clutched at Samei. 'Don't kill us.' He screamed, 'Get away! Don't kill us!'

'Ryn—'

'You killed someone!' Ryn screamed. 'Get away from him!' He was clutching Samei so tight Lidae was afraid he would hurt him. Smother him, break his arms, his bones must be so frail and thin. 'Samei!' Ryn screamed. 'Samei!'

'We'll die.' Lidae sat down on the wet grass. Opened her hands out to them, still and calm, as Emmas had taught her to do with a calf. Her head was ringing, the image of them flickered. Blurring in her eyes. Trying to look into brilliant sunlight in a dark room. When she touched the wound, it was sticky. She could feel the blood scabbing and the scabs coming open again. Ryn's wound would be worse. Much worse.

Five men. She had killed two of them. Five against one, and she been in a nightshift, no helmet, half asleep, in the dark, her head filled with fear for her children. No shame. If I had made a different sword stroke, attacked them rather than defended, if I had moved my sword up instead of down, if I had … had … had … I can't remember the fighting, how I was moving what I did, no one can, just striking it out, but I can see it in my head, if I had done it differently I would have fought them off, not been wounded, they would have gone, I would have killed them, Ryn, Samei, I'm sorry, sorry, sorry, I failed you. All that fighting, all those years fighting.

'Like you were bloody born to this,' Acol says, wondering. 'Never stop being amazed at the things you can do.'

Pride fills her. 'What can I say? I am so bloody good at this, I know.'

Five men, in armour, and she'd been in her nightshift, half asleep. 'Ryn, get under the bed!' If he'd listened. If it happens again, she thought, he must stay under the bed.

The strange way the mind had, all soldiers did it when things had gone badly, replaying it, pretending it could be done again. Next time it happens, I'll kill them, he'll stay under the bed.

It was getting warmer. But she felt the cold creeping into her. I'm dying, she thought. Ryn is dying. The sun was high in the sky now. The buttercups were shining too bright when she looked at them. There were crows and big black-headed gulls gathering in the ruins of her house. She sat in her nightgown all ripped and bloodied, the boys near naked in their nightshifts, helpless.

Emmas died, she thought. Died and left me to this alone. Curse him. If he'd been there: the two of us together against five, home territory, back-to-back, easy. She thought, absurdly, of the times he'd left her alone to manage the children while he was out hunting or working the land, and she'd been so resentful of him.

She thought: but I shouldn't think it would have been different if he was here, that he could have saved them. She thought: I was always better at close fighting like that than him.

She thought: Ryn would have stayed hidden and safe, if Emmas had been the one who said it.

'Lidae?' A voice called, drifting in the sunshine. It sounded frightened, hoarse, wary. Dreading what it would find, preparing itself. 'Lidae?' A girl's voice.

Ayllis, Cythra's daughter, came running up the slope from the house to the village. She was white and crying, her pale golden hair and her face all smeared with ash, dressed like they were in her nightclothes with blood and ashes smeared all over. She ran fast up the grass towards them, trampling the buttercups. Her eyes were wide and sick. When she got to the boys she screamed their names. They clutched her legs, the three of them held each other, the boys pulling themselves at the girl's body, tight and tight and tight. She was shrieking and laughing.

Lidae tried to walk to them. Her head was hurting and she had to crawl. She spat blood before she could speak. The relief flooding over her: someone has come.

'Lidae... Your face...' Ayllis said.

'Is Cythra alive? Ayllis?' Cattle rustlers, chance thieves, knowing she was newly widowed. Soldier, armed and in armour, smelling of blood and smoke, tired, excited. 'Is Cythra alive?' Salith Drylth, she thought, sacked and burned like a great city.

'Mummy killed someone,' said Ryn, burying his face in Ayllis' skirt.

Ayllis didn't look up. 'Mother is alive,' she said. 'So is father.' Her voice was small and dead. She could not look at Lidae or the boys, she looked at the grass where the daisies were growing. Lidae looked at the grass, but her heart leapt. Ayllis said, very slowly, 'Dylas is dead. And Marn. And Niken.' Her brothers. 'We hid beneath the floor. Me and mother. The boys couldn't fit there. They said that we had to hide. That they'd protect us. I heard them. I saw them, through the cracks in the floor. They set the house on fire. They even killed the dogs.' She looked up then, said, suddenly, angrily, 'Ryn is hurt! You're hurt! I need to help you!'

'Water,' said Lidae. Cloth.' She thought: the house was all burned up to nothing.

'We can go back there... mother is alive ... the village ... we can ... we...' Ayllis said. 'It's all burned there, it's— Even the dogs— But there's nowhere else we can go.' She said, 'Mother is there. And Hana. Rena the healer is ... is ... But she ... she taught Hana healing. Your face, Lidae. And Ryn. We have to go to Hana. Hana can heal Ryn.'

'Yes,' said Lidae, because she must say something. They must talk and do things. She thought: Ayllis is a child of thirteen, Hana is a girl of sixteen. Rena her mother brought Hana to help when Emmas was sick, Rena sent her out of the house when Emmas was dying, didn't want her little girl to see a man die.

'Let's ... let's go then.' Lidae tried to stand, went down on her knees, shaking, wanting to vomit, her head black with pain. Come on, Lidae. Don't let them see, Ryn and Samei, they can't see their mother like this. Ayllis was trembling, looking at her. A child of thirteen. Innocent. Lidae, an adult, grown and strong, a soldier-woman with a silver wine cup on her table looted from a king's house, weak and wounded and shaking at Ayllis' feet. Too frightening. And it was shameful also to be helpless like this in front of Ayllis, who was a child still, who had known nothing bad but only a farmer's life and fat peace.

Ayllis tried to help her, but Ryn was clinging to the girl's skirt, his wounded face crushed into her; he screamed when Ayllis tried to ease his grip on her so that she could help Lidae up. Samei let go of Ayllis easily, lay on the grass curled round himself staring at nothing. In the end Ayllis had to pull Ryn off her, he tried to walk but fell down as Lidae had fallen. He flinched away, shouting 'no,' when Lidae his mother tried to pick him up.

'I'll take him,' Ayllis said, 'come here, Ryn, poor boy oh poor little one.'

Ayllis carried him, panting and gasping because he was so heavy, too big to be carried. And there was a relief in Lidae, that she tried to hide, crush away down, shameful, because she was in such pain, it would have been so painful to carry Ryn.

Emmas could carry him still, if Emmas had been here alive, hadn't died and abandoned them. The two of them fighting side-by-side. You bastard, Emmas, for leaving me alone like this.

Samei flinched back from her also, his teeth still bared, his eyes still empty. He made a noise like a dumb thing in the back of his throat when she lifted him. He was unharmed but his skin felt very hot like he was burning with fever. He had wet himself and soiled himself, his body was vile in Lidae's arms. She kissed him over and over, rubbing the clotted blood on her face into his beautiful hair, felt disgust at the feel and the smell of him. He was so heavy. She blinked and gasped as she carried him. The smell of him. Gods, the smell of him. His breath rasped through his teeth and sounded like a sword being drawn.

They came over the brow of the hill and saw the village of Salith Drylth with the may trees all in blossom behind it. All the houses were burned, standing up black and ruined, raw somehow like a mouth of broken teeth. Three lone figures picking around, bent over, keening. The sound of their grief like waves, too loud for them. One figure stopped, as Lidae watched them, ripped at its clothes to rend them in mourning, lay down in the dirt and screamed.

'*What is best in life?*' Maerc had once said, drunk and angry. '*Such a paean we have raised, Lidae.*'

The crows and the gulls were coming. They screamed at each other. Fighting for the spoils. And an eagle, huge on its bronze wings, circling, watching. They are cunning birds, eagles, they can recognise the sounds of war and human carnage. The figure lying bent over got up, shrieked, ran towards a place where a crow was pecking. Lidae saw that it was Cythra. Cythra's voice rose frantic: 'Get away! Get away. My son! Get away from him! Get away!' The crow shrieked back at her. She fell down over her son's body. Lidae saw her fists pounding at her son's dead flesh.

'Mother!' Ayllis cried.

Ryn shouted, 'Aunty Cythra! Uncle Devid!'

Cythra raised her head from her son's body. Even from far off, her face made Lidae flinch. Like Samei, her lips were drawn back, bloodless. Blind and dumb and inhuman. A curse-face. The stone-grief took all understanding from her: and then her face changed, a light came into her, wonderful dazed joy at seeing them. 'Ryn! Samei!' Cythra came running, her eyes red with weeping, her dress torn into mourning rags, dirt and ash and her sons' blood all over her. She clutched Ryn from Ayllis, fell upon him weeping, kissing him, pulled Ayllis and Ryn together into her arms.

Devid reached out to take Samei. 'Here we are, Samei. Here now, little man.' His voice was soft and strong and kind, the voice of a good warm day in the sunshine when there is no shadow of harm in the world. 'Here now, Samei. Little man.' The boy leapt into Devid's arms then, clutched tight into him far tighter than he had gripped Lidae.

Such a relief, not to be holding him, so heavy, Lidae's arms shaking at the weight, her wound screaming, the old wounds in her shoulder and thigh screaming, Samei was hot and stiff and vile with piss and shit, disgusting to hold, she wanted to let go of him, sleep, lie down and sleep. Her face hurt so much and all her old wounds hurt. Ryn and Samei being alive is making them happy, giving them something to think of that isn't what happened, it's a good thing, the boys going to them, them taking the boys from me, like talking to a soldier of home when he has a wound cleaned, a good thing for them…

'You're alive, alive, alive, alive, alive,' Cythra was saying. 'Little things. Little things.' She was laughing and crying like Ayllis had been. 'Alive. Alive. Little things. Little things.' A good thing for Cythra, and the boys, a good thing.

A gull shrieked overhead. Gulls fighting over something. Cythra screamed, almost threw Ryn down. Ran back to the ruins of the village, waving her arms to keep the birds away. A crow flew up, cawing. 'My son!' Cythra screamed. 'Leave him alone. Leave him alone.' She pulled at the boy's body, trying to drag him. Crying, cursing. The body was too heavy for her. She screamed, and then she was unable to scream.

In the silence, a blackbird sang.

Devid said, 'She won't let me touch them. My own sons. She is trying to dig a grave for them. She is trying to move them. But she won't let me touch them.' He touched the bruise on his face. 'This is when I tried to help her with Niken's body.

'They came from the east,' said Devid. His face had the same blank horror as Samei but where Samei was dumb suddenly now Devid could not stop speaking. 'From over towards Baerrryn Drylth. Over Kelurlth Head. I was dragging the boat up the shingle, I saw them coming. A hundred of them, maybe, half of them mounted. They came down slowly. They were dressed in black armour, the crests on their helmets were black like the ones the Lord of Karke's soldiers wear. Their horses were huge. They were silent as they came down, and everything stopped as they came, the gulls had still been flying, they'd come to my boat to steal my catch, but they fell silent when the soldiers came. Even the sea seemed to be silent. I swear it. They were so silent I thought ...' He flushed and said, 'I thought they were ghosts. Soldiers from the old battles. There's a grave up there on Kelurlth Head. Graves out in the hills. You've seen them. I thought they were ghosts. They were carrying torches, some of them, the torches burned without flickering, I swear it, the wind was blowing but the flames burned straight up like they do in a sealed room. When the moonlight showed their faces, I couldn't see their faces, just darkness ... only some of them, I could see their faces, their eyes, they were dead faces. I swear it. They had no life in them, the moonlight shone on them and made their armour bright, they had gold on their armour, some of them ... but their faces were like they were dead. Their horses were ... The horses' heads looked like horse skulls. I couldn't hear even the sounds of the horses' hooves.' He said, his voice very low, 'I hid in the boat. I had the sail down, I hid beneath it. Then I heard ... from the village...' He kissed Samei's hair, sweat-matted and full of dust and ash. His face went blank like dry earth. He said, 'When I got to the village...'

He buried his face in Samei's hair. Lidae heard him whispering, 'Little one. Little man. Little one.'

Cattle thieves. Ten, twenty of them, it's easy to overestimate numbers when they're armed, when some of them are mounted. *'Gods, Lidae, you said two hundred of the buggers, can't be more than fifty of them. Emmas, I could understand, he grew up in the middle of bloody nowhere, two men and a dog's a crowd to him. But you, Lidae, you're a city girl, you should know what fifty fucking people looks like. Got us all excited for nothing.'* 'But they looked like so much more, I'm sorry, they looked so much more, all on horses like that ...'

Cattle thieves. Ten or twenty of them.

Devid raised his head and looked at her. Now his eyes were full of hate. 'The Lord of Karke is building a fortress, they say, on the headland above the harbour.'

The wound on Lidae's face burned up in hot shame. Yes. I saw it. But I … I didn't think … Not a fortress for war. Playing. Like I keep my sword and my helmet. She could not look at him. She could not stay there with Devid's eyes on her, Devid and Ayllis holding her children that she had not been able to protect. I had a sword, she thought, a sword, a sword, a sword, I should have protected them, all of them. They must think that, all of them. Ryn is wounded, she thought, I am wounded, I should see to Ryn, I should see to Samei, I should clean my own wound. But she went down to ruins of the village to find Cythra, still struggling to bury her sons. Bent over, crushed down and small, shrunk down to child-size herself, pulling, pulling, and the body lay stretched out in the dust with the rubble of the house half-covering it. So hacked up Lidae could not tell which of the three of Cythra's sons it was. A man, tall and strong, bloody and dead.

'Let me help you,' said Lidae. 'Cythra.'

Cythra whispered. 'He's my son.' Her voice was like dry earth.

'Let me help you. Please.' Lidae bent down, placed her hand on the body, helped Cythra to drag him. All his wounds were in front. Proper fighting wounds. Pride words, honour words, on the dead grey skin. Lidae thought to tell Cythra this but did not.

They didn't even cut me deeply, she thought. Just knocked me aside and left me.

'Don't touch him.' Cold shaking old woman's hands pushed her away. 'My son. Don't touch him.'

'You helped me lay out my husband's body,' said Lidae. 'You helped me when he was dying, you helped me lay him out when he was dead. Let me help you, Cythra. Please. Or let Devid help you. They're his sons too, Cythra,' Lidae said.

Cythra's curse-face stared at her, blind and silent. A stone where a woman's face had been. In the eastern isles, Lidae thought, they have stories of seal-women with stone-faces, who are a curse to those who have brought grief on them. Cythra saw Lidae the soldier, Lidae the mother of living sons, Lidae who had not been there with her sword to defend them. Drew back withered lips to spit and curse. May your life be as desolate as the winter ocean, may your life be flood and famine and dry bitter earth where no plant will grow, may your life be stones, Lidae, as mine is.

'Dylas heard a noise,' said Cythra. 'Was worried about the cattle. He went out … he came back, told Ayllis and me to hide under the floor. He and Marn and Niken … they… Lidae—' Cythra embraced her. Pressed her face into Lidae's shoulder. 'They…'

'We can bury them beneath the may trees,' said Lidae. 'If you want me to help you. Raise a funeral mound over them.'

Cythra looked down at the broken body. Niken, Lidae thought then, the youngest of Cythra's three sons. Cythra looked up at Lidae. 'Lidae. You're wounded. And Ryn is wounded. Little boy. And Samei must be terrified.' She looked down at the body a long time. She said very slowly, 'We can bury them later. Once we've seen to you and the boys and Ayllis. You living ones.' She drew Ryn and Samei back up into her arms, held them and held them.

Eight

War is not women's work, the men say, in the dark, when they think Lidae can't hear them. These women soldiers, dirty and muscled, dressed like men, killing like men. War is men's work, for which women are unsuited. Leave war to the men.

Women's work is to bear children, the men say in the dark when they think she can't hear them. To raise strong sons for battle, to give comfort to the wounded, to bury the dead.

Nine

'But who were they?'

Devid said, 'Why did they do this?

All of them who has survived looked at Lidae to explain something that could not be explained. 'Because .... Because ...' she said at last, 'in war... these things are done.'

They sat in the woods beyond the village. A good place. The trees were white birch and beech and hazel, good trees, the leaves were still bright and new, green-gold, letting in the spring sunlight, the earth beneath the trees was thick with bluebells just fading, a thicket of brambles coming into flower, wild honeysuckle tangled out not yet in bloom. A clearing like a pool in the trees, the sunlight came down strong, it was getting warmer, almost a hot summer's day today. In a shaft of sunlight filled with seed-fluff floating in the light and almost shining, two butterflies danced together their courtship dance. In this place, enchanted, they sat, the last few survivors from the village, emptied out, dressed in their night clothes and the few scraps they could find in the village, dirty with ash and blood, asking absurd, impossible things. A blackbird sang overhead as they asked these impossible things.

'Why? Why? Who were they?'

What they mean is 'how can they do this?' They looked at Lidae to tell them.

Ryn had screamed when Lidae tried to go near him. But he had let Ayllis and Cythra clean his face, wrap him in a clean shirt that was too big for him, bind cloth in place of shoes around his feet. He sat very still now in the shade of a white birch tree, looking up at the leaves dancing. He had Cythra's cloak over him as a blanket. Hana had given him a healing stone to hold, a round black pebble with a hole worn through it by the sea, hung a spray of new green beech leaves and a spray of willow leaves in a garland over his chest. The leaves moved like leaves dancing in the breeze in time with his breathing. His hair and skin had been washed clean of blood; there was a poultice on his face that smelled of green things and honey. Lidae almost wept to see his left eye was clear and open, the gash on his face just missing it. Saw again and again the sword stroke coming down just a finger's width to the right.

'What have they put on your face? You smell sweet as honey cakes. You'll be healed soon. Healed and well, with a scar to impress the girls, nothing like a good scar my friend Acol used to say, like someone's written how brave you are on your skin, he used to say. I have a scar on my leg, don't I, do you remember when Samei thought it was painting on my skin like they paint the rune words on things?' Lidae took his hand, squeezed it tight, and he snatched it away from her, folded his hands together so that she couldn't hold them. 'I was so frightened for you, you shouldn't have run out, I told you to stay safe under the bed away from them, oh, Ryn, why didn't you listen? I thought you were dead. I thought you were dead.' He said nothing. His face didn't move. He looked like his father had looked when she had lain the body on the pyre. Only the leaves on his chest rusted as his breath came. Lidae sat beside him but he did not look at her.

Samei lay with his face buried Ayllis' lap. Ayllis sat stroking his hair, staring at his hair seeing her three brothers dead. He, too, had flinched away when Lidae first tried to come near. He did not scream, but he had pushed himself into Ayllis lap away from her, his lips drawn back baring his white bloodless gums. 'He's trying to climb back inside you, the little lamb, he'd climb back inside you if he could,' Cythra had said of the way Samei had clambered into Lidae's lap as a baby, nestled himself into his mother's body. Ayllis looked up at Lidae fierce and hating. His own mother, and he fears you, what did you do to him? He says you killed a man, last night, my brothers died, all three of them, they even killed the dogs, Lidae; they all say you were a warrior once, my mother admires you, Lidae, my mother talks about you sometimes with envy, Lidae the soldier, swaggering through the village better than us smiling knowing playing this stupid game of being a farmer sneering at us for being only farmers; where were you, Lidae, when they killed them all even the dogs, where were you, Lidae? Your own sons are sickened by you.

Out of a whole village there was left Cythra, Devid, Ayllis, Lidae and her children, Hana the healer's daughter. But perhaps, Lidae said to herself, perhaps some of the others ran away into the hills. Took their boats out into the night sea. Some of the fishermen, she thought, some of them will come back from a night's fishing, nets shining with their

catch thrashing silver, it was a clear night last night and the sea was calm
and the wind blew soft to the north, good weather for fishing.

But they had treated Ryn's wounds and Lidae's wounds, dragged
the dead into a pile beneath the may trees that grew beside the village,
heaped branches of may blossom over them, gathered together a few
scavenged things left undamaged by the fire and the killing, and still
no one had come back from the hills, or from the sea with silver fish
thrashing in their nets.

'The Lord of Karke will send soldiers to help us, to kill them, as soon
as he learns what has happened,' said Hana.

Silence from Lidae.

'The king, even, in Thalden. He will send his warriors to protect us,'
Hana said. 'They will come on their big horses and protect us.'

'Thalden is a hundred miles away,' said Ayllis.

Silence from Devid and Cythra and Lidae.

Hana said, 'Who were they? Why did they do such a thing?'

It is done in war. That is all I can say. A man orders it, and it's done.
'They did it to frighten people,' Lidae said.

'Frighten people?' Devid said, almost laughing, 'They killed everyone.
There's no one left to be afraid. Because they killed everyone.' He said,
as Ayllis had said, as if it was the worst thing because the mind has to
hold something small as the worst thing, 'They even killed the dogs.' He
said, 'There's no one left to be frightened. Bloody stupid as a plan, then,
wasn't it?'

'To frighten … The Lord of Karke, perhaps, ask him for money,
blood-money to leave here … Other villages … The king and his lords
in Thalden…' Lidae thought: there were great wars once, in the south
and the west, far from here, I fought in them. The greatest battle host
that ever walked the face of the earth, they said of us, numberless as the
stars in the sky. The sound of our feet marching was like a storm, they
said of us, our armour and our spears shone brighter than the light of
the sun. We burned whole villages, fields rich in corn, orchards, flocks,
whole cities we burned, to frightened others into surrendering to us.
But far away and long ago now. The great host was disbanded, I came
here a thousand miles away from the fighting, there are old men here to
whom war is a story their grandfathers once told them. I have married
and borne sons and seen them grow into strong boys, since the fighting
ended. It cannot come again.

A great and terrible grief rose in her. The truth of it, sitting here in
this beautiful, enchanted place. When I was a child, when I lived in the

city of Raena that is now barren dust, when I was a child I remember hearing people talking of the wars far away from us, stories, exciting, frightening, they liked talking about it, how terrible it all was. 'They burned the fields, they killed everyone, even the children,' they would say with relish, thrilling at it. Disappointing, even, almost, when someone said it was not as bad as the rumours said.

'King Durith in Thalden won't be frightened,' said Hana, her voice both so dead and so hopeful it hurt Lidae like her wound hurt her. Hana who had never seen Thalden, to whom 'king' was a word that might as well mean nothing at all, who said 'King Durith' as she said 'a thousand years ago before the world was raised' or 'in a thousand years when the world is drowned'. 'King Durith and Lord Sabryyr and Lord Temyr and the other great ones, they'll protect us.'

'Who were they?' Ayllis said again. 'Why did they do this?'

'I don't know,' Lidae said.

Hana screamed and pointed up into the sky. 'Look! Look!'

The blackbird stopped singing. The wind dropped. Silence over everything.

A shadow. Huge, blocking the sun's warmth. Great wing beats.

Its body was pale gold like faded winter leaves after snowfall, crusted with frost. Its wings were bronze and red and black. It moved with heavy grace, banking in the sky. Spouting out shining fire. Brighter than the sun. They sat in its shadow, frozen, the shadow of its wings like a curse screamed at them. I have never seen anything as beautiful as a dragon, Lidae thought. Once, in thick snowfall, struggling in the battle lines, she had seen two dragons fighting.

The trees swayed in the wind of its wing beats, the leaves rustling. Pretty child song to lull the baby: *dappled, sparkling, dancing, sparkling, whisper, whisper, singing, singing.* It turned, it seemed right above them, a warm breeze on Lidae's face scented of smoke and sweetwood. Its wing beats were flashes of pure light. It lowered its head, its fire spewed out. A flower of fire, unfolding golden petals.

The smell of heat, hot metal, green things burning. Memory smell. As the smell of the dead village had been.

Blurred the sky. Like rain falling from far away. It flew off towards the high hills, and was a daystar shining distant, and was gone.

The blackbird started up singing as if it had never happened. In a shaft of sunlight at the edge of the clearing, two brown butterflies danced their courtship dance. A pigeon flew up from a birch tree in a heavy flap of leaves. A fly buzzed around Lidae's face.

'Firedrake,' Devid said, 'oh gods. Oh gods. That was not a real thing. Please. That was not a real thing.'

'What was it?' Hana cried out. 'What?' As if she had not seen it. 'What was it?' Lidae heard it distantly. A hand tugged at her hand, Ryn's voice saying in his sweet boy's voice, 'What was it? Mummy? What was it?'

'A dragon,' Lidae said, her own voice distant. 'It was a dragon. The greatest and most beautiful of all the things of war. Some say the most beautiful of all things that live.'

'Will it kill us?'

'It's gone,' she said, yearning.

'Will it come back and kill us?' The hand clutched at her so tight it hurt. She shook her hand it get it free. 'Mummy?'

'It—' What am I doing? Ryn's wounded face was staring at her, as she had been staring after the dragon. Softened. Wondering. What are we doing, she thought, piling up corpses as if we can stay to bury them, sitting here without protection, staying here?

She grabbed Ryn's hands. My son! My first-born son! More beautiful even than a dragon! He wanted her to protect him from the dragon.

She said, trying to keep her voice calm, 'Samei, Ryn: we have to get going.' The poultice on Ryn's face glistened. Sticky sweet honey, green leaves, mud. His face was filled with fear again. She said, 'You hurt, I know. You have to be strong for me, Ryn. My old strong boy, yes? We have to go; you have to help me with Samei.' She shouted to the others: 'We have to go. Now. We have to get a few things together and go.' She tried to make her voice sound like Acol's. Like a man. Voice that you did everything it said.

'Will it come back?' Hana said. 'The ... Or the men ... Will they come back?'

This is all real. Suddenly.

Lidae said, 'I don't know.' She said more strongly, try to be strong, look at Samei's face, try to be strong, 'I don't think they will come back, no.' Look to the horizon tonight to the west, she thought. We will see Karke burning. All of Illyrith burning. King Durith in Thalden and Lord Sabryyr and Lord Temyr and the other great ones: no one will come.

'Where is there to go?' said Devid. 'Baerryn Geiamnei? Karke? Thalden?' He put his arm very tight around his daughter Ayllis. She was still holding Samei, and he stroked the boy's pretty hair. 'I don't know,' he said, to nothing and no one.

'I won't leave,' whispered Cythra. 'I won't leave my sons.'

Ryn pulled his hand back from Lidae's, suddenly, quickly, pulled back from her, fled back to Samei who lay unmoving in Ayllis' lap with his face staring away. Lidae saw Ryn's eyes watch her like an animal, because he knew somehow what she was going to say and he was more frightened of her than of the soldiers or of the dragon. Because he had seen her in the night with her sword drawn, killing.

'We have to leave now,' she said. 'Now. We can't go to Baerryn Geiamnei or to Karke, not even to Thalden even if Thalden were not a hundred miles away.' She said, finally, and as she said it she understood that they all knew, deep down, Ryn, baby Samei, Cythra, they had all known all the time they sat here hopelessly, 'They are the Army of Illyrith, the army of King Durith who rules from his throne of gold in the great city of Thalden. I fought with them for ten years. I know what they will do. We have to get away.'

Ten

A time of chaos. A time of warlords. A time of war without end. Axe-age, sword-age, the spears are raised, the banners flutter in the storm wind. Wolf-age, beast-age, age of dragons, joyfully the carrion-eaters sing. The woods are cut down to feed the forge-fires, the sweet green trees blaze up to smelt more iron and bronze. The earth is ripped open for the metals veined within it, the smiths sweat and work until their arms shake. The people must go hungry, to feed the armies marching. They have taken the horses and the oxen, the merchants and the farmers curse them. The villages are abandoned, weeds grow in the streets, for every man has gone off to war. The roads are black with soldiers marching, they raise a dust that hangs heavy in the air. Children are born whose first word is 'battle'. Children grow to adulthood knowing nothing but the music of war. A great empire rises on the blades of their swords, they march across the world killing and the world is thrown down beneath them. Power and death and glory and killing: such fine things. Such good things.

But it is over. It was far from here. Peace and justice, we fought for, once the war is ended and the empire made, they said, we will have peace and justice in which to raise our children, live long rich lives in summer sunshine, all we have to do is win.

And it was ended.

And we did win.

She thought, as she had often thought looking at her children and at Emmas, as Emmas had often said with pleasure in his sweet rich voice: this land, this place of peace, our children playing ... this good land we live in, far from the fighting, this is the kingdom we fought for, these people here in their peaceful little lives, it was in their names, for their lives, that we fought and we won.

Lord Durith is king in Thalden? Out of bloody chaos we made Lord Durith king.

Black-crested helmets, bronze armour, a dragon bright and terrible and golden shining … Plague, they called us. Carrion. Pestilence. Famine. But it was over and ended, we settled down here together, Emmas and I, in peace together, to have children together in a place of peace that we had won.

It was over. It was far from here.

It was won.

Oh Emmas, Lidae thought, I wish that you were here now with me, often we talked of this, dreamed of it, feared it. 'Would you go back to war, Emmas? Do you miss it?' 'No, no, I don't miss it, look what we have here, Lidae, my love, would you go back?' 'No, no, Emmas, I don't miss it, no.'

Oh Emmas, Lidae thought, Emmas my husband, I am glad that you died before you saw this day.

Eleven

All day they walked through the woods, going very slowly and quietly as they had to with two young children one wounded. Lidae's face hurt her, and her shoulder hurt, and her leg hurt where the old wounds had woken. She found that she was sweating and panting for breath. But she had felt so strong, dragging the villagers' bodies, determined to find them all, bury them. If the wound in my face becomes infected, if I get sick ... Ryn and Samei need me well and healed, not bent over sick. I have to protect them. Emmas's dead eyes, screaming at her that she had already failed them when they need protecting. There were five of them, Emmas! I killed two of them. More than you would have managed, alone, in your nightshirt, half-asleep. You died and left me, Emmas, if you'd been there with me we could have fought them off, the children would have obeyed you, Emmas. You died and left me alone, Emmas, and nobody will reproach you for that. But they'll reproach me forever, because I am their mother and I couldn't protect them. There was nothing more I could have done, Emmas. You were a soldier too, you must know that. Five of them! An army! Our army, come here down on them, killing them.

The children stumbled along beside her, lost in this new changed world. Samei is smiling, laughing, then he whimpers, his faces closes into itself, quenched. He flinches, takes his mother's hands, drops it, runs from her, runs back. His hands fragile as bird feathers beating at her, raging, then he hugs her, sobs, crusts her sleeve gleaming dark and silvered with tears and snot. Offerings to her. Warming, even as she tried discreetly to rub it off, 'oh, not my sleeve, baby thing.' His own sleeves and the helm of his shirt and smeared wet with his tears and snot. Disgusting, when he wraps himself against her. His tiny frail skin so hot with fear beneath. Babies, she remembered Devid saying, are soggy things. Ryn does not want to look at her, but his eyes come back to her, haunted, he can't help looking for her, wanting her, his mother, 'tell me it's all right, Mummy, tell me.' He hates himself for wanting her to reassure him. Needing her. His eyes turn cold, baleful stares, the enemy staring out over the borderland, measuring the distance that separates life from death. He makes a spitting sound, like he's copied the rough men in Karke. In Raena, she remembers men who looked at her like that. Samei points at something, a yellow flower he's noticed suddenly with a black feather, a crow's feather, beautiful, caught in the petals, black rainbows and bright summer sunshine and butter spread thick on good bread, his voice is joyful, singing, he waves the feather like a sword, petals crushed beneath his fingers, he thrusts the feather into Lidae's face. She sees Ryn glare at Samei.

I love you, Ryn. I love you so much. It's not my fault, she wants to scream at Ryn, none of this is my fault, how can it be my fault? I tried to protect you, I fought them off, five against one, didn't I try? You saw me. What do you think I can do? Do you think I want this? Enjoy this? What did you want me to do? she thought. Sit and hold you tight in my arms, comfort you, and all three of us would have been cut down?

If Emmas was alive, she thought, then I would have sat and held you, hidden you safe in my arms, while Emmas fought them. Even though I was always better at close fighting like that than Emmas.

Once, far distant, they heard a sound of screaming. Once, far distant, the wind blew from west and they smelled smoke. Otherwise they seemed the only things here living. There will be other people moving in the woods and the wild places, Lidae thought.

'We should go south,' she told the others. 'Try to get out of where the fighting is.' They will be making for Thalden, she thought, that is where the great fighting will be, not here. 'If we go around them, we can shelter for a while, hide in safety, and then when it is over, we can go back to Salith Drylth.' Bury the dead, rebuild the village, sometimes our ploughs will turn up ashes and burned bone, '*It's old*,' we'll say, '*old bones from ancient wars, long, long dead.*'

The others nodded, unquestioning: that Lidae, the solider woman, she's killed people, she knows these things. Even Devid.

'Your sword and your helmet, Lidae,' Devid said suddenly. 'You should go back for them. You should have brought them.'

'What?'

'You need to get them.'

Cythra said, with something in her voice that was harsh as red fire, 'With your sword you can fight, Lidae. If they come again.'

'I can't fight an army. I couldn't fight five men.' She saw Ayllis' eyes go wide in terror. 'It's better,' she said, 'that none of us are armed. If I have a sword and a helmet, we are marked as enemies. Like this, harmless, they will ignore us.' That is a lie, she thought, I know it's a lie.

The thought of the sword and the helmet ... She thought: I killed a man for my sword once.

They walked on for hours, keeping to the wildest parts of the woods where the trees grew thick together and people did not often come. Ryn walked alongside Cythra, holding her hand; it seemed to Lidae that the wounded child was helping the woman along, that without the boy beside her Cythra would fall. Cythra stopped and stared back, very often at first; sometimes she would take a few steps back the way she had come. Each time, she would look at Ryn beside her, smile at him, take his hand again, walk on. Devid and Ayllis walked together. Lidae carried Samei for a long time until her body hurt her too much, and then Devid took him. Ayllis held Samei's hand so that the three of them were pressed together close. Samei was stiff and fever-hot. Not a face but a skull. As if the soldiers had already killed him.

Hana, Rena the healer's daughter, trailed behind them, alone. After a while, Lidae came to walk beside her. They were all walking in silence, looking around them, waiting-listening for black-plumed helmets and swords and blood. Lidae's hands moved down to her hip where her sword would be; in the end she walked with them clasped tight. Hana said something, just a noise of something, a silent weeping sound she made as she walked with her head bent. At the sound Ryn turned from walking beside Cythra. Looked back at Lidae with hate in him and looked away.

Towards evening the light seemed to change. A quality to the light that was frightening. The trees were very thick here, they crept along very slowly crouched and low. Evening was coming. Everything seemed very far off and unreal, creeping along between tangled branches in silence, hard to remember sometimes what had happened to them. A wind began to blow into their faces, pleasantly warm, a summer wind that was good to stand in when the wheat was high and golden and the sheep bells rang across the fields, drowsy warmth blowing from the south with a memory of the warm sweet-scented spice-scented air of childhood. Lidae raised her face trying to see the sky through the thick leaves. A sickly cast to the light, through the dappling green of the trees, a heaviness, the sky was changing.

'Is it a storm?' whispered Hana, with fear in her. She could sense it was a bad thing, this light.

'Yes,' Lidae lied to her. 'A storm, yes.' A kind of storm, she thought. The warm air began to smell of burning. A roar that could have been thunder, a sudden brightening in the sky that could have been lightning. Through the trees, the sky in the west was strange and black-green. The quality of the light was almost like drowning.

'We need to stop for the night,' whispered Lidae. 'Here, where we are hidden.'

Cythra and Devid nodded. They had realised what was happening.

But: 'If there's a storm,' said Hana, 'we need to find shelter. There must be a village... We can't stay out here.'

'No. We stay here,' Lidae said firmly. 'Stop here.'

Hana flinched, cowered at the light in the sky. 'We can't sleep out here!' She shouted, very loudly, 'Why didn't we just go to get help? Why didn't we go to Karke?' The boys cried out at her fear, stared at her. 'Why didn't we stay in the village, or go to Baerryn? Why are we running away from everything?'

Lidae said, carefully and slowly, like talking to Samei, 'We didn't go to Baerryn Geiamnei because Baerryn Geiamnei will be burned like Salith is burned. We didn't go to Karke because Karke will be sealed behind its gates or Karke will be burning. Don't you understand that? King Durith and his lords made war all across the world and now they have come back to make war here.'

The girl said, crying: 'I want to go home. We should go home.'

'We can't go home, Hana,' Lidae shouted back at her. The girl flinched. 'In a while,' Lidae said, trying so hard, 'we can go home.'

Hana looked at her. A stern face, half child half adult, aged and purged by the last few days. But it was Ayllis who spoke. 'Like you went home?' Ayllis said. 'Home to Raena?'

'I chose not to go home. I chose to join the army, leave Raena behind. I didn't want to go back there.'

You're a child, Ayllis I remember you at Ryn's age, crying at your mother because you wanted to play outside not learn how to weave and spin. In Raena, Lidae thought, I was poor, I was nothing, I lived almost as we are doing now, my family had nothing. You have no idea of the world, Ayllis, Hana. This, this life sitting here bowed down and broken by poverty, this is what war rescued me from. I chose to leave, to be strong.

'We can't go home,' she shouted, and the girls and her sons wailed. 'Are you stupid? Don't you understand anything?'

'Listen, Ayllis. Hana, girl, listen to me.' Devid took Hana by the shoulders. A man, talking in all his authority to a child. 'First, you have to stop crying. Stop screaming. Now. Now, girl! Okay? We stay here, stop, shelter for tonight, and tomorrow we'll see. You'll be safe here. I promise.'

Hana screamed, and then she whimpered like Ryn still did in his sleep, and then she was silent. She looked up at the man and nodded. Ayllis nodded. So did Ryn and Samei.

So they stopped just where they were, beneath a tangle of beech trees, the ground beneath them was a deep drift of last autumn's leaves faded pale by frost and snowfall, soft and rustling, dried like feathers. The trees were very thick here. They could not see the sky full of fire. Lidae had to get them organised, they blinked around them, farmers not used to this rough wild living. She showed Devid and Ayllis how to get up a fire, which she didn't like doing but they had to have, just a tiny fire, a light when the dark came down on them. It is a wonder they want a fire, she thought, seeing in her mind her house burning, the flames leaping up between Samei's hunched body and the door. A memory: she had fought creatures of fire once, great beasts like horses but all running with flame, their manes and their tails red flame, men fleeing from the battlefield encased in fire, screaming, Acol had died that day, Emmas had almost died, they had lost that battle. But in the dark in frightened retreat they had made a campfire, huddled around it, stared at the flames. Thus now she showed Devid how to coax a fire from dry twigs. His face lit up and she felt her own heart jolt at the fire when it came, a tiny new spark like a life.

Ryn and Samei sat together stupefied, exhausted. They had not eaten or drunk all day. Water, Lidae thought, oh gods, water, food. She had not thought, they had been so frantic to get away... Oh gods, Lidae thought, what kind of mother cannot give her children food and drink? And leaves them slumped there, untended, while she shows off how to make a campfire, 'look at all the clever things I know to help us survive, to lead you,' we could have sat in the dusk while I hugged them, tended to them. All of her body ached to sit down beside them, fold them in her arms, just sleep now with them wrapped in her arms. We have the fire lit, now find a stream, fetch water in my hands for them ... and there was no stream near them, and she had nothing to carry water in. All these things, these endless caring needed things. I don't know what to do, Emmas. We should have searched the village for waterskins, food, cloaks ... Ten years a soldier, she thought, and I could not do that, the first thing a soldier needs to think of. At home in my burned house I have a silver cup from a lord's table, and a bronze helmet that I used to carry water in sometimes, I brought Acol water in it, when he was burned up and dying … what use is a helmet, I said, here, now, I am no longer a soldier, but I could have brought my children water in it.

'Water,' Cythra said. 'Here's water, everyone. Just a little.' Lidae had thought the woman was sitting in broken bent silence thinking only of her dead sons. But Cythra got up and held up a bag she had brought with her from the village, with a few scraps of food she had rescued and a waterskin. Lidae had not even noticed she carried it.

'Rov,' Samei whispered suddenly. 'Rov. We left Rov.'

Lidae began to speak, say something, she couldn't say what she would say or could say. You can't blame me for that, gods, you can't, ungrateful, hateful, cursed child. It's all my fault, I'm so sorry Samei, I should have thought to rescue Rov from the house, like Cythra rescued waterskins and food, useless, stupid.

Cythra squeezed Samei's hand tight. 'Rov is looking after the house, Samei. Isn't he? Keeping all the rest of your things safe for you and Ryn and your mummy. He's a good friend, isn't he, see?'

And Ayllis said, 'We can make you another doll, like Rov, not to replace him,' she said hurriedly, 'but until we go home again. You look out for a good stick or a bone, won't you?'

The flushed terrified face nodded. Closed back into itself. 'Rov. Rov.' Then silence. Ayllis clasped her hands to her mouth, rubbed her face, as if the lie had exhausted everything she had left. If she knows it's a lie, Lidae thought.

Cythra put her arm around her daughter. 'That's right, Ayllis. We can. Well done.' Ayllis knew that was a lie. Cythra said, 'Ayllis, here, have some bread. Here, Lidae, give this to the boys.'

So, finally, Lidae could go to her sons. 'Samei. Ryn. Here. Have some bread.'

Samei drew back away from her with bared lips. Hugged himself up to Ryn.

A sound in the dusk, and she knew it was only Devid or Cythra moving, it was too close to be anything else. But if I had my sword and my helmet, she thought, I could pretend I could protect them. She said, hopelessly, 'Ryn. Samei. Baby boy. Little boy. Little ones.'

Ryn said, hissing, 'Go away.'

'I had to take the lead today,' she said to Ryn and Samei and to Emmas' dead eyes seeing her, 'I had to get my wound cleaned, I had to help Cythra with her own sons' bodies, I had to lead us all away from the village, take the lead, don't you see, Ryn, Samei, you had to stay with Ayllis and Cythra because I had to do all these things to protect you, that's why I couldn't walk holding you. Can't you see?'

'Get away,' Ryn said. 'Leave him alone. Samei. Samei, don't look at her, Samei. The house burned. She killed someone.'

'I killed a soldier who was trying to kill you!' Lidae cried out. But the boy was so young. All he could see was her sword and the blood. A wall was coming up between them. Two opposed armies digging in against each other, a borderland, narrow and impassable as a knife edge, between life and death. They glare over at each other, unreachable. Sharp killing stakes, fires, trenches paved with men's bones.

When we go home… When all this stops… When we are alive again…

'I told you to hide, and you could have died, Ryn.' She was screaming now, clenching her hands, pounding her fists. 'Never, never ignore what I tell you, Ryn, I thought they'd killed you! You have to do what I tell you, they almost killed you.'

Ryn said, 'You shouted for Samei. Not for me. You were standing in the house and I was lying there wounded, and you shouted for Samei.'

Like a slap. Her anger died. 'I shouted for you, Ryn.' I did. Of course I did.

'You shouted for Samei first.'

'I—' I shouted for you both.

But I had to shout one name first.

'You tried to get Samei first. You looked at me and then you went to Samei.'

'Samei's younger.' And she said, her voice shaking, 'I thought you were dead, Ryn.'

'You shouted for Samei first. You tried to get Samei first.' Ryn said, 'When you were fighting them, you were all covered with blood and your face was lit up and you were smiling. I don't like you.'

'I thought you were dead, Ryn. But I knew Samei was alive.'

She tried to touch Ryn's face and could not. He shoved her hand away, cried out, his hands beat at her. 'Go away. Go away.' Frantic. 'Go away.' She thought of one of them forcing a girl down, the girl's hands beating up frantically trying to push her assailant away. What have I done, my gods, what can I be that my first-born son hates me like this? When you were born, she thought, I thought you were dead. A long moment, the longest I have ever known, an eternity, and I thought you were dead. At night when you were a baby screaming for hours and hours in the dark, I looked back at that moment. The shame made her want to strike him.

'Ryn, Samei,' Cythra said, 'Please, little ones, have some bread.' Her voice was so kind. 'Come on, little ones. For Auntie Cythra, see?'

A long silence.

'For Auntie Cythra, Ryn, sweet thing? You need to eat, sweet thing.'

Finally, Ryn reached out his hand, fragile and feral, not looking at Lidae. Snatched the bread Lidae was holding, gave some to Samei.

Lidae drew breath to shout with rage or cry with happiness. Cythra put her hand on her arm, shook her head.

'Good boy, Ryn,' Cythra said to the boys. 'Well done. Thank you, Samei, Ryn.'

The two boys ate in hunched silence, not looking at Lidae. She felt both pain and joy as she watched them. After they had eaten the boys fell asleep. Samei's face was clammy and filthy but relaxed back into a child's face. Ryn lay beside him, holding his hand. Lidae sat and watched them for a little, and then Cythra looked at her and she carefully moved Samei's sleeping body onto the ground and curled herself around him. He moaned and wriggled, she felt a great horror that he would wake up, scream, push her away. His hands grasped her arm, holding her, his face was soft and fat and calm like a baby's. She remembered suddenly Emmas coming in very late at night after a day hunting or a trip to Karke, looking at the children asleep, smiling down at them: '*How beautiful they are. Look at them, Lidae. How beautiful. Oh, my loves.*' Sitting in the dim light of the banked fire, tears in his eyes, watching them sleep, the greatest wonder of both their lives these two children curled up together asleep.

'*You didn't have to scream at them to go to bed, Emmas, you didn't spend all day waiting for them to finally go to sleep and stop quarrelling and crying and wanting things from you and finally let you have one moment to yourself just to think.*'

'*Yes, I know, I know, Emmas my husband, they do look so beautiful and so perfect. I could watch them forever when they're sleeping.*'

Why can I only feel this for them when they are sleeping? Watching them, far off, away from them, outside them. They run up to me, wake up to see me, and moments later we're quarrelling and I'm shouting.

'I don't know why you find it so difficult,' Emmas sometimes said.

She wrapped her arm over both the boys, fell asleep holding both of them. She thought-hoped-lied-knew that they smiled in their dreams at the feel of her holding them.

Twelve

'What are you fighting for, then, Lidae?'

'Me? I don't know. Nothing. Money. Because I'm alive and I want to stay alive. Because I ... enjoy it. I mean ... I suppose, I do it, I enjoy it ... because... It's something I can do,' Lidae says.

'You certainly can do it,' says Emmas. 'Better than any of us.'

'Well then. That's a reason, isn't it?'

Emmas laughs awkwardly, puts out his hand, almost touches Lidae's hand. A little spark, a little jolting brightness there. Lidae thinks: oh. I see it, what he's asking.

Remembers with a rush her oldest sister, Elyse, on her wedding day, flushed with something as she went out to be married to a drunkard thirty years older than her whom she had barely met. But happy. Excited for something, the future, jokes being made to her that Lidae who was still a child didn't understand, Elyse warm and laughing. All the clothes borrowed or bought with coin they'd had to borrow, 'It will be years,' their mother said, 'before we've paid for Elyse's wedding. Don't think about getting married young, Lidae, don't you dare catch a man's eye.' But her mother had been laughing, kissed Elyse with tears in her eyes, fussed rearranging the veil that Lidae thought was the prettiest thing she had ever seen. 'Joy to the bride! Joy to the bride!' Outside the house, a man danced shaking a walnut shell rattle, even strangers who passed would smile, shout 'Joy to bride!' though the bride was so poor even her borrowed dress was almost rags.

Emmas' hand almost touches Lidae's, pulls back, he says, 'That is a reason, I suppose, yes.'

'Yes,' Lidae says. She moves her hand. Touches Emmas' hand. 'Yes.' His face lights up.

When they marry, she doesn't have a veil to wear or a man dancing with a rattle, the wedding bread and the wedding cake are given them by the squad commander who has replaced Acol, whom they barely know, the bread *is stale and the cake is stale. She had felt afraid, asked herself what she was doing, it can't be undone, she thinks when she comes to eat her potion of the wedding bread and the wedding cake. As they walk away out of the tent a soldier shouts, 'Joy to the bride!' to them.*

The next day when they set out for Illyrith they aren't two soldiers marching but a couple going north together to start a new life. She looks back over her shoulder. I can still go back, she thinks to herself. And in the night, she will lie awake with Emmas sleeping beside her, beginning to be aware that she might be pregnant, I can still go back, she will think to herself.

Thirteen

Morning. Grey and pale, these fine soft spring mornings of petal-pink sky lines, drifts of birds singing, singing with joy in silver voices, a breeze rustling the green fresh new leaves. Dawn light that casts no shadow, all beyond the circle of sleepers a blur of light and dark and white mist. Lidae woke with her arms still around her children. Lay holding them.

No one else was awake, as far she could tell. She could hear them all breathing slowly, one of them, Devid or Cythra, was snoring *put put put* with an open mouth. Lidae's body ached from lying on the ground, the usual places, her shoulder, her knees, her lower back. It was ... familiar. The fresh cool of the air, the taste it had, dawn stillness, waiting. A stem of brilliant green had pressed its way up beside her through the beech mast, swelling opening buds tinted blue that made her think of a woman's pregnant blue-veined stomach. It nodded gently beside Samei's fat baby lips. The pale light somehow caught the hair on his upper lip.

After a while her shoulder was hurting too much and she sat up, very carefully lifting her arms away from the children. Ryn stirred, made a noise in his sleep, Lidae held her breath waiting. He pulled himself tighter into Samei, who stirred also, opened blind eyes at his brother, went back to sleep. Lidae rubbed her shoulder, looked out into the trees. So peaceful, calm and empty, difficult to think of them running with the sky burning. As in a conquered city life would go on for the inhabitants, who still despite everything had work to do, money to earn, families to feed. An old pleasure, waking early on a march with the rest of the squad sleeping around her snoring, sitting alone. A brief, clean moment, all the noise out of reach beyond her own circle of companions.

A crow came down, pecked at the ashes of their campfire fire, hopeful. It called out, made her jump even though she was sitting looking at it, started up with its wings beating noisily, she heard the others stir in their sleep, move in a rustle of beech leaves. Oh no, she thought, please, don't wake up yet, don't ruin it. This peace of being alone in the waking world, her hands and her feet wet on the wet earth, listening, feeling, a rare, sad thing. The crow was gone in a breath of wing beats. In its place, a blackbird and a curlew both began to sing. She looked up into the trees, trying to see the birds singing. The branches were too black and the light too thin. A movement off away to the left caught her eye, a flash of something, she turned, tense, panicked. A deer, a male with new lumps of antlers on its forehead. New green leaves poked from its mouth as it chewed. Its black water eyes flickered, nervous, it backed away and was gone. Lidae felt, oddly, as though she had seen a special and wonderful thing.

She turned back and Hana the healer's daughter was awake also, watching the deer. Lidae smiled at her. 'Did you see it?' Hana smiled back. 'Yes.'

The others woke up soon after. Samei was exhausted, slept until Ryn woke him. Sat up looking around him baffled. 'Where are we?' All the last day … a confused dream. 'Where?' He could not hold what had happened in his mind, he was frightened but could not shape it into anything meaningful, a great dark terror of screaming and fire and blood and running that he couldn't understand but couldn't shake. Almost like the men, Lidae thought, waking the morning after a great sack, drunken, fragmented memories of themselves and the carnage. With a child's eagerness now he looked around the pretty woodland. Lidae wished that he could have seen the deer.

Ryn's anger too seemed faded. He came up to Lidae, hugged her. 'The sun is shining,' he said, which she knew was him trying to tell her he was sorry for his anger.

'It is,' she said, hugging him, a half-understood secret language between them, the closest she could come to telling him she was sorry also.

Perhaps we can go back to the village, she thought. They were all thinking. In this bright morning, peaceful, beneath these fresh green trees. Wondering, as confused as the children: a nightmare, was it, we ran mad, what were we doing?

'It's all over,' Hana said. After a spring storm there is sunshine, the world is clean. 'We can—'

Three soldiers in armour stepped out of the trees.

Lidae's hand went uselessly to her hip where her sword should have been. Despair flooded over her. Devid had a knife that he had taken with him when he went fishing. She knew without seeing that it would not occur to him to take it out. It was perhaps better if he did not take it out.

'Peace,' Lidae said, holding up her hands. Her voice shook, she had to clench every part of herself tight. 'Please.'

In a moment Ryn would run or Samei would run or Ayllis would run. And then they would all be killed here, bleeding away into the fallen beech leaves.

'We have nothing, you can see that. Just spare the children, at least, please.' I need to keep my voice calm, my voice will panic the boys they'll run or Ayllis will run. I could have fought them, gods forgive me, only three of them, I could have fought them, beaten them all, if I had my sword. Gods forgive me. Forgive me, Emmas. She croaked out, 'We have nothing, you can see that. Please.'

'*Born to this, you are, Lidae, aren't you, isn't she lads?*'

'*Born to this, Acol! Yes! Poet of the fucking sword, I am!*' *and the cups clink and we drink.*

Later that night a woman goes walking through the camp past us, a child tugging at her arm and crying, her face bruised her belly swollen in pregnancy, her eyes down too afraid to look up; Lidae-the-solder feels disgusted by her, why don't you fight, you stupid pitiful thing, like I did, if anyone touched me like that I'd kill them.

A silence that rang in the woods for eternity. Black-crested helmets, black armour, three faces staring at Lidae and her children. Eternity, and a single brief heartbeat. I have seen a sword come down on me, on my friends my comrades, I have seen the spear-blade going in to kill a comrade-in-arms I was laughing with. Never have I felt the pain I feel now, seeing the sword blade that will kill my child.

'Ryn,' her mind screamed. 'Ryn. My baby. Samei.'

The soldier put his sword up. His two companions did likewise. Sad welcoming smiles.

'Peace,' the first soldier said. 'Your boys there want a mouthful of stale beer and stale bread?'

And Lidae cried out for desperate joyous relief.

The bread wasn't stale, and neither was the beer. There was cheese and sausage and dried fruit. They sat beneath the spring trees in the dried bronze of old beech leaves, eating in odd awkward silence. They all tried not to look at the swords, or the young girls Ayllis and Hana with their loose hair and long legs. Sitting in the spring morning, eating. Ryn and Samei ate hungrily, Samei almost worrying the food in his mouth like a dog. He made little noises of hunger and pleasure, like a dog.

'Slow down, Samei. It's not going to be taken away. You'll make yourself sick,' Lidae said to him.

'He can eat it how he likes. He's hungry,' said Ryn. He glared at his mother, as though it was her fault that they were hungry. 'You can't take it away from him,' Ryn said, as though she might do that.

'No, obviously, of course, I won't, I'd never, take it away from him, Ryn.'

Ryn said, 'You don't care about me choking.'

'Not eaten for a while, have they, your lads?' said the first soldier, who had introduced himself as Clews. He was old, for a soldier, pale-skinned and grey-haired with heavy lines on his face all battle-scarred. Lidae felt that she should know him.

'Not for a while,' Lidae said carefully. It was the nearest they came to talking about anything. Clews saw that, nodded, didn't speak. 'Want some raisins, boys?' he asked them. Ryn, who had understood everything, shook his head furiously. Samei, who loved raisins, shouted 'Yes!' and then Ryn ate some too because Samei was eating. Samei seemed to almost think it was a picnic outing. And then he would remember it was all wrong and terrifying and inexplicable, and his face would close in again like a door closing against the daylight.

There was a crash of metal, once, far distant, that made the birds fly up from the trees in a clap of wings. They all started, cried out, Ryn dropped the bread he was holding but he did not cry, they all stared over towards the sound, so distant, all of them trembling. Nothing. Still, even then, no one said anything.

'You can't still be hungry?' said Clews after a while. 'That's all we can share, I'm afraid, little man.' He wiped his hands on the dried leaves, stirred them up to make them rustle. Samei laughed. Ryn laughed uncertainly. Clews threw dried leaves towards Samei and Samei grinned at him.

'You've come from ... yonder?' the second of them, Rhosa, asked Lidae. She was a tall woman, creamy pale skin like an eggshell and brown hair like new spring bark on a willow tree, kindness in her face as there was kindness in Clews' face. But the helmet and the armour and the sword, the fresh bread and good beer and the cheese and the meat... Lidae said nothing, but nodded.

'You were there?' said Devid then. 'Yonder?'

A pause. Rhosa frowned. Clews stopped his games.

'No,' the third of them, Myron, said. 'No, we weren't there.'

'Throw the leaves again!' Samei shouted. He saw Myron's face, his own child's face closed up and hardened and he fell silent.

Rhosa said after a moment, 'I'm sorry.'

'Why?' Devid said, as he had said to Lidae, and as pointlessly.

'We were ordered to destroy the villages,' said Myron. 'Burn them and gut them.' He was younger than Clews and Rhosa, his skin was very dark and his hair was black. His dark eyes looked sad. 'Not in front of the children,' he said. 'I can't say in front of them.'

'It's a bit late for that,' said Cythra. 'Don't you think?'

Myron lowered his eyes. 'We didn't do it,' he said. 'Not after the first… the first one. That's why we're here.'

Silence. Waiting. The air and the water and the children's faces are screaming the question that they cannot ask or answer.

Ask it.

'And why are you here?' Lidae said. The three soldiers shifted their faces, looked at each other, tired, guilty, don't want to speak but want to speak and let it out like pissing yourself.

'Take back … what's ours, take it back,' Myron said. The youngest one, maybe still believing. 'King Durith … We made him king, yeah? So: we can unmake him king. We deserve better. That's what they said. What they said.' Big young man eyes. Stared at Devid, challenging him, he's an older and bigger man, strong-muscled arms from farming, fishing, work. 'We deserve better than King Durith,' Myron said. 'That's what they said.'

Lidea thought: we made Lord Durith king.

Lidae said, 'You deserve better?' and Devid said, 'I don't understand. What do you mean? Unmake him king?'

'The boy's garbling it.' Rhosa gestured at Myron to be silent. '"The war reaches its end," King Durith said. "Illyrith is victorious! Or soon will be. After thirty years of war, we are on the brink of victory. The world will be ours." King Durith said. As we marched against the men of Eralath and we defeated them, we took their queen's own sons prisoner, both of them. A mighty victory. Yes?'

'Yes.' The news had come by fast ship, even to Karke, even to Salith Drylth. '*The false queen of Eralath is defeated! Illyrith is triumphant, from sea to sea from north to south King Durith is rightfully king!*' The pretty slave-girl in the marketplace, smooth-skinned and glossy from southern good living, the clever southern slave-man who could read and write and cast up accounts. 'And?' Lidae said.

Myron said, 'And King Durith made a peace treaty with Eralath and gave both the princes back again unharmed, left the false queen on her throne. Said the wars were over, we should go home. Paid off half the army. Took down the horse head from its spear and buried it in the earth. Ordered us home.'

Rhosa said, 'Lord Temyr the king's general, he understood us. He was angry, same as us; he knew what's what. The greatest of the king's warriors: he didn't want some false weak peace.' Rhosa said, cold voice hissing, 'So we took Lord Temyr, and we listened to him, and we made him king in Durith's stead. He raised the luck horse, did Lord Temyr. King Temyr. We marched and fought for him.'

Myron said, 'Curse on Durith the Coward. Temyr for king.'

Devid and Cythra could only stare with absurd impossible confusion. Lidae felt sick. But … we were victorious. Again and again the same bafflement. But … if I had not thought of having a child, she thought, I … perhaps I would not have wanted to stop fighting.

'And … King Durith?' Lidae said.

I know, she thought, I know what happens to kings when they are defeated. The King of Raena, it took him three days to die. But I fought for King Durith. She had seen him once, up close, and he looked a fine enough man; he was very handsome once, Acol used to say, and a great warrior, when he was young. She had fought in his lines, once, when the battle was thickest, so close to him she could see the light blaze on his sword blade, the blood spurt up as he killed. She might feel sorrow, even. The world is changed. How can the world be so changed? King Durith led us to glory. If he has lost, if he is overthrown, if he is dead…

In the Tarbor Mountains in the depths of winter, he led them up slopes that were knee-deep in snow, the snow crusted on his face, he walked in the snow in his war cloak and his armour, he would not go in comfort, he said, while his soldiers suffered for him. In the ruins of Arborn, the City of White Marble, Fairest of Cities, he stood on a great dais of carved sweetwood, robed and crowned in silver, thanked his soldiers for their loyalty to him, told them that all his glory was theirs, that without them he was nothing, ordered the great lords of his empire to kneel there on the dais in thanks to them, sent them away to new peaceful lives with land and wealth. Lidae and Emmas stood together in the front ranks that day also, flowers garlanding their hair, betrothed, 'When I was a child, I worked a rich man's fields from dawn to dusk for a crust,' Emmas said, his face radiant, 'now we will have our own fields, when we have children they will never want for anything. Hail the king! Hail the king!' The first time Lidae heard King Durith's name she had been in the marketplace in Raena, buying food, two men walking ahead of her had spoken his name fearfully, 'They say Durith's army is three days' march away, but still the king and priests do nothing,' one of the men had said. She had not understood what they were saying. Who is 'Durith'? What is he? Ten days later saw seen him for the first time, distant, shining, riding in triumph into the ruins of the city, and she marched out after him.

All I am, Lidae thought, and all I was, I owe to him. He killed my parents, burned my home, destroyed everything that I knew. He gave me everything that I am. He is the King of Illyrith. The King of All Irlawe. Fixed and solid. My children play at being him, as they play at being the heroes of dreams: *'I'm King Durith! Look at my sword! Watch me!' 'I want to be King Durith! Hogging!'* Like the trees and the sea and the sky. And now he is ... dead? Like Emmas is dead.

He shaped my life. He changed everything. He cannot be dead.

She thought then, stupidly, dully: I hope at least that they burned his body when they were done with him.

But: 'King Durith is somewhere down in the south,' said Rhosa. 'With the false Queen of Eralath. That's what they say.'

Lidae blinked. But I suppose ... he must still be alive, she thought then. Because otherwise they would have no reason to come here armed like this, invaders. They must fight now for this one place as we fought for all the world. And as violently.

He shaped my life. Changed my life. If he had not destroyed Raena, I would not be here now and my children would not exist. Of course he cannot be dead.

'I don't understand,' said Cythra. And Devid nodded, and Ayllis, and Hana. 'King Durith is king of Illyrith and all Irlawe. Lidae here fought for him. Ten years, she fought for him, to make him king. I don't understand what you're saying,' said Cythra, and Devid and Ayllis and Hana nodded. 'How can someone else ... how can someone else just be king?'

'Anyone can be king,' said Rhosa, 'if they have enough men to say they are a king. Thirty years ago, before King Durith rode out to rebuild the world, half the soldiers in Irlawe called themselves a king.' The woman frowned then. 'But now King Temyr is the only king.'

Lidae felt the soldiers looking at her with suspicious cold eyes, now they knew she was one of them. If I had my sword, she thought, my armour ... three against one, and they'd kill my children to stop me trying to defend myself against them...

'She was a soldier?' Myron said, astonished, looking at Lidae. 'Her? Don't lie.' He laughed, looking at Lidae. Rhosa rolled her eyes: same old same old, I'm sitting here next to you, Myron boy. But Lidae felt her face burning up. Hurt like a stab wound. She felt herself shaking.

Cythra said, very fierce to Myron, 'Yes, Lidae was a soldier.'

Devid was still trying to understand it. 'But if ... if King Durith isn't king anymore ... if this Lord ... Lord Temyr—'

'King Temyr,' Rhosa said.

'This King Temyr ... is king...' Devid said, in the confusion of a kind man who lived by farming and fishing in a village of rich earth where many flowers grew, 'if this Temyr is king of Illyrith ... why ... why did they ... did you...?'

'We didn't,' Clews said. He hadn't spoken for all of this, had sat watching Samei and Ryn by the stream trying to play while listening not understanding but knowing it was important. 'We didn't do anything,' Clews said. He didn't look at them while they spoke, kept looking at the boys. His face fixed on their faces. 'We left him,' Clews said.

Lidae looked at him, and looked at the last scraps of meat and bread and cheese and beer.

'We did nothing,' Clews said.

'You don't know what was done, to say that,' Cythra said.

Lidae's eyes met Rhosa's a moment. Such pity in them.

Myron said, 'We did as we were ordered, marched here, until the fighting was ... was too ...'

'Our captain, she grew up here,' said Rhosa. 'In the south of Illyrith, on the border. And we went right through her village, and we gutted it. She knew it was her village. Knew where the land was best to camp, best for the horsemen and the footmen to be positioned, where the best things were to be found and looted. We fought a battle, and we sacked the village to celebrate it. And she was part of it. Didn't care.'

Silence.

'The Army of Illyrith is drawn from half the world,' said Lidae slowly. 'Half the army has killed their own people. Gutted their own villages.'

Silence.

Lidae saw her own childhood city of Raena, that she could barely remember. A public garden with a fountain, a temple with silver roof-tiles, a place near the Market Bridge where people went to bathe. If I took the boys to the ruins of it, told them that this was my home, thus partly their home... they would not believe me, and I would not believe it. Elsewhere, she thought. Nowhere that really existed.

Fourteen

Rhosa and Clews and Myron were going south towards the border. If the new King Temyr was marching north, to take Thalden and make himself king, if King Durith was marching to meet him, raging against him... Get away from these things, flee away into the places already scarred with years of fighting. Hide away there where it is safe because the army has already been through there taking and seizing and killing. Devid spoke of going to Thalden, because it was a great city, the seat of the king, and so as a great city it must be safe. Lidae and Rhosa and Clews almost laughed openly at him. The roads will be thick with people fleeing, Lidae thought. The country people fleeing to the towns and cities thinking them places of safety because they are filled with people. The townspeople fleeing to the country where they can hide.

Beggars clamouring at the gates of Raena, begging to be given shelter, camping up against the grey stone walls. She and her friends had gone sometimes to the walls to look down on them, spit at them, throw stones. 'Yah! Beggars, cowards, couldn't fight to defend your own houses, could you? Squat down there in the dust looking to us to help you instead?' Blank faces staring up at them, withered. An old man who wore a ragged coat of red silk and spun gold. 'Yah! Cowards, beggars! Expecting us to protect you!' They scorched in the heat, were soaked in the rain, starved, sickened. She had jeered and spat at the rich men of Raena too, those who had fled the city in the last days, knowing what would come to them, begging and bribing the guards to get out when the gates were sealed. 'Cowards! Deserters! Traitors!' Envy expressed as hate. And she had seen them later, those rich ones who had fled the city before its ruin, clots of them rotting in the roadside as the Army of Illyrith marched past them. Killed them for loot and pleasure. Taken them as slaves. Consumed them. In the empty fields they had lain down to die with the crows picking over them.

'How can Lord Temyr want to be king, mummy?' Samei said

suddenly. Thinking, his face strained. 'King Durith is the king. You can't have two kings.'

'He … King Durith is king, yes. Lord Temyr has betrayed him, calls himself king. But King Durith is the king. That is why there is a war, Samei, little one. Because Temyr knows that he is not the king, you see, because he's frightened and knows he's lying, he is killing people, fighting people, because he knows deep in his heart that he is not king of Illyrith.'

Samei frowned. 'But King Durith is the king.'

'It's hard to explain, smallest one. It's like … it's like when you have a stick, and Ryn says it's his stick, and you know it isn't but Ryn gets angry.'

'Ryn hits,' said Samei. 'Once he bit me. But it was my stick.'

'Yes. But—'

'It was my stick,' Samei said again.

'That's what I mean. I mean … you say it's yours, and Ryn says it's his, and … Being a king isn't … isn't a natural thing, Samei. King Durith's armies conquered cities that were ruled by other kings, made them take King Durith as their king instead. Durith wasn't king in Illyrith, once. Long ago. He had to fight to be worthy of being king.'

Samei thought a long time, and then he said, 'But it was my stick. And Ryn bit me.' And Lidae thought, somewhere, that he understood it far more clearly than she did. *Mine. Not his. Even if he had it first. And he bit me.*

Clews had been listening to all of this, a smile on his face. 'That's exactly it, Samei,' he said, with a look at Lidae. 'If only the great kings and the high lords could see it as clever as you.

'We'll be getting on, then, I suppose,' said Clews after a moment.

The three soldiers got up, awkwardly. Clews held out a hand. 'Well … Goodbye. Good luck. I hope…'

'You should come with us,' Samei said. 'Shouldn't he, Mummy?'

Clews looked surprised. Pleased, Lidae thought.

'We…' He turned to Lidae and to Devid and Cythra. 'I … Well…' He seemed to think. Look at Ryn and Samei. Think. 'If you'd like to travel together?'

Three soldiers armed with swords, to protect the children. She had seen so many children abandoned alone at the roadside, snivelling and stumbling along. If I had Rhosa's sword, Lidae thought, Rhosa's armour, if I had gone back for my sword and my helmet.

Devid said, hesitant, 'If … I mean …' Maybe we are running from nothing, this is all foolish, King Durith and King Temyr fought and one has defeated the other … no, no, King Durith and King Temyr have come to terms, sat down together as friends again. War is madness, the king and the army will have seen that by now, made peace, we should go home, rebuild our house, replant the fields, live. 'If it wouldn't be too much trouble to you…' Devid said. Such a look of dazed relief on his face and on Cythra's face.

Clews nodded, and Rhosa nodded, and Myron said, 'Yes. Come with us. We'll come with you.' Although Myron seemed uncomfortable at it. Cythra clasped Clews' hands as if he was a god-spirit come down to walk with them.

'Mummy! Mummy!'

Samei's voice, shrieking.

They had been walking for perhaps an hour. Samei would not let Lidae carry him, he and Ryn walked on either side of Clews, not looking at her. Samei talked about home, his toys, how his father was a soldier with a sword and had killed a lot of people, been a great man in battle. Ryn was silent. Lidae walked ahead of them, alert and shaking for danger, feeling blades coming down on them killing them. Listening to Samei in wonder. These lies he was telling Clews.

'Soldiers were trying to kill my daddy,' Samei said in a loud voice. He lisped the word 'soldiers', struggled with the 's' sound at the front. 'But my daddy, he's such a good soldier, so brave, he killed all of them. And the king was grateful to him.' What soldiers? What king? Emmas never spoke to them, not once in all her hearing, about their lives soldiering. It was getting hot, too hot for a spring morning, the sky radiant too-brilliant blue. They were walking a road through trampled fields where the wheat would never ripen. The banks of the road smelled of wild garlic and beneath that of blood. There was smoke behind them on the north horizon but they walked away from it, not looking, not daring. Once, that morning, they had passed a burned-out village, that Temyr's army must have gone through when it made this journey. Deserted, a single dog sniffing around, cowered down with its ears back, whining at them. It could have been there ruined a thousand years.

'If this Lord Temyr wants to be a king,' Devid said, dazed, 'why does he do this to his own people?'

'Lord Temyr doesn't want to be a king of the people of Illyrith,' Rhosa said, scorn in her voice that these people could be so stupid, 'he wants to be crowned king in the king's palace in the city of Thalden.'

'He has to keep his men supporting him,' Clews said, 'so he gives them things.'

'Houses can be rebuilt, they're just wood and stone,' Clews said to Samei, a little later. 'All this can be rebuilt, can't it? A good strong chap like you, you can make your house better than it was before, can't you? I had a farm here once myself,' said Clews, 'I sold it, went back to soldiering, and I dare say it'll be in the same state as these, and as your house is. But I'm thinking I might settle again when this is over, stop soldiering, and rebuild it better than I first built it. Yes?'

'Yes,' Samei said brightly. Ryn, with his child's knowledge, said nothing. Clews, who was a good man, surely, began to talk to Samei about what he should keep on his farm, apple trees or pear trees or plum trees, cows or sheep or pigs?

But now Samei's desperate voice came shrieking.

The boy had soiled himself. Orange shit ran down his legs. Crying. His hands grabbed down at himself, trying to hide it or catch it. He stared at his mother with huge eyes.

'Samei, oh, oh, Samei.' Lidae ran to hug him, drew back from the filth-stink, hugged him. He was crying wretchedly, ashamed. 'It's all right, Samei, oh Samei, baby boy.' Orange shit smeared her hands and legs. 'Oh, baby boy. Baby boy.' She buried her face in his hair, all clotted and rank with sweat and ashes, kissed it trying to smell the perfume in it, the odd animal musk of child hair, feral and babyish. She could feel his filth covering her. She set her teeth. Disgusting. Disgusting. And she had never minded changing him, cleaning up after him when he was small, tried to feel in it the depth of her mother-love for him. She thought she was going to vomit. 'But Samei…' and she knew the answer, she knew it but she asked as dumbly as if she didn't know, 'but Samei, why didn't you say? That you needed to go?'

Clews beside them looked horrified. 'He didn't … He didn't say …'

She pulled back to look at the child's face, all creased with tears, red with shame. 'Why didn't you say Samei?' Anger rising up in her because of the shame. Remembered shouting at him only last summer, 'Gods, Samei, you're disgusting, you stink, what's wrong with you?' And Ryn, wetting himself on purpose when she was nursing new-born Samei, looking at her with big angry eyes, and there was nothing she could do but shout in fury at him, Samei clutched to her breast, 'Ryn. Please. Why do you have to do this?' not shouting but begging. Gods, that never-ending time, shit and exhaustion. The rage and fear it was come back.

She could feel Ryn also now, staring at them both. And then Ryn looked at her with almost fury.

'You're making it worse,' Ryn said.

'It's all right, Samei,' Ryn said. 'Poor Samei. Ignore her. She's just being cruel.'

'I killed to save your life, you hateful child, I killed them to save you, look at me, I was injured, I fought like a mad thing to save your life, Ryn. What did you want me to do? What do you think your father would have done differently?'

Her voice came out as a scream of hate.

They were looking at her, the two soldier-men and the soldier-woman, they must have been soaked through with blood and piss and shit enough in their time, Lidae thought, enemy filth and the filth oozing out of a comrade, a friend a lover dying, shrieking, voiding themselves, pus oozing feverish off them. Three sickened faces looking at this woman with her son's shit and tears coating her, they who must have seen and done such things.

'Don't beg him, Lidae,' Cythra said. 'Leave him a while, yes?' Cythra fussed around them all, trying to help, trying to find anything useful to say. Hana and Ayllis both torn between care and giggling revulsion; Devid, appalled, looking at anything that wasn't this.

'I can get some water,' Clews said, kind man, shocked, 'clean him up a bit, get his clothes cleaned, poor thing.'

'*I was better than you*,' she wanted to scream. '*Better than you'd ever be at fighting! I could have killed any one of you!*' And Lidae thought suddenly of her own mother, worn thin and dry as bones, her face shut up like Samei's face. Struggling to feed the children, her husband off somewhere, rich men strolling past in the dusty streets. I'm trying. I'm trying all the time. You think I wanted this? Resentment carved into her mother's face

'Why didn't you say anything? Samei? Why? Look at you. What were you thinking? How could you do this?' Samei began to howl again. 'Samei, baby boy, smallest thing … Samei … Ryn … please…' The boys flinched away from her. All the eyes watching. 'It's all right, Samei.'

She took a deep breath, tried to calm herself again. The three soldiers staring at her. 'I'm sorry, Samei. Ryn. I'm sorry.' And there was grief and an overwhelming joy and shame at herself as the boys came into her arms crying. I love them so much, she thought. So much. So much. None of this is their fault. She rubbed one finger over the trail of dried snot that Samei had wiped onto her sleeve. '*Samei trails*' Emmas would call them, laughing, like the snail trails across the kitchen floor sparkling in the mornings. '*You've been Samei'd.*' Babies are soggy creatures. A blessing, she thought, marking me. Like an offering of milk and wine and honey rubbed on a godstone, on the bark of a sacred tree.

She thought: why can't I find the words to comfort them?

Clews went on ahead fast, came back saying there was a stream a little further on. Lidae and Cythra cleaned the two boys. Then Lidae and Ryn and Samei sat with the soldiers' cloaks wrapped around them while Cythra and Ayllis washed their filthy clothes. Clews had a spare shirt that Ryn could wear, reaching down almost to his ankles and with the sleeves rolled up very fat around his wrists, and it was lucky he was tall for his age, Clews said. They needed to get on, Lidae could see Clews and Myron looking back anxiously down the road, at the field where, just here, the green wheat was still growing. She put her dress on soaking wet, telling the boys her body heat would dry it. 'My hands are nice and warm, aren't they? Well, you see.' It clung horribly to her legs, made a horrible wet noise as they walked. The stream had been dank with pond weed, the dress and her skin smelled of it and she could smell beneath it the reek of Samei's shit. Samei was naked, his shirt wet, his trousers stained and ruined: he wore Clews' cloak wrapped around him. Clews carried him. He had held out his arms for Clews, said he wanted the kind soldier man to carry him. Clews looked at her and at Ryn as they walked with something like pity still. Rhosa did not look at them. Her eyes were very cold.

'He's frightened, poor little soul,' said Cythra. 'You can't be angry with him.'

'I know,' Lidae said. 'Of course I don't blame him. My little one, I should have known what was happening, smallest one, I'm sorry.'

'You see, Samei? Your mummy isn't angry with you. I told you she wouldn't be. But try to think, Samei, little boy,' Cythra said to Samei, 'try to think if you might need to go, won't you? Clever boy like you are.'

'Both of them so brave and clever,' Lidae said loudly, and felt Myron look at her with scorn. She thought: this is what I am, their mother, their protector, I love them more than anything in the world and beyond, nothing matters apart from them. Always. Nothing else matters to me, nothing else means anything.

Even if I had taken my sword with me, nothing else would mean anything.

'You must have children?' Cythra asked Clews and Rhosa as they walked. 'You're so good with the boys,' Cythra said.

'No.' A heaviness in Clews' voice. Regret? 'No. I had a farm, and a man, just like you. Not that far, even, from your village, I don't think. A few hours walk, maybe, no more. Westward, over towards Thalden.' He sighed, suddenly briefly dream-happy a moment even despite everything. 'I always, always wanted to see Thalden. And we could see its towers, the King's Towers, on a clear day, gold and silver gleaming in the sun … We came here to settle, live in peace.

'My man died. I re-enlisted. Went back south. I thought I'd die there, far away back south.' Shook his head. 'My old officer, long ago, the man who first taught me soldiering … he wanted children. Often talked about them.'

Rhosa said, looking at Lidae, 'I don't have children. No.'

They went on through green trees in green fields, the hills gentle here, curving like cows' backs. Untouched: the army of the traitor Temyr had not come through here, left these hills and valleys green and living, in the silver grass beside a pool a flock of sheep grazed, a pear orchard was in blossom, beneath the trees ran fat brown pigs.

'Pigs, then, it's decided,' Clews said to Samei, 'and pears, yes?'

Exhausted, heart-broken, raging, one might refuse to believe in the traitor Temyr and his traitor army. This is some terrible mad thing we are doing because we are run mad. Something we are doing to punish ourselves. To punish Ryn and Samei and Ayllis. But towards evening, they came up on a battlefield, just hidden beyond the hill in front of them. A roar of noise, shouts and the smash of metal, a stink in the air, Lidae froze and Rhosa and Myron and Clews froze. 'Gods. Fuck. Gods.'

The boys started, eyes wide as horses' eyes. Knowing. Cythra and Devid and Ayllis and Hana confused and lost, refusing to know. Clews' face, panicked: women, children, oh sweet gods, what to do?

'Get back away,' Rhosa whispered. 'Back away.' Treading warily, white exhaustion, the curve of the hillside before them. Get back. Back there, on the other side of that green hill, men are dying. Lidae thought of it with bafflement, suddenly. Fighting, killing, she could hear it, taste it, the men fighting had no idea she was there creeping back away from them. She thought of the battles she had fought, the great bright lines meeting and thrashing, the spears and the swords trampling. And men and women and children there on the other side of a green hill, creeping away from it, frightened. She thought of seeing it from the top of a high tower: the battlefield, the men killing, and beyond that, beyond the edge of the battle, other men living at peace. They say in the sack of great cities, she thought, those living in the very depths of the city may not realise the city is sacked and burning. May never know it.

'You said we were behind them,' Devid said to Rhosa. 'Behind their lines. You said.'

'Rearguard,' said Lidae. 'Keeping the communication lines with the south secured.' She said, almost laughing, 'Both sides, keeping the lines of communication with the south secured.' A heaviness in her mouth from the words she was using. The words like stones. Like Samei's shrieks and his shit, like Ryn's silence. Years and years, she thought, my children's lives and more, since I used such words. A different taste to them. A yearning. Myron looked at her almost briefly believing she might once have been a soldier almost like him. She looked at him and she looked over to the sounds of battle, flashes of bright coloured mage fire, blood-stink, and a part of her, a tiny part, thought: let them come. I'll show them.

They went back and round wide to the east; the ground was rough and boggy, thorn scrub, clutching at their feet. Safer, Clews thought, than going south-west, where there was good green turf, good fields with the corn growing, easier passage for soldiers and horses. So they should struggle along where the land was rough and half-dead, towards the sea and the wildness where no one would go unless they were desperate. Marshes, where the people lived in houses raised above the murky water, waded through the mud on long wooden stilt legs like bird men. The sedge was higher than a man's shoulders, drowning them. Mayflies danced amongst the dark stems; Samei pointed, astonished, jerked out of his pain, at a huge iridescent dragonfly larger than his clenched fist.

If it comes to it, Lidae thought, I will kill Ryn and Samei myself, before worse comes to them. She knew then in thinking it that she could not do it. Would hold back from doing it until it was too late. And then she thought pathetically: I have nothing I could use to kill them with. Should I have brought my sword for that? Her own helplessness caught in her throat.

They went on. Dusk had fallen. They needed to stop, Hana and Ayllis were swaying on their feet, eyes empty, Cythra tried to hold her daughter upright, herself stumbling.

'I'm tired,' Samei said.

'We can't stop yet, Samei, little one.'

'I'm tired. Can't we stop? Why can't we stop?'

'I said we can't stop, Samei.'

Ryn said, the first thing he had said for hours, 'Don't talk to her, Samei.'

'Mummy,' Samei said. And then again, in Clews' arms, he soiled himself.

'Oh gods.' And she thought she had felt shame before. 'I'm sorry. Oh gods, why didn't you say? Samei, look what you've done. Samei.' Hit him, shout at him. 'You're a beast, Samei, an animal, look at you, look at this, you're disgusting. I'm so ... I'm sickened by you.'

She's screaming it at him. Hitting him.

'Lidae!' Cythra shouted. 'Lidae! Stop! You're terrifying him.'

And Samei screams, 'Mummy! Stop, no, Mummy.' And her face is so hot and red, she's panting, spittle on her lips as she screams at him. Her mind is red.

'Look at you!'

'He was so frightened,' Clews said. He said after a moment, 'It's more pleasant than blood.'

Yes. Yes. She's shaking now. Trying to calm herself. My little child ... he's crying, sobbing. His face is red, too.

'It's all right, Lidae,' Cythra said. 'We can clean you up, can't we, Samei, hey?'

She's silent. Tries to put her arms around Samei. But Ryn is there between them, glaring up at her like a guard dog.

'Go away,' Ryn says.

She says, weakly, pleading, 'Ryn...'

'You're the disgusting one,' Ryn says.

Clews says very gently, 'You're hurting your mother, Ryn, can't you see that? She's trying her best for you. You're hurting her.'

Ryn says, 'She deserves it. I hate her.' Samei laughs a baby's laugh, shifting and guilty and terrified. 'I hate her.'

'Try to be kind, hey? Little man? Be kind and brave for her.' He was covered in Samei's shit. 'She's trying hard for you, Ryn.'

Something shatters, inside Lidae. No other words for it. She cannot see or speak or hear or feel. They said ... they said to lose a child ... to see a child die ... a wound...

... and she is running.

Fifteen

Better off without me.

They trust a soldier they met this morning. More than me.

Because he's a better parent to them than me.

Because they hate me.

She's running. Running. Running. Keep running on and on and on. Get away.

There's a darkness like all their deaths behind her. And she's certain, as she pushes through trees and it's getting darker, that they're better off without her, that they're happy, pleased she's gone out of their lives. She runs as if she herself is dying. Their shadows are behind her smiling, saying how happy they are now she's gone. She can only hurry on, get away from them. She thinks one or twice she can hear them crying, but it's baby cries, the sounds that woke her in the night, brought her stumbling back to them after she'd left them for one moment to piss, to get a drink of water, one moment, one moment, that's all I wanted, needed, gods, I leave you for one moment so I don't have to wet myself and you're crying like you're dying, what's wrong with you, I left you alone, tiny precious baby, I left you because I'm bad and selfish and put myself first and something has happened, you're frightened, hurt, injured, dying. She almost stops, once, the sound is so clear, her baby, rising howl of its panic and fear, she turns her head, my baby, but she knows she's imagining it, they're happy with Cythra their other mother their better mother, with Clews who's so good and patient with them. Her own selfish mind lying to her that they need her, when they don't need her, they never did.

I should have died, she thinks, not Emmas. She thinks again: if Emmas had been there, he'd have protected them. His sword flashing out, all the enemy going down beneath it, the boys butting up around him with their soft frail limbs, cheering him. She runs and runs and she's exhausted, her breath comes in raw gasps. Not far enough! Keep going! Get away from them! She's running through wet mud, stinking, slipping beneath her, branches tear at her face, whip at her, claw at her feet and legs. Her dress catches, rips: physical pain: she pulls free almost shouting.

It's dark. She'd not noticed. She's exhausted.

Ryn, Samei, I'll come back now. I want to come back.

Ryn? Samei?

She stops, and she's too frightened to go back now, she turns around takes three steps backwards, she has no idea where she's run from or what direction they're in, she can't see anything but dark tree trunks on dark mudland, go back, go back, her heart is screaming but she can't go back because when they see her what will they do and say?

She stops, and she sinks down to the ground cold and damp and vile around her, and she can't even weep.

She thinks: they'll come and look for me. Like she's the child. So she's ashamed of thinking that. Thinking that shows how unfit she is for them. She can hear them in the dark coming towards her, looking, she can see them in the dark, Ryn's gentle face that's almost a young man's face, Samei with his fat lips still so like a baby, Cythra saying 'Look, there she is, see, I told you we'd find her.' She can see herself hugging them. They do not deserve me as their mother, she thinks. And she thinks, deep down inside her in the depths of her, of the days and the nights when she whispered in rage, 'Go away! Leave me alone! I wish you'd never been born! What have I done?'

She looks around in the dark, waiting for them to find her, certain they won't come. I am the most selfish woman living, she thinks. Emmas would never have left them. But because I left them, it shows I am unfit to go back to them.

It's like a trap. Enemy soldiers in front of her, enemy soldiers behind her, two great rows of them, the jaws of a mouth closing. Devours her. A battle that cannot be won.

What am I, she thinks, that they hate me and I love them and I hate them?

Sixteen

Voices that seemed very far away from her. She should turn her head. Look at them. Sound of metal and leather. Sound of a horse—no, of horses—good sounds, the way a horse's headgear rattles, the creak of the saddle, the hollow tread of its hooves, the way you can hear its muscles, feel its coat, when a rider pats its head or its flank to communicate with it and it whinnies in response.

She sat with her back to a tree. She had sat there all night. Staring into the dark blind and deaf and silent, without thoughts without feeling. Her eyes hurt too. Raw and stinging from not having slept. But she must have slept. She tried to remember what direction she had come from. Listen out for the boys coming crashing through the woods. She couldn't have gone that far from them. An hour. No more. She was sitting in a thicket of trees growing close together on a hump of higher ground, willow and alder all budding green-golden, may blossom clotted thick and musky white. Powerful trees, all three, Rena the healer had said. Lidae reached up, broke off a sprig from the alder. The new leaves were sticky. She rolled it between her fingers. Once, when she had first joined them, joined Maerc and Acol, she had got very drunk one night after a battle: she felt as she had the next morning, looking back trying to make sense of her memories.

Another dawn morning. Light washing across the sky like a tide coming in, the sky indeed like pale sand rippling and reflecting the light above it. The trees all whispering and rustling in the wind, the white blossom of the may trees dancing jewelled with spring dew. A line of geese flew over, very high, crying out like dogs baying, warding off the restless dead. And beneath them swifts were flitting, coming back to the north for the summer also, calling with a fragile urgency like fine glass threads. A memory of childhood: Lidae's father standing in the courtyard behind their house, in the dust and the shit and the children begging, his head thrown back in the evening shadows, watching the swifts as they flew. Where the swifts went in the autumn here, flying south to the dry-stone heat in which she had once lived. Her father's face briefly happy, rested, at peace. She closed her eyes. Smiled. A good memory. Few memories of her father. He'd have been so happy, she thought suddenly, to see Samei and Ryn.

She stood up. Her body hurt. Her knees cracked. She had new places that hurt on her face and her hands, a raw pain in her right leg. She lifted up her skirt to find a bruise spreading there. She put her hands to her face and there were scabs, and when she picked them there was fresh blood.

The sounds of men and horses were getting louder. She could make out words, now, men grumbling, joking, singing. She walked forwards.

The battle they had avoided yesterday, the sounds of fighting just out of reach beyond the brow of the green hill: these men. Victorious, from the bright confident look of them. Infantry, their long spears like a forest. Cavalry on fine tall horses, ribbons in the horses' manes and tails, the riders' armour shining. Two, perhaps three hundred of them. At the head of the column, clearly visible now as they came closer, the banners stood proud on ashwood spear-poles. Dark red: King Durith. Green and blue: the colours of Lord Sabryyr. Lidae's heart leapt. The trees gave way to a stretch of marshland, pale reeds and yellow irises; if she had run on any further, she would have fallen into it in the dark. Standing water, dark as old metal, ruffled by the wind. Over the water stood a wooden causeway, and the column of men and horses moved across it.

Smell of metal and leather and horse sweat and man sweat. Good smells, all of them.

Lidae began to walk down towards them. Her heart was beating very fast, a dry sick taste in her mouth. My soldiers, my brothers, my comrades. Wait. Please. Let me join you. I know soldiering, war, killing, I was so very good at it. Some of them, she thought, some of them might recognise her. She could hear it, their voices: '*Gods and demons, it's young Lidae! My friend, my companion! You who were with me at the ships at Ander!*' She could walk forward to them, mingle together, recognise each other, embrace. The light, bright and terrible in her mind: the children are better off without me, they are pleased that I ran away.

She had to splash through marsh water, stinking mud up to her knees, the reeds brushing around her. Their softness felt like Samei's hair. '*Fluffy tails! Mummy!*' She found herself running, slipping on mud and dark water, pushing her way forwards, the sound of leather boots and horses' hooves on the wood of the causeway, voices grumbling and chattering, jingle of metal.

A voice singing, loudly and out of tune: '*They did not fear to ride out to battle, They did not fear spear or sword.*'

'Such a good song, that.'

'Such a good song.'

'Gods, I need a piss.'

'You always need a piss.'

Maerc and Acol and Emmas and all of them, and she could almost see and hear herself marching. A man there, at the back, the way he held himself, his helmet with the boar crest, Acol, Acol had had that helmet once when they first met. And she thought, madly, joyously, I can make it right again. All that I've done, the guilt, the shame, my failure, the children... There they are, Maerc, Acol, Emmas, my past, and I can go back and start again. Acol— I— Wait—

Wordless, endless screaming. The end of everything. The end of every human life. She shrieked out, 'Ryn! Samei!' Her arms went out, searching, clutching out for them, to hold them, shield them, put herself between it and them. A great darkness, a shadow, the sun eclipsed.

The dragon's head lowered as it came over her. Its body reflecting and reflected in the dark water. Brilliant blazing gleaming gold and red. The earth rolled in waves beneath its wing beats.

The fire of it.

The fire of it. Gods.

Her eyes were melting, running off her, tears on her face pouring down hot burning away pain soft steam. There was nothing but white light, liquid, a blindness, she was drowning in its light. Heat pouring over her, waves, she choked it in, she could breathe in the heat that washed her face and her lungs. Her mind was raw she felt it. Cannot think in this pain in this glory. All she could bear. Her mind not working. Her heart not working. The fever had taken Emmas' vision, 'It's dark, why is it dark?' he had screamed with spring sunshine on his face making his hair gleam. And Lidae had seen, once, in a camp outside the high walls of a distant city, she had seen and felt a great crucible of molten bronze explode. 'Ryn! Samei! Emmas!' Lidae found herself screaming. She cannot hear any more she cannot see it, its fires are faces opening and shutting, hands opening, fingers clawing up, voices, shapes. The world bursts into flower. Unfurling. Fingers and hands of fire that open like lilies. The world is the red of beech trees in the autumn, the leaves shimmering, moving, the sunlight of an autumn day the leaves glow against the pale of the sky and the light is dancing and the leaves dance and they speak in the wind. The world is light-on-water, torch-light-on-water in a night's festival and then the dawn sun rising on the water black and silver and bronze and blinding. The hands move. Clawing. The fingers move, like the branches of the tree. She cannot hear or see. It is all distant. She is drowning. The heat and the light and the molten world. She is melting. The hands reach for her, blossoming in fire, leafed in fire, washed in fire, waves of heat and light. The earth was boiling. The vast sound of its beating blazing wings. She had seen the way dragons fought many times once long ago. It hung in the sky far above them. Like a star. 'Beautiful, wonderful, beautiful,' she had once said.

A great silver bird rose to meet the dragon. It sang as it came. Its head was the head of a hawk, a great beak, a hawk's wings, a tail of silver like the tail of a peacock, silver and black flickering. It had antlers like a deer. Its claws were like the claws of a lion. It met the dragon there high above her. Fire poured out of the dragon's mouth. The bird flew on through the fire, singing. It struck at the dragon. Its claws sank into the dragon's breast. The dragon's head whipped around, jaws biting at the silver wings. The two creatures lurched. A terrible long moment when it seemed they would fall together burning into the cold marsh. The dragon threw up its head and spouted fire. The bird sang out.

A second bird god closed on them. This one was bronze. It had long wings like a swallow, a long forked tail, but its face was a woman's face. Its talons ripped at the dragon's red-gold wings. The dragon thrashed and spat at it. The silver bird was gipping on to the dragon, tearing at it with its beak, itself wounded. The bronze bird broke off, spiralled downwards frantic, recovered itself, launched itself again at the dragon, met it face to face. Fire washed over everything. The three of them together were tumbling in the air. The dragon's right wing was injured, bleeding. Where its blood fell, dew-in-summer-morning, the marsh hissed in steam and black smoke.

The dragon screamed. The bronze bird, smaller, broke off from it. The silver bird tore at it, hacking off great lumps of its flesh. Blood and feathers, floating, turning. It thrashed, shrieked, its wings beat torn and ragged. Its body humped in the air. It shot upwards howling. The birds went with it, their song like skylarks. The brilliance of fire and glory was gone. Lidae blinked up, staring. Soldiers, men, wounded, running everywhere, shouts, a trumpet on one note over and over, the splash of water.

She said aloud, 'If the dragon's blood has got in the water, enough of it, the water will be poisoned.'

But they were soldiers, not children, they must know that. A man lay in the mud not too far from her, his arms thrown up over his face, his legs kicking and jerking. He looked all red and black. Lidae's feet stumbled and dragged in the mud as she ran, the marsh water was hot and unpleasant against her skin. The man drummed his legs, shouted. He was slick and wet with blood. It was the man with the boar helmet, whom she had thought was Acol. It is Acol, she thought, Acol died by fire, yes, I remember I saw him, burning, screaming. The helmet was melted onto the man's face. He was dying, clearly, in such pain. Lidae crouched beside him, took his hand. His skin was flecked with molten drops of iron and bronze. He stank, bloody, wounded, killing, slick and glossy with his death clotting on him. Blood smells like iron. Iron smells like blood. Sweet fishy shit smell of a menstrual rag. He drummed his heels, grunted, shrieked. But she thought that he would hear or feel that she was beside him, that he wasn't dying alone.

A trumpet sounded, an urgent, calling blast. She sat up, the dead man in the mud before her. More dead and dying stretched in the hot, smoke-smelling mud. In the distance, the survivors struggled to regroup, flee away on.

She thought: my children. What am I doing, helping this man, this stranger, when my children need me?

She scrambled to her feet, she was covered in mud and blood, another man near her was thrashing and dying in the dark water of the marsh. She thought, her mind suddenly alive again: what have I done? I have to go back to find them.

The dying soldier had a sword, and she bent and took it.

She could find the high dry ground where she had sat all night—she had slept, surely, she must have slept. The green fresh leaves of spring had fallen, lay withered as leaves fall in autumn when the storm comes after the first frost. She turned around and around trying to see where she had come from. A hill. A battle. They had hurried away from it, pushed on, 'south-east' Clews had said, 'we go south-east, into the marshes.' The battle they had avoided yesterday, the men fighting out of reach beyond the green hill. If the soldiers had come across them, Ryn and Samei, little children...

Emmas, once... They'd taken a fortress, it had fallen eventually but they'd suffered to do it, the defenders throwing down mage fire on them, raining

*down hot sand on them from the walls. They went in towards evening, the
darkness gathering, she could remember it very clearly, the fortress walls were
all of white stone that glowed red in the dark in the flames. Their shadows
ran in the dark across the flames. A clot of dark running towards them, they
came at it, it was a woman, very young, with a child in her arms, a baby,
she was fleeing but in her fear she was disorientated. Men on the battlefield,
wounded, sometimes ran the wrong way like that. She went down to their
spears. The baby fell from her arms, rolled in the dust of the street, it was
crying on one note on and on. Emmas picked it up. Looked at it. Took his
spear and... Just a thing men did, soldiers did, in the heat of the moment,
when they were tired and angry and victorious and hurt. And he had been
ashamed, afterwards.*

Or the dragon. Walls of fire, seas of fire, washing over Samei and Ryn.

I can't have gone far from them, she thought, I can't have run far, I
was tired, it was dark, it felt like I was running for a long time, but I
can't have been running for a long time really, they must be close by, they
must. They'll have stayed, she thought, waiting for me to come back. So
she stared and stared around her, trying to find the way back to them,
I must remember it, I must, I can't have gone far, they're here close by,
waiting for me. She'd see them, run towards them, they'd run to her,
arms out, fragile little bird limbs. Ryn would hug her with the fierce
awkwardness of being older, melt into her losing his self-consciousness
in his love, I love you best, best, best, all the best love in the world, Ryn,
my love. Samei would butt his head into her stomach, curled up tiny,
snail-trail of snot wiped over her stomach. My babies, my little ones,
my little ones. We'll get away to the south, away from the fighting here,
start again just the three of us in a little house in the warm. I might have
family surviving somewhere in Raena, she thought, that dirty, dusty
courtyard behind our house, the fountain on the street corner where the
water was brown when it came out at all, the doves in the eaves of the
building opposite, the swallows, the peach tree beside the wine shop. I
will take the children home, she thought. They'll like the warmth, the
golden light of the desert sun. The peach tree would be easy for them to
climb. But they're better off without me, a part of her whispered still,
empty, hopeless. But she stared around and around, walked a few steps
one way and then another, she had no idea which way she had run, there
was no sign of them. She had left them, abandoned them, and they had
gone.

Seventeen

So: find them. Look search, run through the wild landscape, I am their mother, their mother, I must be able to find them. I should know where they are—I will know, the land will open, their tracks will be there, their footprints will be visible to me, lit up in the earth—I must know, I must know. Calm, then: deep breaths, look around, listen. But she could not hear or see them. This great beautiful wide landscape, trees, flowers, high clouds that ran in the sun, and she could not see them or hear them. Emmas' voice, shouting, 'It's dark, why is it dark?' with the spring sunlight bright on his face. I should see them as brilliant as the dragon. Columns of light. Two candles burning. My heart should hear them shouting my name.

Turning and turning. My children. My children.

They are dead, the soldiers killed them, or the dragon killed them. All night, I left them, by now of course they are dead, how can they not be dead?

But she thought, worse and more terrible in its certainty: they are alive, they have gone on with Cythra and Devid, with Clews who was so good with them, without me.

I should be glad then.

So: find them. Look, search, run through the wild landscape, I am their mother, I must be able to find them. The wet earth: black marsh mud, grey reeds, coarse grass tussocks, stagnant water, running water, green fresh things: traces, footprints, here, look, search out the print of a child's hand steadying himself, a trail where his feet have kicked up mud and water, cold filthy limping children's toes. One of them brushing his hands over the reed heads, *'fluffy tails, Mummy!'*, snapping a fragile, bonelike stem in a clumsy movement, by mistake; a stick, yellow with lichen, divided into two halfway down it, a mark on the wet dark wood where a twig had perhaps been ripped off, it doesn't look like it came from the trees here and indeed just here it's grass and marsh scrub, no trees just here, she can see Samei finding it back in the woods near where she left them, peeling the twig off, waving it around as a weapon, dropping it or losing it until she finds it; a thick smear of stinking mud that must have come from a stagnant pool, she can see Ryn slipping, his foot sinking into the mud, wiping his foot with a look of disgust on a tussock of grass. Traces of them her children, look for them, search for them. Nothing and nothing and nothing. In this dead cold marsh, this dead spring morning, nothing and nothing and nothing.

Nothing.

Nothing.

She was exhausted, and she kept searching, going over her own traces; in this vast world there must be a sign of them, a trace of their fingers, their footprints, any moment, any moment she will find it but if she stops searching it will be her failure, if she stops and she had gone on even a moment that's where the trace of them would be. She should feel them, smell them, taste them in the air. But she was crying until she was almost blinded. Her searching erratic and frantic: behind me! Behind me! Check again! Give up. Run on. Turn back. Check again.

I must have a plan, she thought at last. I…

Graspingly, she thought of the soldiers. Marching from somewhere to somewhere, marching south, beneath the banner of King Durith and of Lord Sabryyr. Men with swords, supplies, protection. An endless horde had followed the army when she was a soldier, beggars, traders, whores, hucksters, after every battle there had seemed more of them. A city would fall, a village would be pillaged, the survivors would come creeping and begging in the army's wake. Blank-eyed women at the side of the road, a child clasped in their dusty arms, the column would march past them, they would struggle to their feet, follow a soldier day and night for years if he bought them for a crust of bread. Some of them, the clever ones, could grow rich picking over the battlefields, buying with the knife and selling on. The very soldiers that had destroyed their homes, often, they followed, begging. 'They disgust me,' she had said once to Acol. 'Thieves, beggars, whores.' Their squad captain had had a woman who followed him in the baggage, no matter what he did to her. 'She's safer than she would be without the army,' Acol had said.

The beggars clamouring outside the walls of Raena, whom she and her friends had gone to look down on throw stones, the rich men of Raena, who had fled the city in the last days ... many of them had followed in the army's wake, grateful for anything a soldier might offer them, after the city fell. How much she had despised them. *'They should fight, not beg, they should be strong like I am.'* But now she thought: if Cythra and Devis find the army they will follow it south, trust it for protection. So, I should find the army.

She put her hand on her hip, then, where the sword now hung. Find the army... She went back to the marsh where the dragon fire had burned up the column of men and horses, beside the sword she wore she could salvage from the mire a corselet of good leather, a helmet with a black crest, a knife.

Eighteen

She walked all day through the marsh, going southwards. Towards noon
the sky before her lit up in fire, a second sun, white-pale like the strange
light of a foggy morning, and then later the light died and there was a
thick trunk of black smoke. Magecraft.

Acol, when they first met: *'Have you ever seen mages fighting? Really
fighting? The world is lost in coloured visions, the world is gone.'* Maerc, his
eyes dancing: *'Like gods fighting on the dawn horizon, which I have seen
also, like all the most terrible things of beauty, once you have seen it, you
understand what true beauty is.'*

The land rose again, dry grey hills heavy to walk on, the earth catching
at Lidae's feet in looted boots that were too big; she crested the slope of
a hill and went down the other side through yellow gorse drowsing with
insects, tall grasses, the dry rustle of last summer's heather grey waiting
to bloom, and the smoke was gone. A single great godstone, thick with
lichen, overturned in a streambed with a deer skull wedged beside it,
half-buried. A cairn on the skyline that she climbed towards, stopped to
make an offering of spit. A steep narrow valley green as green marble,
its bottom running water, on the skyline above it another godstone like
a blurred face and a single thorn tree. Gorse flower scent, and the sick
sweetness of bracken. Once or twice, turning to the east as she scrambled
up the higher slopes of a hillside, Lidae saw the thin grey line of the sea.

Over the next hillside, in the late afternoon, golden, she saw before
her the army of King Durith.

Her army.

The hill fell away to dry, wide moorland. The campfires stretched
there in bright welcome. The smell and the sound of an army preparing
itself for an evening. King Durith's red banners flying, Lord Sabryyr's
banner in green and blue. She looked for Lord Brychan's banner that she
had once marched beneath, but could not see it. Very few of the great

lords' banners, the great generals. Too few. But the king's banner, red and brilliant, the king's tent, the king's army, glorious in its confidence. Trembling, her heart pounding, Lidae made her way down towards them. Taste of such joy and excitement. They might be there, she told herself, my children. She could see a great mass of people on the camp's fringes that would be refugees, hangers-on, followers, my children might be there, she told herself. But that was not why her heart beat so fast, and she knew that.

She walked forward, carefully and confidently, no hesitation, and the swell of the army camp was around her, flowed over her, swallowed her up inside it. Camp followers milled about getting themselves settled: women preparing food; children playing; whores and gamesters touting for clients in a rattle of bells and silk and chipped beads. Music drifted on the breeze, victory songs and love songs and tunes to dance to, fast, and rejoice. A dog ran through the camp with a joint of meat in its jaws, two men ran after it shouting for someone to grab its collar; the man in a rough leather jerkin grabbed at the dog, almost caught it; it twisted away, collided with a young man in gilded bronzework who yelled. A cloud of perfumed smoke rose from an offering fire. A wine-seller offered drinks at one in iron a cup, another tried to undercut her at one in iron for two cups, a third shouted that he had better wine in better cups, all three started arguing. Beside a campfire where a squad of infantry were gathered, a man began to sing.

'She was fair, as fair as flowers,
She was sweet as summer showers,
She smiled at me, her love was true.'

A man laughed, the campfire spat, a man's voice said loudly, 'Sing something more cheerful, can't you? Always the sad songs with you.' 'Sing something yourself then,' the singer shouted back and the whole group of them shouted, 'No, no, not that, not that, you know the bugger can't sing.'

A boy no older than Ayllis cut across the argument by playing a tune very beautifully on a silver flute. Lidae stopped, listening, smiling. The boy saw her, gave her a look, she smiled at him, nodded, walked on. A group of tall fine cavalry men, laughing in their haughty way, all smelling of horses and horse-leather, swaggering walk, helmet plumes like deer antler: *'You do know,'* Maerc would say when he saw her mooning at them, *'that all that riding about in tight leather makes them impotent?'* A woman carrying a pile of laundry, a woman with a baby, a man leading a lathered horse, a man shouting and cursing and stamping about because something of his had been damaged somehow. The voice burst up again behind Lidae, louder and almost out of tune.

'Over our bed, the hawks were flying.
Beside our bed, the wolves were running.'

She could almost see them. Lidae and Maerc and Acol and Emmas. She put her hand on her sword and was shocked not to feel the chipped red glass jewel in the hilt.

Trumpets rang. The flute and the singing broke off, the men at the campfire leapt up shouting. The angry man broke off being angry, the lathered horse snorted in excitement, the cavalry men in their helmets whooped. A vast rush of bodies, pulling on armour, dressing and gilding themselves. Lidae found herself moving with them. The men came together, flowed together like water, a dazzle of dark cloaks and polished bronze. Spears hefted. Horse-hair crests dancing. The horsemen had bells tied in their horse trappings, the bells rang out sweet. A drum toiled, echoed back from the green slopes of the hills. The army drew itself up waiting, ah, gods, she remembered, standing in the lines shoulder to shoulder, the weight of the spear, her breath coming deep. She stood now enchanted, her hands clasped to her throat.

The ranks of the army, footmen, horsemen, drummers, the standard bearers with the banners. Camp followers, the tangled refugees that Lidae should be searching amongst, loaded down with all their worldly belongings, on foot and in rags and destitute. She took a step towards them. Ryn— Samei—

Into their ranks, like water parting, a dark figure, tiny and huge both together, cloak fluttering. A flash of light where the sun's rays caught it. Beside it, a man walked carrying a high pole topped with the dark shape of a horse's head.

King Durith.

He walked down slowly. A tall man, bent a little in the back from age and from a lifetime of fighting. He dragged his left leg a little, an old wound from when he was a young general; his face was scarred, his left shoulder dipped with his head held a little crooked: a blow from a dragon's claw once that had nearly killed him. His hair had once been dark almost to blackness, faded now to fine, shining silver; it hung long over his shoulders in a blur like river mist. His skin had the yellow-white of ivory. On his forehead the thin circlet of his silver crown was very bright. Behind him walked his son Kianeth, a tall man in the flower of his manhood, gold ornaments in his hair, gold flowers engraved into his bronze armour. Both were cloaked and decked in the king's colour, deepest red-black.

This great figure of dream and story, who ruled from his throne of gold in the great city of Thalden. *'I'm King Durith! Hurrah!' 'No, I want to be King Durith!' 'He lives in a palace made of gold with towers that reach up to the stars and he once killed a dragon with his own hands and he's the greatest and noblest warrior in the world.'*

The trumpets sounded again, a long peal, triumphant. Great, utter, dazzling glory! Joy and happiness, the power of him, the strength of him. His crown, his unsheathed sword, his cloak blowing in the wind. Three times in his life, in point of fact, King Durith had killed a dragon. Once, in his youth, he had fought even with a demon beast in the shape of a man and defeated it. The marks of its claws were there, men said, in the depths of his face. From the chaos of war without end or purpose, he had hewn a great kingdom. To the poor wild land of Illyrith he had brought great power and great wealth. Prince Kianeth his son, resplendent in his manhood, a warrior without equal, six men, they said, fell in battle with every swing of his blade. Unmatched also in his intellect and learning, wise in judgement, schooled in the arts of poetry, of healing, he had widened and rebuilt the great harbour in Thalden for trade ships, five cities he had founded across his father's empire, all well-planned, pleasing to live in, rich in merchants. His face was grave, and his father King Durith's face was grave, at the task ahead of them, the evil that had been done. But he saw, and his father King Durith saw, the prowess of the men assembled. He knew in his heart that they would triumph over the evil that had beset them.

King Durith raised his shining sword. A red jewel in the hilt, that blazed as fire. Rainbows dancing along the length of the blade. It gleamed with white light. A cheer from the army, ringing across the green hills. Lidae cheered with them.

'The traitor Lord Temyr has broken all his bonds of loyalty. Brought ruin to this sacred land, our kingdom of Illyrith. Brought shame to himself and all who march with him.'

The army shouted, cursed the name of Lord Temyr. Lidae shouted and cursed with them.

'The traitor Temyr has murdered our children. Raped our women. Burned our fields and our homes. From all across Illyrith and all across our Empire, you have come to join me here, now, to defeat him. I thank you, men of Illyrith, men of the Empire. Men who fight for what is right and true. And now that we are gathered here—we will hunt him down, we will be avenged, we will destroy him. The eagles, the most accursed of all creatures, his corpse will lie in the dust unburied and the eagles will tear at him.

'For Illyrith!' King Durith shouted. 'For Illyrith and for your king!'

Every sword, every spear raised. Horse-hair plumes dancing. 'For the king! The king!' Lidae raised her sword along with them. Her heart beat so loud and so fast, wild as dragon's wings. A soldier raised aloft the red banner. The spear-bearer raised the horse head beside it.

The king cried to them, 'The traitor Lord Temyr is coming now to meet us. Drawn back even before he reached our great city of Thalden, whose gates are barred to forbid him entry. Coward: he dares not approach the city, knowing that it would close itself to him, spite him. And we will meet him, and we will destroy him. We must be ready, men of Illyrith! Tomorrow we will march to destroy him!'

The young Prince Kianeth came forward with a great golden cup, flashing with jewels. The king raised it, poured a libation of dark wine onto the good green earth.

'To victory! All you gods, you wild powers of the world, gods and demons, you spirits of earth and stone and water and metal, you powers of life and of death. All that is powerful. All that the world is. We will have victory and right and peace!'

The soldiers cheered. It was so very beautiful that Lidae wept. And she knew, in that moment.

King Durith and Prince Kianeth disappeared back into the king's red tent. The trumpets blew, the men sighed, shook their heads like men waking from a dream, dispersed across the camp. A silence in them, marvelling, then slowly chatter broke out again, talk, laughter, a man said with the awkwardness of someone embarrassed by his own emotion, 'Thank the gods that's over, I need a crap something rotten,' the boy started playing his flute. Lidae sank down on the grass, emptied. The world seemed very cold and grey. A feeling of such loneliness in her throat. She fixed her eyes on the horse head. Their squad had almost, almost been chosen for the honour of carrying the luck horse once.

'You!' A fine man in fine armour, rough faced from years of fighting, like Clews she could so almost recognise him, felt certain he knew her and she knew him. But her heart sank, because his voice too was familiar, the angry bark of an officer about to launch into a tirade against his men. Her whole body tensed ready for the yell: *'Latrine duty! Now, you slackers!' 'Oh for all the gods' sweet sake, again? Third fucking time this week.'* Back and shoulders and shovel hand jumping to be ready for it.

He's not talking to me, relax. Some poor wretch was about to get it.

'You!'

Me?

She leapt to attention. Shaking. Heart pounding. Wilder than dragon wing beats. He thinks I'm a soldier. I— He— Lidae took a breath. *I'm looking for my children, I'm sorry, I took the sword and the helmet for protection, I'm sorry, but, my children, two boys, have you seen them?* When he sees my face—

'Where's your squad, you?'

She thought: he knows I'm a soldier. She said, almost pleading, 'I was part of the column who were attacked by the dragon, in the marshes, my squad are all dead. But my sword … I survived, as you see, gods be praised, I'm here to fight for the king.'

The words came out before she'd realised what she was saying, a great mad rush. The same lie she had told Maerc and Acol, so many years ago, '*my, um, my …. my squad is all dead.*' Ill-fitting bloodied armour, fear in her voice, it must be so obvious she's lying. The officer gave her a long look.

Two boys, seven and five, bronze skin and black hair, have you seen them? She met the officer's eyes, flexed her sword arm a little. 'My squad are all dead. But I'm here to fight for the king.'

Blank face. And then: 'Those men by the campfire there. The ones that are lolling about doing nothing. Yes, you, that's right.'

Flute broke off, singing broke off. *Us? Doing nothing?*

'A new member of your squad, then.'

Nineteen

Lidae awoke the next morning to the sound of the army camp readying itself around her, and it was the most beautiful of music. Her body ached from sleeping on the wet earth all huddled, the smell of a stinking horse blanket someone had lent her itching her face. She was damp with dew. The first thing she saw as she opened her eyes was a spider's web in the grass before her, glittering and shimmering with dew. Beyond it, a flash of colour, two soldiers in red cloaks and bronze armour walking. The first sound she heard clearly was a crow calling, the second the neigh of a horse. The rasping, hissing, dry sound of a hone on a blade, that always set her teeth on edge.

Lidae sat up blinking. The memories were too much.

Her head was aching: there'd been rather a lot of wine drunk the previous evening in welcome. Some surprise at first. Her? A soldier? Really? She'd thought: there was a beggar in Karke once, he stank like a latrine, he was a drunk and a hatha-addict with his face running sores, he shouted that he was a great lord once and sometimes people pitied him and believed him. They'd looked at her like she was lying, but she'd looked back at them, talked the talk and her voice had been shaky with the pride in it, five sentences on holding the line even under dragon fire, marching up a mountainside in the snow, helping your mate off the battlefield when he's missing half his face … and they'd accepted her, seen it, drunk her health and drunk her health and drunk her health.

I'm looking for two children, two boys… But one of them, shockingly old, had been with Lord Brychan ten years ago, yes, he could remember a man called Acol, perhaps it was the same man Lidae was talking about? Crossing the mountains out of Tuva, the snowstorm on that high pass, yes, he had been there, could remember that, terrible, hadn't it been, felt it in his knees and his knuckles still when the wind blew from the north. 'We had to abandon all our loot then, yes, I remember. You remember?'

'Gods, yes!' 'Maerc? Emmas? Lidae?' No, those names meant nothing to him. But Acol … yes … yes … a good man. And Lord Brychan: ah, yes, now, there was a name! He, ah, he was the very best of men! Do you remember when…? And the wine had gone round again, and a song had started up that she hadn't sung for so long. Sitting looking out over the tents, the campfires burning—stars, the poets called the campfires, yes, stars, all that light dancing, and the stars in the sky, brilliant. The Dragon, the Tree, the red star that some men called the King's Star, although none of them could say who the king was to be so honoured. *I'm looking for…* The wine—good wine, rich and sweet—the smell of bronze and iron, leather, of campfire smoke. I'm drunk, with strangers, soldiers, talking soldier things, it would be … shameful, not right, to talk about my children. Tomorrow, she had thought, I'll ask. She awoke the next morning to the sound of the army camp readying itself around her, ready to march, a trumpet already ringing to summon them up, her head ached, it was still … not right, to ask about the children, and they had to get sorted, she needed to scrounge the rest of her armour, the knife she'd taken needed sharpening, sudden orders were shouted, furious to march, march, march. Later, I can ask, if they're here … they'll still be here, this isn't the time, if they are here, they don't want to see me like this, it wouldn't be right.

A man sharpening his sword, the old man from last night offering to lend her some coin to get herself a proper fitting pair of boots, 'You can keep the blanket, Lidae,' 'Want a quick cup of tea, Lidae, before we get going?' *I'm looking for*— 'Oh, please, yes.' 'Head a bit rough, is it?' 'I'll survive.' *Two boys, the oldest's about*— 'Tea. Here.' Gods, it tasted just like the muck Maerc used to make. 'Want some bread, Lidae? I've got some cheese, too, if you like.' 'Oh, yes, thanks.' Gods, the cheese was as vile as the tea. Taste of memories so strong her heart ached.

She felt so light, here. She thought: men leave their children all the time. Abandon them. They're safe and better off with Cythra.

No one would judge Emmas, she thought, for abandoning them.

Again, they lined up in long rows. Began the great bustle of an army on the march. To Lidae's surprise they were going south, not on northwards to meet the traitor ten days' march away, but this did not seem anything strange to the men she was marching with.

'Some plan,' her old comrade shrugged. 'King knows what he's doing. Not exactly up to the likes of us.'

'But why are we doing this, Acol? What's the point?' 'Why nothing, Maerc, mate. No point. They say we march, we march, that's all there is to it.'

She began, 'But…?' but then she thought, I don't care, it doesn't matter, soldiers follow orders, I don't need to know these things. A fresh morning wind, smelling of growing things and cool rainfall. 'Head feeling better, Lidae?' She gave her old comrade a smile. 'Yes. Thanks.'

On a rise in the centre of the camp King Durith was standing, Prince Kianeth beside him. Lord Sabryyr came up with the king's horse, huge and white, its hooves gilded, its flanks hung around with gold; Lord Sabryyr's armour was worked with green enamelled birds, set with blue gemstones, his cloak was green silk, his helmet crest was a peacock's plume. He knelt to the king as he handed over the horse's reins. Prince Kianeth himself helped his father up into the saddle, his hands cupped for the mounting block. King Durith again drew his sword, held it high. A circle of light thrown from the blade, crowning him. Prince Kianeth too mounted, a black horse only a little smaller than the king's. It reared up, treading the air. The prince's cloak rippled in the wind.

'For victory! For Illyrith! We march! We march!'

Spears, swords, cheering. Her comrades around her close.

Two boys, the youngest is about so high. He's my— I mean—

Trumpets. Drums. Overhead, brilliant, a second dawn breaking, the godbirds rose up. Their shadows made Lidae's skin look like pale stone. The wind blew in their faces, before them the plain stretched onwards, there was a great mass of white flowers growing in the sunshine. All was still and wild and very beautiful. A shaft of light came down and struck Lidae's stolen armour, made it flash silver as mage fire, flicker alive like a dragon's skin.

The world was … open. The mist was rising white from a stream-bed. On the crest of the hill, in the distance, the godstone was like a dragon's head. The sun struck it and lit it dark gold. They went past it in their columns, flowers had been heaped before it, a smear down it that was honey or milk; there was a stain of blood and the entrails of a deer beneath the thorn tree. As the king rode past it seemed to shiver, move with the beat of the horse's hooves. The god within it waking to greet the king. It seemed to grow smaller, shrink back before him. The offering stain dried away to nothing.

The singer in the squad, a hard-faced man who surely should not sing so beautifully, started up again:

'She was fair, as fair as flowers,
She was sweet as summer showers.
She smiled at me, her love was true.'
Two boys. Young boys. Have you seen them?

She thought: Cythra needs them, in her grief, her own sons are dead. She needs to care for something. It will be better for Cythra, she thought, to have someone to care for in her grief. Better for all of them. And I remember, sometimes, the way she looked at me … *"don't shout at them like that, Lidae… don't plead with them like that, Lidae… if I were you, I'd… if I were you, I'd never… have you ever thought of…?"*

She thought: they are with Cythra. They are better off without me.

'You know, I do remember you, Lidae,' her old comrade said.

'You do?' Mather, his name was. Lidae had no memory of the name or the face.

'You had a sword with a red jewel in the hilt.' He saw her smile. 'You were damned, damned good at fighting.' He saw her smile widen. 'Damned good.' Shrugged. 'You'd think it would have been impossible to forget you. What with you…'

They went on for a while. Lidae's headache was coming back and her back ached, her shoulders were aching, it was very different holding a spear again to holding a child. She raised her face to the wind. A soldier in the column behind them shouted painfully, heads turned questioning, 'He had a charm round his neck on a cord and the cord snapped,' someone said. Lidae looked at the ground, almost halted to start searching, poor boy, she thought. Then she thought: what's it to do with me?

Mather said after a while, 'We'll reach the river very soon, I'd guess.'

'The river?'

Mather looked at her in surprise. 'The Nimenest. The King's Bridge.'

'We're that far south already?' They had come so much further than she had realised. So strong, fast strong walkers, my children! Lidae thought. Tried to shut the thought away. Beyond the Nimenest were the vast wild lands that men called only 'the Wastes', on and on running towards the distant sea. Beyond the sea was the desert, and somewhere in the desert there was her city of Raena. Or the high mountains of the Emnelenethkyr, the Empty Peaks, darkly forested, dragon-haunted, rich in quicksilver and copper and gold and tin, that she had seen from a distance but never crossed. Acol had fought there for a season, said they were beautiful, less cruel than the mountains of Tarbor; Maerc had talked with longing sometimes of seeing them.

This wide green landscape, grass and gorse and heather… yes, she remembered crossing the Nimenest, the green lands beyond it after the poisoned marshes, feeling her heart rise as she saw the rich grass, the yellow gorse flowers in bloom, the bright hills. And the King's Bridge…

there had been a great and terrible battle here, on the banks of the Nimenest, back at the beginning of the war that had made King Durith king of all Irlawe. He crossed the river here, a great battle was fought, and he was victorious, in its memory King Durith had built here a fine wide bridge. Emmas's first captain, when he was himself first a soldier, had been there, Emmas had said, seen the king lead his host out in glory against the enemies that awaited them, to reclaim Illyrith and build an empire that spread out across the world. She had crossed the King's Bridge with Emmas, already pregnant with Ryn, 'Our new life,' Emmas had shouted when they had stepped onto the stones of the bridge into Illyrith. 'Our new home!' And she had not be able to understand what is was that she had felt.

The stories said the battle there was the greatest and most terrible thing a man could ever have seen. The sky was filled with stars of fire, the waters of the Nimenest burned, they crossed in the morning sun and the sky was dark as night, the stories said.

'Tomorrow morning, we'll cross it, I reckon,' Mather said.

They marched on very fast, 'killing pace' the squad captain called it and meant that in every way. Some of the camp followers tried to keep up with them even at this fast-marching soldier speed, men and women who were desperate, who did not know what they could do if the soldier they marched after got away from them even for a few days. Most of them, thus, being desperate, would be abandoned soon whatever they did. Lidae had seen this, dead-eyed women, their bellies swollen with pregnancy, stumbling after the man they belonged to until they were so hollowed out that the man had no more interest in them. The man already had no interest in them.

'Tomorrow morning, for certain.'

Two boys, young—
I'm looking for—

Camp that night, and the excitement rising. They had marched up north into Illyrith at a fast pace, Lidae learned, gathering others to them as they came. Faster than Temyr could possibly have expected. For three days they had been camped as she had found them, waiting for the remaining lords of Illyrith to come to them. They turned back south now to cross the Nimenest, draw the enemy out of sacred Illyrith to fight him on the dead ground of the Wastes. King Durith would not come as an invader to shed blood on the sacred earth of Illyrith, they said. They put their hands to the hilts of their swords as they said this, they who were drawn from all across the Empire and thus from all across Irlawe. The King knew that Illyrith must be a place of peace, they said.

'Temyr … he is following then?' Lidae asked. 'Marching in pursuit?' Clews is clever, she thought, he will keep them away from Temyr's army, keep them safe, I am sure he will. And he is skilled and strong.

But: 'The traitor doesn't even know we're here,' Mather said, his hand curled in a warding gesture. 'The warmonger is squatting in the north, waiting for word of us. We'll gather ourselves, dig in, and make him come to us.'

'He is despoiling Illyrith, they say,' the flute boy, Garn, said. 'We wait for him, and all of Illyrith will come to fight against him.' All the bright eager certainty of youth.

The hard-faced singer, Granth, sang:
'She was fair, as fair as flowers,
She was sweet as summer showers.
She smiled at me, her love was true.
Over our bed, the ravens gathered.
Beside our bed, the ravens gathered.'

'Always the sad songs, Granth, you cold bastard,' said Mather.

'It's not a sad song,' said Granth. 'Not at all.'

'He leaves her and goes away to war and never sees her again?'

'So?'

No fires, no cooking, nothing to give a sign of where they were, that they were slipping south to dig in and be ready for battle in a place of their choosing. Make the traitor worry, leave him guessing where we are. Thalden is barred against him with gates of iron and walls of gold. He cannot be crowned there, he will claw at the walls until his nails are bleeding, howl like a dog, tear his own face thinking of the power that lies just out of reach. We will wait on the banks of the sacred river, the water before us sparkling, the king in his court ruler of all Irlawe, crowned in silver, throned in gold. The traitor Temyr will have to march back all across Illyrith to meet us, harried at every step, we will stand on the bank of the Nimenest to taunt him, he will lead his men across the water, trembling, we will fall upon him even as he crosses, destroy him, drown him, slaughter him. So die all who dare to challenge the might of the Army of Illyrith, the Army of the King! So the men said, eager, bright-eyed, hopeful, clinging to the words as proof that they understood what was happening to therm. We are not retreating. There is a plan. Glory and victory and hail to the king. Lidae ate dry meat and oat cakes, cold and with damp misting her hair and eyes. I remember. I remember all of this. Glory and victory and excitement.

They were settling in for a few hours' sleep, wrapped in their cloaks on the cold ground, when an order came: 'Work to do, you boys. Arm yourselves, get ready.'

Scrambling up, hearts beating. An attack. Night manoeuvres. A forced march. Is this it? Orders: 'No spears, no shields, swords only. Rub dirt into your hands and face. Keep silent.' Something special. Something secret. Excitement fear excitement mounts and mounts.

Twenty of them mustered on the north edge of the camp. A camp slave came round, gave them bread and salt meat and a cup of wine each. There were thick clouds over the sky, no moon, perfect hiding dark.

Orders: 'Move out. Keep close to the man ahead of you.' No horsemen, no trumpets, no torches. The sound of leather boots on damp grass, treading quietly onwards. 'Keep quiet there, you. Keep your swords sheathed until you have to. Silence, I said.'

'It'll be nothing,' Mather whispered. 'Some poor bastards from a village somewhere, out hunting.

'Deer rutting,' said Granth.

'Villagers rutting,' said Garn.

'Shush,' Lidae mouthed at them. And a man beside her, whose breath came hard and frightened, said, 'There aren't any villages around here.' Excitement, fear, expectation, excitement. Lidae felt her face get warm. Her hand itched over her sword hilt.

They crept on very quietly for a long time, the camp was lost behind them, Lidae found herself marching half asleep in a dream of being a soldier. She chewed a gristly dried meat fragment caught in her teeth. Her mind felt very empty. Listen for the enemy, walk carefully, hold her sword ready. Stare forward into the dark. Play with a piece of gristle between her teeth. Wait. The last time she had been waiting in the dark with a sword, she had been terrified. She smiled now, eager, hopeful. Great and glorious things. She felt … different.

Whisper, hand signal in the dark, the soldiers knowing. It comes. It comes. They halted. Hiss of men's hard breath. Hands in the dark signal: ready. Wait wait wait wait wait. Movement in the dark ahead of them. Whispers in the air ahead. Gasping, itching. Whispers, hands moving, creep round, you men there, surround them. Wait wait wait till they're in place. Eternity. Come on there, they'll hear us, hurry up. Hurry up. Hands in the dark signal: go. They came on like dogs through the trees.

A crackle of branches a shower of white petals. Men, armed, squatted around a campfire, they started up shouting as the soldiers fell on them. Faces lit red with flames, can barely see them. Lidae ran at them. White petals of the may trees on her helmet, magical as a crown.

She thrust with the sword, went hard against someone shouting towards her red and black. Her feet stumbled and dragged on green plant stems. A man's face, eyes wide as horses' eyes, he was on his feet, sword moving, and then he was slick and wet with blood. She lashed at him. Blood smells like iron. Killed him. Blood smells like iron. Iron smells like blood. Another of them broke, tried to run past her, Mather beside her went after him with a growl, took him down with one swing.

The fighting took the enemy as it had taken those the enemy was fighting. They stabbed at her, lashed at her, two of them now, desperate and enraged. They were checked by the cramped space here between the trees. She stabbed and blocked her enemy stabbing. She felt her sword cut against her enemy's body, felt something in him give. A brute face thick with blood grunting at her, it had white flowers caught in its blood-slicked sweat-slicked hair as she did. She used her arm to jab away at its sword blade, knew it left her bleeding, her sword blade met its sword blade and then met its pig-white skin. Her joy was spinning red.

She thought, triumphant: I am fighting and I am winning. She shouted, as she had shouted long before, 'King Durith! King Durith!' Her words were choked with her blood. Oh, it is good! Look, Acol, look, Maerc. Look, Emmas. See me.

Dark figures, bloodied, running towards her, drawn on by the need to kill and die killing. She and they were wild beasts. Her enemy was a humped thing at her feet down and gone. Shower of sparks as the enemy's campfire was kicked up. Orders: 'One there, running!' Granth started, a shout, it was dead. A grunt of rage, a man on hands and knees who crawled away slug-like, she killed him. There were horses on the edge of the clearing, hobbled, they screamed and tried to break away, one of the enemy was ready to mount up. The horses' movements were like water as it flows. We could use the horses, she thought of Clews carrying Samei, but the soldiers cut them down. They were mad with fear in the chaos. 'They're all down,' a voice shouted. Heaped dead, no more fighting, men stood with lowered swords. 'Got them. Well done, boys.' Orders: 'Check them. Make certain.' Lidae bent, checked bodies, drove her sword down into an injured man's throat. He might have been dead already. Best be certain. Faking, unconscious, drag himself off to give them all away.

Mather had found a knapsack, rummaged through it; Garn squatted down to check the purse at a man's belt. 'Just as I remember you,' Lidae could feel Mather thinking about her. The nearest one to her had a fine dagger with an enamelled hilt.

Ten dead enemies. They dragged the bodies into a pile, put the fire out. Garn said with nervous laughter, 'I assume they were the enemy? Not soldiers looking for us?'

'Enemy scouts,' Granth said. He passed a water bottle round for them all to drink. He said curtly to Lidae, 'Well done.'

'I could have been one of them,' Lidae said to Mather as they walked back. 'Sent to infiltrate your camp. To spy. I could have been a farmer's wife with no idea how to use a sword.'

'Why do you think we were sent to do it?' Mather said.

As soon as we get back to the camp, tomorrow, I'll look, I'll look everywhere for them.

A few hours' rest and then they were marching. Lidae lay awake wrapped in her cloak with her heart still pounding. Listening to the others sleep. The ground was wet with dew under her and she felt disgusting. Never sleep. Not after this. So many different things in her mind. All the time she had been fighting, she hadn't thought about them once. So, she thought now: you see, I was right to leave them. She should get up again now in the dark, look for them. She woke suddenly to Granth's voice ordering her up, her shoulders were so stiff it burned to move her arms, her legs felt swollen. Her knees cracked and groaned like stone. After years hauling children around, working the farm, she should be strong. And sick with tiredness, after endless nights being woken by her children needing, wanting things. Granth muttered at her for being so slow, groggily fumbling with her armour straps while everyone else in the squad was ready to march. No nostalgia in waking this morning. A bed, a fire, water to wash my face, a clean shift. She limped; Granth saw her face screwed up with pain.

'Your face is cut,' said Mather.

'Is it?' Lidae touched it: yes, a pain on her left cheek, a raw place. 'Probably just a branch scratched me.' *I'm looking for— Two boys, have you seen them—* Tramp of feet on the march, a group of horsemen rode past going fast. Now Mather had mentioned it, her whole face stung. A barrier of pain between herself and her distant children. But the fierce glory of the memory: I fought a man, I had forgotten how good I was. Am. I can do it so well. Pleasure in her own ability. So long forgotten. *'What do you do?' 'I am a soldier.'* She winced and bit her lip and gasped at the jolt of pain in her leg as she had to move fast, and the men saw it, but they included her in their banter as they marched and she could remember very clear how the banter went as well as how to fight. 'That thing you did with your sword, when the second bloke came at you, right?' one of them asked. 'Can you show me?' What thing I did? I just do it, right, just move my sword and, just, win. 'Oh course I'll show you, remind me this evening.' They marched for the river, going quickly, a few hours and they would march out of Illyrith. She thought: men leave their children all the time, abandon them. And it's often better for the children. It is no different just because I am a woman. I love them so much, but I also love, want, need… She felt emptied and light and numb and hollow and happy.

Twenty

The Army of Illyrith reached the King's Bridge over the Nimenest shortly before noon that day. A very beautiful thing, white marble, gilded, carved with flowers and leaves and swirling branches, roses and honeysuckle and apple trees. Five men could ride abreast across it easily together, it was strong enough to bear the weight of the greatest of war machines and battering rams. It had a span of nine arches, its pillars breaking up the sluggish waters of the river so that it foamed and spun, and each of its nine arches was wide enough to allow a ship to pass beneath it. It was crowned at the north and at the south with guard towers each with room enough for a garrison of thirty men. The northern riverbank was thick with bulrushes and yellow marsh weed and the brilliant pink of willow herb, green birch and alder trees. But on the far bank the reeds grew up tall and straight and whispered of things untouched by men.

A great battle had been fought here once, on the northern bank of the Nimenest, so long ago now no one knew who the armies had been or why they had been fighting. Men had died there in their thousands, if one went out in a boat where the water was deep, a net could be thrown down and pulled up filled with bronze weapons and human bones. The bronze would be green with verdigris but was not corrupted, could almost be used. But the bones would all be cracked and burned black. Here, on the site of the battle, the new young king King Durith had led his army out to war. A road ran away from the bridge north into Illyrith, the heart of the world, the empire they had raised with their sweat and their bloodshed. A road ran away from it south to the great spreading world they had conquered.

The bridge was gone. Ruins. Nothing.

The road ran down to the water's edge and ended there in a raw gash of black earth and white rubble and grey ashes. Huge blocks of carved stone thrown down, shattered, melted. There was a faint taste in the air like the time Devid had shown Emmas how to repair a wall out in the sheep field. Claw marks in the wet mud. On the further shore, the same. Between them, the river flowed calm and undisturbed, the smooth sheen of the water like the perfect movements of Samei's skin. A family of brown ducks were swimming. The army halted, drew up in their lines on the very bank of the Nimenest. King Durith stood proud beside his standard, looking not out over the water as they did but at them, his army. Over their heads back into Illyrith. Lidae was close enough to see his face, the grief and rage in it.

Prince Kianeth rode up to join his father, said something to him. The two heads bent close together, father and son; Kianeth looked, Lidae thought, very much as King Durith had looked when she first saw him outside the walls of Raena. Kianeth also turned to look out at the massed army, at the green of Illyrith stretching away behind them. A shifting, murmuring, in the ranks of soldiers. Weakness. Failure. What king of Illyrith is this, when the river he once crossed in glory is now closed to him. Such an omen in the destruction. At Lidae's aching shoulder, Granth was whispering something.

The ranks of the soldiers opened. A figure in a dark cloak came through them to stand by the very edge of the water beside the king. It carried in its left hand a long staff. Oh. Oh gods. Lidae's heart beating, her blood pounding. The figure in the dark cloak bent, kneeling low on the muddy riverbank, reached its right hand down to touch the water. It straightened, it seemed to look straight at Lidae. It raised the staff.

Lidae wanted to grip Ryn's hand. Say to him, joyfully: 'Watch. Watch. Oh gods, Ryn. That you should see this. My baby boy, dearest one.'

A word, echoing over the water, too distant for Lidae to hear it, but she knew it, heard it ring in her heart and her mind. Blue light burst from the tip of the mage's staff.

The waters of the Nimenest shivered. Little waves, like feathers, ripples on the surface when Emmas had played splashing water to make Samei laugh. The rushes on the far bank swayed as in a high wind. Yellow iris flowers broke off their stems, floated on the water, bobbed on the waves. The water seemed to grow solid, a heaviness to it, a thickness. The colour of the water changed. A deep, old, raw red.

The surface of the water opened. Like a knife cutting down through the water. Cutting it open like cutting a wound. The water peeled back. Like flayed skin.

A road opened in the river. Wide enough that twenty men could march through abreast. The thick black mud of the riverbed, thick with new white rubble from the broken bridge. In the mud there were piled up human bones, and the long bones of horses. Bronze swords and bronze-tipped spears, helmets, armour, arrow heads. A war banner, its shaft gilded, its leather pennant still vivid red.

King Durith sat on his white horse staring. Lidae thought that he, also, could not believe what he saw. Though he was the king, and used to magecraft, and the figure in the dark robes must be the Lady Nayle, his chief mage, who had been with him since Lidae had been a child, who had spoken for him one word and torn the walls of Ander down. So impossible to believe, that a living woman could do these things.

The Lady Nayle seemed to move her head a little. As if she was saying, 'Go! Cross then!' Lidae could hear the voice in the turn of the cloaked head, the same twist of the head she might give to her children when they stopped on the threshold of something new and hesitant. 'Go on, then. Come. Get moving.'

This isn't real, isn't real, it can't be, it can't be, it is real, I have seen these things.

King Durith shook himself. Nudged the horse, and the horse reluctantly went forward, walked down very slowly, awkwardly, into the bed of the great river Nimenest. It stepped forward, its gilded hooves sinking into the soft muck. The smell of the mud it stirred up as it crossed rose, vile, but a safe smell, the smell of fields fertilised for the new planting. It picked its way carefully between bones and bronze weapons. When it came to the fallen banner it stopped, snorted, the king had to dig his knees in, say something. It whinnied. Stepped over the red leather and the gilded wood. Stepped over a horse's skull. Mounted the steep scrambled of the riverbank almost opposite Lidae.

Alone, King Durith sat on his white horse on the far bank of the river. His voice rang out, clear as music: 'As I crossed the Nimenest once to conquer the world for my people, to bring peace to all Irlawe, to make the world bright with glory, so now I cross it again.'

The spear-bearer with the brazen head of the luck horse on his spear-pole came forward, stepped carefully down into the mud of the riverbed. The Army of Illyrith gave a great cheer in one voice, began to cross the river Nimenest. Upstream the water shimmered, bulged, the path the mage had opened up within it rippling. Downstream the riverbed was exposed, wet black muck, bones, flashes of green bronze. All the way to the river mouth, the river would be drawing back, drying, puddles and the stinking riverbed. The force of the water coming down to meet the mage's will must be choking. The water was building into a great cliff against the force of the mage's will. A smooth solid thing. The soldiers tramped across the mud, trying not to look at the wall of water so close to them. If the mage Lady Nayle lost her hold over the river, its waters would come crashing back to close over them. And indeed, as Lidae turned to watch the mage woman, the wall of water buckled, a shower of white churned foam broke over the soldiers crossing, soaking them. Lady Nayle swayed on her feet, threw up her arms. A mist seemed to come over her, a light like a breath of smoke covering her, a shimmer to her. Like rain on a field, seen from a high hill far away. The wall of river water trembled. White spray breaking over the soldiers crossing, shouts from both banks, they scrambled up the near bank faster, pushing at those in front of them. Men ran to help them up the bank; shouts of urgency, the wall of water bending, foaming, toppling…

Lady Nayle stumbled, pulled herself back upright, turned to the river, raised up her arms. Lidae could feel the shock go through the woman's body as she saw the men in the water. Thrashing. Drowning. She trembled.

The wall of water was solid, a smooth hard surface like glass. The riverbed lay bare and exposed, bones, black mud churned up, a path. The men in the river, soaked through, began laughing. Hugged each other. The men on both banks cheered. The king shouted out in delight.

'Not even water, not even a river in spate, nothing will keep the Army of Illyrith from victory! The traitor Temyr, cursed be his name, he thinks that he can defeat us? We fight for the sacred earth of Illyrith, and we will be victorious! If the traitor, the accursed one has destroyed the bridge, it is he who will suffer for it, when he come to cross in our footsteps, desperate, harried, thrown out of sacred Illyrith. Here, where no child of Illyrith can suffer, here beyond our sacred borders, we will await him. Here, we will destroy him. All of you men of Illyrith!'

So easy. Walk through it, walk onwards. Of course I'll regret it, always. Beautiful babies, my beloveds. But the joy, the freedom, as she stepped forward. Pain in her heart. But a great burden of pain and guilt thrown off away. This world here was glorious. She was not ashamed. To see these things. To be a part of these things. One day, the brief years in Salith Drylth will be the unreal dream. They're safe, I'm sure of it. Better off. And I'm free. So easy, it had seemed to Lidae, to leave her life behind her. Anger. Exhaustion. Such vast all-consuming relief. She looked over at the far bank, where the reeds were grey and tall, whispered of battles and wild places and bronze-clad soldiers marching, her comrades' backs disappearing on into the wide world. So close. So impossible. Go back, find them, what am I doing? Cross with my colleagues, step forward, I am a soldier in the Army of Illyrith, I am

myself

free.

Lidae and her squad stepped down onto the mud and began to cross.

Twenty-one

'Mummy! Mummy! Mummy! Mummy!'

Excited.

Frantic.

But it's not real. She had decided, she had just decided, shut her mind to her love for them.

'Mummy?'

She had heard children in the ruins of sacked cities, their voices questioning like that.

The mud sucked at her ankles, it was slippery to walk on, she had to concentrate hard, stepping over old armour, old bones. Where her squad had to walk, there was the skeleton of a horse and rider, still caparisoned all in bronze and gold. They had to go carefully, delicately, over it. Bad legs, sore knees, old wounds: 'Careful, there, Mather,' she said, helping him steady himself. Ranks and ranks of them pressed forward, the king and his lords had already vanished away into the world beyond.

Voices shouted behind them. Desperate, frightened. 'Please,' a voice called out. 'Please, my Lord King.' More and more, a clamour, pitiful. 'Our village has been destroyed. Help us, my Lord King.' 'My children. Please.' 'My Lord King. Don't abandon us. My Lord King.'

Lidae jerked her head. On the bank behind them people were emerging, crept out from hiding amongst the trees, the rubble, they held out their arms to the soldiers, one even held out a baby, they pleaded for aid. Refugees, who had fled from Temyr's soldiers. Trapped here on the riverbank after the destruction of the bridge. They must have run away again, terrified, when the army came. The baby cried frantically in a way that Lidae remembered, when nothing would comfort it. They moaned, called, hands reached out desperately to the army, to the king. 'Help us. There are children here. Help us, please.' And a voice called over the others, very loud and clear in its despair: 'There was a dragon. A dragon attacked us, burned the bridge. A dragon burned the bridge.'

The soldiers' faces fixed ahead of them. Lidae looked down at her feet. I might fall. Mather might fall. They were almost at the other bank now. She glanced at Mather who frowned hearing it. Tried to pretend he could not hear it. The lines of soldiers scrambled up the steep bank, she was almost across.

'Help us. Please. Please.' And the voice, familiar, imagined, terrified, grieving: 'Mummy? Mummy?'

If I went out of the house when the children were sleeping, to look up at the stars, to breath the wide air, two, three steps out of the doorway, the door ajar behind me, I'd imagine I heard their voices shouting in panic, needing me, even if Emmas was there in the house with them. That's all it is. There are children there? Obviously, there are children there. But not my children.

She turned back. Slipping in the mud of the river. Mather cursed her, Garn cursed her. Granth shouted, 'What in all hells are you doing, Lidae?' Her freedom her weightlessness her happiness ripped open. Consumed by a greater heavy joyful hope.

'Lord Sabryyr hangs bloody deserters.'

'Lord Sabryyr hangs spies,' Granth's voice shouted.

But I did, did, did want to be a soldier again. I did want to march with you, fight with you for the king. She'd think she'd heard them crying and she'd put down whatever she was doing, thinking, run to them, even if Emmas was there with them, and a part of her would shout, in fury, 'Can't I have one moment without you? Can't I have anything of my own?', and a part of her would think, 'They are calling for me, not for him.'

There, on the bank. Her children. Her heart leapt up with a song all she could feel was joy and wonder, holding out her arms holding out their arms, and the warmth of them, holding them. All her joy all she could ever feel, what was I thinking? What madness possessed me? Kiss them, hold them, the feel of their thin silky fragile limbs, their hair all matted, pressed into her, she's pressed into them, joined together, press tight until we cannot be separated, they are her, she is them. I love them to the core of my being, my world is nothing, I am nothing, without them I would give up anything everything for them. A pain so deep through to the core of her, and she thought suddenly of her own mother's tired eyes, and she could hear the sound of a door that had so briefly opened closing on her.

Twenty-two

'I didn't think it was you, mummy,' said Samei. 'But then I did know it was you.'

'I knew it was mummy,' said Ryn. 'I knew first, I saw her first.'

'But then I did know it was you all the time,' said Samei.

But how? Lidae thought. In armour, in her helmet, from a distance. They must have been so afraid of the soldiers marching. But they know, she thought, children. 'You both knew,' she said, 'because you are such clever children, aren't you?'

Samei said, with the cruelty of innocent children: 'You ran away.'

Lidae said, flailing, her words as uncertain as the riverbed, she had rehearsed this answer, a long speech that they would forgive her, I can never justify it, what I did, I can't be forgiven, they'll understand, it will all be over they'll see, 'I– Because– You– We–' I didn't mean to run away. In a moment, she thought, I'll start shouting at them, blaming them, like I do when I look away, let go of their hands, leave a knife on the table, a hot pan on the floor. Because it's too painful, because I'm so afraid in case I ... in case I might have wanted to .... And to cover that fear I'll start shouting at them. Because I'm so ashamed, and that shame, you see, you gods, you world, that shame is because I love them.

'I– Because– I– Samei– Ryn–'

Ryn said, with the cruelty of a child's knowledge: 'It doesn't matter. She'll have some excuse. And she's sorry, she'll keep saying she's sorry. But we didn't miss her anyway, did we, Samei?

'She'll run away again,' Ryn said, 'I bet.'

'No, I won't,' Lidae said, the only thing she could say.

Samei squeezed himself into her, face pressed into her waist, pushing into her, 'Don't run away again Mummy don't ever, ever, ever go away.'

'I won't go away. I won't ever go away. Please don't say that, Ryn. Please.' And she thought: why am I begging him? She heard Cythra in her mind: *'You shouldn't plead with them.' 'You're too weak with them, Lidae,'* Emmas would say, *'just tell them, be firm with them.'* She thought: I killed a man, at least one man, yesterday. 'Don't say that, Ryn, you're frightening Samei.' A note of anger in her voice, creeping in, already. *'Be calm, Lidae, you're frightening them,'* Cythra was about to say, *'it's all right, Ryn, please Ryn think of your poor mummy.'*

'I won't leave you again, I promise,' she said, 'ever. Ever.'

'That's not true,' said Ryn.

She wanted to hit him, scream: no, it's not true, of course it's not true, but I'm sorry. I was angry and I was ashamed, and it was wrong and I'm sorry it can't be forgiven, no, and what else can I say to you? I did something terrible, and it can't be forgiven, I'll never forget, you'll never forget, no. I failed you. And there's nothing, nothing, nothing I can say.

Samei said, 'You promise Mummy? You promise Mummy?'

They were frozen there, the three of them, hugging so tight they were one person, bound tight by love and rage at each other. Until suddenly there were people all around them, different voices, Cythra, Devid, Clews, Mather, Granth. Lidae had never felt such anger and such relief at them surrounding her. The boys pulled away from her, looked at Mather and Granth in confusion. Clews, Lidae saw, put a hand on each of the boys' shoulders, reassuring them. Like Emmas would have done. He had shed this armour, as had Rhosa and Myron, didn't even carry his sword.

'What in all gods is going on?' Granth said. 'I mean … it's obvious what's going on. But … what the fuck is going on, Lidae?'

'These are your children?' Mather said. 'You've got children, Lidae?'

'Yes. These are my children.' He looked at her differently. *You gave birth, you are a mother, Lidae?* He was shocked, she saw: I thought you were a soldier, Lidae? He could see her body, her sex, the children pressed up against her: he could see them inside her womb, her vast body and her sex when she was pregnant with them, he looked at her crotch where she'd bloody grunting groaning pushed them. Camp slaves and camp followers got pregnant, gave birth during battles during fast retreats during forced marches, crouched lowing like cattle, thighs splayed, dragged their children, fussed over them filthy and selfish and howling while war made the sky black overhead. Lidae and the other women soldiers would turn away from them, revolted. How stupid, they'd think, how hopeless, to let that happen.

'You have children?'

'Samei,' she said, 'and Ryn.'

Clews said, urgently, 'The river—this is King Durith's army?'

'Yes, of course. What do you think it is?' Lidae understood then what he meant, she said equally urgently to Granth, 'We're crossing with you. We can talk about … about what I do, once we've crossed.' And Granth went pale, that terrified reluctant old look: *women and children, refugees?* But he nodded.

'Children,' Lidae said to Ryn and Samei, her voice strong and calm, pretend that they're soldiers, that this is me giving orders when the squad leader's down and dead, 'children, little ones, I'm sorry I went away—' and she can't say *ran away*, she can't, people go away all the time, they have to, they need to '—I'm sorry, but listen, now, children, this isn't the time, these are my … my friends see, and you'll be safe with them, but we have to cross the river now, okay?'

She held the boys' hands tight, led them down to the riverbank. Samei looked at Clews, she thought, very briefly, asking him from reassurance, checking he was coming with them, afraid. Ryn stared at her, cold eyed, his face very old and thin. His hand clasped her hand very tightly. It felt so cold, dry with picked skin horrible around his fingertips and his knuckles, and then it felt warm.

The wall of water rose up beside them. It was a terrible struggle for their children's legs in the deep stinking mud.

'Watch where you're stepping, come on, please, come on, quickly,' Lidae fretted.

Cythra and Devid and Ayllis and Hana followed them. Clews and Rhosa and Myron. A handful of others who must have been trapped there; the baby she had heard before wailed as its mother clutched it too tight because she was slipping. Granth made a noise, trying to stop all of these people, an old man with a gold brooch to pin his cloak, a couple perhaps his adult son and the son's wife, you can't come across here, can't follow us, this is an army marching to war, but the soldiers eyed the gold at the man's neck, the woman's long-fingered hands, women and children, old men, desperate, look at them, help them across.

'There's a slippy bit there, Mummy,' said Samei very gravely. 'A deep-mud bit, be careful.'

'Goodness, yes, thank you, Samei. Very deep. What a kind boy you are, looking after me. Big steps now, can you manage it, biiiiig steps.'

'Biiiiiggggg steps.'

Ryn almost slipped over, hung on her arm as she pulled him up. His face flashed love at her, Mummy who saved him. 'Biiiiiggggg steps.' The vast churning wall of water, it was terrifying to Lidae, Ryn tried not to look at it, hurried saying, 'It might fall on us, quick, quick, quick.' The soldiers were between the children and the water, thankfully, so that the children could not properly look at it.

'It's magecraft,' Lidae said. 'Did you see? Did you see it? See her?'

'She was magic, Mummy!' Samei said. 'I want to touch it.' He pointed 'A fish! Look! A fish!'

'Oh yes. How pretty. Biiiggg steps again now, Samei, Ryn, the bank here is very steep, very steep, see. Careful. Hold my hand and …. Biiiigggggg steps.'

Hand in hand together they went across the riverbed, climbed the bank. 'We're outside Illyrith now,' Lidae said. 'In a new country. Not even a country, really, King Durith rules it, but no one lives here. Imagine that, Ryn, Samei, it goes in for a thousand miles and no one lives here, it just goes on, wild…' The boy stared, wide-eyed. She thought: a new land, and I can care for them.

Granth was a kind man, it seemed. Most people are of course indeed kind. He let them march beside the squad, not just the boys but Cythra, Devid, Clews, the woman with the baby and the old man and his son and daughter-in-law whom no one knew. Sometimes Samei held his mother's hand, sometimes asked Clews to carry him 'just a little', then wriggled down with a whoop, enjoying the sense of this new wild place. The spring in him, making him happy, living empty of thought in this moment, like a beast. He skipped ahead of them, legs raised high: she felt it like the sun inside her, catching at her throat. That the world could be this, still, for him. 'Haaa-ya!' he jumped, 'Biiiigggg steps!' Clews was watching him too with the same painful joyful longing. Such happiness Lidae could almost feel herself briefly in a moment of forgetfulness: *dappled, sparkling, dancing, sparkling, whisper, whisper, singing; the sun is out, the air is sweet, my small child warbles birdsong. And a biiiiiiiigggg step at the end of each verse.* Our favourite thing to do on a spring day, boys, isn't it? Let's look out for a biiiiiggggg stick! Ryn caught her hand and laughed and pointed at a tree trunk that he said looked like a face. 'Biiiiiiiigggggggg steps!' Samei shouted at him, and Lidae thought oh gods, this will be the new thing he shouts all day every day when I'm trying to get him to calm down and behave. 'Biiiiiiigggggg steps!' Ryn shouted back, doing stupidly high big stepping. 'You look like a horse,' said Samei. The soldiers watched and smiled.

'They're lovely boys, your sons,' said Mather.

'How old are they?' asked Garn.

'Four and seven.'

'Fine boys. My sister has one of five, and a girl of two.'

'Granth has a boy of seven back home in Albor.'

'Cal, his name is,' Granth said. 'He'll be eight this Sun's Height.'

'Ryn will be eight at Sun's Height, too' said Lidae. 'Hear that, Ryn, my comrade Granth here has a son just the same age as you?'

'A daughter, too, back in the baggage somewhere,' said Garn. 'A baby, she is.'

'Yes, yes,' Granth said. He fumbled in the purse at his belt, 'Want some raisins, lads?'

One of the soldiers flirted with the woman with the baby, gave her some food, helped her when the baby needed to be changed.

'We did look for you, Lidae,' Devid said, 'I did, and Myron and Rhosa. But ... the boys were screaming, my Ayllis was screaming, and I ... It was growing dark. It was too dangerous, you see that?' He hung his head in shame, looked at his daughter. 'I couldn't follow you further into the woods. You might ... you might have come back,' he said. 'In the night, or in the morning. But then we had to get on. We saw ... The dragon was there, overhead, we could hear ... And Clews said .... We couldn't wait, you see that? Clews told the boys you'd gone ahead scouting, were going to meet us at the river, and they believed it, sort of, I think. But it we couldn't stay there, see? You see that, Lidae? The... the firedrake... and I had to think of my Ayllis.'

'It doesn't matter,' Lidae said. 'I do understand, Devid.'

They went on for several hours, through moorlands thick with heather, in every sheltered cleft, on every southern slope, there were trees lace-leaved for summer, wildflowers burst up in a richness more vivid, bleaker somehow, almost frightening in the contrast with the bare crags, the sudden rearing outcrops of grey rock, giants' bones, demons' bones. In the valleys there was a great marsh, Lidae could remember that clearly, beautiful and poisoned, dark water that shone like bronze mirrors, mile upon mile of white reeds, yellow irises, the air had been perfumed with mint, with flowers, but the water was death. Swifts and starlings, drifts of them, circling and circling in the air, darting, turning, thought-fast, arrow-fast, spiralling, shooting, sparking. Magecraft, these birds flying. Too fast to be caught by human hands. Faster even than dragons. A hawk, she thought, hanging motionless, diving to catch a bird on the wing. An arrowhead of wild geese, flying high to get away to safety, and cranes, surely, from the wide span of their graceful wings. But nothing that walked on the beautiful green earth here to eat the plants or drink the water that gleamed so very welcoming.

'Keep close to us,' she called to Ryn and Samei, as the first butterflies flashed purple and crimson, bees droned around them. Lidae looked up at the sky sometimes, if a cloud caused a shadow to fall on them or for no reason at all. She remembered standing on the hilltop out trapping birds, hoping, dreaming. She marched along with Mather on one side, Garn on the other, Granth ahead with the squad commander, sword, spear, helmet on. Samei said, giggling, 'You look like a soldier, Mummy,' and she laughed, 'Do I really, Samei, goodness, I wonder why that might be?' and the other soldiers laughed with her, 'She does, do you think, little man?' Granth said. And she thought: I ... We ... This could, maybe, work?

But: 'I want to go home, I want Daddy,' Samei began to scream, when a moment before he had been riding on Clews' shoulders, singing, still saying 'biiiigg', a branch of may blossom waving in his hand. He soiled himself again when Clews put him down at his scream. The scream and the stink made the men around them notice. Lidae tried to feel anything beyond fear and shame. Clews was different, now they were surrounded by soldiers. Didn't help her with Samei's filth. He looked sad, ashamed, awkward in his refusal. Men and dragons: she understood, did not reproach him. Even Devid would not help her, among all these men. 'Oh Samei, Samei,' she cried out, dismayed and humiliated, and Ryn bared his teeth at her, picked at his dry fingertips. She and Cythra and Ayllis struggled with Samei, kissed him, hugged him, Lidae had to carry him, struggling beneath his weight. Ryn only watched the grey sky, glared at them.

They struggled on, a copse of beech trees in a sheltered hollow, the beechmast crunched under their feet, mounds of faded bronze leaves, rich damp smell of them rotting, Samei was happy again, whooped and jumped, threw the dead leaves over his head. They looked to Lidae like old flakes of bronze armour, like the pieces dug from the earth around Baerryn Geiamnei, and that was a bad omen, but she tried to smile at Samei playing in them. The soldiers went back to smiling at him. She stirred up the damp leaves with her sword blade, and Granth laughed and kicked them at Samei and Ryn. The new leaves on the beech trees were green-golden. 'Never leave us, Mummy, never again.' But this might work, this could work, she thought.

The trumpet sounded to make camp for the night. The children were tired, Cythra looked drained, palid, hunched tensely into herself. Worse than she'd been when they were fleeing and in danger, Lidae thought. Kept staring about her at the soldiers, so did the woman with the baby, so did the old man's daughter-in-law. She frowned, bit her lip, wrung her hands, when the order came to stop, and Granth said that they could camp with the squad.

'Thank you,' Lidae said, 'thank you, Granth, for letting them stay with us.'

'It's nothing. Poor children.' But she thought Granth looked at her in an odd way.

The old man and his son and daughter-in-law had a few coins, offered to buy food to share if someone could tell them who and where to buy from. Ask Sydela, Mather told them, Sydela the sutler woman, the best of them, wouldn't cheat or sell bad meat, he'd take them to her in a little when he was done doing things.

'Sydela?' said Lidae.

'Sydela. Yes.'

'Black skin and black hair.'

'White hair,' said Mather. 'I suppose it might once have been black.'

'I sold her four silver cups once,' Lidae said.

The old man with the son and daughter-in-law looked at her, raised an eyebrow, shook his head. 'Maybe you should sell her that sword, then?'

It was like a slap in the face. Trying to make friendly chat and banter. Reminisce. My sword? What? What has it to do with you, old man, anyway? She said, dumbly, 'Sell it?'

Blink. 'Sell that sword. It would fetch a few coins.' He said, the old man said, 'Sell it to buy bread.' He said with infinite patience, as though she was stupid, 'For your children.'

'My children will be fine and fed, thank you.' Her face stung as though he'd slapped it.

A commotion, the woman with the baby made a noise, the baby started yelling, she heard Samei's voice shout. Oh gods. Relief flooded through Lidae. Vile old man, run to Samei and get away from him.

'Your son is crying,' the old man said. 'And that baby, too.' He winced. The sound was dreadful.

Lidae had left Samei and Ryn playing while she worked with Mather and Granth. And Samei had somehow just managed to hit the baby with a stick. So Cythra ran to see what the trouble was, Ayllis ran up, Samei pushed up patting at the baby, repeated on and on that it was an accident until Lidae had to shout at him to stop, he started crying, the poor mother had to tell him it was all right, it was nothing, even as the baby yelled its head off. The soldiers stared, of course, men exchanged glances, the old man with them.

She hugged Samei, he wiped snot all over her, somehow managed to scratch himself on her armour, howled. He had a smell that made her fear he'd soiled himself again. Ryn shouted at her for her cruelty to Samei. The baby was purple with rage, almost choking; the wretched mother had to strip her top half naked to get it to latch to her breast. 'It was an accident, an accident,' Samei howled. 'If that boy was mine, I'd wallop him,' a man's voice muttered. 'It wasn't his fault, he should never have been left unsupervised,' a man's voice said.

Granth came over, draped his cloak carefully over mother and baby. 'My daughter's colicky. Screams the bloody camp down. Her mother says the best thing in her life will be the day she's weaned.' The poor woman flushed, her face going crimson. She was looking down, trying not to look at the man in his armour. 'Thank you,' she said. She did not sound grateful. Her voice trembled with rage. But the baby quieted finally, and Samei hadn't soiled himself.

And kindness again, out of it: Garn and Mather properly noticed the state they were all in, went off to try to find clothes or at least blankets for the children. Ayllis had been travelling all these days in her night shift and a blanket for a cloak; Garn came over to her now with a long man's jacket that came down almost to her knees. 'Keep you warm,' Garn said. Warm wasn't quite what he meant. Devid nodded. Thanked Garn. The first time Devid had spoken to the soldiers. He'd refused to eat at first, Lidae had noticed, watched Ayllis's face as she ate, the hard thin lines of fear softening a little, only then had Devid eaten anything himself.

'It itches,' Ayllis said, tugging at the jacket sleeves. They hung down over her hands; Cythra had to roll the sleeves up and then they were thick and awkward around Ayllis' wrists.

'You look like Samei wearing Emmas' coat,' said Lidae.

'You look like a soldier, Ayllis!' said Samei. 'Can I have a soldier's coat?' He tugged at the sleeves, got one unrolled, flapped it about like it was a wing. 'Floppy Ayllis!'

'I look stupid, and it itches,' said Ayllis, taking it off. A squad of soldiers was marching past them, heard the voices, turned to look, curious. Two or three of them looked at Ayllis, certainly not seeing a soldier. One of them shouted out, 'Oi, oi!' Cythra cried out like an old woman. Ayllis put the coat back on, wrapping it around her.

'It's all right, Ayllis,' Lidae said quickly. 'They don't mean anything by it.'

Lidae thought: how I despised them, when I was a soldier, those weak people, camp followers, refugees, beggars, grown men and women so helpless and weak.

The old man's son returned with bread and cheese and raisins, it was more expensive than he'd thought, he said, fingering the purse he wore around his neck, they'd share it, yes, but … The old man's gold cloakpin was in a style Lidae recognised very well, as she should given it was typical of Raena. The woman with the baby wore a dress of green silk, dirty and crumpled but fine, rich cloth with a pattern of red and black flowers woven in. Southern work from Eralath, they didn't make cloth like that in Illyrith. I suppose, Lidae thought, I suppose merchants have always traded southern cloth and metalwork. But she thought of the marketplace in Karke, the stalls laden with looted jewellery and cloth and fine things, cimma fruit for a lord's table that cost as much as a life did. The bread and cheese and raisins were a pittance, a mouthful each at most. The woman with the baby cried, when they handed her a crust of bread.

The soldiers had been given rations that morning, still had a few scraps left; Lidae divided hers into three, it looked so little that she gave the boys half of her own share each, Samei offering to share his with Ayllis any moment.

Lidae's squad looked at each other. Fidgeted, all of them went to speak at once, tried not to look. Granth said, 'Look, lads. Lidae there was bloody brilliant yesterday.' Still a pittance. But it tasted very good.

Even after night fell, the camp was a mass of noise and bustle, digging in, settling itself to wait for the enemy to come to them desperately fleeing the people of Illyrith, caught on the blades of the true king's vengeance. All the excitement, men talking and singing about the wonder, the river, the mage Lady Nayle, the waited battle. Ryn and Samei calmed down, the baby slept, the boys and Ayllis tried on Lidae's helmet, waved her sword around. 'Strong Mummy!' Samei said in amazement, 'are you going to fight the bad men?' And maybe this was all going to be all right with them. Finally the boys fell asleep, exhausted, their bodies humped up together. Lidae worked alongside Mather doing what needed doing.

'You should be with your boys, Lidae,' Mather said, but she shook her head.

'Cythra's with them. And Clews.' They were sorting a batch of spear heads, getting them sharp, checking any that might be damaged. Good work, they had a fine smell to it, the feel of the metal was very good.

Lidae liked this kind of work. Calming, even as the click of the bronze made her heart pound for what it meant.

After a while Granth came over. Stood beside Lidae. 'Fine boys, your boys are,' he said again.

'They are,' Lidae said.

Granth said, 'Lidae? A word, please?'

'Yes?'

'Maybe ... not here?'

'What?'

'Let's walk a bit, maybe.'

'What?'

They walked a bit, under the darkening sky. Off in the distance a man's voice was singing, loud and out of tune: *They did not fear to ride out to battle, Nor did they fear spear and sword.*' Lidae said, 'What, Granth?'

The man frowned, rubbed his face, coughed awkwardly. 'Look Lidae... I mean I can understand, you were desperate, I can see that, your man there, he's obviously not exactly soldier material himself... and your children, well, I mean...'

'My man?'

'That chap with your boys... He's not your man? Sorry. I just assumed. Sorry.'

'He's not my man, no.' In her mind she saw herself nine months' pregnant, her breasts swollen, her thighs and ankles heavy, the thick blue veins and the silver tracery of stretchmarks running across her huge hard stomach, the disgust she had felt at how quickly and violently she had orgasmed when she and Emmas made love when she was mad keen to make love even as she could not bear to see her huge stomach as she made love. Panting and lowing in labour, the vast physicality of her, her spread sweat-covered legs, her uninhabitable body, her sex. She touched her sword, stood like a solider with her solider armour, tried to make Granth see her armour, sexless fierce soldier-Lidae.

A moment's pause. 'Well, so, anyway, I can see ... Well. Anyway.'

'Yes?'

'Look, Lidae.'

No. No, please. Not this. Not after yesterday. She was silent, understanding everything, trying to understand a word. She had, she remembered, overheard Acol give a similar speech, once.

'You found our dead soldiers, and you thought ... I can understand that, Lidae. I can.'

She said, more fiercely than she meant, her face burning, 'I was a soldier, Granth. I was.'

'Yes. If you say so. I mean...' He shrugged. 'You were damned good yesterday, to be honest with you. I'd have been proud, even, to have you in the squad.'

Her face was so hot it was as hot as dragon, as dragon fire, and she wanted to soil herself and scream like Samei, curse him like Ryn. She said, her voice shaking, 'But?' And she thought: I do love my children. So much.

The man was silent a while, he had to decency to look ashamed and away from her face. 'But ... everything, Lidae.' He rubbed his face, shifted his weight from foot to foot. After a while again the man said, with very obvious reluctance, looking straight into her face, because he thought of himself as a good man, 'Look... you can stay near the squad if you want. You and those people with you. Even the baby, though the lads will probably kill me, and I can't believe I'm saying it. Unless anyone else more senior says you can't.' And he looked away again, ashamed, because he was a good man, Lidae thought.

'I was helping Mather with the spears,' she said, weakly.

'Leave that. Look, Lidae... just go and... keep out of the way with your children.'

And in the end she had to thank him, because it was more, maybe, than she and Acol and Maerc might have done.

And that's it. So quick and final.

Of course that's it.

That's always it.

She should go back to the boys. Look at them, hear their breath, Samei's pouting face and lips, it's worth it, I'm so happy I found them again. My beloveds beyond reason. What madness possessed me? Nothing matters beyond them, say that again and again and again. As she got to them, she saw that Samei was awake, sitting with Clews, the two of them talking. She stopped, stood and watched them. It was like watching Emmas sometimes with one of the boys, calm and gentle. Ryn was sleeping, she couldn't see his face, he was so small, so hunched, so pitiful, she came closer to lie down beside him, put her arms around him, sleep pressed up to him. Best beloved, most beloved. Self-pity for herself, pity for him. What will they think, tomorrow morning? I ran away but I even failed at that. Ah gods, they were indeed better off without me.

Samei saw her, hugged her. 'Samei woke up,' Clews said. 'He was frightened. But we sorted it out, didn't we?' He shifted up, let Lidae sit down beside her son. Samei climbed into her lap.

'Look what Clews made me,' said Samei proudly. He held up a carved wooden figure, a little soldier man with a rough face, long thin head and body and legs. 'He's even better than Rov,' said Samei. 'A real soldier, that a real soldier gave me! And he's got a sword, look, and look, Mummy, his sword is tied with a belt and you can take it off!'

'He's lovely,' Lidae said. Choking back tears. 'I hope you thanked Clews properly.'

'I'm sorry...' Clews said. 'I ... hadn't thought. I just thought ... he'd like it.'

She said, because like Granth she wanted to think she was a good person, 'No, no, it's fine. It's beautiful. He did thank you?'

'He did.'

'Clews said you found King Durith for us, Mummy,' said Samei. 'He said that's why you went away.' He said, sleepily, very gravely, 'It was very good of you, Clews said, to find the king for us.'

Neither of her children, she thought, had said anything much about her disappearance. Like a comrade left alive but wounded on the battlefield, she thought, some things were not to be talked about. Those few days—days! she thought, days!—like a comrade's face, alive, and you go past him, and you have to forget, pretend. She lay down between Ryn and Samei, and she cried herself to sleep, her body felt as though she had been struck. *Poet of the sword, you are, Lidae girl, isn't she lads?* She could hear Acol and Maerc and Emmas pissing themselves laughing, *'Bloody good, bloody talented... But look, you know, you're just not ... not ... there's something ... I mean... I mean,'* they're saying, quietly, they don't realise it themselves, but they fear it, know it, I mean: if their poor mothers had been soldiers like she was, travelled the wide world seeking things... they probably wouldn't have had children themselves, those women, the men's own mothers. Women bear the soldiers, women die by the sword. That's woman's work, that is. Walking past the refugees from her wars shuffling along the roads from ruined city to ruined city, following a soldier for a crust of bread or a coin, sitting by the roadside in the dust and the mud too despairing to go on. How I despised them, when I was a soldier, those weak people, grown men and women, mothers with children, and they sat slumped with their children crying, they gave up, gave in. Weakness. Helplessness. I thought then that I was so much better than them.

A group of soldiers went past at a distance, men on horseback, trying to laugh and make their horses kick, they looked so young, Lidae thought, so very young, barely more than children. But she huddled herself fearfully as they rode past her, so large on their horses, noisy, filling the air around them. Tried to make herself small, hunched her body in. Why am I afraid? she thought suddenly. They went on past without noticing her. She was holding her body the same way that Cythra held herself, she realised. Hunched against men seeing her.

Twenty-three

All day the soldiers worked, preparing the battlefield for when the traitor Temyr was forced to confront them. 'He's desperate,' Granth told them, he'd been told this by his squad commander, who'd been summoned to a meeting in the king's very tent. 'He thought all of Illyrith would open its arms to him, really thought that, stupid arrogant bastard traitor. Thought Thalden would open its gates, shower petals down on him, crown him. Now he's caught, the men of Illyrith harry him everywhere, every town and city, the lowest peasant hovels, are closed to him, he is forced back in fear—and we are here, with the river before us, to destroy him. His army shrinks in number every day. So: he will perish! In the very place that King Durith rode out once to stamp his glory on the world, we will defeat him. It is only right and fitting, King Durith says.'

'They are preparing the battlefield exactly as it suits our army,' Lidae told Ryn and Samei and the others, 'you see, there, they are digging defences, ways to funnel and harry the enemy, expose them to our arrows, our magecraft while our men are well protected, setting redoubts that the traitor Temyr will have to batter his men against without a hope of taking them. It is always better,' she told Ryn and Samei and the others, 'to be the one who waits, rested, dug-in, having chosen the battlefield, than to be the one who must march to battle, uncertain of what it is that they face.'

Clews and Rhosa and Myron nodded, 'It is indeed, Durith is a wise commander, very experienced,' Rhosa said. Clews pointed out all the preparations to Ryn and Samei, took them through how he though the enemy would try to cross the Nimenest, how well defended King Durith's army would be.

'Don't sell your sword, Lidae,' Clews said quietly, later, 'unless you have to. Hide it. Keep it near you.'

'I don't know. What's the point?'

She sold the sword and the helmet to Sydela for almost nothing, paid the old man for his kindness in sharing his bread with them through gritted teeth. *Do you remember me? Lidae with the red glass sword?'* she had almost asked Sydela, but had not dared. As she was coming back she found Ayllis standing alone beside a white blossoming may tree, shaking.

'Ayllis?' It was bright daylight. The camp was churning with people, the sky was clear, the girl had on the coat that Garn had found for her, warm and thick about her, shoes now, even, on her feet. She was holding an empty waterskin. 'Ayllis?' Lidae asked. 'What's happened?'

Ayllis looked down at the ground. Her face was very red, she had been crying. She began to cry again now. 'Are you hurt, Ayllis?' Lidae said. 'Tell me what's happened.' Her body tensed, like it did before a battle. Clenching itself, closing itself against danger. A new sense of fear on her. A stone on her.

'I went down to the river...' Ayllis shook her head, snorted, tried to stop herself crying. 'And ... A man...'

She had gone to the river to get water earlier, she finally told Lidae, and two soldiers walking past had called out to her. She had turned away, hurried off with her waterskin still empty. One of the soldiers had called out, 'We're not going to eat you!'

'Don't tell mother,' Ayllis said. 'She's so frightened. She cries every night about Marn and Dylas and Niken. You mustn't tell her.'

'They only make a joke? They didn't...?'

'They didn't touch me,' Ayllis said fiercely. 'A joke?' she said then, 'a joke? Is that what you think it was, Lidae-who-used-to-be-a-soldier? A joke?' Her voice rose in a mixture of scorn and shame: 'If I had a knife, I'd have killed them.'

'I'll come with you,' Lidae said. 'To fill the waterskin.'

We have to say it's a joke, Ayllis. I always did.

'I'll do it on my own,' Ayllis said. She hurried off towards the river away from Lidae. She stopped, turned back, spat out at Lidae, 'I'll tell any soldiers I meet that they're joking.'

That evening the king paraded the troops again, a brilliant pageant of them to show their glory. The soldiers marched and wheeled in bright brilliant lines to show their manoeuvres, drums beating, banners raised, horse-hair crests proud in the wind.

The boys cheered, Devid and Cythra cheered, the old man and his son; Samei waved his wooden figure, shook it like a spear. How fine, how beautiful, to stand with her children have a chance to show them this. But Ayllis said, 'If I was this Lord Temyr, I'd have set the dragon on them all there and then.'

Samei said confidently, 'Lord Temyr wouldn't dare. If the dragon comes again, King Durith will kill it.'

'Yes, Samei,' said Lidae.

'The dragon could burn half of them up before King Durith even drew his sword,' said Ayllis. 'It's stupid. It's all stupid.'

Samei whimpered. 'Will the dragon come, mummy?' Will the fighting come?' All his joy in it vanished. Lidae said angrily to Ayllis, 'Stop it. Stop frightening my children.'

Ayllis looked away, her face flushed, ashamed. But Cythra said, as angry as Lidae was, 'No, Ayllis, you're right. It's stupid.'

'It's necessary,' Lidae said.

'Necessary?'

'It inspires the men,' Lidae said. 'Reminds them what they're fighting for. Encourages them.'

A silence. Then Cythra said, 'Marn and Dylas and Niken didn't need to make a speech or dress up,' said Cythra, 'before they fought to save their mother's life and their sister's life.'

'That's different,' Lidae almost shouted at her.

'Is it? This Lord Temyr, he'll be doing exactly the same thing marching to meet them. In the ruins of our village, even. And King Durith won't be sending those bird things against him when he does. They let each other do these things. Can't not be able to do these things' Cythra looked at the two boys watching the soldiers. 'They can't just fight, they have to dress it up so that it means something. So that people can see them.' She said with a snort, like talking about idiot children, 'They have to be able to parade themselves, shout, wave their spears, make their camp and do all complicated special things.'

'No, but—' But— 'They have to inspire the soldiers for the battle,' Lidae said again.

Ignore her. She's angry, she's bitter, what does she know of war? Samei clutched at her hand, frightened by her anger. 'Will the dragon come, Mummy. Will there be fighting?' Samei and Ryn asked in fear.

'Not now, little ones. Not now. Look! There's the king! And the king's son!' Both armed, both glorious: what must it feel, to be a warrior such as King Durith, looking at your strong fierce son, knowing him as great a warrior as you are, marching down into battle beside him?

'The king!' Samei cheered. 'The king!'

Ryn said, 'Look at his horse, it's huge! And his armour is so shiny it looks like a mirror, I bet you could see your face in it.'

'Isn't that a fine thing, you see?' Lidae said to them.

'Is that what Daddy looked like once, Mummy?' Samei asked. His eyes were huge with wonder. 'Like the king?'

A door, closed forever. Yesterday, Lidae thought, yesterday, you saw me dressed like that, Samei. Like the king. Shining.

Samei said, 'How funny Daddy must have looked, Mummy! With his armour all shining.' The soldiers marched and wheeled, sarriss rose and dipped, rose and dipped. Thunder of hooves as a unit of cavalry charged in a tight wedge like a spear point, scattered, turned, reformed, charged again. The king himself applauded them. Samei clapped his hands, held his soldier-doll up to look; Ryn's face was very bright. He was watching Samei, and he was happy because Samei was happy.

'They do look fine, don't they, boys?' Devid said. He came up close to Lidae and said quietly, 'I'm sorry. For what Cythra said. It hurt you, I saw it. I'm sorry.'

'It doesn't matter. Honestly. I'm sorry I was angry with Ayllis.'

'She didn't sleep last night,' said Devid. 'Sat up all night watching over Ayllis. That's all it is, why she said those things. She's angry and frightened. But she's not angry at you. She'd be upset if she knew she'd hurt you.'

'King Durith will win, Devid,' Lidae said. 'Please, tell Ayllis, tell Cythra: the dragon won't come as they fear, the army are here around us, there will be a battle, yes, but not for days still, and even when it comes, we'll win.'

Devid only shook his head.

Lidae thought. I know exactly what she's afraid of. Gods, I know. The sounds at night in her camp still rang in her ears. From Emmas' tent, once or twice. 'War music,' Maerc had said of it. And at the beginning it had frightened her and made her angry. Why, why, why do men do these things? 'Try to get used to it,' Maerc had said. 'Or cover your ears with your cloak like I do.' The slave-women in the baggage train, the women sitting begging at the roadside, offered a crust of bread for their children in exchange for following a soldier into his tent. The army swallowing them up, armed men, strangers; *We won't eat you, don't worry,* to a girl of thirteen. The woman with the baby, who had had to smile in gratitude for the help a man was giving her, even as he rubbed his hand over her bare breast. Hana, Ayllis, young and homeless and destitute, I suppose, Lidae thought, I could try to teach them fight. Soldier Hana. Soldier Ayllis.

Cythra's right, she thought, so right to be afraid of what will happen to them.

'This is the army of Illyrith and there is nothing to be afraid of,' she said in a cold voice to Devid, 'look at them, how glorious they are, look at them, and we'll win and then all will be well.'

You stupid helpless weaklings, Lidae-the-soldier would mutter, I am not like you, I will never be like you. Why don't you fight, you stupid pitiful things, like I did? If anyone touched me like that I'd kill them. Look at you, so vulnerable: become a soldier, you there, girl, weak one, victim. Be strong, fight, take up a sword, learn to kill. I hid beneath my own parents' dead bodies, I dressed myself in the armour of one of the men who killed them, I marched with those men and I was part of them, and look at me, look how strong I am, how much I have made of my life, my life is better than it would have been had they not come. Our house was one room with a courtyard outside that was filled with rubbish, when it rained all the sewage in the street ran in under the door. My sister married a drunkard thirty years older than her, because he had a house and a garden with an almond tree. My father worked sweeping shit from the street. My mother worked washing pots in an inn. By the time King Durith came to Raena my father was drinking every day.

War? The best bloody thing that ever happened to me.

She put her arms around her sons' shoulders: 'Look at them, Ryn, Samei, don't they look glorious, wonderful, like heroes, all of them?'

Twenty-four

'Lidae,' Clews said that night after the boys had fallen asleep to his stories about old campaigns and great battles, 'Lidae ... you sold your sword, I know, but... Lidae...' He looked very weary. He'd been nervous watching the men parade, she'd felt the tension in him, his eyes flicking across the gathered army, up to the sky, out towards the distant line of Illyrith's hills. Behind them, towards the endless moors and marshlands of the Wastes. Now, beside their campfire, he still looked out into the dark, down at the boys sleeping, out into the dark again.

'What is it?' She thought: he was with Temyr's army. And she thought: oh gods, what does he know? She had been caught up in the boys, in soldiering. What does he know about Temyr's army that I don't know?

'If Temyr is so desperate, if Illyrith has rejected him, barred every gate to him...' Clews ran his hands through his hair, shifted, bit his lip. Oh gods, what does he know? His body seemed to scream something.

'Tell me.'

He said, 'Your boys are fine boys, Lidae.'

'They're a spoiled nightmare, the pair of them, Clews. Samei shat himself on you.'

He tried to smile. His body was screaming desperation at her. 'He did, they are, true. Lidae, I have to tell you: Rhosa and Myron and I, we'll be fighting with Durith's army. I'll tell the boys properly in the morning, of course, but I wanted to tell you now, before you heard or guessed anything.'

'Oh.' Heartbreak. Slap in the face. 'You and Rhosa and Myron.'

'And... Devid. And that young man with the mean-faced father. He's never held a sword in his life, it's written all over him, he'll be doing something awful like latrine duties, that should at least please you.'

'Oh.' Devid has children. The young man has an old father and a young wife. But no one says they need to stay to care for them. They'll

give Devid a sword tomorrow, and if he sells it to buy bread for his
daughter, they'll hang him. Oh gods, she thought, I'll have to help
Cythra now, she'll be broken with it, help to look after Hana and Ayllis
as well.

She said, trying to keep her voice light, 'Thank you for telling me,
Clews. That was thoughtful of you.'

'I'm sorry they won't let you join them. I can see...' He smiled at her
again. 'They're foolish. Really foolish, wasting your skills. I can see you're
a better soldier than most of them. Probably better than I was. If I—' He
shook his head. 'I'm sorry, anyway.'

Stick the knife in. Twist it. I know I'm better than any of them,
Clews. 'It doesn't matter. Ryn and Samei are what matters, obviously.'

She heard her own mother suddenly, a horrible memory echo, *'Aren't
you eating anything, Mummy?' 'I'll eat later, little ones. When your father
gets home.' 'But aren't you hungry? It smells so tasty, Mummy, how can
you not want some?' 'Yes, but you eat it, Lidae, Elyse, that's what matters,
obviously.'*

'Thank you for telling me,' she said. 'Thank you, Clews. The boys
would have ... We'd have been lost, without you, if we hadn't run into
you.'

'They're fine boys, as I said. Mostly, anyway. Excellent judges of sticks
and dried leaf piles, very good at big stepping, and both certainly got fine
voices on them.' He went to get up, and then he said, 'Maybe it's good,
that they won't let you fight, Lidae. You should be grateful. You...' His
face was filled with pain. 'You... I've said too much. Ignore me.'

'Clews?'

'Durith falls back here, flees from sacred Illyrith the very heart of his
empire ... if the people of Illyrith have rejected the traitor Temyr, why
does Durith wait here in the wilds rather than marching? When the
battle comes, Lidae, and it will come very soon, I think, when it comes
stay very close to your boys, keep Cythra and Ayllis and Hana with you.
Be ready to run, Lidae. You hear me?'

He knows, she thought. 'Who are you, Clews? Why are you here
with Durith's army? King Durith will win, Clews,' she said. 'He will. He
has to.' Because I am here and my children are here, and if he loses it will
be the end for us.

Clews said, 'Durith is a great king, Lidae, and a great warrior. He
may still win. But be ready to run, when the battle comes, Lidae.' And
she wanted to weep: what do you know, Clews?

She should be raging against him, cursing him. *'You brought them here to the riverbank, Clews, to wait for the king. You should have taken them far away, protected them. I ran away and left them, Clews, because it was better, I should never have left them, I should never have followed the army, no, I am a bad mother, selfish, wrong, I don't love my children enough, I want my freedom, all those terrible things. But you, Clews, if you knew, you should never have dragged them here into danger back to me.'* But it was the other thing she thought of, now. A girl walking through the camp now past Lidae, her face bruised her belly swollen in pregnancy, her eyes down too afraid to look up, how stupid, Lidae-the-soldier had muttered looking at such women, how can you allow yourselves to become like that? Just be strong, you stupid woman. And pregnancy ... children... How stupid you are? There are herbs, potions, sponges, most of the sutler women have them; look at them, in fact, the sutler women, most of them use them, all the women soldiers use them, you just have to go and buy them. Why don't you just ... take control of your life, make choices, be strong? Why do you look so afraid? What's wrong with you?

And she realised thinking back in shame to Cythra's anger: that was the first time Cythra has spoken her son's names since they died, and she had been so caught up with the soldiers parading, she had not noticed it. Let the names drift past her, unheeded.

But I am a soldier, she thought. I am, I was.

Twenty-five

The battle. It comes. It comes. Two days passed, they awoke on the third morning to find that the traitor Temyr had outflanked them. Trapped them.

The dragon circled on the horizon. It could be a bird, a hawk circling, a goose. If one's eyes were so good, to see in the far swimming distance. Ryn pointed, indeed, saying 'look, a bird!' And then his hand dropped, his mouth fell open in wonder and fear. In the dragon's shadow, almost treading the earth like human soldiers, great creatures walked on cloven limbs. On the brow of a great green hillside human soldiers were arrayed with the morning sun brilliant on their armour, blazing into their eyes, so that as they day went on the sinking sun would be behind them. Blazing into the eyes of the army of King Durith marching against them. The hillside ran down to the stream where Ayllis had fled from the soldiers, marsh and boulders, flashes of yellow irises growing. Temyr's left flank was anchored by marshland, standing water, green pools, black mud banks, a wild, god-haunted place. On Temyr's right flank, a steep sheer crag rose up crowned in black rock. A single thorn tree stood on the top of the crag, dead and bare, yellow with lichen, twisted by the wind. Beside it, tiny, terrifying, a single figure, a dark shape in a dark cloak.

An arrowhead of white geese flew over King Durith's army, calling mournfully, flew over the ranks of Temyr's army and into the Wastes, lit by the sun. Following the dead paths over the wild, driving away the spirits of the dead. A flock of black swallows flew up from the south, frightened, flew over the army of the traitor, on over King Durith's army and over the wide fast-flowing river Nimenest that ran like a wall behind them.

Perhaps a mile separating the Army of Illyrith from the army of the traitor. A long way, the enemy lines were small as toys, tiny figures moved in the front ranks, if one's eyesight was poor the whole enemy army would be a blur. Like rain in the hills.

They were many of them.

Many, many of them.

So near, so close, the enemy. No distance at all, in the span of a man's life.

'They knew. They knew.'

'How did they get here?'

'Magecraft.'

'Trickery. Deception.'

'Betrayal,' a voice said, dark and heavy. 'All the king's plans were betrayed to them.'

'Don't be foolish,' Lidae said. Knowing that they were betrayed. 'It must have been obvious to any man with eyes what the king was doing, what the king's enemy should do.' They have come down the coast in black sips, fast and angry, marched hard to meet us here. King Durith should have known. Must have known. All the ships in Thalden's harbour: I do not think that Thalden has closed its gates to the traitor Temyr.

Who is betrayed? she thought. King Durith? Or all of those who fight for him? Who trusted him? He has led us to this place, he holds all our lives in his hands. He holds my children's lives in his hands, if he has lied to us, I will... I will...

The trumpets sounded, called them urgently to battle order. The army waking, leaping to its feet, panicked. Up swords! Up spears! Gather, run, ready yourselves, the enemy has outwitted us, we stand here now and we must fight and we will fight! For peace! For right! For justice! For the king! Distant cheers, the beat of swords and spear, from the enemy opposite. They, also, would be hearing the same thing said. For the king! For glory! For the king!

Cythra screamed, saying goodbye to Devid; he was crying also with fear, Ayllis clung to his arms.

'Come on, he has to go,' Granth shouted. Pulled the family apart. 'If he doesn't come to the line, gods help him, I'll kill him.'

'It's all right, Cythra. Don't frightened the girl. I'm coming.'

Cythra dragged at her husband's body, screamed. 'Curse King Durith,' she shouted.

'Get off me,' Devid said, angry, humiliated, other soldiers' wives and women don't do this, woman, 'I have to go, don't you see that?' One more sword, one more spear, to defend his family.

'You'll be killed,' Cythra screamed, 'he'll be killed, Lidae,' as Lidae dragged her away.

'He has to go with them,' Lidae said.

'He's never held a sword in his life,' Cythra screamed. 'You could go and fight, Lidae, why do they make him fight and keep you here safe with your boys when my boys are dead, Lidae? My boys are dead my husband will be dead.'

'Daddy,' Ayllis screamed, 'Daddy.' Cythra screamed, 'My boys are dead why can't they leave him with me?'

'Gods.' Clews looked eaten with pain at the scene. 'Gods.'

Lidae said, 'You've not seen this before?'

Their eyes met. 'Not quite like this. After a city falls, perhaps.'

Husbands ripped from their wives' arms, children dragged from their parents, we kill the men and the boys, we enslave the girls and the women. Lidae wanted to say, *You did this, Clews, somehow, didn't you?*

'Well… goodbye, Lidae.'

Rhosa called to him then to hurry himself, get moving. The long lines of soldiers winding their way to battle. The shadow of the dragon and the bird gods, challenging, wrestling.

Clews' walk changed, as he came nearer to the men he would be fighting with. He seemed very hunched, head bent eyes down, weight on his shoulders. Getting smaller as he got nearer the ranks of soldiers. Then, just as he got to them, pulling himself up straight, head up eyes up, proud in his armour and his helmet crest standing proud, raising his spear to cut the wind.

How do I feel? Lidae thought. Do I envy him?

'Clews is going to fight,' Samei said. 'I don't want him to fight.'

'Yes, Samei.' Ryn was holding his brother's hand tightly. 'Clews is going to fight.'

'But he'll be all right? Won't he, Mummy? Won't he, Ryn?'

'You were a soldier, Mummy,' said Samei. 'Will they ask you to fight?'

'No,' said Lidae quickly. 'No. no, Samei, small one. Of course not.'

'King Durith will win, though, won't he, Mummy?'

'Yes. Of course he will.'

Trumpets. From the enemy lines, the beat of drums. The dragon spat red fire. Their own lines sang out the paean. At the front of their lines, sword raised, King Durith rode to show himself to his army and to the traitors, his cloak swirling; beside him rode his son with the red banner raised. The enemy shouted, clashed swords and spears together. Great ringing heartbeats of iron and bronze. Arrows loosed from the enemy ranks, too far away to be a danger but the arrowheads were wrought to make a whistling sound, low and moaning, ghost noises.

'Mummy. Mummy.' Children's hands clutching at her. 'Mummy. They might hit us.'

'They can't hit us, little ones. They are too far away, you see? Far away. I like the noise they make.'

Ryn's face was trembling, trying not to cry. He looked like he did when he was a baby. Be brave for them.

Samei said, 'But they might hit Clews!'

'They're too far away to hit Clews either, little one.' And, indeed, their army was jeering and laughing at the arrows, 'A little girl wouldn't be scared of that display, you cowards. You want to hear some noise, you come down here and fight.' And their own army loosed their own whistling arrows back towards Temyr, sang out the paean again. Prince Kianeth made his horse rear up, hooves treading the air, so that the banner dipped and shone. 'For Illyrith! For Illyrith! Death to the traitors!'

A great shout, all the army crying out together, 'Vengeance! The King! The King!' Trumpets rang out. 'Be ready! Men of Illyrith! Against treachery! For vengeance!'

I could have been down there. If the children hadn't found me again. If I'd managed to run away. I would have been there with them.

I don't envy them.

I do envy them.

And the crowds in Karke, shoving her children aside, barely even noticing. And the men in the streets, back when she was a child in Raena. 'It's not safe out, after dark,' her mother saying to her, 'don't be stupid, Lidae. Take care.' Flinching, being cautious, planning how she would walk home, even in daylight, her mother who worked in a tavern and had a weight to her, her body tensed up, hunching her shoulders against something every time she went out of the door. The woman forced to smile in gratitude for the blanket a man was giving her, even as he rubbed his hand over her bare breast.

As if you could just not chose it.

Twenty-six

Temyr's position on the crest of the hill was defensive. He would not attack, unless he wanted to throw away his advantage. He would wait, make Durith march his troops up the slope to him. In the camp bonfires burned, the camp followers and the camp slaves set up branches crowned with a bone or a sprig of new green leaves; tied on ribbons or a lock of hair, poured out a libation of wine or water, cut their left hand with a knife and smeared out a few drops of blood. At the centre of the camp the king's servants raised a horse's skull on a spear pole, a powerful thing. It was very old, the bone very yellow and damaged, missing its lower jaw and most of its teeth. They had fixed white pebbles into the eye sockets that stared blindly keenly around it. It was small, a colt's skull or a pony's skull, not a warhorse. But it had a sense to it very strongly that it had died by violence. A true luck horse. A wonder, Lidae thought. She wanted to go over to it, kneel by the fire, make the luck offering. But she could not leave Ryn and Samei, nor take them with her, because they looked at it and were frightened. I could crawl over there, kneel, kiss the ashwood spear and make an offering of a trail of spittle from my lips. I could ask for luck for them, for the king, for Clews and Rhosa, for any here in either army I ever fought beside. I could steal a sword away, slip to join them, I could … I could… A trumpet sounded, Samei started crying, Ryn had a look on his face of fear and excitement, they knew, both of them, innocent little children, they knew that the trumpets meant war, death, fight. Now! Fight!

I could…

Her skin prickled, her breath came heavy. Thrilling. Like a hand caressing her skin. Oh, you gods and powers, I could, I wish… Always the wretched children snivelling at her feet stopping her, stopping her doing anything, Emmas going off for days hunting in the high hills, Emmas going to Karke for a few days to sell the extra produce, make a few coins, *'I'll bring you all back something.'*

The Army of King Durith was drawing up in tight ranks, looking over at the Army of King Temyr awaiting them. Between the two armies, the breeze blew spring flowers, set their petals dancing, the grass was dew-jewelled, spring insects buzzed in the damp and the swifts flew down low to feed on them. A long time, waiting, the two armies stood facing each other in silence. As if one or the other would turn and break. Again, two flights of whistling arrows. They brought down a handful of the carrion birds circling above them. The swifts fled.

The Army of King Durith raised up the paean. Began to move forward. Slow and steady. Bronze helmets covering their faces. Their teeth showing, bared, their eyes dark and hidden.

The dragon came over, to burn them. Devour them. The bird spirits flew up to meet it, singing. Samei raised his head to stare, as if Lidae had pointed out a rainbow. Mouth open in wonder. It was wonderous. A river of flame beaten back by great bronze wings. Warm air on their faces, sweet gentle, the smell and feel of the air in the south in the desert. The dragon screamed in rage, its fire pouring out to fill the sky. The men were marching beneath sheets of fire, marching up the hill slow and steady, spears waiting. Their armour glowed red in the heat. The birds sang to dance the fire away. The men were terrified, amazed, walking forward, doing this as they had before over and over. I have walked beneath the shadow of a dragon's wings, I have walked into dragon fire, Lidae thought.

She had never seen a battle from a distance. And the strange realisation that there was so much space around them, these men coming together almost as children playing, and beyond them, around them, all this great space of the world, green moors, deep marshes, trees growing, wildflowers, and they did not see it, they walked into dragon fire, beautiful and golden, and all they had to do, all they had to do was stop playing, walk away. Men were dying. Burning. Melting, liquid, their bodies running, flesh and bronze armour liquid together. Consumed by fire to their very bones; the dogs and the carrion birds could not feed on them. Here, watching, the heat of the dragon fire merely made the blossom on the trees rustle in a warm wind. White petals coming down, Samei had some in his hair, crowning him. The lines went on through the fire. The dragon spewed flame. The bird spirits lunged at it singing. A rain of arrows, iron points, bronze points, bone points, poisoned. A rain of arrows from our lines meeting them. The dragon and the bird spirits wrestled. Blood and feathers raining down. On the high ridge the enemy braced and waiting. All that we can do is go forward to meet them. Crossing the stream bed, water lapping at men's ankles. Keep the line! Keep the line! Muddy, and sandy, and Clews crossing might think perhaps of fetching water after Samei had soiled himself. Little fish in the water. Leeches. Yellow iris flowers like flags. A smell of mint, watercress, perhaps in peacetime we might play here very happy.

Keep the line! Keep going! Dragon fire shines on the water. Fat and flesh and metal all liquid, hissing, an iron sword plunged into water to temper it. The best iron, you know that? the best iron is tempered not in water but in blood. Gaps in the lines already, come on, please, Lidae's praying now, come on, please. We were glorious, we held the line, we walked through fire, come on now, do this, hold the line, hold the line, meet them. Run, Lidae's praying, stop this, run, run you mad fools run from this, this cannot be, it was not like this, she thinks, not like this when I fought, when Acol fought, Maerc, Emmas, they are gone mad they are walking through dragon fire towards men's spears, eyes waiting, watching to kill them, if they were not mad they would scream and flee. Stop! What are you doing! Think of my children! And watching this unfold before her, it is not real, it is like watching the children playing from the shadow of the doorway, the tiny figures falling, dying, they are not real they are not dead. If Clews had carved a whole regiment of little wooden figures, soldier men, it would look like this. Or a line of bone Rov dolls. And all of them are dead white bone.

'I don't want to look, Mummy,' Samei is crying. Samei screams. 'Make it stop, mummy! Make it stop! Make it go away! I'm frightened! Mummy!' But he cannot stop watching, Ryn cannot stop watching, none of them. Cythra has her hands raw in her mouth, bites on her knuckles until the blood comes because Devid is down there, killing, dying, but she cannot look away. I am sick, Samei, sick to the depths of my soul, I cannot tear my eyes away.

A burst of light, shattering into the enemy: Lady Nayle, Lidae thinks, Lady Nayle who tore the walls of Ander to dust merely by speaking. Men in the enemy ranks fall, shining; the mage cuts the enemy apart into fragments. A kind of joy in Lidae, the light gleaming: I remember how it felt, fighting in the ranks pushing and crushing when the magelord Lord Kimek washed fire over the enemy to break them. Pride in it. The thrill of it. I remember Lady Nayle when she first came to fight for us, she was young and thin, fragile; Lord Kimek was newly dead and Acol and Emmas laughed at her, how small and pretty she was. She could raise the mage fire in waves so bright we had to look away. Lady Nayle pours out her fire now and the enemy screams in fury.

Excitement dances in Lidae's heart.

Winning.

Winning! Ryn, Samei!

A shout. Up from the right, distant. Through thundering with the grass thrown up by their hooves, white horses, black horses, caparisoned and plumed. Riding out of nowhere, out of the green forest, leaves and blossoms like Samei's blossoms all caught in their hair. A spearpoint, screaming and thundering. The bit cuts into their mouths makes their spittle red. Their eyes mad wild red dripping blood. So close to the enemy lines already, the foot-soldiers toiling up the hillside wet and muddied have a new light to them, their lines grow tighter, heft the spear with some more hopefulness, the dragon wheels in the air to come upon the horses, the bird spirits pull back to it choke its fires with song. A blue light bursts out over them. Blue fire. It cuts into the enemy lines braced and waiting, fearing. Prince Kianeth and his cavalry come crashing into the enemy lines screaming blue fire-burning over them. Horses broken on great ashwood spears. Sariss longer than a man, iron-tipped. Horses and men skewered, opened, dying. But breaking through the enemy lines. Breaking, opening them.

Yes! Yes! Ryn! Samei! Lidae clutches their hands. Look! Oh, my children! See it. Every part of her heart and soul crying out to be there with her comrades in glory.

The far line of the enemy ranks opens, a doorway, the enemy cavalry on their great horses charge out, screaming, ringing. A great lord in golden armour at their head. They are a point to break in through the lines coming at them, the soldiers of King Durith, our soldiers, toiling in bloody fear up the green hill. They swing round, tight arc, pushing to meet Prince Kianeth throwing himself against their footmen. Kianeth's men cut through the ranks of the enemy, smash them down, men dying, Kianeth's men and horses dying. Pull around, screaming, bloodied men bloodied horses, howling back to meet the enemy horsemen. Trumpets, drumbeats, the two packs of horsemen like the creatures in air together wrestling. Durith's men toiling up the green hillside. The enemy spears readied for them.

The enemy cavalry wheels. Leap back from Kianeth's charge, spin together. Like water. Crash down on Durith's lines toiling up towards them.

Lady Nayle looses her fires. On the high ridge, standing dark beside the thorn tree, Temyr's mage looses fire back on Durith's men.

White fire. Washes over them.

The enemy horsemen burst through the struggling lines of Durith's soldiers. Careering down the hillside towards the stream that still flows bright. Swing round, pull up together. And now Prince Kianeth's cavalry are swooping down towards their own lines to meet them. Durith's men scramble to let them pass.

This is madness. Men and horses impaled. Men trampled down, almost drowning. Dragon fire and mage fire. Great shining feathers and dragon blood.

The horses shriek as the cavalry collides together. The two lines of spear men come together with a shout and a crash. Men dying. Men killing. Thrashing. Shattering. Running blood. I envy them. I do envy them. Cythra wails out, 'Devid! Oh gods, Devid!' curse Devid, curse him, Lidae thinks, that he should be there in place of me. A sword, my fingers would close around it, I would stride down run after them, be part of this. Go down there, fight, be with the soldiers, kill! My comrades, my brothers, my friends! Her hands shape a sword in the spring air. She can feel the warmth of the hilt, fine bronze with leather wrapped around for the grip, red leather, and there is a flash, a wink, red glass on the hilt, she can see it. To stride out with the sword bare in her hand, to kill, to rescue them. To be glorious. Her cloak and her hair blowing blood-soaked in the warm wind. I have walked into dragon fire. I have been all that is laid there bloody before me, and far more. For ten years, I won every battle I fought in, I never wavered, my sword danced in my hand. All I want. In all the world. To go down there. To take up the sword and fight with the banners standing proud.

She can feel the sword in her hands. She can see it. Just a moment longer. Just a moment, to make it real. Red glass, winkling. The smell of metal. The smell of sweat and blood and filth. The warm slick of it on her skin.

Twenty-seven

Five hours. Wrestling. Close. Filthy struggle. Hacking, hefting, sword stroke against sword stroke slugged out weary. From this distance in nodding wildflowers, it looks like nothingness. Horse charge. Dying. Broken. Beat it off. The dragon is ripped and bleeding. The bird spirits are shattered and one has died, its body is huddled in the bright stream.

Samei screams, 'Make it stop! I don't want to see!'

Where Lidae stands, the grass is green and pleasant, and wildflowers nod in the warm wind. Lidae watches. Her heart is shrieking. We should run, as Clews said. This is the end. Run away. Again. Again. Flee.

No! Impossible! King Durith will win, I know he will, because, because, because I am a good mother and I love my children.

'You victims. You weak ones. You deserve it. How can you let this happen to you? Why don't you just be strong?'

'I am a soldier. I am, I was, I will be. Born to be a soldier.'

Cythra screams, 'Devid. No. No. No. No. Devid. He's dead. He's dead.'

'What a paean we have raised, Lidae.'

Samei screams, 'Make it stop! Make it stop Mummy! I don't want to see!'

This is not fighting. These stupid men scrabbling to kill each other over nothing. 'Fight! Fight, Lidae!' Rena the healer shouted in the dark of Lidae's house, as Lidae squatted bent against the bed shrieking, gasping, weeping, her body dying. 'Fight! Come on!' Pushing and pushing. Samei sticking inside her, Lidae tearing her body apart to push him out of her, 'Fight, Lidae, push! Come on!' Rena and Cythra pleading. 'Fight, Lidae, push! Come on!'

Bringing a child into life, bearing a child, birthing it. That was fighting.

This is not fighting.

Cythra screams, 'Devid.'

Samei screams, 'I don't want to see!'

We should run.

'Make it stop! Make it stop, Mummy! I don't want to see!'

Twenty-eight

The dragon broke Durith's lines to weary nothing, Durith's horsemen wheeled and wheeled, like birds circling to fly south as the morning air grows cold. The enemy horsemen charged them. The grass of the field seemed to grasp at the men's feet and the horses' hooves. Holding them. A weary old man, grown old with fighting. Temyr, in his place, can offer more war, more pillage. Early on in the fighting Prince Kianeth went down with his horse, blood trampled over him. King Durith's men fought on bravely. But the knowledge of the young prince's death was within them.

The cavalry broke first, because it was easier for them to break in their circling. Or for other reasons, because these were men of wealth with money for horse and armour. They broke and went spilling into the woods, into the wilds. The footmen in their struggling lines pushed and trembling, hacking with swords, their ashwood man-killing spears long spent. Weary weakness. Fearful. The cry going up, despairing, as the cavalry broke to abandon them. Men in the ranks hacking at their enemy to stay the death stroke, ignorant of all but the sword in front of them killing, the cry goes up, the knowledge that the cavalry has abandoned them that Prince Kianeth is dead. For some, in their ignorance, they might believe from this that King Durith himself is dead. The lines began to crumble. Men retreating. Fleeing. And the dragon broke its fires over them. Lady Nayle, fighting, brave and glorious. Fire pouring from her hands. But she was weakened, wounded, fighting the river god of the Nimenest had damaged her. She swayed, buckled, the fire in her hands was fading. On the high ridge beside the thorn tree, Temyr's mage shifted, turned himself to meet her. White light came from his body. Beat out over her. She shrieked, and burned, and fled.

The terror of it, the marvel, from which the eyes cannot look away. Men killing men.

I want … even as they are dying… I want to be a part of them … I fought with them … I would have died with them. They cannot lose, Lidae thinks, still, as she can see them losing. They cannot lose, because they are my comrades. This cannot happen to them, to me, to my children. 'Run,' she heard Clews warning her, but she won't run, we'll win, we will, because…

But a shriek, behind her, Ryn's voice howling. A soldier in bloodied armour, eyes showing black through a burnished helmet, black horsehair crest tattered and smashed. She spun around, hand useless where her sword should be, teeth bared, go at the enemy, her heart screaming, save my children, go at the enemy with hands and nails and teeth.

She slumped, knowing. She cannot defend them. She could kill until her arms were aching, and she could not in the end defend them.

A part of her thought: they stop me from doing anything, they choke me, hobble me. The absurdity, she thinks: their weakness is what stops me from protecting them. The enemy will kill them. I will have to watch it happen.

The enemy moved its head a little. The black horsehair crest nodding. The horsehair plumes twisted, a mouth like a wound opened, long dog teeth barking.

No. No. No. No. No. Spiralling screaming circling in her like the birds circle, like horsemen as they sweep in for the kill. Thunder in her head shrieking. She cannot see for her terror. But this cannot happen. This cannot happen. Not to me, to my children.

All those I've killed. All those I've watch dying. But this cannot happen to me and to my children.

'Don't kill them. Please,' Lidae whispered at the enemy. 'Kill me. Not them. Not my children. Spare my children.' It sounds so false and comic. She has heard these words said before by others. And a tiny voice in her heart, even now, triumphantly within her: you do love them, you see? You say what a good mother says, you do love them. Someone, somewhere, the god powers that walk the earth as we lie sleeping… they see this, that you are a good mother to your children. 'I'll kill you,' she screamed, she had heard so many women scream that, *'I'll kill you, if you touch them, my children,'* the soldiers ignored her, as soldier-Lidae with her sword had ignored so many women. Helpless, useless. *But I'll kill you, I'll kill you, spare my children…* A hand shoved at her, a sword pointed at her throat, a sword pointed at her children, *Ooh, I'm so scared, what you going to do, woman?* Another soldier identical to the first, black burnished armour eyes hidden beneath its helmet, beast-jawed, beast-armed, wolf, crow, monstrous, murdering. Cythra between it and Ayllis, trembling hand outstretched, 'You can't kill her. Please. Please.' Her voice weak.

The enemy soldier said, in his gentle voice very like Clews' voice, or Acol's, 'We're not going to kill her, woman. Or any of you.'

There was a flash of red as the man lowered his sword to gesture to his men. Lidae turned to stare. Burst out into wild laughing. The sword he was holding had in its hilt a piece of red glass like a jewel. Her sword, that she had left in the ruins of her house in Salith Drylth. All this way, running from the soldiers, we will be safe, don't worry, there is nowhere safe to go to, everywhere is burning, get up, walk on, run, we will be safe, the war will end, we can come back home, we can keep going south away from here and start our lives again. And here he was, one of the soldiers who had sacked Salith Drylth, killed Cythra's three grown boys, stolen Lidae's sword from the ashes of the house she had built using coin she had once looted.

I remember seeing the captives, Lidae thought, trailing through the camp, I remember thinking so scornfully that if they were anything at all they would just run away. She tried still to think only of her children. Even in slavery, as long as I can love my children…

'We're not going to kill you. Really. Honestly,' the enemy soldier said. 'I can see you've been through it a bit. Captured by these animals who refuse to accept King Temyr as the king … but you're safe now. King Temyr is king of Illyrith, and he loves his subjects.' No different to Clews, indeed, or Granth or Mather or any of them. Soldiers, good men, people, looking out for a poor weak woman and her children, reminds them of their own mother, themselves when they were little boys playing. 'Obviously we're not going to kill your children.' Moved off, shouting to the men with him: 'Go through the baggage there! See what they've got! Let's get all those tents secured, yes? Come on, get moving.'

Samei said, 'Has the fighting stopped? We won?'

Lidae squeezed Samei's hand very tightly. Squeezed Ryn's hand. 'Yes, Samei, Ryn. The fighting is over.'

'And we won?'

'Get that stuff secured there, you lot,' the enemy soldier said. 'You, women, look, just get on off with you.'

The world was dissolving into celebrations. King Temyr's soldiers cheering, clasping hands; camp followers from all across the world greeting the soldiers joyfully, women and children laughing, shouting, hugging, throwing up their hands in delight that their prayers have been answered their loved ones are safe. The dragon flew overhead, celebrated its own victory. An officer walked past them, all bloody with the radiance in his face from battle, his helmet plume red and nodding. The officer's cloak fluttered behind him, as King Durith's cloak had fluttered, his sword was at his hip so that he walked with the casual knowledge of man who can kill. Lidae walked slowly, dazed, wondering, baffled. This morning we were in one camp, cheering our army, men have died, now we are surrounded by another army, cheering.

Cythra whispered, 'Devid.'

'We'll find him,' Lidae said.

There was a stir of movement at the centre of the battlefield, a murmur of voices, awed, astonished. A shout of rejoicing started up, voices bawling out the paean, but beneath that there was fear, something uncertain. Shame. A slow procession formed up, four soldiers carrying a bier of their spears, faces set under the dead weight. A voice shouted, very solemn, frightened, 'We've found him.'

King Durith was fully armed still, his armour hacked up in many places. His helmet had been pulled off, to show his face. His grey beard jutted upwards. His hair hung back matted with sweat and blood. One corner of his red cloak trailed down almost to ground, flapping around the legs of man carrying him. Once, Lidae had stood near enough to him to see his eyes move as he gave his orders, and once she had fought near enough to him in the line of battle to see his sword blade move as he struck. He had a wife, Lidae thought. A daughter, Princess Elayne. I wonder if they are still alive. If they will know that he is dead. Did he know, I wonder, Lidae thought, that his son Prince Kianeth was dead? She thought: I hope not. But he must have known it was all lost. I wonder how he died. I hope it was a good death. She was too far away to see anything, the body on its ashwood bier disappeared into the ranks of the army that had betrayed and defeated him. He who had ridden into Raena in bloody triumph to order every living thing within its walls slaughtered, who had led the great charge outside Gaeth when she had killed six men and realised she was a warrior born, who had got his whole army safely across the river Immlane in the dark when dragon fire and magefire rained down on them when all she could see was death. Such power. Such power there is in one man's death.

'You're crying?' said Cythra. Her hands made a curse sign, she spat towards the distant procession. 'My husband is dead there somewhere. And you cry for the man who killed him?'

Lidae wiped her eyes. 'I fought for Durith. He was betrayed. No one should die like that. And Devid may not be dead, Cythra.' She pointed down to the battlefield, the men churning across it, Temyr's camp in the distance, prisoners from Durith's army already being marched off in the dead king's wake. 'We can look for him, he'll may well be a prisoner down there, come.'

Ryn said, 'So if the fighting's over … Once we find Uncle Devid … Can we go home, then?'

'Go home?' Lidae said. She thought then: once we have found Devid we can go home now, I suppose, yes. The war is won the battle's over. Such death, such ruination. But it's done, it's ended. We can go back home, bury the dead, rebuild the village, live in peace. Keep pigs and plant a plum tree.

A few days walk, no more, a trip to sell goods at a market, a jaunt in spring sunshine to visit friends. Cross the river, walk through green hills to our village, the buttercups will still be glowing golden, the cows and the calf in the byre, the fishing boats drawn up on the shingle beach. In a few years' time, Lidae thought, once the house is rebuilt, it will be as if nothing happened. The king will rule in Thalden, the Army of Illyrith will march south to war, the winter winds will bring snowfall, the corn will ripen in the fields, the apple tree will blossom each spring.

Twenty-nine

They walked down towards the battlefield, perhaps twenty paces. Men and women already gathering there to pick over the dead. Ayllis said, 'He's alive. He'll be alive, mother, I'm sure of it, he'll come to find us any moment, you'll see.' A column of prisoners, frightened raw eyes, bloodied clothing, Lidae searched their faces, Ayllis said, 'He'll be a prisoner, I know it, you'll see.'

They went forward another twenty paces, braced themselves staring at the bodies, and then Lidae stopped walking. The children stopped walking. Samei cried out, 'Clews!'

Clews and Rhosa. They both turned. Samei ran to them.

'Samei!' Clews said, ruffling the boy's hair, smiling at Ryn. 'Hello.'

'I knew you'd be safe,' said Samei.

Ryn said, 'Were you fighting?'

Clews' armour and his sword were clean, for a man who's been in the depths of battle. But he had the smell and feel of blood on him. 'I was fighting, Ryn, yes,' he said.

'And you won!' said Samei.

A grave smile. 'We won.'

'I knew you would.'

'Yes.' He smiled again, wearily: Samei's innocence shaming him. Samei held up his wooden soldier-man. 'New Rov watched everything. Cheered for you.'

'Thank you, New Rov,' Clews said gravely.

'Come on,' Lidae said. 'Come away, Samei. Ryn.'

'But Clews—'

'I said come away.'

'Lidae! Wait! Please. Durith was a great man,' said Clews. 'A great king.' He looked down at Ryn and Samei, and then looked away. 'But he was too old, Lidae. My Lord Temyr had no choice. The world was burning, and for thirty years Durith showed his strength to master it. But his strength was fading. He talked more and more of peace. But the army will not have peace, Lidae. The army would have turned on him for showing weakness. Despised him. And we would have been back where we were before he was king, when all was chaos.' He rubbed his face wearily. 'You were a soldier, Lidae. You know.'

She said, fiercely, still trying to beat back tears, 'I left the army.'

He looked full in Lidae's face then. 'You did, yes.' He who had stayed with her children when she ran away.

So she was angry with him and said stupidly, 'You used us, Clews. You used my children.' As though he would say he was sorry.

Rhosa said, 'Of course we used you. We could never have walked into Durith's army without you to disguise us, no. Refugees, poor vulnerable women and children, kind run-away good-hearted disgusted-with-their-orders foot soldiers protecting them. And what would have happened to you, do you think, if we hadn't protected you? Every road in Illyrith must be choked with refugees, Lidae. With children.'

They all stood awkward, silent. Samei pulled at Lidae's hand. 'Come on then.'

'Come on?'

'We're looking for Devid,' Ryn said. He understood something about Clews, or about Lidae, because he said, 'But I think he's probably dead.'

'Devid? Oh gods, yes, Devid.' Clews looked around him now, as if he could magic Devid up unharmed before them. 'You'll find him,' Clews said. 'I know you will. You and Ryn.' As if it was as easy to find a man as it was to destroy one.

'Of course we will. He's Uncle Daevid! And then when we've found Uncle Devid, we're going home!' Samei said. 'Me and Ryn and Ayllis and New Rov.'

'Yes. Yes. That's good.'

Lidae said. 'I assume it safe, to go home now? You won't be burning and looting our village again?' Not in front of the boys, don't say that, but so much anger in her, and it must be said.

'That sickened me. I told you.'

'Did it? Really? Why did your king do it, then?'

Rhosa said, 'The men needed to be paid and fed, Lidae. As you should know.'

Silence.

Yes.

Lidae said, 'Say goodbye to Clews, children.' *Wish him luck, I suppose, even so, because…*

'Lidae. Wait. Please.' Clews said, 'My Lord Temyr will be riding north to be crowned king in Thalden and I will go with him. In a day or two, no more. As Rhosa says, you helped us achieve this. We owe you something for that, I think. I can find you a tent, food, new clothing, a place in the baggage train near the king's own household. Or I'll try, anyway.'

Cythra: 'Can you rebuild our village, Clews?' *Can you bring my sons back to life, Clews?*

'No.' A pause. 'I'll have men find Devid for you, Cythra.'

'He's dead,' Cythra said. 'Aren't they all dead, Durith's men?'

'He may well be alive and prisoner, I'll find him for you, I promise you.'

And they stayed, of course. And he did. Lidae sat with the children in Temyr's camp, watching the soldiers. They looked like the birds that came down into the fields after the harvest. They all seemed … frightened, a little, their celebrations heavy with the knowledge of what it meant. A group of them went past, men on horseback, and it came to her that they were almost children, closer in age to Ryn than to herself. A soldier brought them clean clothes, brought them a tent as Clews had ordered, a good one, clean, big. They sat and waited, and after they had waited for a long time two soldiers came leading Devid unharmed and clean and well-dressed back to them. Devid fell at Cythra's feet weeping. Shat himself like Samei. Howled with grief at what he had done. 'I killed a man. I killed a man, Cythra. And the man next to me died, I saw his chest cut open, I saw him dying, I saw him dead.' As if he hadn't killed cows and sheep and birds and pigs. He vomited and cried, and Cythra and Ayllis held him, wept with him. 'I can't,' he screamed, 'I can't fight again, I'll never fight again. Don't make me go back there again. I killed a man,' he screamed again and again.

The boys were so frightened, seeing a grown man cry like that. Lidae said, 'It's all right, children, little ones. Poor Devid. Poor, poor Uncle Devid.' They went over to him, hugged him. 'We'll go home now, remember, Uncle Devid?' Samei said.

A little later the soldiers came again with food for them, fresh and hot and well-cooked, white bread, roast meat. They thanked the soldiers. Ate.

Thirty

That evening the army burned King Durith. His pyre was raised on the very top of the hillside, for all to see.

'Everyone must know that he is dead,' Clews said. He had found Lidae standing outside the tent, straining to watch the pyre being raised, asked if she wanted to come and watch with him. Many of Temyr's army were still out in the hills, hunting down the last remnants of Durith's soldiers who had fled. Those who had surrendered were kept apart, in small groups under guard for the night. Placed where they could see the pyre clearly from a distance, understand what it meant. 'He should not only be watched by those who betrayed him,' Clews said.

Clews led her to a bare patch of ground looking across at the great pyre. Heaped up branches, white flash of white birch bark that glowed in the failing light. Spear shafts to form a bier for a king's body. The whole thing was gleaming with oil to help it burn, the smell of it was rancid and thick. Durith was in his full armour apart from his helmet, his red cloak folded about him. They had placed his sword in his hands. Heaped may blossom at his feet and his head.

She thought of dragging Emmas's body onto the pyre of stones she had built for him. The weight of Emmas' dead limbs.

Temyr stood near the mound, staring out at his soldiers. Did not look at the body of his murdered king. Where Durith had been glorious in his old age, white-bearded, wise, stately, Temyr was in the full vigour of his manhood, his golden hair and beard just tinged with grey. His armour was black and gold and scarlet, worked with a pattern of flowers, his cloak was red trimmed with gold, he wore on his head a helmet with a great golden crest. Jewels flashed on his cloak and his armour, on the hilt of his great sword. He was a tall man, strong built: Durith's body looked smaller, very fragile, beside him. There was a weariness and a pride mixed together, Lidae thought, in his face. He looked very fine. So very much a king. Almost as Durith had looked, she thought, riding into Raena, seeing all about him what he in his great victory had done. She had never seen Temyr before, in all her years of fighting, she stared and stared, marvelling, though he stood so that the evening sun was behind him, making him a great figure of dark and shadow, outlined and gilded, too dazzling to look long upon.

The last rays of the sun vanished below the hilltop. The living king and the dead king were outlined against red fire fading. A soldier all in black brought up the horse for the sacrifice that was proper at the death of a king. Durith's own horse: they must have taken him still mounted before they killed him. It reared up, when it saw the body, lashed its gilded hooves out at Temyr, almost struck him. A fine omen, Lidae thought. The soldier struggled with it to get it quiet. Temyr drew his great sword, in the twilight black against the sky it looked huge also, as the man and the pyre looked huge. Jewels flashed in its hilt. Blue flame on its blade, moving. The horse bucked and neighed. Temyr's stroke was ragged, the horse kicked out, bleeding. Lidae saw hands move to make a warding sign against ill luck. The horse went down, slipping in its own blood, beside the pyre. A great shout and the pyre was lit. The final light in the west faded. The right time, the luck time for such a vast thing. She remembered Emmas all in gold when he had been chosen once to light the pyre. The smell of smoke and burning fat that clung to him afterwards, the sweat dripping on his forehead. Durith's own face, grave but without tears, when he had lit the pyre to burn his eldest son. The flames went up high and fast: they must have soaked the pyre with so much oil, she thought, where did they get it from, out here in the wild hills? But they must burn him all to ashes, make sure nothing was left. Not his bones, not his sword. The smell was horrible. Even from a long way back, she could feel the heat of the flames. Always burning. Always burning. Emmas's pyre. The fire leaping up when her house burned.

Clews said, 'I had hoped that he would die in the fighting, last year. So did he, I think, in the end.' Clews' face was red, from the firelight. He too seemed to be burning away.

Temyr—King Temyr—stepped back a little way from the heat of the pyre, a knot of his men around him; the firelight gleamed on his great king's helmet and on his gilded armour. In the dark high above the wild geese flew past, flying north, calling. The flames lit them red. The dragon flew down to hang beside the pyre, sending up great showers of sparks with the beat of its wings. It was grieving, Lidae thought. Though it had fought against its master, because like the soldiers it was not a thing of peace. It was wounded, its wings ragged, its golden body wrapped in new deep scars. It shrieked its grief. Its tail lashed, beat against the ground hard enough to make the earth tremble. King Temyr and the knot of men around him drew back and back. The dragon gave a last great cry and flew off up into the darkness, following the geese north. It was a star, blazing, and it was gone. Lidae found that she had been holding in her breath.

Clews shivered. He said suddenly, 'It's ashamed that Durith is dead. I hope it dies.'

Lidae said, 'Did you really have a farm in Illyrith? And a man? Did you really leave the army for a while, for a life of peace?'

A shadow flickered in Clews' eyes. 'I once knew a man who did. Who had all of those things.'

Lidae said, 'Yes.'

In the smoke and the heat she remembered, so clear and sudden, the market square in Raena, hot and dusty in the late afternoon, the girl Lidae going to the market with a few precious coins clutched in her hands, trying to bargain the market women down for the cheapest cuts that were spoiling in the heat, the men's voice, angry, frightened, 'Durith's army is three days' march away,' not understanding what it meant but feeling herself afraid. Six days later the walls of Raena had fallen, King Durith rode in triumph and her family was dead.

She was crying again, as she had been when they brough Durith's body in from the battlefield.

It is not Durith that I am mourning for, she thought.

'There's a man here somewhere who has my sword,' she said absently to Clews. 'Looted it from the ruins of my house.'

'I could find him,' Clews said. 'Find it. If you want.'

Her heart leaped. Saw the red glass in her mind. Winking. But she said, 'Find him and ask him if he looted Rov, perhaps.' Clews laughed a bitter laugh at that.

'I have to get back to my children.' They were sleeping in the tent, safe with Cythra and Devid and Ayllis. 'I have to go back to them.' The camp was filled with movement, soldiers drifting in the darkness in and out of Lidae's steps. 'Get out of the way there,' Clews had to shout at a group of them, drunk and eager to celebrate. They went to shout back, saw his red cloak, hurried away meekly.

'They are mourning him, in their way, I suppose,' Clews said. They are ... we are like a greedy son when his sick old father dies, I suppose, tonight.'

I wonder, Lidae thought again, I wonder if I know any of them here? She scanned the faces as she walked with Clews, hoping. *Lidae, why, it's Lidae! My friend, my companion, you who were by me at the ships at Ander!*

'When I was a child, I lived in a village by the sea,' Clews said, 'my father was a farm hand, worked all his life in another man's service. The furthest point in the island to the furthest east of Irlawe ... if you looked north or east from the house doorway, there was nothing but the sea. Nothing, just the sea. If you looked south or west, behind the house, there were fields and then woods, and I never went beyond the woods, my father had never been beyond the woods in his life. There were hills, he said his master said. And a town, although he could not imagine how a town might look. When I was sixteen, men came round all the villages recruiting. I've never gone back. My father is dead now. The sea came up one night in a storm, drowned all the island, they say. There's sea, now, where we lived, they say.

'I asked Devid about whether you had really been a soldier. He told me about you. I was at Raena,' Clews said, 'when it fell. I was... I was one of the first in through the gates.' A shamed, proud smile on his face. 'My squad... we opened the gates.'

Yes.

'I'm sorry, Lidae.'

'Someone had to open the gates.' Lidae said after a while, 'Raena could have surrendered. The king and the priests. Opened the gates and let you in. They didn't have to fight.'

Clews said, 'No.'

She thought: you and Emmas and Acol, all of you, you think your story is no different to mine, you were poor, you were nothing, you went away to be a soldier because it offered you a better life, and so you think you are no different to me.

A pause. Clews said at last, 'If my Lord Temyr had not acted, the army would have split, there would not be one new king, but two or three or twenty, every city in Irlawe would be throwing off our rule, striving for power against each other. It was the only way, Lidae. I think ... I think in the end, in the battle, I think even King Durith understood why we did it.

'I fought for him for thirty years,' said Clews. 'All my life since I was a young man. Until last year, when I began to see that he was weakening.' He looked very hard at Lidae, and then he looked away. 'Durith was weakening. And war is a hard thing ...' He said slowly, 'As I said, I hoped he would fall in battle last year, in the south. A better end. He came close to it. He knew, I think … I am sorry that it had to be like this. So is my Lord Temyr. Truly.'

A fine speech. How many times had he gone over it, rehearsed it in the dark in the bitter watches of the night, listening to Samei's sleeping breath? *If I hadn't hit him, he was going to hit me … If I hadn't lost it, he was going to break it anyway…*

'Is Durith's wife still alive?' Lidae asked. 'His daughter Princess Elayne?'

'I don't know. Who knows?' They walked on a little. 'Why?'

'Nothing.' She thought: we burn those who die in war. But those who die at peace, little slow nothing deaths, we bury them close to our house, to be near them.

They were coming to the tent, big and new and smelling clean. Acol and Maerc would have killed someone for that tent. Lidae didn't want to go in. Stay out in the night with the soldiers. Keep her children safe from out here, doing some good great thing for them by talking to Clews who had got them all these things. Not go into the tent and see them there, and have it all end.

'Samei and Ryn are fine boys, Lidae, truly. Take pride in them.'

You and I, she thought, both of us have killed boys just like Ryn and Samei. I don't care about the cities of the south making war on each other. Two, three, twenty, a hundred warring kings. I had my house and my children, and I had peace.

There was a noise, suddenly, from a little way off, a shriek. Clews shook his head. 'Durith would have kept better discipline.' A woman came running towards them, in the light of the campfires her face showed bruised. Hana's face. That morning she had been a child safe in Durith's camp. The soldier chasing after her caught up with her, grabbed her hand, pulled her off without looking at them, his hand already reaching down her dress. Hana said something, giggled in a false loud voice. Her head turned towards Lidae, her eyes huge, before the man pulled her away.

Clews said, in the dark, looking after Hana, 'Lidae … have you thought …? It's a waste, you know, Lidae. You were good, I can see it.'

Lidae said, almost cried to him, 'Don't ask. Please. Don't.'

Cross the river, walk through green hills to our village, the buttercups will still be glowing golden, the cows and the calf in the byre, the fishing boats drawn up on the shingle beach. In spring the apple tree will blossom, in summer the corn will ripen in the fields, in autumn the leaves be bright as my sons' hair, in winter it will snow thick and deep. Inside the house, we'll sit by the fire and tell stories. Outside the window the birds will sing.

When she drew back the door curtain a long bar of light from a campfire fell on the boys' faces. They were huddled up together, Samei on his back with the side of his face pressed against Ryn's shoulder. Ayllis, Cythra and Devid lay very close to them, Ayllis between her parents, Cythra's arm over her. The woman and the baby were sleeping in a little hump. For a moment Lidae saw them as dead bodies piled up. A heap of bodies, limbs scattered. Old women, children, strong warrior men. Burrowing beneath them, keep still, hide, bury myself beneath my mother's body, hide here until it is safe to come out. Samei was sleeping on his back, his arms thrown up above his head. He looked so very little, a tiny baby, his face fat and soft. Ryn's arm was thrown across his brother's chest, defensive. Ryn's face was turned away from Lidae, she could the curve of his cheek and temple, with the scar running over it; his hair, matted with dirt, was pushed back and she looked for a while at his earlobe. 'Like a tiny shell.' Emmas had once said. In the far corner of the tent the baby began to whimper. Samei opened his eyes, looked straight up at Lidae, smiled, closed his eyes again, smiled in his sleep. Cythra groaned at the baby whimpering. The baby's mother crooned to the baby. Quiet again, as she put the baby to her breast.

Lidae thought with shame the old lie: better to do it than to suffer it done.

She thought: I love you, Samei, my baby, baby boy, Ryn, my most best beloved one. So much. So much.

She bent and kissed Ryn's cheek, very gently so as not to wake him. Went back out into the night after Clews to ask him. He had been walking very slowly, waiting for her to come back to ask him. He held something out to her, wrapped in a long dark cloth.

They had lit the pyre for their own dead now, the soldiers of King Temyr who had been victorious, the glorious hallowed dead who longed only for war. Men stood around it, black and small. In the dark, flushed red by the fire, Lidae looked no different to any of them. Red glass flashed at her hip.

Guilt overwhelmed her.

She felt bright and joyous and free.

Part Three

The Son

Thirty-one

A light dusting of snow was blowing off the high mountain peaks to the west. In the dark she could not see it, only feel it against her skin. The sound of the sea on the shingle at the foot of the wall was familiar, soft and gentle. They said that if it continued so cold, the sea would freeze.

Ilas at his post stamped his feet hard. His armour, which was finely decorated with enamelled flowers, made a ringing sound. There was snow caught in his helmet-crest. He blew on his fingers loudly. The flakes were big, like feathers. 'Bees', Samei had once described the snow.

'Nothing will happen tonight.'

'Won't it?'

'Of course not. If they do come, they'll come at dawn when I've just got into bed and warmed up. But they won't come.' He beat his hands by his side, puffing out his breath. 'I'm a dragon, look.'

'My children would do that. When they were children.'

Ilas yawned, showing a red mouth. Tipped his head back to catch a snowflake on his tongue. The black horsehair crest looked like a crane's wings as it was dancing. They had spent many watch duties out here in the summer evenings, on the sea wall of the fortress of Navikyre, following the cranes dance on the shore of the Ylanlynei Sea, the Closed Sea.

'When the sea freezes,' he said, 'the army of Eralath will come. Over the ice. That's what the captain says.'

'The ice would have to freeze very thick, to take an army's weight. We can wait a long time, then.'

'Or that's a story they tell, to make us think we're safe here until then.'

'Stop thinking about it,' Lidae said. 'When they come, they'll come.' She could remember someone telling her that, a very long time ago. Maerc maybe, or Acol. 'You can't guess these things. You'll go mad, trying to guess it. When they come, they come. Don't think about it until then.' And Cythra, she could remember, telling her the same thing about childbirth, in the long last days before Ryn was born. 'Like the birds coming back for summer,' Lidae said to Ilas. 'When they come, they'll come.

Ilas said after a while, 'It's getting heavier.' Smaller, harder flakes. Yes, the ground was white with them now. Ilas's black coat turning white. The waters of the Ylanlynei Sea showed as darkness, where the shore now had a faint white light. The lights of the fishing village were almost blocked out by the snow falling. If it kept falling, Lidae thought, they would be sent out tomorrow morning to dig the road out.

She tried to cheer Ilas. 'This isn't real snow. When we were in Tuva, crossing the mountains in winter, the snow in the high passes up to our waists…' Stamped her feet also. The bones in her legs creaked, I am getting so old, she thought, talking about my children, my joints aching and creaking.

'It's still cold, however deep it is. My spear's getting frozen,' Ilas said, and then looked at Lidae in horrified embarrassment as she laughed at him.

'Maybe try not to say that in front of anyone apart from me, Ilas.' And then she felt more embarrassed than the boy did, for giving him motherly advice rather than laughing at him.

I'm old enough to be his mother, she thought, and more. Almost old enough to be his grandmother, if his parents had him young. He might not be embarrassed to say things like that in front of the others, either. Things a man can say in front of other men that he can't say in front of a woman old enough to be his grandmother. Even if she is serving on the same guard duty as him.

Ilas pointed. 'What's that?' Lights moving in the darkness, over where the sea was. A boat coming in across the water. Small, from the lights. They were coming against the wind, sails furled: through the snow quiet Lidae could hear, now she listened, the sound of the oars, the beat of the drum.

A voice shouted from the walls, 'Who goes?'

Who's out on the sea in the dark in the snow and the wind? The answer was inaudible. She knew what the question was, so could hear it in the snow and the wind. A light was raised in the prow, drawing out a signal.

'Something important,' Ilas said, excited, as the boat came around, began to move in through the water gate. 'Not just a supply ship. An envoy from the false queen of Eralath. The king. It could be the king.'

'A supply ship would be more welcome,' Lidae said. 'Fresh grain. Fresh fruit.'

Ilas looked at her and shrugged. 'Well, I say it's a magelord or Prince Fiol or the king.' They craned their necks, trying to see. Figures, cloaked, muffled up against the cold. A voice, whispering, 'She says ... but he ...' Lidae thought she heard it say. A single brief glimpse of a man's face. Lidae thought: it looks like Clews. It could be, I'm sure it is. The voice whispered, 'He'll change his mind ... it ... when ...' Worried. Even frightened. Him changing his mind would be a bad thing, I assume? But then the figures were gone in the snow. It wasn't Clews. Dark ripples on the water from the boat and the water gate closing. The lights of the fortress running on the ripples like broken glass. Then the snow coming thicker, until the dark of the sea was almost lost. A white world out here, looking out at the great expanse of the sea. Ilas yawned, stamped his feet. Lidae thought: why did I say that, that I hope it is something so dull as a supply ship? Why should it not be the king? There were noises and lights across the far side of the fortress, a bustle of movement again lost in the thickening snow. Torches flickered casting arcs on the stonework. The bulk of the fortress swallowed the lights up.

Ilas said, 'If it's a magelord or King Temyr or Prince Fiol, maybe it means something will happen. An attack.'

'If it's a magelord or King Temyr or Prince Fiol we'll find out tomorrow. If it's a something else, an envoy from the Queen of Eralath, we'll never know. So don't agonise yourself trying to guess that, either.' Who else here, Lidae thought, will give him motherly advice? Ilas nodded meekly to her wise old patronising wisdom. Stamped his feet, blew on his hands to try to warm them, puffed out white breath. There were snowflakes caught in his eyelashes. Lidae's shoulder and her knees ached, her legs and her fingers felt puffed up with the cold. Gods he looked so young.

They were relieved and went back to the sleeping hall. Shaking snow off their cloaks. Warm air warm bodies smell. The warmth made Lidae's fingers burn so that she struggled to get her armour off. She scratched absently at the scar on her cheek. A servant brought them warm wine in good bronze cups. The wine was half water. Yawning face as he served them. Ilas put his boots to dry too close to the fire, where the leather would be damaged by the heat. Lidae went off to piss; in the cold of the latrine her piss and her body smelled very strong, almost pleasant. Snow and sea-salt, wood-smoke, wine, wet leather, men's sleeping bodies, rough blankets; woman's body and piss. My body even smells like an old mother's body, she thought, like the smell after my mother had had a piss, the sound of it, the smell of heavy, worn-out skin of her hands and her thighs. So like her mother, whom she had loved, she thought, the mottled blue veins of her thighs, the silver lines of her belly, the heaviness of her calves and her feet. When she was a farmer's wife in Salith Drylth she had marvelled sometimes at the smell of her body, the feel of it, how is it so different, she thought, from when I was a soldier, how am I so changed? Marching in bright columns, in the fresh air with her face raised to the wind … She'd heard a man talking about her recently, one of the squad, young, handsome, no different to anyone else, 'Frigid old woman,' he'd said, 'I'd be doing her a favour.' They knew she was a mother with grown children.

It was so easy, in the real fighting, with Acol, before she knew these things. Little naïve girl, who didn't notice. They talked about it then too, I'm sure they did. But I didn't notice. Poet of the sword, you are, Lidae girl. Nudge, nudge, wink, wink. She's so innocent so naïve she thinks we mean it. Humour her, lads, yes?

Wasn't like that. I was good at fighting. I am good. Better than most of them. But it was all different when I was young, and my bones didn't creak and ache.

The red glass in the hilt of her sword winked at her, smiled. She slept.

The snow had stopped when she woke next morning. The air and the light had the white softness of snowfall, but the sky through the window was blue and clear. Snow as deep as her thumb on the windowsill. In the anteroom the washwater had a thin crust of ice since it was last used. The bare fields around the fortress were perfect white, tracks of men and horses black across it; the earthworks around the fortress walls showed up as rings of blue shadow. But they went out on a patrol that afternoon and it was all already melting, her wet boots splashed through dirty slush. The country around the fortress was empty, abandoned villages with boarded-up doorways, reed thatching beginning to rot, in one village a dog had been left chained up, wild and starving, it growled at them in fury, its paws scrabbling in the snowmelt, pulling at the chain. Their captain, in pity, stuck his spear into it. Moments later a crow had come down to feed on it. The only signs of life: but in the melting snow slush there were tracks still visible, a herd of deer had run here, a fox, there were feathers and blood where a fox or a hawk had brought down a pigeon, human tracks where the hidden people from the villages had crossed the snow out of sight of the soldiers in the fortress.

'Hope they do come soon,' someone muttered. 'It was boring enough before it started getting cold.' A night and a day since the boat came in and they had not seen or heard anything unusual, it couldn't have been a magelord or King Temyr or Prince Fiol, or indeed an envoy from the Queen of Eralath, nothing unusual was happening. A rumour indeed, running around the fortress, that something hadn't happened, or wasn't happening, but no one knew what it might have been, if that was a good thing or a bad thing.

After the patrol, Lidae had time to herself before the night's guard duty. A sign of the trust the captain put in her, the guard duty, four nights of it, to help break the new young ones in. Be proud, Lidae! And not the worst shift, getting up in the middle of the night, saved that for the old veteran men who had to get up six times a night to piss. She only woke up once or twice when she was running with night sweats. She went down to the shore of the sea, near the water gate where the boat had come in in the night. A little stretch of mud and shingle, studded with old timbers from an earlier, wooden version of the Navikyre Fortress. Some of the men came down here to fish. She liked to watch the water. In the shadow of the fortress walls the mud had a crust of ice still in places. Too thin to crunch beneath her boots. A pair of geese bobbed on the water, cold even to watch them, they had come south for the winter, she thought, flown south from Illyrith, could have been living in the saltmarsh in the shelter of Kelurlth Head. Twelve years ago, she thought, she might have been hunting them, bringing their feathers in a sack to Karke marketplace to sell to make soldiers' beds.

Soon, she thought, I'll be too old for fighting, really too old, I can see what the new young ones like Ilas think of me, an old woman, fighting. Not that we've done much fighting here, keep the old veterans and the green new ones safe on garrison duty away from where the fighting is. And one day soon I'll be too old for that, even, and I'll have to go back to a life that isn't soldiering. Go to live in a village outside Karke again, perhaps, or back to Raena where they say people are living again. In all the years since she went back to soldiering she had not been back to Karke or to Raena. All the gods and powers be praised.

Thinking this now, she bent and picked up a pebble. White, smoothed into an oval like an egg by the waves stirred up by the boats coming and going from the water gate. A vein of white crystal ran through it, dividing it in two. When Ryn was a little boy, she thought, he would have liked it. A good stone. And a shell, when she bent again, a mussel shell broken off at one end but with a hole bored through it, and thus lucky also.

'Let me never have to go back to Raena or Karke as a soldier. Never. Please.' She clenched her left hand tight around the stone and the shell, threw them both out into the grey waters of the Ylanlynei Sea. They made a good noise as they stuck the water, sank down with barely a ripple. The two geese moved their heads at the sound.

She thought: and let me never think about Ryn.

Then a meal, back into her armour for guard duty on the seawall of the fortress keeping watch for birds flying over the water. Warships and dragons and spirits and great shining half-visible things of shadow, coming to destroy the fortress from over the Ylanlynei Sea. One of the Tarbor Mountains had fire on its peak, which terrified poor Ilas. 'It's a dragon! A dragon!' he cried out breathlessly.

'A fire mountain, erupting. The Tarbor Mountains spit out fire and flame. I crossed them once, with King Durith. Snow up to our waists, snow blinding us, blowing in our faces, and in the distance the greatest of the peaks was erupting in flame. And even if it is a dragon ... it's far away. Very far away. Too far away,' she said, 'to be a dragon, believe me.' *'You don't know what it was like, back in the old days, when the war was young, real fighting.' 'You young ones ... when we were fighting in the south, under the old king.' 'My sword's fought more battles than you lot put together.' 'Stop worrying.' 'You sound like my children.'* I must bore him senseless, she thought, droning on.

Twelve years, King Temyr has been king of Illyrith and of all Irlawe, the true and rightful successor of King Durith may his ashes lie beneath their cairn in gentle peace. Twelve years, his army has marched across Irlawe from the ice of the north to the southern deserts, from the rising sun in the east to the setting sun in the west.

Twelve years, Lidae has marched in his army, stood in the ranks awaiting battle, fought for her king with the killing bronze of sword and spear. Twelve years, Ryn and Samei have marched in the baggage train behind her, until they in their turn have grown from children into soldiers. Twelve years, Devid has learned to love soldiering, become a fine warrior as he once dreamed of, died alone on a battlefield, left his wife and child with nothing, they trail on alone now after his squad washing his old comrades' clothes.

In the south, the false Queen of Eralath is old and weary, her sons lead her armies into battle in her place. In the east, the men of Arborn and the Immlane river flock to the banner of their dead magelord, whom they claim is undefeated and undying, returned to them. In the west, the old cities that were once each a kingdom rise up against Illyrith's rule, each crowning themselves a king. In the north, in Illyrith itself, there are whispers of betrayal. King Durith, men remember, has a daughter still living, Elayne: she is full grown now to adulthood, talks of revenge. But the wars, King Temyr tells his soldiers, the wars will soon be won. If we do not keep fighting, King Temyr tells his soldiers, we will lose everything. Old men who have fought all their lives since they were children. Boys who hunger to come to manhood, for fear there should be no more conquests left for them. They stand in their rows, bronze swords shining, bronze tipped ashwood spears raised high. Black horse-hair crests to their helmets nodding.

Thirty-two

'Millet porridge for dinner. Again.'

'And?'

'And I'm fed up with it.'

'You're fed up with everything.'

'You're not bored of this? Really?'

'I don't complain.'

'It's inedible. Gods! Millet porridge and snow. They could at least get us meat. How are we supposed to fight, eating this stuff? It's like they're trying to make us too weak to fight.'

'Somehow, you know, Deljan, I doubt that.'

'I had a girl back home who wanted to marry me. I told her I'd rather go off to war. I didn't tell her I'd rather go off to sit around shovelling snow and eating millet porridge, did I?'

'Perhaps, then, you should have checked the meaning of the word 'war' before you left.'

'Gods, you prick. You smug prick.'

'Say that again? You'll be on latrine duty again, if you don't watch out.'

'Fuck you, you smug prick.'

'He got a letter from his mother three days ago,' Lidae said quietly later. 'The girl's married his younger brother. She's pregnant. Let it be this time. Just ignore him.'

Their squad captain said, 'Stupid bastard should have married her and got her pregnant himself before he went off to war, then, shouldn't he?'

News came the next morning. The false Queen of Eralath was at the south coast of the Ylanlynei Sea. Moving up the shore of the Ylanlynei Sea towards them. It was announced that half the garrison was to march in two days, should ready themselves. The rest would stay behind, hold the fortress. The boat, Lidae thought, had indeed brought news of some kind. *She says... but he...* A spy from the enemy army, even. A little pitiful burst of excitement, shared between her and Ilas, that they had seen the boat come in. Knew something more than the others. A secret message in the night that the enemy was moving, and they would march out quickly, head the enemy off in a place of their own choosing, break it.

And if they were marching south... Lord Sabryyr, the king's highest ranking general, was in the south with his men. She thought with joy: I might see Samei! Two years, since she had seen Samei. Clews had taken the boy under his protection. Looked out for him. Samei was not one of the ranks footsoldiers, like she was.

'Born to it, naturally,' Clews had said about him, 'clever and skilled and keen.'

Samei had been handling swords since he was five years old. Sat in Clews' tent since he was a child talking tactics and strategy over with him. Two years, since she had last seen Samei. Though a letter had come from him a year ago, he had learned not just to read but even to write. The pride she had felt, taking it to one of the few men in the fortress who could read: 'My son has written this to me, two iron pennies if you'll read it to me.'

Two years since she had last seen Ryn, she thought. Her mind closed to it. Shame. Anger. Don't think about Ryn.

That evening they were drawn up in the courtyard of the Navikyre Fortress. Parade dress, their armour polished, red ribbons decorating their spear shafts. Blue lips, poor heartbroken Deljan joked, to go with the red ribbons. They stamped their feet on stones that glittered with frost, looked very fine, Lidae thought, the snow on their black cloaks was like stars glittering in the night sky, or like the spangled silks the great ladies had worn in Raena that the child Lidae had loved to look at, except that now, years and years and years later, she understood that they had not been great ladies but street whores. The snow on their helmet plumes made them look dusted with silver. It will never stop being beautiful, she thought, ranks of soldiers drawn up in order, armed, proud in their calling. If it ever ceases to strike me with wonder, she thought, the joy at its beauty, the luck I have had to be a part of this.

There must have been soldiers on the streets of Raena when she was a child, but those she did not remember, because they had lost. Just men on the streets of Raena, awkward in their armour, 'keep away from them,' her mother and her father had warned her, 'keep away from the king's soldiers, Lidae, child. Don't speak to them.' And some of the children she played with had laughed at the soldiers, shouted insults at them, made rude gestures at them behind their backs. But the soldiers of Durith's army, when they had marched into Raena in triumph, and the girl Lidae had been crouched in the filth of her parents' bodies, crushed, trembling, terrified, had looked up, seen them…

Glorious. Power and strength beyond her imagining. I am a part of them. I am one of them. What I saw that day, I have become, and my sons now have become. If I ever stop feeling wonder at it, may the earth open up to swallow me.

She thought sometimes, as in a dream, of the years with Emmas on the farm near the village of Salith Drylth, 'Bright Field', named after the buttercups that grew there. For a while, she thought, the earth did swallow me up.

'Soldiers of King Temyr! Soldiers of Illyrith!' The trumpets rang, and the order was given that they would march west in the first light of the morning, to defend the green fields of Illyrith, the farmers and the children who lived their peacefully, the wild hills and plains where they bred horses, the good earth and fat flock; to bring the enemy peoples of the south who suffered under false rule back to the true king. There was, their squad captain told them, great treasure in the Queen of Eralath's baggage train. It was well known. What would be wonderful, Lidae thought, would be if she and Samei could be there side-by-side, fighting.

The western shore of the Ylanlynei Sea was dun hills rising out a flat dun plain, dry and barren, their slopes very sheer, narrow green valleys where crops could grow folded within them. The landscape looked, Lidae thought, like the folds of a woman's body, or the fat folds around a baby's knees and wrists. The people here lived by fishing, and by farming millet and little wiry-coated brown sheep. They had all fled, like the people around Navikyre Fortress, as the army began to march. The sheep were left, wild little things that ran from the sound of men's footsteps; there was a knack to rounding them up by whistling to them on a bone pipe that the squad captain had learned, he showed them and that night by their fire they had fresh meat. Stringy and greasy, not good eating, and a salty aftertaste from the shepherds driving their flocks down to shore to graze on the salt flats there.

'They like it, gods know why.'

'They do the same on the coast of Illyrith,' Lidae said, 'graze the sheep on the beaches, feed them on seaweed and seagrass, to make the flesh salt-sweet.'

'Gods know why they do it there either, then.'

'Hunt us some wild fowl, Lidae, tomorrow. Catch us a fat roast duck.'

'I haven't hunted wild birds for years,' Lidae said. 'I need lures and nets.' Her bones ached from sleeping on cold earth, after so long at the fortress on a bed, her shoulder, her knees, her hands, her legs felt heavy and stiff. War wounds, she told herself. Not because she was growing old, getting worn out by life.

They came down very close to the shoreline the next day, that evening some of the soldiers at the next campfire went fishing, so everything downwind caught the smell of cooking fish. The next few days they were up in the dry hills, scrambling over rocks glazed in frost, dry snow wind blowing from off the sea behind them, the cold taste of the air in their face. One morning it snowed properly, snow halfway up Lidae's calves, all the sheep and the wildfowl disappeared, the going was very slow. A wagon overturned, spilled out blankets into a snowdrift, there was much shouting, half the columns seemed to be held up by it; that evening, half the squad had strips of blanket cloth tied around their legs. The higher slopes of the hills had a type of bush with berries still in season; they stained the men's lips blue and were very sour, gave the men stomach aches, but still they insisted on eating them. The squad captain had to issue orders, which were ignored, to stop eating them. Every few hours marching they would come upon a godstone squatting on a hilltop staring down at them, almost, almost carved with a head and arms and a face. Once, outside an abandoned village, snow blowing over them like dust but not settling, they had to march past the skull of a wolf set up on a stone column, surrounded by a circle of sharp wooden stakes. Ilas cut his hand with his sword, rubbed his blood on one of the stakes. The squad captain and several of the others made offerings of coins, or dried meat and water from their packs. Lidae happened to be marching beside Deljan: he watched them, and she thought he would sneer, but he cut his hand like Ilas, rubbed his blood on the same stake, muttered something. Lidae thought she heard him say 'happy', and 'safe'.

She herself left a lock of her hair, spat at the base of a stake, whispered a luck prayer for Samei. I'll see Samei again, perhaps. Soon. Any day. My beautiful, beautiful, beloved baby Samei. My precious smallest Samei. Luck to him. Glory to him.

The thought butted into her mind like a great beast: *and luck for Ryn*.

'Luck for Samei, and for me, and may we soon meet again.'

Nervous excitement mounting in Lidae every day. The snow day, when they went very slowly, the footmen sent ahead of the cavalry to guard the horses from injuring themselves in hidden holes in the snow, that day was agony for her.

The country growing softer, more wooded, leaving the thin brown sheep and the sour blue snowberries behind them, out of the wind and the dry snow, marching through pine woods where the air was perfumed with resin and the ground beneath their feet was soft with pinemast. But an empty place now. No villages, no godstones, nothing but pine trees. The few streams ran very clear, the water very cold, with a brown-red tint to it. No fish in the water. No wildflowers. A sad place. That afternoon they turned westward, heading away from the sea, and a rumour sprang up that they would be meeting with Lord Sabryyr's men that evening. They halted by one of the cold dead streams, seemed to be waiting for something. Two horsemen took off riding hard into the woods, ahead of them, for a long time, they could hear the sound of hooves beating hard on the soft pinemast earth. A rumour came that a horseman had come out of the wood, met with their commander, must have come from Lord Sabryyr.

Lidae's heart beat and beat. As the horses' hooves beat and beat. They seemed to wait forever, Deljan began muttering things, stamping his feet. It was starting to get dark, would soon be more difficult to begin settling for a camp.

'They could at least let us sit down and cook some dinner,' Deljan muttered. 'Or tell us what's happening.'

'Stop complaining. Come on, Deljan. Stop it.'

'What's going on? Come on. It could be Sabryyr's men, or the enemy, or gods know what, I wish they'd bloody tell us.'

'We'll know when we know,' said Ilas. 'Stop fretting.' And looked at Lidae as if she'd approve or disapprove of what he said.

The old mother of the squad. She saw Ilas and Deljan sniggering.

A trumpet sounded, giving the order to go forwards.

'You see?' Ilas said to Deljan. 'Stop fretting and it comes. Wisdom.'

Lidae tried not to hear. Her heart was pounding. On for another hour. It was really getting dark now. Too late to see him tonight, even if he is there, Lidae thought. Not until tomorrow morning now at the earliest. Even if he is there. Why had they had to stop and wait? They came out of the trees, climbed a ridge, looked down into the eastern twilight at grassland that blurred into the skyline, grey and green and twilight blue where the first stars were opening. And suddenly there before them campfires were burning.

Lord Sabryyr's camp.

He won't be there. Samei's letter had said that he was with Lord Sabryyr, but Samei's letter was a year old. Samei was on the other side of Irlawe. Not until tomorrow morning, now, at the very earliest. Her heart was so loud and she was shaking. Run forward out of her file, run into the camp, find him. Samei, Samei, Samei, smallest baby one. He won't be there. I won't see him until tomorrow morning, now, at the very earliest. Tents and campfires, the horselines off on the far side, figures moving about. A ringing sound, a smith in the camp working; a sutler wagon, well-laden, an old man sitting among the bundles of food and drink and cloth and cook pots. Washing water in a bronze cauldron, shirts and leggings drying on a wicker clothes frame. A shriek of laughter as a group of raggedy children ran past and a woman's voice called out sharply, 'Get out of the men's way, there, children. What did I say?' The children giggled. 'Can't you keep them under control, woman?' a soldier muttered. Three dogs ran up growling and barking. One had a wound on its shoulder that made it limp and Lidae thought it would die soon. But the other two were glossy and well-fed, almost fat. Lidae's column had to march up the slope of a hill clear of the pine trees, a trumpet rang in welcome, an officer's voice roared at them to form lines, send them off to pitch their tents off to the western edge of the camp annoyingly close to the horselines and the smithy and the latrine pits. Promise of a good ration of salt meat and wine to go round when they'd got dug in; general moving forward of women and gamesters and sutlers with equipment, Ilas asking everyone to search out a washerwoman for him.

Samei. Samei. Samei. Lidae was settled by the tent, eating bread and pork, grease running down her chin. He won't come. He won't come. He's a thousand miles away.

A tall young man stepped forward out of the dark.

'Mother?' Samei said.

At first, she couldn't recognise him.

He was absurdly tall. Was he always that tall? He had shot up like a young tree, Lidae thought, in the two years since she last saw him. She leapt to her feet, went to hug him, and he was half a head taller than she was. But he still, she saw with relief even beneath his armour, sixteen years old, very nearly, he still had a boy's thinness to him. In his armour, his bronze skin lit by the campfire, three days' stubble on his face, he looked so much like Emmas. So much like Ryn, he could be Ryn as she last saw him. His hair had darkened, the beautiful golden curls that she had run her fingers through, charmed, marvelling, when he was an infant at her breast. He wore his hair long to his shoulders, braided with red leather to keep it out of his face. The down on his upper lip was almost a moustache. He had a bruise under his left eye, a scab on his left cheek. His armour had a fine pattern of leaves worked across the chest in green enamel, and his cloak was deep red.

He said, 'Mother?' Almost as if he did not recognise her. As if she too had grown tall and strange in two years.

'Samei.' He did not open his arms. They hesitated in front of each other. Lidae thought: after two years, I thought things might be different. 'I— That is— Come and sit down. You've eaten?'

'We ate earlier.'

'Wine. I've got some wine here. I'll find another cup, wait …' She was fumbling in her bag. Shaking, and her heart was shaking.

Samei said, 'It's fine. I had some wine earlier, too. It's fine.'

But I have to get you something. Lidae said, 'You're well? You look well. How long have you been camped here?'

'A few days. I'm well, yes.'

How's—? Have you heard from—?

His voice had broken. He sounded like a man. She thought with a shock: he's sixteen. He's older than Ryn was when— He's the same age I was when Raena fell. But then his eyes moved, looking at something off to one side of them, the firelight caught on his cheek, she thought: he's still my child, look at him, his child's face, how he looked when he was small, so interested in things, his upper lip sticking out like that.

'What are you looking at? Oh, the sword… That's Deljan's, it's beautiful, isn't it? He won it, in his first skirmish. He wanted to sell it, but I told him to keep it.' It was a very good one, iron, there were bone plaques on the hilt, the carving had been chipped and worn away so that the pattern was very faint, a rough outline of birds, delicate as patterns seen in clouds or in the shape of a tree in leaf. It was propped in the entrance to Deljan and Ilas's tent, so that everyone passing could see it.

'I'd buy it,' said Samei. 'If he was still interested in selling it.'

'I'll ask him.'

'Four in gold, tell him.'

'Four in gold?' She said, 'Where do you have that kind of coin?' He's a child, she thought.

Samei shrugged. Again, he looked so like Emmas. So unlike the child Samei. 'We were in a fight, a while back, found some good stuff, afterwards, in their baggage.'

A silence. The way he said it. So casual. *We were in a fight. We went through their baggage.* The brooch fastening his cloak was silver, southern work from Eralath or Turain. She said, 'Is that where you got that scar?'

Samei touched his face. 'This? No. No.'

'What happened, then?'

He shrugged. 'Nothing.'

'Samei?'

'Nothing. Really, nothing.'

'Have you been fighting?'

'I'm in the army, mother. We fight.'

'No, I mean: someone attacked you? Samei? Smallest one? Is everything all right?'

'Of course everything's all right.'

He got up. Very tall, looming up over her. 'You've got so tall,' Lidae said.

'Have I?' She stood up also, it was too difficult to sit with him standing over her so vast like she was the child. But he was half a head taller still, it disturbed him, Lidae saw, that he was taller than her, looking down at her. His mother, small and old and grey, her knees had creaked like twigs breaking when she stood up to greet him. She thought: he sees what Deljan and Ilas see. An old woman.

'I have to go back to my squad.' A pause, Samei's face twitched, he looked around the camp.

How's——? Have you heard from——?

Samei said, 'We have duties, tomorrow first thing. But I'm free for a while in the afternoon, we're staying put here tomorrow, I'm sure, to let your men rest. I'll come and see you then. I can stay longer then.'

'That would be lovely. Maybe you could stay, eat with me then? I'll ask Deljan about the sword.'

'Thank you.' He did embrace her then, stiffly, her face was buried in his shoulder, he's too tall, she thought, too tall, what happened? He smelled different to her memory of him, the child smell of his limbs when she kissed him. A man, she thought. He smells like a man.

Have you heard——? Ryn——?

'Sleep well. Good night Samei. Thank you.'

'Good night.'

Thank you? What for? For coming to speak to me? She watched him walk away, thin and tall and awkward in his armour. A calf still, just, not a bull. Another soldier came to join him, a friend, she thought, they walked on together and suddenly it wasn't her son at all it was two men, two soldiers, disappearing into the camp and she had seen it so many times before, soldiers in armour walking together, talking together, the easy way they walked in armour in an army camp, but she felt a kind of horror, because one of them was her son.

Crouched in the filth of her parents' bodies, crushed, trembling, terrified, watching the soldiers walking through her street in Raena talking and laughing.

'That's your son?'

She smiled at Ilas. 'That's Samei, my younger son, yes.'

Pride, also. So much pride. My son, in a red cloak, my son with four in gold to buy a new sword with, my son with his soldier friends! A song that Acol sang sometimes in the evening when the campfire had burned low: *'The bright-faced ones, shining sword-men, 'Be as he is', mothers bade their young sons.'* All a woman could ever hope for, a tall son in well-made armour, confident, brave, strong.

They were lined up the next morning on display to the king, stood in full armour with sword and spear, the cavalry mounted up with their horses in full battle dress. Lord Sabryyr rode up and down the lines inspecting them. A tall man, strongly built in his arms and shoulders; his hair bright golden. He could not walk, she knew that about him, was carried about in a litter or pushed himself around in a wheeled chair; he was a great horseman, naturally enough as riding a horse gave him four strong legs to move on, and a great general of cavalry. His helmet was decorated with white feathers; pale opals shimmered, like eyes, on his armour, like white pebbles gleaming wet on a shingle beach. His skin was dark almost to blackness, as luminous as the gems. Lord Sabryyr welcomed them into his soldiers, told them they would be marching south in two days to fight the false queen. His soldiers had skirmished with her army twice already, he assured them, the second time the enemy had been commanded by the younger of the false queen's own sons. Both times they had been victorious. The queen's own son himself had indeed fled. The enemy baggage was rich pickings, the men of Eralath were soft, wanted luxury even on the march. It would be a glorious campaign.

The necessary cheers, fanfare of trumpets, the paean roared out to the beat of drums. They marched back to camp, heads held high. Put down spears and swords and helmets, sat down to drink tea and bicker by their tents.

'It's odd,' said Deljan, 'that we went all that way so quickly and now we're sitting here waiting for the enemy to find us.'

'Two days to rest up after the march,' said Lidae. Everything was odd, Lord Sabryyr camped here waiting. The camp had the look of having been well dug in. An odd tension in the air around them, like a house where an argument has broken out. Someone said they had seen horsemen riding that morning, going fast, heading east.

'Two days to warm up after the snow,' said Ilas.

'No, it is odd, you're right,' said another of the squad, the woman Eralene, Lidae's tent-mate, white as new milk and strong and tall.

'It's not odd. An army needs to rest,' said another of the squad, the man Arael, sand-coloured, dust-coloured, fading grey in his skin and his hair and his voice. But there's an explanation, we're just being rested after the march, or that's an excuse because Lord Sabryyr has some plan in his head that involves us waiting here a few days, letting the enemy know where we are. There's nothing to worry about. They all felt it. Pretend there was no unease.

It explains why Samei was tense yesterday, Lidae thought. If they've been sat here a few days waiting, wondering, like this. He might even know more about it, can't tell me, it must burden him.

That was ... No, she thought, don't think that. He's a child being trained as a junior officer; he can't know anything more than I do.

He'd tell me, she thought. His mother.

She thought then, in a rush of fear: what if he is ... he is placed in command over us? My little son, an officer, knowing secrets, giving orders, telling me to do things.

'They're just letting us rest a few days after the march, it's not odd,' she said to Deljan. 'That's all. It's quite usual. When we were in the east across the Immlane River, we made a forced march and the enemy was almost on top of us, but we were rested for three days before the battle. In Tuva, the king waited on purpose for six days, drawing the enemy up to us, to trap them. It's normal. Nothing to worry yourself about.'

Deljan nodded, unconvinced. Eralene looked unconvinced. She had taken a walk around Lord Sabryyr's camp first thing that morning, Lidae thought, said she knew someone in Lord Sabryyr's service, she had perhaps heard things.

'War is mostly waiting around not knowing,' said Lidae, like any old hand might. Like Acol had said to her once and then rolled his eyes saying it. Deljan gave her a look, like her children might when she told them to get to bed. Yes, yes. We know. Be good.

'Well, we can warm up,' said Ilas. 'At least.'

'Take advantage of the rest,' said Lidae. 'If we are about to fight.' This uncertainty. Don't voice it. Eralene jerked her head, as if Lidae had said something she shouldn't have guessed. 'As we are about to fight.'

Eralene and Deljan went off together later, Deljan was looking to buy a new shirt because his spare one had got torn the first night out of Navikyre fortress.

'All the cursed luck.'

'You jammed it in your pack and pulled it out, it's no wonder it ripped. You could sew it.'

'No, look, it's ruined. Stupid.'

'There are traders in the camp from the villages to the north,' said Eralene. 'I'll take you. They might have something.'

The two of them set off and Lidae felt guilty that she hadn't asked Deljan about his sword. On her tongue from waking, she had almost asked him over breakfast and when they were arming themselves to parade for Lord Sabryyr and just now before he went off to buy a shirt, this would have been the ideal time, she thought, to ask him, when he was thinking about coin. She couldn't put into words her reluctance to ask him. It will make Samei happy, he wanted it. If I had the coin, I'd buy it for him, I used to love giving him things he wanted. Treats and toys, a jacket he wanted once that Sydela the sutler woman said had come all the way from Marna in the far south: that cost me far too much. I'd come back from a siege with a gift for each of them, 'Mummy, Mummy, we haven't seen you for days! Have you got something for us, Mummy? 'You spoil them, Cythra said. But a sword is … A looted sword, a man died holding that sword, and it's so fine, so old, it has killed many men.

When Deljan comes back with his shirt, she thought. That's a better time, he'll have spent some of his coin, he'll be thinking of coin, of the things he could buy at the traders' market, I'll ask him then. Unless Samei is here by then, she thought, he said he'd come back this afternoon, if Samei comes here before they get back and I haven't even mentioned it to Deljan yet. How stupid. If Samei's own sword is damaged, she thought, not good somehow, he lacks confidence in it, and we'll be going into battle soon, and I didn't take the chance to get him a better sword. If…

Her mind froze against it. He won't … It … If … if battle comes … He's my son. My little son. As soon as Deljan comes back, she thought, I'll ask him.

Thirty-three

'No.'

She looked at Deljan dumbly. 'No?'

'No. It's my sword.'

'But he's offering four in gold. If that's not enough...' I have one gold coin myself, she thought, 'five in gold?' she said to Deljan. 'Five?'

'I'm not selling it.'

'But...'

'I don't want to sell it.'

'But Samei...'

'I won it. After my first battle. I'm not selling it to someone I've never even met.'

'Samei's my son.'

'I'm still not selling him my sword. I don't want to sell it.'

'But...'

Lidae could feel the others watching. 'But...'

Deljan had a good new shirt, well-fitting, and a new pair of leather gloves. He'd treated himself and Eralene to honey cakes and wine, there was a smell of wine and spices on his breath. He must be in need of coin, now, she thought. 'Five in gold,' she said. 'Please, Deljan?'

'If he wants another sword that badly, he can buy himself one anywhere in the camp,' said Deljan. 'Or you can give him yours. No.'

But he's my son, Lidae thought. How can you not want to sell it to my son, who needs it? She sat down by the campfire. What will I tell Samei?

But she waited, and Samei didn't come. He must be busy, she told herself. But he didn't come. Two soldiers in red cloaks went strolling past, talking and joking, she watched them in grief looking around for Samei.

The squad captain came back to join them, from walking around

Lord Sabryyr's camp. He sat down by the campfire, asked Ilas to make him some tea. 'Something's up,' he said. 'I went over to where Lord Sabryyr's own men are stationed. Near enough to Lord Sabryyr's own tents. They're stirring around like ants over there. Wouldn't say anything. Looked at me.' He stretched his hands to the fire. 'Hurry up with that tea there, Ilas. Come on. They were thinking about something, I'm certain. Worried. Then a rider went off, fast.'

'They've been camped here for ten days,' said Eralene. 'My friend said they've seen four riders going off in the last two days. Going north.'

'Generals send messages all the time,' said Arael, who had been in the army long enough that he had had two sons grown to be men and soldiers and seen one of them dead and gone. But who was stupid. 'It's nothing.'

There are always things going on. So many things, Lidae thought, the leaders keep from their men. Better and easier we their men don't know. But there was something here, she thought, in the air of the camp, yes. She thought again of the boat coming in in the night.

That's why Samei doesn't come, she thought later. She drank two cups of tea, sitting by the fire outside her tent waiting. Nervous about going for a piss, even, in case he came to her tent while she was off in the distance pissing, and he walked past didn't see her and didn't recognise the tent. He's my son, she thought. My youngest son, my baby. Why am I nervous? *Little lamb. He's so huggy, oh look at him. He'd climb back inside you if he could.'* I should have gone to the market with Deljan, she thought, got him something nice, honey cakes, candied cimma fruit, something. Why didn't I do that? *I couldn't get you a sword, Samei, but I've got you some cake to eat.*

Two years! Nothing, no time at all. Days had passed, sometimes months on end, when they'd been apart when he was a child, she'd been off fighting and he'd been with Cythra in the baggage train, safe. Some of the men here had children in Illyrith or Tarbor or Cen Elorn that they'd barely even met. Their squad captain, Ilas gossiped, had a son in Cen Elorn that he'd never even met. But it grew towards evening, the sun was low and red in the sky making the pine trees glow as if with dragon fire, and still Samei didn't come, and Lidae's heart felt as though it would break. Deljan and Eralene started bickering about cooking something for supper, and still Samei didn't come, and Lidae felt as though she would weep. She was afraid that someone would ask her something, 'Is it Eralene's turn to cook the stew, or Deljan's?' and she would weep.

He's busy. Things. Important things. How pleasing to me, that my son should have such important things to do, whatever it is that's happening.

She got up. 'Save some supper for me, Deljan, if you would?'

'He's busy,' said Eralene. 'Got caught up, that's all.' Like Eralene was talking about a lover, like she'd spoken to Arael when he'd been moping because a laundry girl in Navikyre fortress hadn't kept a meeting with him. But her dark eyes in her white face were full of comfort and concern.

'Do you know where the Winged Blades are camped?' She had to wander through Lord Sabryyr's camp asking, soldiers and camp followers shook their heads blankly, pointed her off left or right to the where they thought the Blades were posted, turned out of course to be quite wrong.

She somehow ended up by the horselines, a camp servant carrying a saddle off for mending shook his head at her. 'The Winged Blades? I don't know. I'm sorry, I don't know.' She turned and walked back towards her own encampment, defeated. Nobody knows.

She walked on, almost crying, and Clews stepped out of a tent ahead of her. Stopped.

'Lidae?'

'Clews?' Two years since she'd seen him, also. He was older, the scars on his face standing out harshly. His face was thinner, she thought, had hardened into an old man's face with a beaked nose to it like a bird. An eagle, most accursed of all creatures that fly beneath the sun. There were shadows beneath his eyes. She thought: is he ill? He looks ill. Or just tired.

Sad, she thought. He looks sad. Like he has done a wrong thing.

'Lidae. What are you doing here?' Stupid question, they both laughed awkwardly at it, *what does it look like I'm doing here, I'm doing the usual things*. 'I didn't know you were here … Are you all right?' Clews said, looking at her closely. 'You've been crying?'

'It's nothing.' I am a soldier! Soldiers don't cry because they can't find someone's tent in an army camp. But she remembered him holding Samei, drying shit on his chest, his kindness then, he had not looked sad then, she thought. 'I … I'm trying to find Samei's tent,' she said. 'It's so foolish, I can't find it here, of course.'

'Samei's here too?'

'He's in the Winged Blades.' So proud, but the name made her wince slightly every time she said it. A very old and prestigious squad, Samei had told her solemnly, it was an honour to be posted to it, she must have heard the name, yes, yes, of course she had heard the name. It made her smile. Such a child name. He had smiled when he said it, tasting it, '*The*

Winged Blades. Such a name.' 'But you know that, obviously,' Lidae said to Clews, stupid statement, he was the one that got Samei posted there. She thought: what's wrong with me today?

'I hadn't realised the Blades were here,' said Clews. 'I—'

'What?' He looked pained, suddenly. A shadow on his face. 'Clews?'

He shook his head. 'Never mind. It's nothing important. I'll take you to Samei now, if you want. Help you find the Blades. I hear nothing but good of Samei. You should be very proud of him.'

'Thank you.' They walked together. Clews seemed thoughtful, biting his lip, Lidae wanted to speak to him, but she felt afraid somehow. He looked at her awkwardly, frowning. 'I thought you were off in the west?'

'We were. Guarding Navikyre Fortress from nothing. We marched only a few days ago.' She said, 'The battle will be any day now?'

'Any day now?' He seems startled. 'Who told you that?'

'Lord Sabryyr...'

'Lord Sabryyr told—? Oh. Oh, yes. Yes. You look well, Lidae,' he said hurriedly then. 'You're keeping well?'

'I...' There was nothing else to say, so Lidae said, 'Yes.'

'Have you heard from ... Ryn, at all?'

'No.' A rancid taste in her mouth, saying it. Spat it out. *Don't ask, don't talk about him, I have one son and that is Samei. Don't you know?* Clews saw, knew, remembered, guessed. Said nothing. They walked on a little in silence, past an encampment of fine leather tents that must belong to a squad of cavalry. Clews said, 'We're almost there, I think. I'll ask someone.'

Clews stopped a young cavalryman, all shining gold hair and kind eyes looking down at old grey Lidae. The Blades were camped just up ahead.

'What's happening, Clews?' Lidae asked him. 'What's happened? What is it?'

Shadows. Clews rubbed his face wearily. 'I can't... Don't ask. You know I can't tell you. I'll tell you tomorrow. Not now. Please, Lidae.'

Something wretched has happened, Lidae thought. So much of my life, she thought, is people begging each other to do something or not do something. Please, please... Thank you, please... A soldier's life, that knowing-not knowing: they're planning something, they know something dreadful, killing, losing, but we can't know. Trust us, he says, and he's lying, but I have no choice but to trust.

Parent and child. Leader and soldiers. Life is such a pitiless secret thing.

'Samei's tent should be just here,' said Clews to break the silence. 'Here. They've got fine tents, you see? Keep him warm and comfortable.'

'Yes.' *'Keep a king's loyal soldier warm on a cold night, they complain about the cold on campaign all the time, the soldiers,'* somewhere she had heard someone say that, and she could remember the children's faces grinning about it.

'Well... I'll leave you then, Lidae.' He looked so awkward; terror clutched her, something has happened to Ryn or Samei, he can't tell me, Samei can't tell me ...

'What is it? Is it Samei? Ryn? What's wrong, Clews? Tell me. Please, just tell me, whatever it is.'

'It's nothing, Lidae.' He smiled. 'Samei is here and well, with great things to tell you. Give him my greetings, and my congratulations for doing so well.' And he was gone, and she was standing on the edge of the Winged Blades' encampment.

They did indeed have fine well-made, well-kept leather tents. A bright campfire burning, a young woman with lovely shining hair bent over it stirring a large bronze cookpot. Cooking onions. Lidae's mouth watered. The woman was singing to herself. A man was sitting outside a tent polishing a jewelled corselet, whistling along to the woman's singing. Pale hair and pale skin, pale questioning eyes, something cold within him. He put the armour down carefully. Looked at this old grey woman with distaste. She thought, stupidly: he's a grown man, not a child. What's he doing here with Samei in the same camp?

'Yes?'

'Samei ... Sameirith of the Winged Blades. I'm looking for him?'

'Are you?'

'Yes. I'm his ... his mother.' What is wrong with me? Lidae thought. Why am I afraid? Her heart was beating so fast and hard, her mind seemed to shake within her. Samei's world, without her, this cold pale young man Samei's friend.

Another man came out of a tent, looked Lidae over. 'He said his mother was a solider,' the man said, 'didn't he?'

'He did.' Cold eyes looked her over, made her think of white snow. Men's faces long ago in Karke, in an army camp long ago when she was a poor woman with two children... I'm a soldier, Lidae thought. A soldier, no different to you. Killed more people than you, I should think, being so much older than you. Her body was tense and folded. Weight on her shoulders, pulling her down into herself. What am I afraid of? These young men are fellow soldiers and Samei's friends. My son's friends.

I shouldn't have come to see him, she thought. I should have waited for him to come to see me again.

'His tent's over there,' the pale young man said. Samei's friend. 'He's not here.'

'I'll wait.'

Cold eyes: 'If you want, I suppose, then.'

The second man was watching, laughed. 'Leave her be. If she's his mother.'

She went up to the tent, called out 'Samei?' in case he was there somehow. It was good and clean, fine leather, they must have wagons, she thought, to carry their baggage. Twice as large as the dirty canvas she shared with Eralene, and they were lucky it was the two of them, many of the men slept three to a tent. How extraordinary, Samei with all this, more than she had had in her life ever. Oh, Samei, she thought, my littlest one.

She opened it to look inside, Samei's things: he'll keep it tidy, she thought, Ryn never cared where he left things, said he knew where they were when he needed them and that was all that mattered, but Samei was so careful with his things. A carved wooden chest. A green glass ewer. A silver wine cup. Propped beside the cup, still cherished, the wooden soldier-figure, Rov. I should get him another blanket, she thought, or—

There was a woman sitting on the floor, on the blanket that served as the bed.

'Oh! I'm sorry!' Lidae started back. 'I thought … they said this was Samei's tent.'

The woman said,' This is … my Lord Sameirith's tent.'

She was not a girl. A woman, strong and tall, a long tangle of yellow hair down her back, green eyes that looked away from Lidae, refusing to meet her face. She must have been thirty, there were already streaks of grey in her hair and her hands had a coarseness to them that came from work. Mother's hands, strong and red. She was wearing a loose gown of pale blue, spring sky colour, spring flowers, cut very low to show her heavy breasts.

'He's not here.' Her voice was dry and quiet. Dead.

'Tell him I came to look for him. Oh, no, of course, I'm his, his mother. Tell him I came looking for him, when he comes back, tell him.' The woman did not reply. But her head jerked up, staring at Lidae wide-eyed at the word 'mother'. A look of hatred flashed across her face.

Eyes lowered. The dead voice said quietly, 'I'll tell him.'

'Thank you.'

The woman let out a breath at that, like a laugh. Her hands clawed together at her wrists.

Lidae stumbled out into the night. Sickness overwhelmed her. That would complete it, the pale man and the laughing man and the woman seeing her vomit, saying to Samei later, 'Your old mother came by, looking for you. Mad old bat. She was sick outside your tent.' The woman would have to clean it up, she thought. Samei's slavewoman cleaning up her vomit.

What made me think I could possibly come here? She thought: the squad captain has a slavewoman in the baggage somewhere; Arael had a slavewoman for ten years until she died, she bore him two children. It's hardly a rare thing. The boys in Raena, fifteen, sixteen, boasting about things; the girls in Raena, desperate: 'Give me a copper piece, then, and I'll let you lift up my dress.'

She thought: I'm going to be sick, I'm going to collapse, I can't see.

Thirty-four

Samei was at her tent waiting for her, when she got back there. He stood up, smiling, when he saw her, he looked easier and happier than he had the previous day.

'Hello Mother,' he said, easily, happily, smiling.

'Told you,' said Eralene. 'Didn't I?' She had been talking with Samei, she had a brightness to her from talking to him. Lidae thought: she likes him.

'Samei.'

The boy frowned. 'Mother? What's wrong?'

'Nothing. Nothing's wrong.' She said in a rush, 'Deljan doesn't want to sell the sword, Samei. I'm sorry.'

'Oh, no, it's fine.' He smiled again, standing tall over her looking down, innocent sweet boy's face. He held up the sword. 'I asked Deljan myself, explained, he was happy to sell it. It's lovely. Your squad are all very kind and friendly.'

'Oh. That's good.' Even in this, she thought. *Look, Samei, my littlest one, I got that sword you wanted, sweet boy, here it is.*

'Mother?'

She was about to cry. For shame at him or herself. My failure as a mother, my fault. That woman in his tent. Red mother's hands, that woman has. She said, 'It is a beautiful sword, Samei. It suits you.' It has killed more men than he has spent years alive on this earth, she thought. But it looked right in his hands in the dark, with the firelight playing on his face and on its blade, a tall soldier with a slavewoman a spear-prize in his tent.

Say nothing. Pretend. 'Try to get used to it,' Maerc had once said. 'Or cover your ears with your cloak like I do.' I covered my ears last night, she thought, at the noises from Ilas's tent, where did I think the girl he had with him last night came from?

I was keen for him to be a soldier. I brought him into the baggage train of an army when he was four years old, for over ten years he has walked beside slave women. I have known soldiers all my life, she thought. What did I expect?

She said, 'You're disgusting. You disgust me, Samei.'

His face was rigid with shock. Like she'd stabbed him.

'I went to your tent,' she said.

'My tent?' He looked so stupid, dazed, his baby innocent face when she accused him of something Ryn said he'd done.

She spat out, 'That woman, Samei. Disgusting.'

'Oh gods,' he said. So innocent, shocked, shaken. I hadn't realised, he'll say in a moment, I didn't think, and it's not that, not what it seems. I'm a child, mother. How can you think that?

Eralene gigged. Nervous girl's fear-laughter. The campfire flared up and Lidae thought how late it was and how dark and how they would be marching soon.

'I won her,' Samei said. His voice wasn't angry. He was confused. His upper lip trembled. 'She's my prize. I won her by my own spear.' Little boy: he was going to cry, because she was angry. She thought suddenly of his face crumpling up in the same way when he was little, doing something that had upset her that he'd thought was good.

'You disgust me,' she screamed at him. She thought: he thought I would be proud of him.

Look, Samei, my littlest one, I got you a slavewoman, sweet boy, here she is.

'I won her. In war. I'm a soldier. My prize.'

'You're a child!'

'A child?' And he was almost crying. Like a child.

'You disgust me. That … that woman—'

'You wanted me to be a soldier. What do soldiers do? We marched in the baggage train beside women like her enough times. Just like her. *"Just the captain's slavewoman, just ignore her, Samei."* We used to order her about, tell her to fetch things for us.' And he spat out, finally, finally, 'If Ryn—'

'Don't you say his name. Don't you dare!'

'If Ryn had a spear prize—'

'Don't you dare.' Her hands came up, as they had when he was a child, to strike him. As they had when he was a child, she had to fight herself not to strike him. She shrieked, 'Ryn would never do anything like this.'

He made a little choking noise, deep in his throat.

She lowered her hands.

Ryn's name lay between them like vomit.

'I'm leaving. I can't listen to this.' And he said as he left, Eralene gigging her nervous laughter, every soldier in earshot staring open mouthed nudging each other listening and laughing this mad woman shrieking spittle on her lips shrieking at her son, 'You wanted me to be a soldier, Mother,' he said, and he was gone. Her tall strong brilliant son.

She shouted after him, 'You're disgusting.'

The men watching had no sympathy for her. She said to Eralene, her voice shaking, 'He … He had a woman. In his tent. A slavewoman. He's my son.'

Eralene and Deljan walked away together. Embarrassed.

In the tent it was very dark, Lidae lay with her face pressed close to the stinking canvas, pretending she was asleep, Eralene moving around trying to pretend she was asleep because it was so awkward.

'We're marching tomorrow,' a rumour had gone around the camp suddenly in the night, 'we're marching tomorrow, lads, change of plan, get some sleep.'

'Good. Thank the gods.' Luck signs, cheers: the moon had appeared, huge and full, as the rumour went around. A fine omen. Many of the men had made offering of a coin or a lock of hair buried in the earth, spat for luck. A voice drifted up singing from the next campfire, *'You who are strong as mountain streams, Warriors, lion-men, storm-bringers, spear-clad.'*

Thirty-five

Is it my fault, somehow? How have I raised him? Things I said to him? Things I should have said?

But he's a man. He has to go among men, do men things.

Maerc says, angry, in the ruins of Gaeth, 'Don't kill her, stupid: she's the only thing we have here to make coin out of. Young and pretty, a rich man's daughter: even with the glut of slaves there'll be in the markets, she'll be worth something.'

'He wants to marry you,' her father says to her sister, a rich man in the wineshop he drinks at, has paid her father's drinking debts more than once, 'he's got a house and a garden, he'll treat you all right,' her sister looks around the hovel they live in, at her father, nods; on the wedding day her sister almost looks happy, her sister's husband is smiling and attentive and keeps saying how lucky he is like you'd think your sister had been the one to propose to him.

Oi, oi! We won't eat you.

'Frigid old woman,' she's heard men in the squad mutter at her, 'I'd be doing you a favour, what's wrong with you?'

War is written onto women's bodies. War is women's business. She knows this. She has known this since she was sixteen. Tries to forget. It has defined her life and the life of both of her sons.

Thirty-six

She was awoken by a child's voice shouting.

'Found you! Found you! You need to think of a better hiding place!'

'Cari's useless at hiding!' a girl's voice shouted.

'Oi, look, you lot, we're trying to get this stuff shifted. Bugger off, the lot of you. Unless you want to help us.'

'Can we? Can we? We'll help!'

'No, no, no, no, no, no, Cari, Lana, no, that was a joke … just … okay, but … be careful … Cari! Careful with that! Gods!'

Eralene rolled over, groaned, muttered something about children. Lidae crawled out of the tent.

'What's going on?'

'We're packing up indeed. Marching!'

It was all a rush, then. Trumpets. More trumpets. Great and mighty alarums. Ilas shouted, 'Come on, Lidae, Eralene, you lazy buggers, they're ready to go. We're ready to go. Get your bag up on your back, then.'

'Yes.' I wanted to buy Samei a present, she thought, something good, and now we're marching.

She thought: I might never see him again.

Men heaving their baggage, talking loudly now, trying to sound normal, 'The false Queen, and her sons, those butcher boys!' 'Eralath, the rich southern cities!' 'Eralath, in summer warmth!' Fear nagging and clawing beneath them, something strange is happening, we know it, we feel it, what is it, suddenly, that is happening? A man tried to shout, another to laugh loudly, a woman's voice in the distance roared out screaming at her children. 'Get some breakfast on.' 'Tea's up, who wants some?' 'Pack that baggage up. Come on there.' 'Quickly.' 'Get ready, you!' It's all so quick. Forced march, camp, hang around, panic, break camp, forced march. The actual words of every cheer, every chant for victory: what the fuck's going on? The tension in them, the question beating around them heavy on them … It came to Lidae that she was imagining it, nothing was wrong, only her exhausted grief and shame and rage for Samei. At herself. Making everything around her strange to her, heavy, as though she was sealed away from the rest of them. Then she looked at Eralene, at Ilas, and she was sure they were confused, afraid, uncertain, just as she was.

Things walked on the far edges of the columns, spindle-legged, winged, beast-headed. Almost visible, sometimes, as human shapes. Shining light sometimes, very high in the sky, burning. They marched due east into the morning, and that was good, the wind blew in their faces the ground was good for marching, hard with frost and soft earth beneath. The metal smell of the cold, the warm good stink of horseshit. Lidae ate bread and a wizened dried-up apple while they were marching. Getting away from the camp where Samei had been, marching, she could pretend last night had never been. She's his camp servant, she thought. Keeps his things nice for him, cleans, washes for him. She looked up and saw the birds again, flying very high, very black, flowing. As many birds as there were soldiers. The memory, very sudden, Lidae's father standing in the courtyard behind their house, in the dust and the shit, his head thrown back in the evening shadows, watching the swifts as they flew. The same birds, Lidae thought, over Illyrith and over Raena, the same birds making the same journey she was making, had made over and over again. There were white flowers in bloom on some of the trees that grew little and stunted and alone on the great grey sweep of the plain, they had a strong sweet honey scent that stood out like snowflakes against the black wood.

'Winterblossom,' someone called the flowers, 'Queen's Blossom. I've never seen it grow so thick.'

It had grown in Raena, Lidae thought, remembering, though they had called it a different name. The smell made her think of… something. Something gone, unreachable, from her childhood.

'Pretty those flowers.'

'Yes.'

'Perfumed.' Eralene tucked a sprig of them into her helmet.

She thought: Raena is out here somewhere, also. They say it is accursed now, grass will not grow over its tumbled walls, bare white bones lie still unburied in the ruins of its houses, at night black dogs howl in the empty streets. Shadows walk at night in its streets.

She thought: many other cities have been rebuilt. Why is Raena so special? Or so valueless? Perhaps, she thought, they would march past it tomorrow, or the next day, or the next day. She could march past it with Samei. 'Look, Samei! The city of your forefathers!' And she would say, with bitter relish: 'If I had not become a soldier, Samei, this is where you and I would live. Shadows in the ruined streets.' But she had no idea how near it was or how far, it could be a thousand miles distant.

One thing was becoming certain to all of them, on this great dry grey plain where wild horses ran in the distance and birds circled overhead. In the pale morning they marched with the sun in their eyes, their shadows falling behind them. In the afternoon they walked with golden light on the backs of their necks, the shadows falling very long before them, the sky in the west spreading itself gold-blue-grey. A little thing, a foolish thing, a man must walk in one direction or another, the sun is before him in his eyes and he complains that it is bright and blinding, or it is behind him on his back: but if it is behind him a soldier-man of Illyrith will murmur uncomfortably, make the luck sign with his left hand when he thinks no one is looking, because when he marches to war he does not like walking on his own shadow with the night falling dark ahead of him. The shadows coming up to meet him.

They were not going south towards Eralath and her rich summer cities.

They were going north-east. Back, back towards the Wastes and Illyrith and Thalden.

'Come on, you lot. Get moving there. Come on.'

'Going to be a frost tonight.'

'And there was me looking forward to going south.'

Arael said, 'We're fighting soon. Warming.'

Deljan said, 'Very warming, being dead.'

'Stop it.'

Give you a nice fire and everything.

'Just stop.'

'Just get bloody moving.'

Delin said, 'Got a hole in my boot. Gods bugger it.'

Pause.

'Gods what?'

'No. No.'

'Snorting with laughter. Dying laughing. "Gods bugger it"?'

'You are so stupid, Delin.'

She said, 'When we stop tonight, I'll …. have a look at your boot.'

Feeling so embarrassed he wishes the ground would swallow him: 'Thanks.'

Arael said, 'When we're in the line, someone make sure the bloke they're squared up to has got the right sized feet.'

Deljan said, 'What size are Delin's feet?'

'Bit bigger than my feet.'

She said, 'Always happens the day after you break camp. Always. Soldiers' luck.'

Feeling so embarrassed he wishes the ground would swallow him: 'It does. It is.'

'Going to be a frost tonight. Bet on it.'

'Two in iron says it snows tomorrow.'

'Done.'

Areal said, 'Gods, look, up there ... that must be the dragon...'

Deljan said, 'It's a raven. Or maybe an eagle.'

Delin said, 'It's a pigeon, is what it is.'

Lidae thought: soldiers must have their prizes. 'Cold and lonely life, being a soldier, if you think about it,' we say, 'a soldier-man needs a camp woman to keep him warm at night. It's natural, like.'

If she has a child, Lidae thought, I will be a grandmother.

There are herbs I could get her, Lidae thought. Potions, sponges.

Smoke on the horizon, rising grey over the grey of the plain.

A village.

There's that special smell, woodsmoke, hearth fires for cooking and baking, all soldiers come to recognise it. A good smell. It hung in the air now before them. It was snowing, thin flakes, barely settling, the sky was grey and yellow, gloomy, tasted of a greater cold coming, the smell of the village was sweet as hay-breath.

The squad-captain called halt. 'We're stopping here for the night, lads. Foraging party being sent out. We've been volunteered for it. Who's up?'

Deljan, brash and excited, volunteered immediately. His first real chance at fighting, after a year guarding the walls of Navikyre fortress watching the sea.

'I'll do it,' Lidae says, also eager. Been a while, stuck guarding stone walls. Show them what she could do.

The squad-captain paused. Frowned. 'The Winged Blades are leading it, Lidae.'

Lidae said, 'And?'

'You sure you want to do, Lidae?'

'Yes, I'm sure,' she said. A pause. 'I've fought beside the man I married. I've fought beside my friends. I'm sure I can fight beside my son.'

'Yes…'

'Any number of men, all the time, in every war, have fought beside their son. The king,' she said, 'fights beside his son. Entrusts whole armies to his son. I wanted my sons to be soldiers,' she said.

'Yes.' A frown. Arael and Eralene and Deljan frowning. She thought with sudden rage: Arael has a soldier son and has buried a soldier son.

'When battle is joined, which we all know will be soon, I will be fighting alongside my son. Unless you want me to stay back in the camp with the baggage?'

She thought: I sound like his mother, making a speech to him. An old woman ranting on about her dignity to him. She thought with rage: but it's true, men fight all the time beside their sons, want them to be soldiers. May he be greater in war, men say, than his father is, may I live to see him victorious by my side.

'If you're certain,' the squad captain said.

'I wanted him to be a soldier.' Mad old woman. Her anger makes her seem less capable of fighting beside Samei the hero, not more. 'How would you feel,' she said, 'if I thought you couldn't fight beside someone you care for?' She thought briefly and fearfully: what if I do shame him, because I am frightened, cannot fight beside him?

The squad captain was looking bored now. 'Yeah, yeah, all right. Go on then.'

They set out for the village. Lidae, Ilas, Eralene, Arael, Deljan. Armed only with their swords; this is not spear-work, close work, blade work, this. In the gathering dusk outside the village, they met the leaders. The pale young man from the Winged Blades, 'his mother?' and his laughing friend, older but somehow rawer, 'he did say his mother was a soldier woman.' Others, that she saw as a blur of armour and faces, twenty or so swordsmen.

Samei, gleaming, golden, who looked at her and then could not look at her, turned his head away, ignored her loftily as a commander ignoring the men under him, shuffled away to hide from her behind his friends.

She thought: oh gods, how absurd, how foolish. What a child he is.

Then they were off to the village, and she could not see his face, but she could feel him ahead of her. She could recognise him in his helmet and his cloak and his armour from the way he moved, his height, the way he sometimes very slightly jerked his head. Then he turned back to say something to the man beside him, and she saw that the man she'd been watching wasn't Samei at all. One of the gleaming men ahead of her, unrecognisable, was Samei.

Deljan touched her arm. 'What's wrong?'

'Nothing. Shush.'

'Silence, there,' someone hissed at them.

It was night now. The moon rose through snowclouds that parted raggedly to show it thin and white. Frosted ground that felt like metal. Smelled almost like metal. Thorn scrub and sage scrub, dry and leafless and dead as driftwood. Winterblossom in thick banks. Tall soft grasses growing beside a stream, their leaves crusted white with frost. Lidae ran her fingers over the leaves, felt them cold and limp, furred. They left a white dust of frost on her skin. The banks of the stream were churned from animal's hooves trampling there, mud with a skin of ice over it, there feet sank a little and the mud smelled sweet, animal and earth smell; on the far bank there were flat stones where the women must come to wash clothes. Some of the village goats were moving, awake near the stream: Eralene hissed that there would be shepherds to raise the alarm but Lidae shook her head because the Winged Blades, her Samei, would already have dealt with them.

A godstone: even in the dark Lidae could see that the image of the god had been carved and painted onto it, a horse rearing up, strongly muscled, a war horse, from its back sprouted bird's wings. It was all rubbed smooth around the horse's head, where the villagers must touch it for luck; lower down it was smooth in a band where the goats must scratch themselves against it. There were a few bones and a broken pot at its base, a dark smear that might be dried blood. It felt very old. Lidae did not like it. Deljan went close up to it, kicked the offerings at its base away with his foot, spat at it where its red-painted eyes watched him. Stop the god from seeing. The first of the village houses were up in the dark ahead.

Lidae tried to look ahead again for Samei, which she knew she should not do. Deljan whispered, 'Ready?' And she remembered suddenly Cythra struggling to bury her three sons. She thought: does Arael feel this fear for his son? Does King Temyr feel this for Prince Fiol? Surely not. And she remembered suddenly King Durith dying in ignorance that his son was dead.

They went into the village.

Thirty-seven

Poet of the sword Lidae, her blade shining. Ten houses at most, a huddle of them around a storehouse and a well with a shrine place beside it, another godstone, grey and shapeless, they tore through like a fire blazing. Lidae felt, as she felt every time they did this, that she was close here to being a dragon, this was how a dragon must be, ripping the world open. All my life, she felt deep inside, all my life I have longed for these things. Grown men and women screaming, running, sobbing, at her approach. I am as a dragon. I am as a god. How strange. Wonderous. Marvellous. 'Don't try to run,' she shouted, 'get down, kneel. Kneel.' Men and women, children, crouched on the cold ground kneeling to her as if she was a great king.

The pale young man shouted, 'Get the storehouse doors open.' He pointed to the cowering villagers. 'Start getting the stuff out. Now.'

She could see Samei, over by the storehouse already, he shouted like his friend, 'Everything. Now. Get moving.'

A man, in command. If I didn't know he was a child, she thought, I'd see… He gestured at Lidae with his sword, which was bloody, the clean strong way he gave the order made her jump to obey him.

'Get the people moving,' he shouted crisply, 'come on.' He turned his back to say something to his comrade and for a moment he disappeared again. Two men in good armour, her superiors, giving orders to the men under them. Then he made a gesture in a way that she recognised as Samei so strongly it struck her like a blow.

Deljan and Ilas and the rest ran to his orders. Lining up the villagers, getting them looting their own village. Two young men from the village lay dead and the rest stepped around them, over them, until one woman knelt down and began to scream. Ilas went over to her, raised his sword. Too lost in grief to hear him. Ilas pulled her roughly to her feet, pointed at the storehouse. She hung on his arm in a dead weight, shaking, he dragged her, almost threw her, shouted. She stumbled to join the other villagers. Lidae saw her face as she passed, red scratches down her cheeks where she had torn herself with her nails in grief. Samei and the pale young man his friend stood by the storehouse doors watching everything.

'That's it, quickly, now,' Samei said.

Lidae followed his orders smiling. There's something here like a game. *'I'm the king, Mummy, you're my army, you do what I tell you to: let's play!' 'Alright, great king, what do you want me to do? But just a little while, Samei, I have to start the dinner cooking,'* and these games got so boring so quickly, because he could never really imagine what he wanted his army to do.

Finally, Lidae went up to him. His face was bloodied, it must have been him, she thought, who had killed the young men. But he too was smiling. His face changed, when he saw her, he frowned like a child, he was guilty and frightened, and then he was angry. He turned away from her, began shouting at two of the villagers for nothing so that they were even more frightened, dropped the sack they were carrying, wheat spilled out oddly dark against the trampled snow. His companion shouted also, at that. Went over to the two wretched men, raised his sword, Lidae saw that he was going to kill them.

She thought suddenly: I can't see this. I can't watch. Not Samei, killing.

She who had killed and killed, who had watched her own parents die.

Samei went over to his companion. He did not look at Lidae, but she knew that he could feel her watching him, his body moved in a way that showed he was so aware of her. Pretending he was ignoring her. The two villagers stood in a pool of spilled wheat, waiting for the sword stroke. Samei said something quietly to his companion, gestured with his arm at the two villagers. His companion said something in return. Samei nodded. His companion lowered his sword blade, said something to the two villagers, walked away with his head held up in the same self-conscious way as Samei. He too was a young man, very young. The two villagers got down on their knees, one of them grasped at Samei's left hand to kiss it. Samei raised his head, searched around the village until he saw Lidae. His eyes met Lidae's. He looked shocked. Astonished. He mouthed something. 'Mother,' she thought. That's what he's saying. She smiled at him. He looked away, shook the two men he had saved off him, walked off after his companion. Fast, his head high, and again she could not recognise him.

The two village men knelt in the pool of spilled wheat.

Lidae went over to Deljan and Eralene, began leading the surviving villagers back towards the camp. Deljan was delighted, because they'd found a whole sack of dried apricots in the storehouse.

'Are you all right?' Eralene asked.

'Of course.' Lidae realised that she was shaking.

A flicker of flame went up behind them, the Winged Blades setting fire to the village.

'Pointless,' said Eralene. 'Why do that? Why not leave it?'

'Because,' said Areal.

'It doesn't matter,' said Lidae. 'No one will come back here.' She thought: I've done this before. So many times. This is what's done, in war. Destroy things, burn things.

'Your Samei's good,' said Deljan. 'Really good.'

'You must be so proud,' said Eralene. 'Gods!'

'Yes.' Lidae said, 'A whole sack of dried fruit?'

'A whole sack. At least.' She thought: we'll let the villagers go once they've carried the things back to the camp, they can flee away into the hills.

'The strong ones, the men, we'll stick them in the front ranks,' said Ilas. 'Better than herding goats and picking fruit, trust me.' His voice, too, sounded distant. 'And the women...' His body changed, his hips moving in a swagger that looked so stupid. 'That one who was upset about her man... Did you see her? Sweet.'

'Look at this place,' said Deljan. 'Look at it. Huts in the desert. They'll be better off.'

Lidae said, 'Yes.'

Thirty-eight

The whole raid must have taken … less than an hour? To gut a village. About as long as it might take to gut and joint a sheep. A column of slave captives, filing through the desert night, the soldiers of Illyrith around them. It began to snow just as they left the village. Thick, soft white-feather flakes. When they filed past the godstone carved with the image of the horse one of the villagers cried out in a shrill voice, not a word but a raw sound like a beast. The woman whose man had died. Another woman took up her cry. The children all began to scream.

'Shut up. Stop. Keep walking.'

The sound was horrible. The falling snow, growing thicker, caught it up around them as though they were in a small, crowded room. Deljan had a sick look, started up gazing around him. One of the Winged Blades marched forward, struck the woman hard in the face. Her cries continued. Not screaming. Calling out for something.

'Shut up. Stop. Stop. You, the rest of you, keep walking. Make them walk.'

Just by the godstone. In the snow and the dark the stone was huge. The winged figure of the horse was clearly visible.

It was very dark. It shouldn't be visible.

Lidae showed her sword to the captives near her. 'Walk. Come on. Now. Walk.' There are godstones all the length and breadth of Irlawe, broken, ignored, sometimes they are uprooted and cast down and are used later as rubble to build a field-wall. It means nothing. Nothing.

'Shut up. Stop.' All the other villagers had fallen silent. Walked fast onwards with bowed heads. The crying woman broke away, ran back towards the stone. Her face was bleeding where she had torn at her cheeks in her grief. Her voice rose, very loud, too loud.

'Gods,' Deljan held his hands over his ears. 'Gods.'

Bronze flashed in the darkness. The sound of it, music of bronze and iron, a sword blade hissing as it was drawn, the woman's cry rising to a terrified triumphant shriek, cut off.

'Shut up, shut up, shut up. Get walking. Come on. Come on.' The man who had killed the woman almost ran to reach the head of the column, away from the body crumpled near the godstone.

'Stupid noise. Gods.'

Eralene screamed.

Thunder of hooves coming towards them. Horsemen. Riding out of the desert from the east. The soldiers swung around; voices shouted curses.

'Swords!' Lidae called. 'Swords!'

'Winged Blades! Draw up!' Samei's voice, so assured.

They all knew.

Straining into the dark, the snow was falling very thickly suddenly, white blinding them. Far off, a movement in the dark. Writhing. Shifting. Something coming out of the dark and the snow. Like birds, Lidae thought, a great flock of birds flying in the dark and calling.

Horsemen, armed, their horses armoured, they wore bells on the horse's trappings that rang out madly. Voices shouted out a war cry.

At their head, five great black horses. Five riders in black plumed helmets.

Blue fire blazed around them.

A great fear seized Lidae, a pain in her body. We have seen such things, we march ourselves beside such things sometimes in the heart of a great battle. Dragons, god-spirits, shadow creatures that walk the hilltops and the forests. Dead things, we have seen and fought against and fought beside. But she was so afraid. The comfort, the truth that she told herself now, lying: always, when they fight such things, men are afraid. The villagers' gods, demons from the empty desert places, come to punish their worshippers' enemies. The horses' hooves threw up the snow, it looked almost as though the horses were running through water kicking up white foam, but there was no sound of hoof beats. They came closer and closer, they were huge, bigger and thicker than the largest war horse Lidae had ever seen, the riders in their black iron armour taller than any man. Their swords ran with blue fire, and their swords were as long as spears.

The horses' heads were black empty skulls, with empty eye sockets.

The riders' faces, beneath their helmets...

'What are they?' Eralene whispered. There was no answer. They are killing things. Wild things that ride in the desert, old things like the horse carved on the godstone. Wonders, thought Lidae. Monsters. Like so many things we have seen and fought with. The comfort, the truth she clung onto: it is only of these things, these monsters, that I am afraid.

They were so silent they could be an illusion in the darkness. And, indeed, in the darkness they glowed with blue light and they could be seen clearly, their ornate armour, the horses' chest pieces and head pieces worked with silver and pearls, the sheen of the riders' cloaks hanging in fine folds. They should be dark shapes in the night's darkness. The blue fire that blazed around them cast no shadows on the snow. But Lidae could feel them coming closer, the rush of wind they stirred up, the living strength of them, bone and blood and muscle, hear the creak of leather and metal and the panting of the horses' breath.

The five horsemen struck into the soldiers and the captive villagers. A wave breaking, a great dark wave in a night sea. It was very cold, all around them. Hooves and horses' breath trampling out white frost. They smelled and sounded of raw deep frozen dead cold. The horses did not make a noise even as they collided with the men in a crash of bodies, the riders did not shout or speak. On foot, men and villagers running, pushing out of their way, men went down under the horses' hooves, screaming, men were struck down by the vast swords, fell bleeding, men swinging around with swords to fight. Lidae threw herself sideways, a black horse went past her in a howl of frozen air. Snow in her face, so cold her eyes were running with tears. Her skin hurt and her bones hurt. She staggered on her feet clutching her sword. Her hand on the hilt looked blue and numb. The red glass on the hilt was covered over with white frost, its fires hidden.

Behind the five, the line of living men and living horses that followed, shouting, whistling, bells ringing, a second great wave that smashed and broke over Lidae in a great roar of metal and meat. She was flung around, spinning, pain again in her arms, her legs. The stink of the horses. A horse's head, eyes huge and wild, crashing against her, its mouth was open very wide with blood on it where the bit had cut in. She struck out with her sword and her hand. Shouted, 'Samei! Samei!' The first shout calling for him to help him, baby Samei. The second shout calling for him to help her, Samei the hero.

Like a sea. Thrown on the waves, a maelstrom ebbing twisting pulling, if I fall, she thought, go down under hooves and men's feet, I'll die like a man being drowned. She couldn't breathe, her body was crushed, she was falling. The sword struck against a horseman's sword, or one of her own comrade's swords, a horse's flank lathed and bloody, the rider's boot kicked into her face. Killing. Kill it. Aching. Sick.

The riders were gone through them, hooves kicking up the snow. Wheeled around, drew up in a line. Between Lidae and her comrades and their camp. Fifteen of them, no more. Horses' hooves mired in blood. The line parted, the five great black horses came through to stand in the front. They made the living horses, the real horses, look like toys, absurd and small. Cold white breath came out of their red mouths, thick as mist.

A single banner flew over the line, lifeless, muffled in the dark and the snow.

It was dark red. The king's colour, the empire's colour.

The banner of Illyrith.

Six of the soldiers lay dead and trampled, cut open. Many of the villagers lay broken and dead. Two enemy horses were down struggling on the ground, dying.

The enemy readied itself to charge again.

'We are the soldiers of Illyrith!' Ilas yelled. They all yelled madly, 'We're the soldiers of Illyrith! We fight for the king!'

The enemy charged them.

Red banner flying proud overhead.

'We're on the same side as you, you dumb fuckers!' Deljan screamed. 'What are you doing?'

The horses were coming. The ground was shaking.

'Form up,' one of the Winged Blades should shout to them all. 'Form up, ranks, tight there, form a wall. Brace against them.' Even without orders they should form up close, close in on each other, this was a thing they had trained for and been taught to do again and again. 'Form the line, close there, brace against them.' But the only sound now in their ranks was a low wheezing moan, in and out, in and out, from a man somewhere dying. They stood scattered, struck dumb, men on foot no different to the captive villagers.

The horses broke over them. Lidae swung her sword, half falling half running. A man screamed. A sword that seemed made of ice swerved past her. Huge as a man. She felt the air hiss as it came so close. The horse was gone, running past her, its great hooves throwing up snow that was now stained red. When she looked up, Ilas was lying in the snow with the sack of dried apricots beside him.

The horsemen wheeled round. Drew up in a line looking at them.

This isn't even fighting.

The black horses breathed out frost white air. In the dark, the horses' skull eyes glowed blue.

Cold silence.

We should have seen the godstone and fled. But the world is full of gods and wonders. They fight us, we fight them, we are always afraid. She thought: they are men of Illyrith. No different than we are. Men!

We should run away. Split, flee in all directions, shrieking, they cannot pursue us all. We could bring them down, kill all of them. On foot, barely armed, we could bring them down, we have fought horsemen before like this, on foot.

The villagers … these are their gods? They cower, they are dying, they do not flee, their own gods are killing them.

The black horses charged again. A black horse and a black rider, and the blue flame on the sword blade was all Lidae could see. Distant, like she was sleeping, dreaming. Cold death dream. Emmas was caught out in the snow once on the hills behind our farm. Hurt his ankle, lay in the snow in the dark, and it seemed peaceful and right and good, to lie down and die in the snow. Is this what this is? Dying in the cold snow? A pain burst through her. She was falling. She could see the black horse crashing over her, hooves shod in iron that was gleaming ice-blue. She could see a man in bronze armour, red helmet plume, a sword in his hand, and he struck the great black horse with the sword deep into its neck and its shoulder, like a man making the horse sacrifice. An arc of red spraying up and, in her confusion, she saw it as red light. The sun setting there over her. The horse screamed. The man screamed, too loud to hear it fully. Her head and her hands were covered in blood. The black horse reared, screamed with a sound that was not the noise a horse could make, came down with a great crash with its legs tangled into itself, its head flopping and lolling with a wound cutting it open from flank to neck. It thrashed in the snow on its side, dying. White frost breath gasped horribly out of it.

Its rider was struggling, crushed and caught beneath it. Black armour jerked like a beetle. Armoured limbs moved in a way that was not real and human. A grating of iron. A sound, finally, from the rider, a harsh gasp of breath. The great, black-plumed helmet rolled from side to side, trying to pull itself up.

Lidae was on her hands and knees, her mouth choked with snow and blood. She was still holding her sword, the hilt of the sword seemed part of her hand. The red glass winked. She crawled towards the fallen rider. Drove the sword into the rider's face through the helmet.

Dark eyes, human eyes, stared up at her. She thought: it's not huge, it's not even as big as a grown man. A small, fragile, slender thing. The sword went in with a crunch of flesh and bone. The sound of metal shrieking on metal and the helmet rolled away from the breastplate, empty, and there was nothing there. Iron armour, burnished black, and the old bones of a horse. Frost over them, tracing the patterns in the armour, making the bones shine.

Lidae's hands were shaking in the cold. She looked at the man in the bronze armour, so ashamed of her failure, grateful that he had saved her life, and he was in command, he had responsibility for her, she followed and fought and he fought and led, but it was shaming, stumbling to her feet in the ruins of the enemy horsemen, he had killed the enemy and saved her, she who put her life into fighting had fallen unable to fight. His eyes met hers, through the red-plumed helmet, and of course she saw it was Samei who had saved her life. He didn't speak, and his face was so young, and she saw that he was terrified.

He gestured with his sword. 'Form lines, hold lines. Come on. Come on.'

Four black horses. Four black horsemen. They had retreated back a little, the horses pawed the ground and shook their head. The living horsemen drew up close behind them, their horses too stamped and shook their heads. Lidae thought: they're frightened.

'You,' Samei shouted. 'Form the line. Now. Come on.'

Me? She thought: but you're my son.

Her sword was frozen in her hand, pain wrenching up her arm as she moved. She could feel all the men with her staring, they all knew Samei was her son, she was Samei's mother, they had watched him shout at her for her uselessness, she had humiliated Samei in front of them.

'Hold the line,' Samei shouted.

A wall of men, armed, swords raised in front of them, close together. Lidae thought: I wish we had spears. The four huge black horses came on against them, the living enemy following.

Hold the line. A crash of bone as the horsemen struck them. The shock set Lidae's teeth ringing. She stumbled backwards. Pressed hard against the man behind her. Jostling. Like being in a crowded street, in a market, pushing. A rich man comes down the street with his guards and the people have to push and shove together, hurting each other, to get out of his way, a child tugs at her hand so tight it hurts, frightened.

Horses' hooves in her face, lashing out. She heard and saw the man next to her struck by them. She struck her sword at something at the dark in front of her, the jolt of it went up her arm as the blade bit home. She could hear Samei in the background shouting in a voice she barely recognised.

Samei was fighting one of the black horsemen. The huge bulk of the horse and the rider, the mage blade, the ringing crash of metal. Samei, his tall thin boy's figure, his body moving so fast so smoothly, twisting, striking; she could see, in the cold dark, as if Samei was glowing with light, radiant, sunlit. He warded off a blow from the enemy sword, struck back. The horse threw back its head and screamed. The men pushed and ebbed around Lidae, she went forward with them, 'keep the line, take it down,' flowing around a black horse that was wounded, surrounding it, mobbing it, stopping it. The rider towered over them. They pressed up close, formed a circle around the horse so that the rider couldn't use the horse's strength and speed against them. The rider thrashed left and right with his sword, one of Lidae's comrades went down, a shout somewhere behind her, she struck hard and her blade met the enemy's mage blade. She almost dropped her sword the pain was so sudden and so great. Her head rang like the metal. I am fighting magecraft. I am fighting a demon or a god. She struck again, and the blade cut hard into something. It did not feel like cutting a man did. Dry, solid, like cutting salt meat.

Always, in front of her, on the edge of her eyes, Samei. Gleaming. Shining.

The horse and the rider shrieked in a sound like a sheet of ice shattering. The frozen surface of a pond breaks and a child falls through. A shadow before Lidae's eyes, a rush of wind that stung her. The black horse went down with its legs flailing, crushing its rider under it. Horse and rider broke apart into old bones wrapped in old rust-flawed armour. The mage blade lay in the snow with a skeleton hand beside it, the blue fire slowly flickering away to nothing.

Samei shouted, 'Yes! Yes! Men of Illyrith! Kill them!'

The second wave, the living enemy, came down then, smashing with a howl of pain and fury into the soldiers of Illyrith struggling with the black horsemen. Like a storm wave that breaks over a shingle beach in fury, rips up the pebbles and the litter the fishermen have abandoned there, ebbs back away with the pebbles clattering, nets and ropes entangled, and a second wave breaks, greater and stronger than the first, the water foams up in a maelstrom, fighting against itself, the nets are torn to pieces, the pebbles clash together, the sea boils white. Great wide sweep of horsemen, spread out, surrounding them, men's faces cold and hating, sword blades flickering red.

'Men of Illyrith! Hold!'

My son. In command. His voice sounds so strong. No, no, no, no, no, not Samei in command, not Samei, he's a child still, a child, he's too young, so young, they'll kill him.

A voice shouted in response, the first words the enemy had spoken: 'Traitors! Betrayers! Kill them!' And another, loud and raging, 'Kill them!' And another, sweet, almost gentle in its fury, 'For the Queen! Kill them!'

In the smash of it all, Lidae was fighting almost thrown off her feet, keep the line, brace, hold, swords! but her heart screaming. In the churn of horses and men's bronze-framed faces, she saw Samei, grinning the death grin, bloodied. But he was gone in a moment, the chaos of battle swirling to claim him, another horse and rider were up killing her and being killed by her, she could not be sure it had been him.

There were too many of them. Twenty horsemen, against a foraging party on foot, burdened down with goods and prisoners. A slaughter, not a battle. 'Hold the lines! Hold!' But a man shrieked in pain, a man beside her went down, her own sword lashed and struck home, and a horse screamed out, its white eyes rolled in her face, its mouth was open showing blood foamed up on its lips and teeth. Its rider was shouting, pulling at it, trying to hold it. Lidae saw a young face, white skin like milk and blue eyes but in its youth and sweetness she thought that it too was Samei. A sword—not her sword—went into it. It slumped down over the horse, and the horse went down with a crash and a scream, bringing Lidae down under it. A vast spreading pain in her bones, a stink of horse sweat and of shit. Poor boy, she was thinking somehow. She lay crumpled beneath the horse's bulk, the dead boy's head face-down over her, the slaughter beating on in its waves around her. Hooves and feet trampling over her.

Thirty-nine

So a girl had lain once, huddled beneath her parents' bodies, her father's body crushed down over her, covering her face so that she could hardly breathe. Heard the soldier men strolling past, laughing, joking.

Forty

Hands lifted a great weight from her. Her body felt very strange without the weight on it. She felt stiff, moved her legs awkwardly. Terror that she had been injured. She was covered in dried blood crusted onto her.

A voice said, 'Mother?'

'Ryn?'

Samei's voice said, 'No, Mother. Samei.'

She said after a while, 'I thought we were all dead.'

Samei hissed. He might even be laughing. 'Only most of us.'

'I ... I thought you were dead, Samei. I saw you leading the fighting. I thought you'd be dead.'

'Are you all right? Can you stand?'

'I'll try. No, don't help me, I can manage. There. See?' She smiled at him.

'Your arm's wounded.'

'It's fine. *Your* arm's wounded.'

'Seras bandaged it. I'll live.

'Seras?' She said suddenly, remembering, 'You killed the ... the god thing.'

'I did.'

'I thought you'd be dead, for certain. When you took command, I could see them all, coming at you, trying to kill you, bring the commander down ... Samei, why did you do that?'

He shrugged. 'Someone had to, didn't they? Sit there, I'll get someone to come and bandage your arm.'

'I don't need to sit down. You could have been killed! Samei!'

He was already walking away. Stopped, looked at her with an old face. 'So could you.' So many things in that one sentence.

'You did so well, Samei.'

He shrugged, went over to inspect a pile of bodies crumpled up together where the fighting must have been very thick. 'Demons.' He spat on the cold ground.

'But the others. The enemy. They were...'

Samei shook his head. 'They're dead.'

'They were fighting under our banner, Samei! They were part of our army. Our comrades.'

I've heard that before, she thought with horror. Heard it and seen it.

'They weren't. They were enemies.' Samei's voice was very cold and flat. 'They were our enemies, Mother.'

'They were flying the king's banner, Samei.'

Shouted it: 'I said you're mistaken.'

Samei assumed total command now. The other surviving Winged Blades almost bowed to him as their leader. He wore it lightly, walking through the battle's traces, sighing like a man over their dead. But Lidae could see his awareness, the shock in him: I am a leader. They look to me. They trust me. He moved with the grace of a child's self-consciousness. There was a tension in his face, the way his mouth was set, where the child Samei was screaming with fear. Go up to him. Comfort him. He almost saw me die, Lidae thought, he almost died, he killed, some of his companions are dead. A simple foraging expedition, a chance for him to feel some excitement, he is so afraid inside, I can see it. He's a child, she thought, a child still, they should be letting him sit in silence, afraid, overcome.

A part of her, astonished: he saved my life. I am his mother. I should have saved his life, he is the child I am the parent.

'Demons.' Nine of the foraging party were dead or dying. Nine out of twenty. A disaster.

A few of the villagers had somehow also survived, and Samei barked out a command to them: 'Gather up the enemy's remains. Make a pile of them.'

Ten, twenty of the villagers were dead, their dead and dying lay beside the soldiers. It astonished Lidae that they had not all run away. Their own gods, she thought, as the wretched people hurried to obey Samei's order. Five of the enemy soldiers were down, and three horses. Out of fifteen: an astonishing achievement. Two of the five black horsemen had been destroyed, each lay in a great mass of bone and metal. The ground beneath them was frozen but the snow would not settle there. The remains looked very old, like the bits of bone and metal and pottery that the plough would occasionally turn up. A woman cried out in pain, dropped the black helmet she was holding, clutched her hand. 'It burns! It burns!' Her hand was raw and red, marked with frostbite.

Samei said, 'Pick it up. Now. Go on. Pile it up. All of it. Demons! We'll put a marker there, that we destroyed two of them. Then our dead. We'll burn them.'

'No. We should take them back to the camp,' the pale young man his friend said. Seras, Lidae thought. 'We need to burn them there, properly.'

Samei frowned and then nodded. Angry at being told he was wrong, but thinking, accepting he was wrong. 'You're right.' He shouted to the villagers, 'When the demons' remains are gathered up, you pile our dead together ... there,' he pointed to a good place, a hollow that would shelter the dead, 'and then you sit here, guard them until someone from our camp comes for them.'

Bowed heads, the villagers working with the ghost faces of people in great pain. Scraps of bone and iron piled together in a mound, the villagers' dead gods, the villagers' hands burned and maimed.

Eralene said, 'Lidae? Ilas is dead.'

Deljan knelt beside his body, staring down at him. His face was cut open, the skin frozen and black.

'Oh gods. Ilas.'

'Stupid. He tried to fight one of those things. Stupid.'

Arael was dead too. His face was perfect, his eyes open in astonishment. 'He didn't try to fight those things,' said Eralene. 'He got kicked by a horse.'

A woman came creeping up to take Ilas' body. Deljan said harshly, 'Don't touch him, you. We'll take him.'

'No.' Samei was there, resplendent, the woman bowed her head, averted her eyes from him. Like he was a king or a god. Her whole body shook, Lidae saw, being near him. 'The villagers see to the dead. They are responsible for their deaths, they see to them. We'll come back for them.'

'He's our friend,' Deljan began. 'We—'

'I gave my orders.' He was looking at Lidae as he spoke. He might never have seen her before. He paused, said in a kinder voice, 'If there is anything left to salvage, grain, meat, that dried fruit you were so pleased about, gather it together. You can carry that back to the camp. Not the dead.' Samei's voice cracked, finally, a boy's voice, on the final word 'dead'.

Lidae put out her hand, touched his arm. 'Samei.' Samei took a step towards her, towards her arms to cry there and be comforted. Drew himself up, stepped back away: *I am a captain in the Winged Blades and in command here. You are a common foot soldier.*

'Now,' he said. 'As I ordered.'

The snow stopped; the air felt warmer. It was coming on for dawn. A disaster. They were all so tired. Beginning to think, all of them that had survived, what would happen when they limped back to the camp. Nine dead men lying together in a hollow, a handful of villagers sitting terrified around them. All of the survivors wounded, armour and swords damaged. Samei walked at the front as leader, looking straight ahead of him, his back very straight his head up. Lidae thought: go to him. Walk beside him. Talk to him. But she didn't dare.

'These things happen,' Deljan kept saying. 'Stupid. Bloody stupid. But your Samei, Lidae … gods. He'll be … I can't imagine. They'll make him a general maybe.'

'The way he killed that second rider,' said Eralene. 'I've never seen anything like it. The strength of him! The courage!'

'The second rider?'

'He killed both of the … the things, Lidae,' said Eralene. 'Didn't you know?'

'I was … I didn't know. He didn't say.' That sounds pathetic.

Deljan said, 'Their banner—'

Staring eyes over towards Samei. 'Don't say anything, Deljan. You imaged it.'

'But their banner, Lidae.'

'I said, don't say anything.'

The camp was coming up before them, campfires burning, the smell of men and horses, the sounds of men and horses. They seemed to walk more slowly, trying to keep from getting there, even Samei, especially Samei, who must report it all, confess. I am getting old, Lidae thought. My son is a man. I don't want him to be a man. I want him to be my son. I want to be the one protecting him. A sentry called out the watchword, Samei held up his hand, named the foraging party and the name of their dead commander, 'Acting captain Sameirith in command,' stepped up closer to give the counterword, say something. In the dark, Lidae could imagine the sentry's face. Passed into the camp, the grief that Ilas wasn't there to be glad about getting back to his bed.

Samei and Seras were marched off to report. Samei's whole body slumped, Lidae could see that he was terrified. Go to him. Insist on staying with him, 'he did so well, look, you, Lord Sabryyr, you weren't there, you have no idea what happened, twenty of us, on foot, Samei did so well to get any of us out, if you'd seen him…' The man Seras said something to Samei, touched Samei's arm, just gently, brushing it. Samei turned to look at his friend. His body seemed to brighten. Lidae could imagine him his face relaxing, smiling. The two of them went off together, Samei's shoulders lightened.

'Come on,' Deljan said, almost in pain. 'Lidae.' Yes. Gods. They were exhausted and wounded and thirsty and starving. Frightened. Her men. A camp servant dressing Lidae's arm properly, the squad waking, swarming up around them, having to tell them about Ilas and everything. Yes, huge black horses, gods from the desert. Yes, Arael and Ilas were dead, yes, she was wounded, yes, her Samei had saved them, yes, she was proud of him.

It felt like the day of her wedding, bright smiles at every shout of 'Joy to the bride!' until her face ached.

'He's got a woman, hasn't he? Someone'll have to tell her.'
'Ilas?'
'No, Areal.'
'Oh, yes. Yes. But she's only a slavewoman.'
'He's had her forever. Had his children.
'When the baggage catches up then.'
'One of his sons is still alive. I think.'
'Tell him too, then. If we ever run into him.'
'So, what's he got in his tent, then?'
'Fuck all, as far as I can see.'
'No, wait, look, a decent blanket. Get it washed a bit…'
'Gods, what did he keep this shirt for? All rags.'
'A gold cup! The sneaking tightwad bastard.'

Lidae slept a little; always hard, in the light with all the voices of the camp moving around, to get to sleep no matter how tired she was. Sleep now, be awake tonight, tomorrow morning if they marched she'd be tired again. And the strangeness, always, trying to sleep after one of them was dead. The light and the cold and the muffled quiet of snowfall too made it difficult to sleep.

Later, she was sitting outside the tent drinking tea, watching the snow fading, waiting for dusk when they would burn their fallen. A pitifully small pyre: sometimes that was a glorious thing but tonight it would be a shameful thing. Her back and her knees were both aching. Walking with her arm injured had somehow made her back hurt worse. She had noticed, walking back to the camp afterwards, that she had been trailing behind the rest of them, felt at times that Samei had had to slow down their pace to make sure that she wasn't left behind the rest of them. The snowy ground slipping beneath her feet.

Samei stepped into their ring of tents, stood awkwardly in front of her. Snow slush on his boots.

'Mother.'

'Samei.' She said quickly, 'Is everything all right?'

'All right? Yes. Yes, it is.'

'You're not ... blamed?'

'Why would we be blamed?' He looked genuinely puzzled. So innocent, Lidae thought. So confident in himself.

She said, 'We have to blame someone.'

'They must have known we would be there. Or, like that man said: the woman called them. But we can't turn back, every time we pass a godstone or a shrine, can we?'

'No.'

A brief silence. She was very aware that the last time they spoke she'd ... been angry with him. Shouted at him. She thought: is he waiting for me to start shouting again? I should, I should. But it's growing dim now, the memory of the woman's face, frightened, crouching in the tent, she can see so much more clearly her youngest baby son's face, hurt, astonished, when she shouted. She thought: he's my son, he's kind to her, of course he is. He's a child. It's not what it looked. He's my son. And she wanted to ask about the red banner, what he knew, her son keeping secrets from her, knowing things.

'Sit down, Samei?'

'I...' He smiled awkwardly, shifted, sat down beside his mother. His hair was very clean, smelled of lavender. It had had an odd smell to it, not quite pleasant, when he was little, she suddenly thought of that, holding him sometimes and not quite liking the smell of his hair, she'd changed the stuff she washed it with twice. He was clean and rubbed down with good oil, his shirt was fine cloth, dark green, he had a bronze brooch she had never seen before fastening his cloak.

'They've made me a lieutenant-captain,' he said.

'Oh Samei! Well done!'

'Did you see?' His whole body lit up as he said it, he fidgeted with his hands, held them out to her eagerly, shaping out the story. 'That great stupid thing on the horse, too big to move fast, it was huge, wasn't it?

Did you hear the noise it made when I brought it down? Gods! That feeling, standing with it riding up against me, and I knew, I knew I could take it down, I could feel it, it was like my sword and my armour … it was like the sky, the battlefield, everything, they were telling me that I'd win, I could bring it down so easily, and I did!'

He waved his hands as he had done as a child when he stumbled over his words in his excitement, couldn't find the words to tell her about some great amazing thing. 'And it came down! It was nothing, I knew it. Just old bones, did you see, Seras was frightened of them, I think, but I knew…' He flushed. 'Don't tell Seras I thought he was frightened of them.'

'I saw it.' Never, in all his life, she thought, have I protected him. Failing, when the black horse rode at her, paralysed and frozen, trapped like a frightened beast.

She thought: Emmas would not have frozen, Emmas would have put himself between the horse and our child.

A pause. Samei began, 'Mother, when—' just at the same moment Lidae said quickly, 'Eralene says it was the finest thing she ever saw.'

'Eralene? Oh, the other woman in your company?' A good thing to say, that, it brought him back to thinking about his glory: 'It was the finest thing I've ever done! The way it went down, I didn't even think I'd hit it that hard, just … whoosh! with the sword, and it went down …

'I knew I could do it, I knew it, just … whoosh! with the sword and it went down, really hard, the crash it made! Just … whoosh! The crash it made when I hit it! With my new sword! It was so easy! Like … This is what I was made to do…'

'Yes. I know how it feels.' Their eyes met, both alight. Biiiiiigggg smiles. 'The best feeling,' Lidae said.

'Lieutenant-captain!' Samei said. 'Lieutenant-captain of the Winged Blades! Can you imagine?'

'I'm not surprised. You deserve it.'

'We'll be marching soon. There's a rumour soon as tomorrow, as soon as the … the dead…' His child face was hidden a moment, the brightness gone out of it, he frowned, rubbed his hands on his knees, '… when that's done … we'll be marching, everyone says, and I'll have a command! And in the battle … If anything happens to the captain, I mean, not if he dies, or anything, just if he … hurts his arm, or something, gets ill, it happens a lot, you know it does, and I'd be captain! In the battle!'

Lidae said, 'Yes.' Little child. '*If anything happens…*' Little boy who can't think of men really dying, only of a world that's made for him. 'Yes,

Samei. That would be wonderful, yes.' She said, very awkwardly, 'Samei
... when I saw you, and I thought you were Ryn. I didn't mean ... It was
just ... because you've got so tall...'

'Did you? I didn't hear you.' He was lying. He was desperate to hear
her say that. She shouldn't have said it to ruin his triumph. He said, 'I
have to go to the pyre, now. Seras will be lighting the pyre, isn't that
amazing?'

'Yes.' *It was just ... when I said his name and not yours it was because—
you are so tall now, tall as he is and I was confused, knocked down and dizzy,
I didn't mean, it's not that I...*

'I should go.' He got up and Lidae got up too. Eyes met: he looked
away from her. I've always been good, she thought, at digging the latrine
trench.

'I'll walk with you, Samei.'

He frowned. 'If you want.'

They walked out of the circle of tents, through the camp. 'That's a
lovely dog, there,' Lidae said, pointing to a camp dog resting by a tent,
a big red thing with long legs and big ears. 'It looks like the one that
followed Cythra's wagon around for a while, do you remember?'

'Something smells good,' Lidae said, as they passed a cookfire where
a man was bending over a pot. 'Tasty. We'll see if we can find something
good after, shall we?'

'It's a great honour,' said Lidae, 'that Seras has been chosen to light
the fire. Your father was chosen once, he was so proud to do it. A great
honour.'

At last, at that, Samei grunted.

They had almost reached the pyre. Men gathered waiting, she could
see Deljan, Eralene and the rest, the pile of bodies so pathetically
shamingly small on a ridge with the sky falling golden now behind them,
torches burning blue and red. Samei walked off to stand with the other
surviving Winged Blades. Torches flickered on bronze armour. A shout
went up as fire filled the sky. Smell of hair and skin burning.

Forty-one

Ryn.

Two years before. The boy Ryn—the man Ryn. All bright and happy, armed, in armour, red horsehair plumes nodding on his helmet, the autumn wind blowing down from the north blowing snow-scent, beech leaves like fire reflected in his helmet on the breastplate of his armour, his eyes too are filled with golden flame. He is so beautiful, she thinks, in his armour.

Her oldest, her first, I remember the moment I saw you for the first time when I had birthed you, your black eyes staring at the world so fierce, trying to see it all, your eyes staring at me, and now look at you, a man grown.

I thought you were dead, Ryn, when I birthed you. You must be dead, I'd carried you, felt you kick inside me, whispered to you, my littlest babe, my love, my baby thing, when you're born, when I can hold you, little thing, when you're born: the world is so good! And I was so certain, when I birthed you, that you were dead, you must be dead because I, I mean, me, Lidae, how could I manage to do this impossible magical thing. A king can summon up dragons, a mage can still a river's flow, break down the walls of a city: but I, Lidae, I am an ex-foot soldier, nothing more, how can I do so wondrous a thing? 'Is it dead? It's dead, isn't it? It's dead,' I said to Rena the healer, holding you out to me. You moved. Kicked your legs. The smell of you, the feel of you. 'He's alive!' I whispered, like it was the greatest wonder of human life that I had done what women do every day, every hour, fret and agonise and pay coin to try to prevent. And you didn't cry, you simply stared up at me, so fierce, your hands moving, opening and closing, your legs kicking.

And now you are a warrior in bronze armour, cased in bronze armour over your beautiful shining bronze skin. You look like I did the first time

I saw myself in armour, reflected in a bronze mirror so that my skin and my eyes were bronze. You look like your long-dead father, who I never loved but who I knew was a good man and a good soldier, who I thought so handsome with his golden curls and his bronze skin. I cried, I remember, when you came up to me for the first time in your fine armour, Ryn. My first-born child. I loved you like nothing else in the world, Ryn. I will always love you like nothing else in the world, Ryn.

Those few years when it was just you and me, and Emmas in the distance, when you were my world—if I could have one time in my life again, Ryn, my beloved, it would be that time, when you were a baby and I was alone with you, wondering at you.

'I hate you, Mother. I hate this. All of this. I don't want to be a soldier. I never did. Why did you do this? We had a house and land and a cow and a calf in the byre, and we could have gone back and rebuilt that. Like Cythra and Devid did.'

'They didn't go back and Devid died,' Lidae says. But she can see it. White may blossom. Glowing yellow buttercups. Brown speckled hen's eggs. The smell of manure, cow's eyes watching her, puffed out warm hay-breath. An apple tree by the door. Bread baking.

'But we have all those things,' she says. Whispers. 'And more than that. More than we'd ever have had.' And it's true, all of it, they're barracked outside Tyrae, a rich city with rich fertile country around, many years ago she helped to sack it and it's rebuilt itself richer than before, as it has over and over, there's fresh meat and fresh milk every day, honey cakes hot from the oven, when Samei spreads butter on his bread, Clews says laughing, there's more butter than bread. Clews has found them a house to lodge in, good soft beds, a view of fruit trees and wheat fields and roses. They drink out of bronze cups, eat off silver plates.

Ryn says, 'We could have lived in peace under King Durith and our house would never have been burned and there would have been no need to be anything other than what we were. But King Temyr wanted to be king, and you wanted to be a soldier.

'You're selfish, Mother.

'King Temyr is a monster, Mother.

'I refuse to fight for him. I curse him.'

A chasm opens between them, deep into the earth, at the bottom there are human ashes, human bones. A high wall she cannot break. The sound of her voice shouting for Samei. A smear of snot on a dress sleeve, like a snail trail across kitchen flagstones. Flies buzzing around a cimma fruit, that cost two in iron, that was dropped in the dust after one bite.

'I tried,' she screams at him. 'I tried, I tried, I tried, you think I didn't? You can't imagine how hard it was.' Ashes and tears choke her mouth. She can't speak.

Ryn says, his teeth bared at her, snarling, hating, 'Father used to say how fine it was, to have left the army, to be living in peace on the farm, how this life we had, me and you and Samei and the green fields around us, this life was all he'd ever dreamed of. But I remember your face when you killed that night, Mother,' Ryn says. 'How happy you were. How pleased you were, to be a soldier.

Teach Samei to be a soldier for King Temyr, Mother. I'm leaving, I'm going back to Illyrith, to live the life Father dreamed of. I hope I never see you again, and you can be happy, you soldiers, you and Samei.'

You didn't cry when you were born, Ryn, my beloved. Stared at me. Your black eyes like black stones stared at me. You didn't cry when you left me, Ryn, my beloved.

The voice in her heart: if I had told Clews he was wrong, taken them home to Illyrith, stayed in the baggage train with Cythra, brought the boys up to be sutlers or gamesters or blacksmiths? A real mother, so many voices whispered, would have stayed with her children. But Devid went off to be a soldier, left his wife and daughter in the baggage train, died of it, and people praised him.

The voice in her heart: curse Emmas. Emmas is years dead. Very easy, to say what he would have done.

Forty-two

'He did so well,' Clews said.

'What?'

He had come up behind her while she was watching the pyre. 'Samei. "A hero in the making," I've heard people say of him. Important people.'

'You're an important person.'

'Far more important people than I am.' The light from the pyre beat on his face, made it different, older, younger, both at once. He looked uneasy: what is it? Lidae thought, something is wrong with him. Him, also, she wanted to ask about the red banner, the enemy banner, the secrets Samei was keeping. 'He's been rewarded, I know. And that's just the beginning.'

She could see Samei near the pyre, talking with Seras his friend. The two of them very close together, she had direct sight of Samei's face briefly as people flowed around him. He looked happy. Seras made a gesture with his hand that made Samei's face crinkle up laughing. A third man, the older man from the Winged Blades' camp, came up, clapped them both on the shoulders, Samei and Seras said something back to him. She could recognise the exchange: 'Who wants a drink then?' 'A drink, gods yes!' The pyre burned in a sudden mass of sparks, there was a swirl of people around it, a clamour of cheers and shouts.

'Seras is another fine young man,' Clews said. 'His mother is a distant cousin of Lord Sabryyr himself.'

Lidae found that she had started walking, away from the pyre and the celebrations for the dead that would doubtless last all night. Clews walked beside her. They came up towards to Lidae's tent. Most of the squad were off with the rest drinking to remember Ilas and Arael. A woman's fake moaning came from one of the tents nearby. It stopped very suddenly when a baby started to wail, then started up again. Lidae tried not to look at Clews. She expected him to walk off now but instead he sat down beside her tent, gestured to her to sit with him. Casually, used to command: it did not occur to him that it was her tent. To her great surprise he said, 'Would you like some wine? I've got a bottle of something drinkable, if you've got cups.'

'Somewhere.' Tin, with the enamel chipping off so the flowers around the rims looked like they were wilting. It was a good wine, sweet and dry. 'To Samei,' Clews said.

'To Samei.' How strange it felt.

They sat in silence a little while, drinking wine. Sitting looking out over the tents, the campfires burning, stars the poets called the campfires, yes, stars, all that light dancing, and the stars in the sky, in the east, brilliant. The Dragon, the Tree, the red star that some of the men called the King's Star, although none of them could say who the king was to be so honoured.

'I heard a story once,' said Clews, 'that if you sail to the edge of the world, the sea and sky meet, and you can sail up into the sky into another world. Kingdoms, fields, forests, mountains. The stars are hearth fires, campfires.'

Lidae said, 'One of the men in my squad, Maerc, he used to say that. When we've conquered the world, he said, we can march off the edge of the world and conquer the lands up there in the sky.'

'When we've conquered the world...' Clews refilled his cup, drank. 'Wasn't there a king once who swore he'd conquer the world and the moon and the stars and the sun?'

Lidae laughed, 'That was one of Ryn's favourite stories when he was little.' Saying the name made her shiver. Slipped out, like a beast, from where it crouched on her heart and her tongue. *'Careful! Oh, Ryn! Samei! You let the calf out again!' 'It was behind the door, it was waiting there to get out, it wasn't our fault, Mummy.'* But Clews didn't seem to have noticed.

'You think it's just a story?'

'A children's story. Of course it is.'

'I believe it,' Clews said. He drank, refilled his cup. 'My squad captain once ... the way he told it, I always thought it was true. A children's story...' He shook his head. It occurred to Lidae that he was heading towards being drunk. She had never seen him drunk before, barely even drinking.

'Clews ... What is it?'

'Don't ask me.' He rubbed his face, sighed, and Lidae thought: he looks like an old man. He is an old man, she thought. She remembered suddenly his story about his man and his farm. His story about being the first man into Raena to open the gates. Spent his whole life in fighting, going behind the enemy lines, going out in front to infiltrate the enemy and betray them. She remembered his speech to her: *'If my Lord Temyr had not acted, the army would have split, there would not be one new king but two or three or twenty, every city in Irlawe would be throwing off our rule. Even Durith understood in the end that it was necessary to do as we did.'* And she could still remember the way he had looked when she first met him, the lie he had told that he was shamed by war. Every time, for twelve years, it surprised her that he was what he was.

'Tell me,' she said to Clews. He wanted to tell her, that's why he was here half-drunk talking on about her son. 'Tell me, Clews.'

'Nothing. There's nothing to tell.'

'They were fighting under our banner, Clew. I saw it.'

'You were mistaken. Forget it, Lidae. Leave it.'

'No. I can't forget it. I saw my men die under our own banner.' She said fiercely, 'What does Samei know?'

'I only came to tell you how well Samei did, how you should be proud of him.' He got to his feet, looked down at Lidae bleakly. 'Don't ask me, Lidae. Please.'

'Clews! Tell me what's going on. If something's happening, I have to know. My children, Clews. I have to know for them. Tell me!'

He looked down at her and his face was broken. 'Just leave it. Please, Lidae.' Then a smile again: 'Look, let me tell you about Samei, more about Samei. Good things. He saved my life, you know, not too long ago. Two columns under the command of Prince Fiol got cut off, somehow, out in the hills west of Gaeth. The country is very dry there, we spread the men out to scout for water. A stupid mistake. It was getting late, the men were tired, the ground was very dry, no streams, hard rock, and the going was bad. Five thousand enemy horsemen came down on us howling, welding mage blades. Prince Fiol panicked. Sat on his horse while his men got cut to pieces around him. Then he went down, his horse killed under him, and the surviving men lost their heads completely. I thought he was dead.

'Frankly, I thought I was dead.

'The enemy commander was a huge man all in black armour, there was magecraft in his armour; his armour was gleaming blue, his horse was breathing blue fire. I saw it. Lord Maeth, I think he was, one of the greatest of Eralath's great warlords. The fighting was ... appalling. But Samei's lines held, he kept his men together, even pushed back. Samei...' Clews closed his eyes, smiled. 'Samei was ... shining. He looked like a star, his face radiant, there was a light around him. He was on foot, against cavalry, but he ... he must have killed ten of them, at least.

'Lord Maeth, if that was who it was, Lord Maeth was cutting our men down. Samei challenged him. Lord Maeth ignored it. But Samei shouted to him again, and again a third time, and he looked at Samei's face, shining, and on the third time he accepted.

'The fighting stopped, all of us, to watch. It was dark, the only light was from the moon, and from the blue blades of the enemy. Such an eerie light. I should have been terrified for Samei. He looked like a child, still, beside this great giant of a man terrible with blue flame. But I ... I had no fear for him. I knew. The two of them fought, and neither of them could break the other. If Lord Maeth had his size and his strength and all his experience in battle, Samei had speed and courage and that wondrous shining light.'

A pause. 'I'd like to say that Samei killed him. But ... I think, honestly, that if the fight had gone on much longer Lord Maeth would have killed Samei. But a few of our men had got away, at the beginning, and Samei had managed to hold the enemy for long enough... The king himself came to our rescue. Samei and Lord Maeth were still fighting, when over the brow of the hill out of the darkness the king and five thousand men came down upon us. They cut the enemy to pieces. The king himself killed Lord Maeth. But when all was secure, and men were seeing to the prince's wounds, Prince Fiol told them to see that Samei was well first.

'And Samei knelt before Prince Fiol, and told him that it would have broken his heart, to think of the king his father weeping because his son was dead and lost to him.'

Clews took a long drink, shook his head in wonder. 'That little boy, shitting himself all down me, crying with fear...'

Lidae said, amazed, 'He didn't tell me any of this. I didn't know.' What had happened last night, she'd thought it was the first time he'd fought properly, against an enemy with real swords wanting real blood. *The way I spoke to him*, she thought. *No wonder he was hurt. Samei, have you been fighting?* Patronising him, talking down to him, oh how special he's doing, my little boy, anyone would think he was really doing these things. *'We were in a fight, a while back. We went through their baggage.'*

'Be proud, Lidae,' Clews said. 'Be so very proud.'

My son the monster.

My son the rapist.

'I am very proud,' she said.

Forty-three

She woke early the next morning. Her body and her eyes were sore as if she had been crying. A frost had formed in the last hours, black metallic earth with a ghost sheen. In the east, a thin band of golden light almost a fire, a tree on the far horizon stood out against it black and jagged. A cough, a muttering, dogs barking, a crash as someone dropped something metallic and the sound rang out too loud. She lay a long time awake in silence, looking out through the tent opening at the little patch of earth and sky. A line of birds came flying far off over the sunrise, flowing together and moving. The light came on very suddenly, bright daylight and the night-shadows banished, the birds went wheeling away. The frost on the black earth shimmered like mist on water. She kept thinking that she had done something terribly wrong and shameful.

'Lidae.' Deljan, who hadn't gone to bed yet, called to her from where he sat by the ashes of the campfire. From a tent one of the others shouted to be quiet, stop disturbing everyone. Lidae scrambled out of the tent, Eralene grumbling at her. 'A woman looking for you,' Deljan said.

A young woman, dressed in dark plain loose clothes. Her body was heavy, thick and swollen, but her face was thin with a strained look to it. Her hair was hacked off short. She walked towards Lidae in a way that was somehow both eager and very hesitant. Flinching back even as she came on. Like a woman made of glass, brittle and about to shatter; and Lidae thought, as she came nearer, her face bent away her eyes averted from Lidae's face, she seemed almost to have a shadow over her, as if she was a demon thing, a dead thing out in the dark of the lich roads, a great horror came over Lidae and she wanted to run away. She thought, stupidly: this is what I was ashamed of.

The woman said, 'Lidae?'

She was half a head taller than Lidae. She had a smell of cold earth, the unkempt look of someone who had been sleeping rough in the cold frost. Her short hair, Lidae realised, was hacked off in mourning, in the manner of Raena and the south. A necklace of green glass beads clicked around her throat.

Lidae saw that the woman was Ayllis. Ayllis, grown to adulthood.

She must be … what … twenty? No, older, surely: it was years since Lidae had last seen her, she had been almost grown then… Her lovely hair, the same pale gold as dried apples, just like her mother's hair, hacked off in mourning. She has come from Ryn, Lidae thought. Because in all this huge world, she can only have come to me about my son, because my son is all that matters to me, she must, she must be bringing me a message about him. The clear pale air and the ground were black around her. Ryn's dead, she thought. Ryn's dead.

'Lidae?'

She had been staring. She felt as though she had fallen some great, vast distance. 'Ayllis? Is it you? Really?' She said, trying to keep herself from screaming out, 'You look … But where have you come from? What are you doing here?'

She could see suddenly and very clearly in her mind so many things. Ayllis in the sunshine outside the farmhouse in Salith Drylth, stroking baby Samei's face so very gently. Ayllis running up the slope of the field, all covered in blood and ashes, and the look of joy on her face when Lidae and the boys were alive.

'Is Cythra here with you?' Impossible to think of Ayllis without her mother beside her. How good it would be, Lidae thought, to see Cythra again. How happy it would make Samei. To say to Cythra in a proud mother's voice, *'Samei is a lieutenant captain in the Winged Blades, and a hero, and known to Prince Fiol himself.'* How delighted Ayllis and Cythra would be!

Ayllis put her hand up to her cropped hair. A grown woman's hand that worked hard, not a child's hand, the skin red and coarse, the nails broken and flaked. 'Mother's dead.'

'No. Oh. Oh, Ayllis. I'm sorry.' Stupid, stupid, stupid, stupid. 'I'm so sorry.'

The girl shrugged. 'It's fine. It was almost three years ago. I thought you'd know, somehow.' She said, in a voice that was Ayllis's voice for the first time, fierce and bright, 'I thought Clews would have told you.'

Three years! Lidae said, stupidly, dully. 'No. He didn't, he didn't tell me, no.' She thought: I could have paid a scribe to write her a letter. 'I'm sorry,' she said again. Found herself staring around her, hoping for

Samei or Clews or Eralene, anyone, to appear beside her, rescue her. It was so very awkward, this woman with heavy breasts and tired eyes who was the girl Ayllis that Ryn and Samei had played with, talking to her as if she was a woman, and all the time the ringing voice still in her ears: Ryn! Ryn! Ask her about Ryn! *I've stood on the battlefield while dragons fought in the sky above me, felt the heat of their fires overhead. I've stood in my line, unmoving, while white mage fire runs over the bodies of the men next to me, burns them away to nothing. I've stood my ground while the sky grows black with shadows, they came down on me with claws and great bloodied teeth and I held the line, hacked away at them. How's my son, Ayllis? Oh, he's well, Lidae, very well, very happy.* But Ayllis stood awkwardly in silence, looking down. Lidae said awkwardly, 'But, I mean, you must be tired, I mean, sit down, I'll get you something to eat, some tea.'

'That would be good, thank you.' The girl rubbed her face, a very weary gesture. 'You're a washerwoman, still?' Lidae said, prattling, trying to find things to say that weren't anything. 'Your squad's here, presumably? Where are you camped, then?' *How did Cythra die? How's Ryn?* A smith started up working somewhere nearby, to groans from all across the camp. His hammer rang and rang, and then a hiss, hot metal plunged into water to cool it. Someone was cooking something sharp and greasy and well-spiced.

'Tea,' Lidae said, trying to gather herself. She could see it, the farmhouse, the walls whitewashed clean. A man standing in the doorway, tall, but her mind would not let her see Ryn's face. 'Deljan,' she said, crossly, squad mother telling off her useless young ones, 'stop staring, the poor woman has travelled a thousand miles, get her some tea to drink, some bread.' *I am in control of this, strong, see?*

'Three years,' she said again. They both sat down by the remains of the campfire, Deljan hurried about, the others in the squad came out of their tents, pretended they weren't looking.

'She spoke about you,' Ayllis said. 'When she was dying. She was sad that she hadn't got a chance to see you again.' There was a little clump of yellow groundsel flowers growing just by where they were sitting, Ayllis poked it with the toe of her shoe. 'She got sick and died. It was quick, in the end. She was asleep, and then she was dead.'

'That's good then.' There's a kind of comfort, Lidae had seen many times before, in saying how someone died. She heard the words very distantly. Have to say something. A great sick ringing horror: Cythra dead. That strong kindness: dead. How many years, then, since Devid died? Gods, the boys were still children when Devid died. I should have thought about her more. Asked Clews to find out about her. And now I'll have to tell Samei.

'Is Samei … Is Samei here?' Ayllis asked, and Lidae started as if the girl had been seeing her thoughts, but how foolish, of course Ayllis would be thinking about Samei, and she would have some message for Samei from Ryn. 'I heard … There's a story I heard, that Samei is a great hero,' Ayllis said. 'Is he really?'

'He is! It's the talk of the camp!' Lidae told her the story of the battle, the terrible demon horsemen, Samei taking command. Ayllis sat very still and quiet, listening.

'I knew he'd be a great warrior, Lidae,' Ayllis said when Lidae had finished, 'Mother did, too. "Like he was born to it," Mother said.'

Cythra said that? About Samei?

'He reminded her of Niken, she said.' Cythra's … youngest son. 'Niken wanted to be a soldier. He'd have been proud, Mother said, to see Samei. He always liked Samei.'

'Did he?' Lidae thought: I barely remember Cythra's sons. I had no idea they thought anything about my children.

'Niken was the one who … that night, the one who first said they should fight.' Ayllis looked fixedly down at the groundsel flowers, touched them with the toe of her shoe to make the petals shake. Her fingers twisted and twisted in her lap. 'Lidae … why I've come … I've come from Ryn. I mean, Ryn doesn't know, doesn't know I've come to find you, but I—'

'He's alive? Ryn's alive?' Her voice was very loud, pleading, she sounded like she was begging Ayllis not to do some terrible thing. Deljan, sitting pretending he wasn't staring, started, his hand went to his sword belt.

'He's alive,' Ayllis said. Her foot pushed down harder on the groundsel flower. Half crushing it. There was something very horrible to Lidae, very frightening, about the sight of the yellow flowers crushed beneath Ayllis's feet. 'He's alive, but he— He—' Her face turned up to look at Lidae finally, her wide girl's eyes filled with grief. 'Lidae, Ryn has sworn to find Samei, in the battle, kill him. If Samei is here, Lidae, I have to warn him, that's why I came. I have to warn him. Ryn has sworn to kill him.'

Forty-four

She, Lidae, she does not doubt it.

What have I done, to bring up my sons to hate each other? When they were children, they loved each other so much. Worse than any sword wound, worse than Emmas dying, worse than seeing her mother die. Cythra bent over her son's bodies, in the memory Cythra was not a woman but a shadow, a monster, terrifying in its grief. Like a stench, a sickness, too horrible to look at. In the memory Cythra's face was deformed. Monstrous bared skull teeth. Howling like a dog. What words are there to say this to me? Your tongue will rot in your mouth, the words will choke you.

If I had brought the boys up to be sutlers or gamesters or weaponsmiths. If I had taken the boys back to Illyrith, rebuilt the farm. If they had been born as beggar children, squatting in the streets of Raena. All those women who had sat in the dust of a ruined city, followed the army as beggars and slaves, whose children … whose children … But I loved my children. I love them. What more could I have done? What else could I have done?

What have I done, to make them hate each other like this? So many things, so many things I did wrong.

'You're lying. You're lying to me.'

Ayllis said, 'He took his sword, cut his left hand, let the blood drop to the ground, swore that he would find Samei in the coming battle and kill him. He was so angry when he heard the name 'Samei' in the battle in the village, he cursed that he hadn't been there, all he wants, all he can think about, he joined the queen's army, all of it, just to kill Samei. We all know the battle will be days away, if that, he's counting the hours, determined.'

Just let me die, you gods. So long ago I could have died. There was a pit beneath her, she was falling, the world opened up to suck her down. She could not hear, she could not speak. A single combat, two men gripping each other, so tight they might be lovers. Blood and sweat running down them. Arms and legs and thighs meshed. Face against face, bright hair mingling. Breathing on to each other's lips. And they go down together, gasping in exhaustion, they lie together in the dust as one. The stronger of them stirs and gets up slowly, limping, aching. Looks down at the man he's killed. Spits. Weeps.

'That's not true. Not true. What do you mean, "the queen's army"? Ryn is with … with … with the enemy? A soldier? Fighting against the king?' Pick the story apart, make it not true. Refuse it, even as she knows without question the truth of it.

'He's with the queen's army, yes,' Ayllis said again. Almost as if Lidae was stupid. 'A year, he's been a soldier. Don't you know?'

'You're lying.' And she said, lost in confusion, picking the edges of the story apart so that the thing that is true, also, the core of it, will not be true, 'Why would Ryn be fighting with the Queen of Eralath against Illyrith? He went back to Illyrith to be a farmer, why would he be in Eralath, fighting? And you, Ayllis, why would you …? You've come … from Ryn in the false Queen of Eralath's camp? Why would you be there? You're a washerwoman in your father's old squad of foot soldiers, why would you go over to Eralath? Why would Ryn?' This is all impossible lies. You know it. *You're lying to me.*

'Ryn is not a traitor,' Lidae screamed.

You're just jealous, Cythra, because your own sons are long dead. May your life be as desolate as the winter ocean, may your life be flood and famine and dry bitter earth where no plant will grow, may your life be stones, Lidae, as mine is. But what has Samei ever done to you, Cythra, for you to be saying this? Or done to Ryn? Or, but, I mean, the thing he's done, the woman, he … but, he's never said, he's never said he hates me, Cythra. Not like Ryn. Go back to Ryn, then, Cythra, he's no son of mine, Samei is my son, Samei the hero, tell Ryn that Samei will kill him if Ryn tries to fight him, if Ryn dares to fight him. Open her mouth to scream it aloud: 'How dare you, how dare you tell me these things?' The ground should open to swallow you, for saying these things. You walked through the camp and the men should have turned their eyes from you in revulsion. Blinded, sickened by you as you passed them.

The earth beneath your feet should be rotten, and the sky above your head should weep. You are lying when you say these things.

Ayllis, Lidae thought, it's Ayllis, not Cythra, the girl Ayllis is sitting here beside me head bent, her hands on her stomach. Cythra is dead.

'Is Ryn happy, Ayllis? Is he well? Does he … does he ever speak about me, Ayllis?' Ask her these things. Open my mouth, ask her these things.

Forty-five

A shout from behind her. Men with swords, surrounding them, cruel blades, cruel eyes. A woman's voice said, 'You, there. Spy. Get up. Or we'll kill you where you sit.'

What?

Rhosa, with ten men beside her, their cloaks and their helmet plumes pure snow-white. 'Come away from her, Lidae,' Rhosa said. 'Get away from her, Lidae, step away. Slowly. She may be armed.'

Ayllis? Armed?

This is madness. Endless madness.

Rhosa was unchanged. Unaged. Like a child's memory of an adult, ancient, ageless, the same older face seen twelve years later, as old then as it was twelve years ago. Her hair was still brown, spring tree bark and spring branches, her face still milky white and kind. She had seemed both younger and older than Lidae, when they met before, when Rhosa was a high-ranking soldier on a secret mission to destroy King Durith and Lidae was nothing and Ayllis was beyond nothing.

Ayllis got to her feet very slowly. Her face was sick white. Terrified. 'I'm not a spy. I swear. I just came to warn Samei and Lidae. Please.' Her hand went to her stomach, fingers spread holding herself. The way Ayllis placed her hands, the heavy swell of her body in its loose gown, made Lidae finally see what should have been obvious, that Ayllis was pregnant.

Lidae drew her own sword, stood between Ayllis and Rhosa's sword blade. The red glass in the hilt winked at her. Her and Rhosa and Ayllis.

'Don't be a fool,' Rhosa said. 'She's an enemy spy. I'm ordering you to put your sword down, Lidae.'

Clews was there also, walking towards them stern and very grey, armed men around him. 'Lidae,' he called out to her. 'Lidae, get away from her. You remember her as a child, I know. But get away.'

Lidae held her sword out at Rhosa, the blade shaking in her hand. She's lying, yes! About Ryn, about Cythra, about everything. 'You can't harm her,' Lidae said to Rhosa, 'I won't let you harm her.'

'She's a spy and a traitor.' Rhosa's voice had the same cold, flat kindness it had had when Lidae had first known her, pretending to be a simply runaway soldier, talking without emotion but without cruelty to Cythra and Devid and the children. 'Put your sword down and step away from her, Lidae. Now.' And Lidae thought suddenly of Clews, trying to tell her not tell her something, Samei, knowing something, too frightened to speak of it. Red banners, the king's banners, flying over the enemy horsemen. A boat coming into Navikyre Fortress in the dark, bringing secrets. Clews's face, there, briefly glimpsed. '*She says ... But he ...*' Just forget, Lidae. Don't ask. Please.

'Ayllis?' Great spreading fear. 'Where have you come from, Ayllis? What army is this that you've come from, you and Ryn? You're a spy, Ayllis?'

She's a child. Running towards me in the dawn sunshine, the first living face I've seen, rejoicing, yellow flowers crushed beneath her feet. She's pregnant, Rhosa, for all the gods' sweet sakes. Cythra, like a black dog, howling. But Lidae took three long steps away from Ayllis who had loved her sons like a sister. Lowered her sword.

An enemy. A spy. Yes. And therefore she is lying.

Just let me die, you gods. So long ago I could have died. There was pit beneath her, she was falling, the world opened up to suck her down. She could not hear, she could not speak.

She whispered, 'You can't harm her, Rhosa. Swear it to me.'

Rhosa only gave her a sad, shamed, knowing look.

'Swear! You knew her as a child too, Rhosa.'

Rhosa said in her gentle cold voice, 'She won't be harmed.'

But what else can she do? Kill every soldier in the camp? 'I did know her, you're right,' Rhosa said, 'I remember her, she won't be harmed, Lidae. And think, Lidae,' Rhosa said, 'about Samei.'

White cloaked soldiers surrounded Ayllis, bound her hands, placed a rope like a halter around her neck. Her face, stricken, turned back to Lidae. 'Tell Samei. Tell him,' she called. 'Warn him. Please. For Ryn.'

Devid's voice, embarrassed, ashamed, defensive, furiously righteously rightly with her for endangering his own family: 'I did look for you, Lidae ... But ... It was too dangerous, you see that, Lidae? When you left them? Ran away? You might have come back, and it was too dangerous to look for you. You see that?

I see.

Lidae watched the soldiers until they were gone from sight, Ayllis lost in the snow-white helmet plumes, so small in comparison, a child still indeed, the soldiers themselves swallowed up in the great mass of the camp. Lidae's own squad surrounded her at a distance, still staring trying not to look. Whispering, questioning, wanting to make sense of all this.

'I didn't know she had another son.'

'What can he have done?'

'What must she have done to him?'

Turn round, shout at the top of her lungs, a desperate war cry, 'I did nothing! Nothing! I loved him more than all the world, my first-born, my most perfect, my most beloved, all my heart. I loved him!'

Clews stood very awkward a little way off. Eralene walked up towards Lidae, opened her mouth to say something, gods knew what she could say. Clews moved his hand, a small, quiet gesture of command. Eralene stepped away. The whole squad shrank away.

In the distance, still, the smith was hammering away making his horseshoes. The hammer rang out. Lidae tried to listen. Beat. Beat. Beat.

'Perhaps,' Clews said, and he sounded so tired his voice was a croak. She thought: he'll always sound a good man to me. 'Perhaps, someone could get some water, for myself and for Lidae? Or a cup of wine, even?' He rubbed his face the way men do when they are very tired. Closed his eyes and looked away from her, winced in pain as if he had been wounded.

Lidae said, 'You knew about Ryn.'

He rubbed his face again. Hiding his face from her. 'How could I tell you? I wanted to tell you. I couldn't manage to drink enough to bear to tell you. Like a stone in my throat. I'd have had to drink until I couldn't speak, spew it up over you. How can a man say that about— I wanted to get you posted somewhere far away, Lidae, you and Samei. If I'd known that you were stationed at Navikyre Fortress, when I brought the message there, if I'd known, seen you, I would have ...

'I'd have tried...'

He trailed off, barked a laugh into the cup of wine Deljan had hurriedly brought him. 'She decided on it. There's nothing I could have done then, or can do now,' he said. 'Hope it still somehow doesn't come to battle. That's all there is left to do. Hope she—' He drank down half the cup of wine in one swallow. 'There's nothing I can do.'

Lidae looked up and down at the tents, the squad's hidden eyes and

ears fixed on her. Listened to the hammer as it rang. She stepped up close
to Clews. A knife hung at her belt, the same knife she taken from the
dragon-dead out by the banks of the Nimenest. She came up very close
to Clews and pressed the knife into his stomach, the tip up against his
skin, hard into it. He went rigid, coughed on his wine. But the things he
had done, the life he had led, backstabber, betrayer, schemer, killer, he
neither moved nor spoke.

'Stop your own pity. Tell me. Tell what is happening and what I can
do for Samei and Ryn.'

Clews said, 'You can't anything, Lidae.'

'I'll break Samei's sword arm, if I have to, so he can't fight, I'll walk to
the Queen of Eralath's army and I'll break Ryn's sword arm. My children,
Clews! My children.' She heard him gasp, as she pushed the blade in so
that it broke the skin, she felt ashamed, sickened, even as she felt a kind
of long buried pleasure in hurting him.

Clews said, 'Put your knife down, Lidae.'

'Not until you've told me everything. All of it.'

Clews said, 'Walk with me, then, Lidae.' From a distance it must
have looked as if Lidae was supporting him, like a woman supporting
her aged father, or a woman caring for a husband who was sick. They
walked a long way to the edge of the camp. Stood in the heart of a clump
of thick bare trees. Their feet half-buried in beech mast. Children from
the camp had been playing there, bent branches down to form a shelter,
a secret den.

'So tell me. Or I'll kill you.'

Deep breath. Clews, and Lidae.

Clews said, 'It is not the Queen of Eralath we're fighting. We have
agreed a peace with Eralath and the Queen of Eralath is our ally now.'
Deep breath. Pause. Deep breath again. 'It is Civil War again now, Lidae.'

'Civil war?' Lidae echoed dully.

'King Durith's daughter Elayne has declared herself Queen of Illyrith.
All Illyrith has risen for her. She has seized Thalden, crowned herself
queen there. She is perhaps ten days' march from us. Her army, I believe,
outnumbers ours two to one.

'Ryn is with her army, yes. A strong, brave, young captain. That
fine story I told you about Samei? I could tell you similar stories, more
glorious even, about Ryn.

'But they would not be glorious, of course, because they are about
our enemy.'

He leaned closer against Lidae. The knife blade pressed against his skin. She had to move the blade back, loosen her hand awkwardly, to stop it from injuring him. 'Her envoy was to meet with Lord Sabryyr, at Navikyre Fortress. Make some kind of settlement. I hoped, I planned— She refused to send anyone. Half the empire, marriage to Prince Fiol, Temyr grovelling at her feet ... she is interested in none of it.'

He said, very slowly, 'I advised Temyr to kill her before he ever moved against King Durith. All those years ago, long before I met you and Samei and Ryn. More powerful voices them mine disagreed. She was Durith's daughter, after all. And a child. And he was ... our king.'

'Why do you want to King Durith to win?' Lidae remembered Cythra asking her in the dark the night before the battle that had killed King Durith, as the fire burned down in ashes.

'Everything I had, my home, everything is because of King Durith. For ten years, I fought for him.'

'Everything you had is gone, Lidae.' And Cythra had said as the fire burned down and the dark claimed them, 'You had a home and a family before, in Raena. When you were a child. What did King Durith do to them?'

There was a king in Raena, my king, I lived there the first sixteen years of my life as his subject, Raena was filled with statues of him. I can't remember his name now, no one can remember his name or his face or his great deeds. I don't know this Queen Elayne. I have never seen her. Barely heard her name. I cannot say, cannot care, whether she or King Temyr is a traitor or the rightful king. Except that my children will suffer either way.

She can hardly be alone in thinking this. After so many years of warfare every man and woman and child in Irlawe must know this.

Samei, shouting, howling, as a little boy: *if Ryn has the stick he'll break the stick, so I'm going to break the stick. Ryn made me do it, Mummy. It's his fault I enjoyed myself by breaking the stick.*

Names that mean nothing. A king, a queen, another queen, probably soon after that another king. March south, march east, march north, march west. We survive, or we don't. Fighting for someone. We care ... about as much as you do. As in: nothing.

But Lidae thought: but my sons ... both of my sons are heroes.

'Lidae ... could you put the knife down now?' Clews said. 'Please? Could you?'

Forty-six

'Will you let me go now?'

No. Tell him, don't ask him. 'I want to see Ayllis,' Lidae said. 'Even if she is from the Queen … Queen Elayne's camp, she … She's a child. An army washerwoman, Clews. You know her. You heard her, she came here to warn Samei. That's all.'

'I knew her when she was a child,' Clews said. 'When was the last time you saw her, Lidae? You don't know anything about her, what she is now. You're too trusting.'

Sneak up in the dark in blackened armour, faces smeared with mud, barely dare breathing, crawling on our bellies like snakes, hearts pound loud enough to wake the whole enemy army, if one man sees us we're done it's over and done. Scouts out patrolling the margins, eager alert sentries, guard-posts, watch-lines and watch-words and counter-words and challenges. Slither on our bellies like snakes, run bent double on all fours like beaten dogs, cut the enemies' throats before they see us, the flash of light on our blades enough to kill us all.

And Clews walked into King Durith's camp once with a little boy's shit and snot caking his clothes, sneered at by bold tough soldier men, and he killed the king.

'How little we regard the poor wretches who follow an army,' he had said years afterwards, talking it over to Ryn and Samei. 'Men and women and children. They swarm around the camp, and we don't look at them, don't see them, assume they're harmless useless nothings. That woman there, going past, what did she look like Ryn?' And Ryn couldn't say because it was just another old camp woman carrying washing, he didn't see to notice anything. 'Remember that, you two. Think on it.'

They had nodded in agreement, yes, Clews, we will, Clews, just as they did when he talked of night marches, outflanking manoeuvres, coded messages. Hurried him on to talk more about those other more exciting things. 'Think on it, you two boys.'

'But we don't want to hear about old women and babies, Clews, tell us about the siege of Telea again.' *And Clews smiles, is easily persuaded, because it is a good story, it is definitely not about old women and children.*

'I have to see Ayllis, Clews.'

'Oh Lidae. You are too—' the man shook his head, frowned, sighed. 'Briefly, then. Be careful, if she starts asking you anything about our troops here, numbers, anything, talking to you about Queen Elayne.' He looked at Lidae, as if he was expecting her to say something: *'I don't believe you about this enemy, this "Queen Elayne". Prove it to me, that that's who we're fighting. Tell me why I shouldn't go over to this "Queen Elayne" then.'* He said wearily, 'She may try to win you over to them.'

Lidae shrugged. 'Who do you think I am, Clews? I do what I'm told, fight who I'm told to fight. Someone points me, tells me, "There's the enemy, there, at my signal kill them," someone gives the signal, I kill them, or I'm killed myself. I know you're lying and I follow your orders even though I know they're lies, even if I have no idea on this earth why or for what or for who. Someone I've never heard of before. Someone who was our ally yesterday. The false Queen of Eralath, the undead magelord king of Aborn, King Durith's daughter, King Durith's mother, uncle, cook's neighbour's wife's sister: I fight until we've won or until we've lost or until I'm dead.'

'"King Durith's cook's neighbour's wife's sister?"' And then Clews laughed, really laughed, like that was the funniest thing he'd heard from a long time, and gods help him, Lidae thought, perhaps it was. 'Oh Lidae. You sound so like the men I knew when I was first a soldier. *"For the king and for each other, until the sun falls and the world ends."*' And then his laughter stopped, and his face was grey and tired again. 'I remember you mourning King Durith. You grieved for him. You were loyal to him, believed in him. I remember how much I envied you, that you had been loyal to him.'

Lidae thought: when the battle comes, my squad might switch sides in a heartbeat, if someone like you orders it. Order us to retreat without fighting, watch our comrades die without helping them. Turn around and fight our own comrades until we kill them or are killed by them. That's what our loyalty is. Yesterday they were our best friends, today without any reason given they're enemy meat. And we do it, because that's all there is for us. We don't understand a word of it. But we go along with it. Suspicious. Or resentful. Or entirely, pathetically, desperately, full of trust. Like... But it's too obvious...

So she said nothing.

'King Durith's cook's neighbour's wife's sister. I'll remember that.' Clews said. 'Lidae, do you think you could put your knife away, now, at least?'

He led her though the camp to Ayllis. She marvelled, as she did whenever she was with him, at the way his cloak and helmet meant that crowds drew back, melted away almost in fear from him. Looked bright and respectful at him. Samei will be like this soon, she thought with pride. Already is like this, perhaps. And he said, Clews said, Ryn must be like this in Elayne's army, also. Of course he is.

She thought with a shadow coming over her: does Ryn have a woman captive in his tent as well as Samei? Shall I ask Ayllis that— tell me, Ayllis, is my oldest son a rapist as well as my younger one?

Don't be absurd, she thought. She looked at Clews and his face was kind, I've always thought of him as a kind man, she thought. Samei's woman is … willing. Nothing special. Just a soldier thing. And Ryn…

Ryn could never do such a thing to anyone. Absolute certainty.

A pedlar woman was wandering around the camp selling luck charms. She repeated over and over to the men around her, calling, wheedling, begging them: 'These bones, you see them? These bones are from the earth here, a great battle was fought here, too many years ago to recall. That cleft there in the earth, by the river there, that was where they fought, you see it? They broke the earth apart with their fighting. And these are their bones, the heroes who fought here, I dug them out of it. Luck! Luck, they'll bring you. Three in copper, for an amulet made out of heroes' bones.'

'There was never a battle fought here,' said Clews. 'I've heard her before. Everywhere we camp, she says the same thing.' There was no cleft in the earth to dig in. The nearest river was perhaps five miles distant.

She came up very close to Lidae, holding out her goods, dirty white splinters of bone on greasy cords to hang around the neck. Her fingers were black with soil, it clung to her skin and her clothes. 'Three in copper.' Lidae took a charm. Felt stupid even before she handed over the coins.

'Bird bones,' said Clews. 'Look how thin they are. Last night's dinner, I should think. If that.'

'I know they're not real. I only want to give her coin.' She threw them away onto the ground. In a hundred years' time another beggar woman can find them, tell lies about them.

A great grand tent in the distance, Lord Sabryyr's tent. Beautiful deep blue, like the sea on a fine day in summer in the shallows near Kelurlth Head.

'It's hot and uncomfortable,' Clews said. 'The cloth gets hot in the sun, smells odd.'

Lidae hoped they'd go nearer. See Lord Sabryyr in the distance. There was a lovely food smell, sweet bread baking, and beneath it a general scent of perfumes, oils, herbs, spices, rich things, clean things. A woman walked past, very grandly and beautifully dressed in soft pale pink, the colour of the inside of the big, curved shells Ryn would search for on the beach at Salith Drylth. She was carrying a birdcage with a bird in it. The cage was made of gold, studded all with rubies, but when Lidae looked at the bird to see what wonders it might be it was plain brown and drab.

'If Ayllis hadn't trampled that poor groundsel plant to nothing,' said Clews, 'they could have fed the bird on its seeds.'

Then they turned away from the grand tents, left the fine clean smells behind them. 'The Winged Blades,' Clews said, awkwardly, 'are camped over there, to the left there, if you want to see Samei.'

'I—' She had been trying to think what she might say to him. And then he'd ask, of course he would, as Ayllis and Clews and everyone who had been listening must be asking, the one question, clear and stark and she could answer it, oh gods: 'And if it comes to it, mother, if we fight … which of us do you want to win?'

'After … Afterwards.' She hoped Clews would say that he would come with her, but he said nothing.

'What did you say to him,' Clews said at last, 'the first time you let him go into battle?'

'What?' Of all the things he might have been thinking about, all the terrible things '…I don't know. Don't remember. "Be strong, for me", or some equally absurd thing. The usual things people say, I suppose. At least, I never heard Arael say anything different to his children.'

'Yes,' Clews said, as if he had hoped she'd say something different.

'Here we are then,' Clews said. 'There.' He pointed up at a place where a group of cages were placed with men guarding them, they looked almost like pig houses, little and low, with a strong vile sick smell. Lidae recoiled, felt her body curl itself up grown tense, her shoulders hunch her legs shake. A place to keep enemies, traitors, those who have offended and schemed against the king. A black dog was sniffing around the cages. The sight of it made Lidae want to scream out. She grasped Clews' hand, stumbled, leaned against him as he had seemed to lean against her when she held the knife to his chest. Every soldier knows of this place, is terrified of it worse than death. But it's an unreal place, also, to soldiers like Lidae who are unimportant and will never end up here. A thought struck her, looking at it with Clews: are you ever afraid, Clews, that you'll end up here? But, again, she could not say it. The guards nodded at him, he walked through the cages confidently, a man who knew where he was going, was not afraid of this place. He said, in that way he had of talking to Lidae as if she was himself, 'Sometimes I come here, walk here among them, just to think about ... about things.'

Lidae remembered his kindness, his care for her children. A great feeling of pity for him. But she said, 'Ayllis is a child, Clews. And you put her here.'

'She's older than Queen Elayne,' Clews said, as if Queen Elayne was a real young woman like Ayllis.

Rhosa was there waiting for them. Hair like spring tree bark and spring branches, face milk white. And she and Lidae, Lidae realised, must be around the same age. She nodded at Clews with her kind smile. 'I assumed you'd come to see her,' Rhosa said. 'That Lidae would persuade you.'

'She's not a spy,' Lidae cried out, almost a child herself. 'Let her go, Rhosa. Please.'

'You know that, do you?' said Rhosa. 'Do you, Lidae? You know what she is, what your son is?'

'Her mother was my friend,' Lidae could only say, uselessly, hopelessly. 'Her mother was my friend, and she used to play with my children.' I know nothing about her beyond that, who she is, what she wants, what she thinks. A child, who used to play with my children. Please. Let her ... let her come with me, stay in my tent, I'll guard her, if she tries to run away, I'll...

'You can have a few moments talking with her,' Rhosa said. 'I suppose, Clews and I, we owe you and her that much.'

Lidae thought: Clews will die in a cage in a place like this. But Rhosa will never end up here.

Lidae stepped up to the cage. Squatted down. 'Ayllis? Are you ...? Will you speak to me, Ayllis?'

The woman in the cage was silent. Huddled in on herself, head bent. She sat up at Lidae's approach. Her eyes were red with crying, but she smiled when she saw Lidae. She looked so much Cythra, she was caught in Lidae's memory between the child Ayllis, pretty and pale, running and laughing with her skirt hitched up to free her long thin legs, and Cythra sitting wise and all-knowing at Lidae's table, helping her with the children, advising her, so kind, so helpful to Lidae.

I didn't ask her anything about her life, Lidae though. Her pregnancy—how can I not have noticed? Ayllis, the pretty little child, pregnant! Impossible. But when I last saw her, Lidae thought, she was already older, then, than I was when I first became a soldier. She is certainly old enough to marry, to have children. But: her hair cut short in mourning—the baby's father, Lidae thought, of course, that's who she is mourning. Relief sweeping over her. She sat down on the wet ground in front of the cage.

'You haven't been … harmed, at all?'

'No.' It was less than an hour since they had taken Ayllis away.

Tell me about Ryn. Is he well? Is he happy?

I'll get you out of here somehow. Don't be afraid, Ayllis, I won't let anything happen to you.

They say you're a filthy lying traitorous spy, and you're lying about Ryn.

'I'm sorry about Cythra,' Lidae said. 'I wish I'd known. I'm sorry.'

A release, for both of them, talking about Cythra. See her sitting at the table in Lidae's house in Salith Drylth, her hands working on something, making the boys giggle together.

Lidae thought then: Ryn knows, of course. The first thing he'll have asked Ayllis: how's Cythra, Ayllis, is she here? I'd love to see her again. I remember sometimes Ryn and Samei would call Cythra 'mummy'. How much it hurt me.

And a tiny part of her thought: I hated Cythra. For knowing what to do with them. Be more like Cythra, Lidae! Try, come on! Tomorrow, tomorrow—lying awake in the dark, listening to the boys' breathing, wanting to cry with shame, with pity for them that they were her sons and not Cythra's boys who had such a good mother to raise them, tomorrow it will be different, tomorrow I'll do better, be more like Cythra, a proper mother, I promise you. I don't know what to do, tell me what to do, Cythra. Help me be more like you.

A guilt and a shame that would never be lifted now, and a terrible rush of relief in her, that Cythra was gone and dead.

Ayllis said, 'She never really recovered from Father dying. Spoke more and more about Marn and Dylas and Niken. And now she'll never — if it's a boy, I was going to call him Niken.' She broke off, her hands over her stomach, bit her lip. 'Except now if it's a boy I'll have to name it after my husband.'

'I'm sorry,' Lidae said again, almost not listening.

'She didn't want me to marry young,' Ayllis said. 'If she was alive, she might even be angry. I got married very soon after she died,' Ayllis said. She touched her short-cropped hair. 'My husband was a hero of Elayne's army. *"Poet of the sword, glorious, his name will live forever in song."* His mother was from Raena. He'd never seen Raena. But I remembered you cutting your hair off in mourning.'

'I'm sorry,' Lidae said again. They fell silent. Both waiting, both too frightened to mention the … the other thing. That night talking with Cythra after Lidae had buried Emmas, when the geese had flown over the house calling the dead. Death so close around them, making her say things, ask things. *'We bear them, we care for them, we bury them,'* Cythra had said.

'Queen Elayne has promised peace,' said Ayllis. 'We make peace with Eralath and the southern cities, we stop fighting, she's going to pay off the army, disband it. That's why Ryn joined her. My husband also. As soon as Temyr is defeated, we'll have peace again, Lidae.'

She really seemed to believe it. Her face was radiant as she spoke. 'Did you know, Lidae, the old king her father, poor King Durith, he was going to make peace with Eralath, his envoys and theirs had agreed everything, he was going to disband the army, let them go home? That was why Temyr killed him, did you know that?' She lowered her voice, almost conspiratorially to Lidae, 'You don't know, but your friends, Clews and Rhosa: they were part if it, Lidae. Ryn knows, he told me. He was so angry when he found out. I'm so sorry, to have to tell you. So, you see, you must see, why it's so important, why we should fight for Queen Elayne?'

Lidae said, very slowly, 'I see.'

'If you tell Samei all this,' said Ayllis, 'maybe he'll see it too, do you think? And then it might, I mean, once he understands…' She looked over, narrow-eyed, to where Rosa and Clews were talking. 'Lidae, I am sorry about Clews. I know he's your friend. But he's not what you think, not just a soldier.' And there she was a child again, so naïve, so … so kind, Lidae thought. Gods, how could someone live through all this grief and be so kind still? But Clews and Rhosa had been shocked by how trusting she was herself, and what must it be like for them, trusting and believing nothing? I don't know anything, Lidae thought, except that Clews has treated my sons well and kindly, whatever it is he is.

'That's enough now,' Rhosa called over to her. 'Leave her alone now.'

'Queen Elayne is only fighting for peace,' Ayllis said. 'Lidae, when the battle comes … Ryn, and Samei…'

'They're my sons, Ayllis. I … I wish…' What am I trying to say? What can I say? The woman sitting huddled there could not be the child Ayllis, it was Cythra, or her own mother, or herself, pregnant with Ryn, sitting there.

She wanted to reach through the bars, say to the woman, fierce and urgent: 'If a battle comes, if men come, after the battle … just go with them. Do what they want. Don't anger them. You've seen what happens to women, after a battle, you know what … what to do.' She couldn't say it. What a pitiful thing to have to think to say. Ayllis as someone's slavewoman. Like Samei's woman without a name. Cythra spoke to her, she thought, I'm sure, told her what to do if it ever came. She was a camp follower, a washerwoman, an army wife now: the women there in the baggage, they must talk about these things.

It was all so easy, in the real fighting, with Acol, before she knew these things.

'Come away, Lidae,' Rhosa said. 'Now.'

'Be safe, Lidae,' Ayllis called. 'You and Samei and Ryn.'

'Be safe,' Lidae said to her.

'Come away. Now,' Rhosa's soft, sad, kind voice said.

Forty-seven

'You see?' Lidae said to Clews. 'She's not a spy, she came to protect Ryn and Samei.' When I ran away from my children, she thought, Ayllis was the one who comforted them.

'Perhaps she did, even.' Clews said, 'I suppose it is good sometimes, to have to remember that there are good people in the world.'

Lidae said after a moment, 'Why do you do what you do, Clews?'

'What?'

'Why do you do this? Plots and counterplots and betrayal? Why not go back off and farm, or whatever it is you want?' The truth of his life struck her so clearly. You see those cages, and you know you'll die like that just as well as I do.

'I found I was good at it. I enjoy it.' *I might not in the end die like that.*

They walked on together, because neither of them had anywhere really to go.

'Will she make peace?' Lidae asked.

'Who, Elayne?' You mean 'would she', I think, Lidae? Would she, if she were to defeat King Temyr, our king, which she will not, would she make peace? I don't know. I don't imagine so.'

'King Durith, her father, you said, wanted peace.'

'Did I?'

'That was why Temyr rose up against King Durith, you said. Because King Durith was weak, wanted to disband the army, make peace.'

'I... Yes. Yes, you're right. I had forgotten.'

They walked on a little further, walking aimlessly, the Winged Blades are camped just near here, in fact, if you remember. 'What will you tell Samei? If you want,' Clews said, 'I could do it, Lidae. If you wanted me to. It might be easier, perhaps, coming from me.'

'Yes! You're right, yes, it would be.' But Lidae stopped walking, turned away from Clews. 'No. I'll do it.' Whatever I can find to say, I'll say.

She thought: curse Emmas. Curse Cythra. They would have no idea in the world what to say, either of them. I've told men their comrade's been killed. Samei was stuck inside me, dying, Cythra said he would die, it tore my body but I birthed him. I can find the words to tell him this, and the way to make it all well.

'Are you sure you don't want me to do it?' Like he wanted to do it. It was so tempting. Comforting. He'd do it well, better than she could, man to man, and none of the memories.

'I have to do it.' When this is over and Elayne is defeated, she thought, Ryn and Samei and I, we can make something different.

Tomorrow, she could hear her voice whispering. Tomorrow, next time, I promise, it will be different.

Samei's camp was half-deserted. Lidae started around her in fear, because they must have been sent out on a raiding mission, a skirmish, Ayllis had said the enemy was only a few days march away. Black clad horsemen breathing out cold fire, cutting Samei down, he'd ride at them, refuse to retreat. She waited fearfully also for Samei's slavewoman to come out of his tent. There was a whoop of young man's laughter—boy's laughter— from behind the tents off in a thicket of trees. It was growing colder, threatening rain, but when Lidae followed the sounds she found a group of young men playing about there, they'd thrown a stick up into the high branches of a tree and were playing the ancient boys' game of trying to knock it down by throwing other sticks up at it. Not a very edifying game, Lidae thought, for these well-born young soldier-heroes.

'Hey!' One of them had found a dead branch as long as a spear shaft.

'Oh, come on, that's utter cheating.'

'Yes, but he'll never get it high enough.'

'Throw it! Throw it!'

It went up, hit the tree nowhere near the stick, came down narrowly missing one of them. He picked it up, waved it at his friends, then a brilliant idea struck him, he made a little run, used the branch to help him jump. 'Vault!' The branch snapped clean in half in a shower of rotten wood-dust. The boy himself went down on his right knee with a yell of surprise, got up with a shamefaced expression and a grazed leg.

'Stupid bloody stick.'

'Seras, you stupid!'

'Might have worked.'

Samei made a great leap, higher and further than his friend Seras. He whooped, seemed delighted-surprised he's jumped so high, did it again.

'That's jumping, Seras!'

'No, that's showing off, Samei.'

Samei whooped and leaped again. A wonder to her, that she had birthed such a thing: why me, out of all mothers, to be so blessed in him?

Seras shouted 'Yes! I hit the stick!'

'Doesn't count, no one saw it.'

'Oh, what?'

'Yes, what. We were too busy watching Samei jumping.'

'Oh what? Oh, what?' He threw another stick, the stick went nowhere near the first stick and itself got stuck in the tree, then they saw Lidae watching.

A pause, young boys' embarrassment, several of them had twigs and dried leaves in their hair, they all had the dusty tree bark and soil and lichen coating to them that made Lidae's hands itch. Shaking the boys' shirts out, sighing over the rips and the dirt, the faint mouldy smell to it, a horror that she'd find beetle larvae, the way it got into the seams. Samei shuffled forward, utterly embarrassed about everything, but she thought with such happiness that he was pleased to see her also. He looked about ten years old suddenly. He felt about ten years old, hugged her suddenly. She braced herself for his friends to laugh, her son to step back embarrassed, tell her to go away. They didn't laugh, and he didn't step away.

'What's wrong?' Samei asked. Full of concern and care, he drew back a little to look down at her face. 'Mother?'

And she couldn't say it, *'come over here, Samei, we should go, not to your tent, somewhere else, because, and I have to tell you, you know your brother? Of course you know your brother, what am I even saying? You remember Ayllis? Gods, of course you remember Ayllis, but your brother, and Ayllis, well...'*

'Nothing's wrong,' Lidae said. 'Nothing. You've got a twig in your hair, Samei.' She pulled it out, she had to reach up now, what beautiful hair he has, she thought. It was very clean and shining. Apart from the dirt and the leaf litter. 'And a woodlouse, oh Samei.'

'That's his favourite pet,' his friend Seras said.

'I've got some honey cakes back at my tent,' said Samei, 'would you like a honey cake, Mother? Not you, Seras, you already ate half of them.'

'Let me get the woodlouse of your hair first, littlest one?' That did make him flush and stiffen. 'Hero Sameirith, I mean I'm sorry.'

'"Littlest one" is less embarrassing,' he muttered at no one.

Lidae thought then of the woman in Samei's tent. She was frightened and unwilling at first, Lidae thought, yes, it's natural, I was frightened the first time, with Emmas, and I chose him. But, this boy, smiling, he tried to rest his head on his mother's shoulder as they sat eating the cakes even though he was taller than Lidae was, and the cakes themselves were stale but he hadn't noticed they were stale just because. The woman belongs to a great hero. She must feel honoured now. Proud, to have been chosen as a prize by such as Samei, a hero's woman. Eralene would like very much to share Samei's tent for a night. How much better it felt, to be able confidently and calmly to think that.

'These cakes are inedible, Samei,' she said, instead of all the things in the dark she'd thought of saying, the grief and shame and rage at him, 'how can you not have noticed?'

'Now you mention it,' Samei said, 'they are inedible. But Seras ate six of them without complaining.'

'Good for Seras.'

Ayllis is lying, she thought, she's a spy trying to unsettle us. Sameirith the hero! Bring him down, attack him, make him weak. Ryn gets angry, he says these things. I hate him, Mummy, I hate him, why did he have to be born? I wish he was dead, over the most stupid little things, you're disgusting, Ryn, how can you say that about your baby brother? Look how much he loves you, if you ever say that again, I'll, I'll, gods help me, Ryn.

'It's what all children say, my boys couldn't go an hour, some days, without one of them yelling at the other two like that,' Cythra would say, when Lidae fretted over it, *'What have I done, Cythra, should I only have had the one, why do they feel this what did I do bringing them up to make them feel like this? I try so hard Cythra, what is it I'm doing wrong?'* Cythra's boys seemed so normal, so contented.

'If a battle comes, Samei,' she said, 'when it comes, I mean,' for she had seen his face, he knew battle was coming and when, it was strange and exciting to be talking to him about this secret they both shared, like talking to him about a Sun Return gift for Ryn. 'When the battle comes, Samei.' But the words after that … she tried to force it, like forcing standing in line when the dragon fire and the magefire comes. The words crowded on her tongue howling to come out but she could not speak them.

They should have caught Ayllis, Lidae thought, sneaking into our camp, how could anyone not see her coming, bringing such horror into our camp? She should have burned like those dark riders. Reeked of carrion.

'When the battle comes, Samei.'

It's a vast army, Clews said, Queen Elayne outnumbers us two to one, what are the chances really, ever, of Ryn and Samei coming anywhere near each other? Two men in a battle, like two pebbles on the shore meeting.

'When the battle comes, Samei.'

Ayllis was lying. Lying. Lying. Ryn is my son. My best beloved son.

'When the battle comes, Samei... Be careful, Samei. Please.'

He was eating one of the stale cakes, deeply contemplative. 'These really are stale, aren't they? I paid good coin for them. Do you think I was conned? Seras, how could you eat these, you clown? They're like sawdust.'

'Be careful, I said, Samei. Samei, are you listening?'

He turned his face to her young and smiling. 'Be careful. Obviously, yes.' She couldn't tell him. So innocent. He'll never know, it never need bother him.

Later, when she left him, she saw his woman go over to him, not tied up or forced or anything, walk straight up to him, and she thought triumphantly: you see?

Forty-eight

A meadow in early summer, when the grass is lush and green, flowers grow up in the sunlight silvered with dew on their petals that are soft as a child's hair. The cattle plunge through to go down to the streambank where whitelace grows in thick piles, lick at the mud and the water; a boy goes with them, herding them gently, his feet are bare and the dew and the flowers stain his skin. Cowslip, pale golden, primroses, paler still, a riot of glowing buttercups, the milky flush of children flower, lark's feather cool and delicate. The hedgerow is thick with honeysuckle, perfumed with wild garlic, still holds the last of autumn leaves at its roots; on the other side of the stream there are purple irises, pink mallows, and then woodland, the new leaves bursting joyfully green-golden, filled with birdsong, bluebells lie like deep pools. Downstream an orchard is in full blossom, white petals tinged with blushing pink. In a cottage garden there is lavender for healing, dog roses for beauty, bean plants bloom crimson red. The wind blows softly, sets all the colour dancing, clouds come over the sun and the light changes, the sky in the west grows darker with a fine fresh rain. A traveller stops on the roadway, looks over the country with pleasure, smiles; a long time he has been walking, and the sight is sweet and good.

So was the army of Queen Elayne, drawn up vast before them in the sun when they awoke the next morning. Bright armour, high-stepping horses, strong handsome young soldiers, red banners fluttering.

Queen Elayne herself has hair as black as midnight, her skin is white as snow and her lips are red with the blood she has shed. Queen Elayne is unnatural, monstrous, a woman in battle, she is beautiful as death itself, her armour is trimmed with pearls and emeralds and lily flowers, any man who sees her falls in love with her even as she kills him. She lights a candle every day in memory of her murdered parents, she has dedicated her heart and her maidenhead to righteous vengeance, she walked alone up to the gates of Thalden dressed in white and crowned in flowers and implored the people to open the gates to her in her dead father's beloved name. She whored herself to the footsoldiers at the gates of Thalden, the merchants of Thalden in their rich houses, the very beggars in the city streets, and that is why they opened the gates to her, she chooses a fresh soldier every night for her lover she has given herself to every Lord of Illyrith and that is how she has raised her army and bound it to her in treachery. She has burned Lord Sabryyr's estates, killed King Temyr's wife and Prince Fiol's young children, sworn that every man who fights against her is guilty of her father's murder and must be punished for it. She has promised any man who abandons King Temyr's army a bag of gold and a farm and chance to live in peace. She is the daughter of the true king, King Durith, therefore she is queen by right of birth. King Temyr has proved himself in battle, has brought Illyrith such glory, while this woman, Elayne, she is … well…

Such words ran around the camp as the soldiers woke and blinked and stared and cried in rage and cried in fear as they learned who this enemy was and why it was they were fighting.

'A young warrior queen…' Eralene said, breathless.

'A young warrior queen…' Deljan said, marvelling.

The Army of Queen Elayne has a fine position, perhaps two miles from where King Temyr was camped, squatted on the road back to Illyrith. A wide rolling plain riddled with gullies, marshy, awkward under foot, a short gentle rise of dry ground where they waited, a river, narrow but with deep, steep banks and a fast current, anchoring their right flank. In the winter cold the ground is crusted with frost. Moss and reeds and coarse grass sparkling, catching the first light. The earth is armed against them, wrapped hard in metal. Pools of brown-tinged water have a thin black skin of ice. Under the weight of a man's feet the ice will crack, the hard earth will open, mud will suck around soldiers' ankles as they march. It's a long march through the frozen mud. There is frost on the enemy's fine gleaming armour, the points of their spears crusted with it. The sun is behind them, low and brilliant, will be in their assailants' eyes as they march up.

The better position by far, defensive yet aggressive—but they have marched all night in armour, they stand now in their ranks, frozen, weary, watching, waiting for the attack. Lord Sabryyr should take the initiative, lead his troops at once to attack. Let the enemy wait and they will be dug in solidly there, throw up ditches and palisades and horse-breaking man-killing spikes. But the men are taken by surprise, confused, confounded, 'King Durith's daughter!' men whisper in the camp. A long march up to engage them, men can stumble in the marshes, loose themselves, foul themselves in gullies and ice-rimed pools. A cavalry charge uphill is a nightmare. An assault by massed infantry, on rough boggy ground, uphill, is worse. But they have marched all night in armour in the cold. But we could make them stand all day now waiting. But then they will get themselves established, dug in. But our spies say she has left her baggage far behind her, will have little food with her, make her wait, sit tight by our fires with hot food and hot wine and comforts, make her men grow hungry and envious as they wait. But 'King Durith's daughter…' voices in the army whisper with longing.

But we— But they— But, on the other hand— Queen Elayne has the better position, uphill, well defended, with the marsh before her, the river to her flank. Our men are rested, warmer, better fed. The ground is crusted with frost, the sky is heavy, a cold thin rain soaks its way into the men's bones.

Lidae stared down into the colours and movement trying to see Ryn. Staring across at the tiny figures, a blur of movement and sometimes sounds would drift over, shouting, sometimes smoke from the enemy campfires would be blown on the wind. That man there, or there, or there—any one of them could be my son. I should be able to see Ryn there shining out at me.

Forty-nine

All day they sat and waited, while the enemy stood and waited on the hill beyond for them.

The rasping sound of Deljan sharpening and sharpening his sword. Lucky whetstone, he said. Spat on the ground, rubbed his hands, spat again, worked on the sword past any point of needing to sharpen it. The sound set Lidae's teeth on edge, droning on and on and on, but they left him alone with it because he needed to do it. Some of them sat quiet, even slept. Some of them needed to do something to keep from running screaming. Bed a woman. Sharpen a sword. Polish their armour till it shone. Maerc had tried to mend something of his that wasn't needed for battle—a spare shoe, his blanket, a new handle for his eating knife, something, anything. Acol had said he broke things on purpose, in the days before a battle, so he had something to mend. One of the others had done the opposite, tried his hardest to accidentally break something he didn't need for the battle, his spoon or his cup or his haircomb, say loudly 'well, doesn't matter, does it? This time tomorrow I'll be dead.'

The greatest magecraft of all. A lot of them ran to bed a woman or drink or gamble for the same reason, said loudly, 'It's the last time, this is the last time, this time tomorrow I'll be dead.' Lidae looked over towards the distant lines of the enemy camp. Ryn would be there. Remaking his promise? Regretting it? These two huge armies, Lidae thought. They won't meet. We won't meet.

Around noon a great shout of joy rang out across the camp.

King Temyr and Prince Fiol had arrived with a thousand spearmen and a thousand horsemen. King Temyr had fought a skirmish with the enemy, routed them. His banner flashed brilliant red, a new one, huge, it took two men to hold the great ivory that held it. His tent was set up, so vast and so covered in gold embroidery it was too bright to look at. A great council of war was held.

'Half the horses are ridden to death, won't be any use to anyone.'

'Half the spearmen are wounded.'

'The other half haven't got their spears.'

'By 'routed them', they mean, 'lost''.

'He's frightened. Cacking it. A friend of a friend, she saw him ride in.'

'The young prince, too. Been injured and everything.'

'And alone like that… Where are the other lords? All the rest of the king's great army? This it?'

'We're it?'

She says … But he … He'll change his mind … It … When…

No one quite knew where these rumours came from. The squad captain had orders to have anyone whipped, who repeated them.

'Hurrah!' they cheered, at the squad captain's order. 'Hurrah for the king.' It was freezing cold. A few flakes of snow in the air. The enemy must be cold, too, without tents to shelter in?

Eralene said to Lidae, 'I'd pay good coin for someone to smash Deljan's whetstone. Really, I would.' She looked over at the horizon. Two women, waiting for tomorrow's dying. Longing for it. Fearing it. Oddly, Lidae thought then of Samei's woman sitting so afraid in her master's tent waiting for her master to come back. *'Bed a woman.'* What horrible words to use, she thought. 'Drink some wine, play some dice, bed a woman.' If Emmas had ever said that about me, I would have— *'You really think you can bed Lidae, Emmas? Five in iron says you can't.'*

'He'll break his bloody sword,' said Eralene, 'if he keeps sharpening it like that. It'll be so sharp there's nothing left of it.'

At dusk they lined up to watch King Temyr raise the luck horse for them.

It was many years since Lidae had last seen him. Four? Five? Cythra had been alive then, she thought, and Ryn had still been with her, teaching Samei how to use a sword properly, 'Like this, Samei. It's easy, see, if I show you?' She remembered Temyr in his glory, the first time she saw him as her king. Bloodied after battle, golden, glowing. He had seemed huge, in her mind, great and vast as if he had towered over the lesser men around him. As true heroes and kings did. He had been brilliant in his power, she remembered so clearly, the light that danced around him, the knowledge of power and victory that cloaked him. Follow me! Follow me! I will reward you! I will give you wondrous things! That is a man and a leader, she had thought. That is a warrior. That is a king.

He had aged, she saw now. His golden hair and long golden beard had turned grey. His face was tired, with pouched eyes that reminded her suddenly of her father. Queen Elayne had killed his wife and his young grandchildren, she remembered. As he had once killed Elayne's family: and he must think of that. He was smaller than she remembered him. If I did not know he was the king, she thought, the greatest king and warleader in Irlawe, would I pick him out as our king? He looks like any other man. Tired and old.

He looks like King Durith, she thought, before the battle in which Durith died and Temyr was made king. And one day Queen Elayne will grow old, and another man will rise up to be king. *It's my kingdom. Mine. No, it's mine, mine, mine, Mummy, Mummy, tell him.* As long as I survive and my children survive, Lidae thought, what do I care? As long as I can earn coin and live. Ten years, I fought for King Durith, twelve years I have fought for King Temyr, my king, my lord, my sworn captain, I will hold the line, I will not fear, I will kill for him, I will die for him.

The horse was led forward. It was very fine, as it must be, caparisoned in scarlet so that it looked bathed in fire, or in blood. The king looked very old and shrunken, next to the great warhorse. And Prince Fiol, who stood watching, only a few years older than Samei... Prince Fiol's young wife and infant children had been murdered, he was young and facing war: Lidae thought, I am being unfair, it is to be expected that he looks so drawn and sick just as his father does, his mother and his wife and his children are newly dead, he is a fighting a terrible new war. But Prince Fiol saw it too, she could tell in the way he held himself.

King Temyr raised his great sword high, and the torchlight flashed on the blade. Rune words written there, cut deep into the iron: *strength*, the king's sword said, and *triumph*, and *power over all men*. Samei's face moved, Lidae saw that he was looking not at the king himself but at the runes. The horse whinnied, afraid, stamped its hooves; Lidae had a rush of fear that it would rear up or bolt away, leaving Samei humiliated. The great blade came down, the horse was still and silent for the stroke, crumpled down, Samei stood with the body huge before him, all soaked in hot blood. King Temyr raised the sword to the sky with the horse's blood running down it. Brought the blade down again and again to hack off the horse's head.

The horse's head on a spear shaft, driven into the hard earth. The army flooded back to their tents, to sit and wait for the final orders to fight. Lidae stared around, trying to see Samei again, but he was gone in the mass of soldiers that flowed like a live thing. A trumpet sounded two notes, bright and silvered, the call for the cavalry to ready themselves for action. They said tomorrow, Lidae thought, we're nowhere near being ready to form up. Now? Every man in the squad looking around them, eyes fearful. Not now, we haven't got ourselves properly ready, everyone said we had until dawn. A few, perhaps, with the hungry face, eager: 'that was our trumpet-call, no, listen, it sounds like our trumpet call, it does, if they're going up, we'll be going…' A brief flurry of action in parts of the camp, men moving in eddies, something was happening, their own time would very soon come. Battle in the dark. Lidae hated fighting in the dark.

'Those traitors, then, over there—they got eyes that can see at night?'

'Magecraft. Turned them all into, like, bats.'

'Madness.'

Men were moving, yes, something was happening. 'Get yourselves ready, you lot, get sharp to it,' the squad captain shouted to them. 'Come on. Come on.'

I should tell Samei, Lidae thought. Tell him about Ryn. Sit here for long hours, cold and anxious, 'Ryn, Samei, my beloveds,' waiting, waiting, he's near, but I can't leave here; any moment the order could come…

In the dark, men pressed up together, bronze helmets hiding their faces: they could kill each other without even knowing. I could kill Ryn myself, she thought, and never know, and never even know for certain that he is dead. His child's body, crumpled in the dark, firelight playing on his golden curls, when Temyr's soldiers came and she had thought that he was dead. When he was born, she thought, I was sure that he was dead. My blade dancing around me, poet of the sword, light in my eyes, these dark shapes up against me, killing them, in the dark they're not even men just shadows, they see me as shadows, as nothing. Dragon fire and mage fire on their helmets. I cut my son down, cut him open, he dies without knowing it was me, I never know that I killed him.

But the order to fight didn't come, the stirring in the camp quieted, they went back to their tents, sat by their fire waiting. At dawn, the squad captain said. Waiting. Waiting. Go and find him. Look out towards the enemy lines—I should be able to see Ryn.

'When the battle's over,' Eralene said, 'I'm going to buy myself a new dress. Rosy pink, with gold embroidery on the bodice. I'll wear it in the evenings, when we're back doing nothing at Navikyre Fortress.'

Deljan spat for luck, held his hand in a warding gesture. 'Don't talk like that, gods, don't tempt death like that.'

'Silk ribbons for my hair,' Eralene said. 'Pink, to match.'

Then someone's boot buckle snapped, for no reason, he was cursing and Eralene pointed out that it was lucky beyond lucky that it had happened now at the last moment he could try and fix it, not just as they drew up to meet a cavalry charge, she'd told him he needed to get the thing fixed days ago. Weeks ago.

'Weeks ago?'

'Maybe not weeks ago. Days ago. But I did tell you, Delin. Twice at least.'

'I thought it would hold.'

'You mean you bodged it with some string.'

'You mean you're too cheap to buy a new one in case you die tomorrow.'

'I mean I thought I'd fixed it.'

'Well, you obviously didn't fix it, did you? Gods, stop being so hopeless, you. I'll have a look at it. Bodge it better with some more string.'

'Be easy to recognise his corpse tomorrow, anyway.'

Silence.

'That's going to far, Deljan. Not funny.'

'No. No, sorry.'

'Of course it was funny. That'll learn Delin, won't it, if he's only recognisable by his broken boot.'

'Send his boot back to his old mum. *"This was all we could find of him..."*'

'Now that's really not funny, Deljan.'

'No. No. sorry.'

They cooked a meal, camp servants came around with wine. King Temyr had sent around wine for everyone in the army. Lidae had been polishing her armour, pointlessly but she must do something, in the weak light of their campfire it looked brilliant as mirrors and she couldn't see where it might need cleaning so keep on and on cleaning it. Broke off when the slave came with the wine to eat and drink.

'An hour or two more,' the squad captain said. 'Then we're up.'

'You said dawn half an hour ago.'

'That was half an hour ago. What I'm saying now is, an hour or so more then we're up.'

'Bet you he's still saying that an hour before dawn,' someone muttered.

'An hour after dawn, more like.'

It was very dark, no stars, no moon. Their campfire burned very low; the flames had a green tinge to them. It made the tents look like they were made of green leaves. The bronze of their armour looked like it was soiled with verdigris. Keep polishing it.

'Something's happening,' Eralene said.

A crash and a shriek, very high above them. They shivered, hunched close by the fire, looked up at the sky once and then tried not to look. Dark shadows, darker than the clouds. Movements in the air, swirls, shapes. A trick of the darkness, of the firelight, because they were afraid, that was all they could see. Thank the gods the clouds were low and heavy, Lidae thought. In bright moonlight, the things we might see. Think we could see. The battle had begun already, then, while they sat awaiting their final orders, not men fighting but dragons and god-beasts. In the thick clouds the king's dragon and the queen's dragon met with claws and teeth and fire, tearing each other, rending each other, burning. Burning. A thing like a man, horse-headed, long-clawed, dark as shadows, its limbs as long and as fragile as birch trees; Lidae had glimpsed it in the twilight once, following the army, half-insubstantial, its hooves leaving no marks on the snowy ground. It loomed now in the sky to the north, grown vast as a hillside, wrestling and stalking a beast all of white light. The western horizon rang with fire. An endless painful shrieking. Then a silence like a blow, more painful and more frightening than the shrieks themselves. Then a flash of red light, a smell of burning, and another scream. A smell in the air, cloying, perfumed. Spices, meat going rotten, honey. Childbirth, shit, the sickbed. A sound, briefly, almost overhead, of heavy wings.

We have a great magelord who will take the dragon. Lady Nayle, grown old in King Temyr's service, her hair they say is grey now, her hands shake on her staff; but she can fight a dragon, blast it with white fire into nothing, although she looks so small and frail. The king's aged mother, you would think her. She has fought gods and monsters for three kings. Look to the west, we will see her raising magefire white and blue and bright silver, ripping wounds in the dragon's skin. Lidae and all of them craning up, staring, hoping.

A scream, and a flash of white light. Somewhere in their camp a human voice moaned in terror. A trumpet rang, very distant, off to the north. Or she imagined it.

'Oh gods,' Deljan cried out. 'What's happening?'

The first great battle Deljan had fought, Lidae remembered. Or Eralene, or most of them. She smiled at Deljan, and at Eralene. Kind, motherly, reassuring smile. 'The strangest thing in the world, this, sitting around waiting to go into battle. Just … sit and try to do something, like the captain said.' Nobody else would say it, so she said after a moment, 'It's natural, you know, to be scared. Most people are scared. I heard a story once about a great general, a great warrior, never lost a battle, and he wet himself before every battle, he was so scared.'

A snigger, eyes rolled awkwardness, 'That's not true.'

'Gods, that's disgusting.'

Mealy-mouthed, old-woman, motherly use of the words 'wet himself'. *Pissed himself. Shat himself.* But they both looked easier, once she'd said it, Deljan's hunched shoulders relaxed a little, he took out his whetstone again before Eralene glared at him and he put it back away. Old motherly old woman words, Lidae thought, they'll laugh again behind my back tomorrow, if I die tomorrow. But she thought they had listened with more respect, now that she was the mother of a hero.

'I've fixed your boot for you, Delin, you hopeless,' Eralene said. 'Gods know how you thought you'd mended it. But here. Try it on.' A useful, pleasing thing to do. A reassuring thing to do.

'Thank you. Well done.' They all watched very solemn while Delin, who had also never seen a real battle before, tried the boot on. He got up, stamped around, and the buckle came loose again. 'Damn.'

'Let me look at it again.'

'No … No, there's no point.'

'No, look, you can't go into battle like that, with it flapping.'

'I'll tie it. It's fine. It's fine.' His voice broke, on the last word 'fine'. He got up, went into his tent. He was crying. Trying not to show he was crying.

Silence.

'How long before the order comes, do you think?' Deljan said.

A crash overhead. And a trumpet and a drum, off away somewhere very distant. A flash of white. A sound that might have been men fighting. Metal, iron striking bronze.

'They're fighting?' Deljan said in panic, 'Why aren't we fighting?' Like they'd been forgotten, battle joined and men dying, and someone forgot about all the infantry waiting by their tents.

'Skirmishing. Things off in the plain, in the hills to the north. I don't know.'

'Why don't they give the order? Gods.' Deljan's heels were drumming on the ground, he almost started up the whetstone again. 'Why are we waiting around when it's happening?'

A scream, somewhere far away. A distant beat of wings. That smell in the air, faint and brief.

'Soon,' Lidae said.

Delin came out of his tent, trying to look happy. 'The boots are fine, now, look, I tied them. Pissed himself! I bet you made that story up to tell your kids.'

'Ryn threw my stick into Cythra's pigpen, Mummy.' His face all wet with tears. Endless outraged crying.

'That's not true! Samei threw the stick himself and I said he'd have to go and get it out himself if he wanted it back. But Samei's such a coward, when I said he'd have to go and get it back himself he cried.'

'That's not true! Ryn threw it!'

'Samei threw it. But then he was so scared of the pigs he cried.'

'It's all right, babies. Little ones. Samei, you foolish baby thing.'

'I wasn't scared! Ryn did it!'

'It's not good to lie, Samei, little one, is it?'

He wails, howls, beats his hands in the air. 'I wasn't frightened.'

That's why he did it, she thinks. And later Emmas tells them a story about a great general who gets scared before every battle, even though he's never lost a battle, cries with fear, even wets himself, and they laugh. Acol told her the story as a joke, when she first joined, these stupid grand leaders in their fancy armour she moons over. Years later Emmas told her the same story, all serious and not realising it was made up, because he got scared, she'd realised, every time, he hated fighting. He'd held her hand when they scraped pus from the wound in her thigh, she owed him, so she never told him.

But she's never talked to her children about feeling anything in battle, no. How it feels. How sometimes it's so very frightening. Never told them that story, even to make them laugh, never thought to tell them, talk to them.

'A great soldier told it to me,' Lidae said. 'I don't know.'

A crash overhead, louder. Green lights and red and gold and shining star-bright silver. A scream, loud and sudden. The sky was lit up like the sun. Sunlight flashing on water. Winter sunlight in Illyrith that caught the tops of the high hills behind the village, made the bare rocks golden, the clouds golden, the birds circling there, sparks of light. The scream came again, ringing with pain and triumph. Far, far distant overhead.

Deljan cried out, 'What is it? What's happening?'

Lidae said, reassuring, herself awed, 'Dragons. It's the dragons fighting.' Dragon fire brilliant as the sunrise. Deljan's face was lit up glowing.

A burst of green light, a roll of silver like a wave breaking, a shower of golden sparks, a crash. Deljan clutched his hands to his ears. A strong, horrible smell of blood. Men's voices, distant, roaring something. A war cry, triumphant, but tinged with great shame and sorrow. A shriek in the sky, so loud she could see it as a jagged flicker in her mind. Something beautiful and terrible is so quickly dead. Wash of fire, the whole of the sky lit golden, Eralene's pale face was golden, beautiful in the flames. Fire rolling across the sky, eddies of fire, and white mage fire, blue mage light. Lidae thought: Deljan is right, why is the trumpet not ringing out to call us to battle? They are fighting, the great beasts, why do we not fight? They fight and die … I want to fight.

But the fire and the lights faded a little, the screams and the roar grew less, the battle moved away into the east. I wonder, Lidae thought, are we winning? We must be. But if we are winning, then Ryn … Ryn…

We'll win but he won't die and neither will Samei. I could turn my coat, she thought. Lord Sabryyr might go over to the enemy, with all of us under him. Elayne is King Durith's daughter, King Durith was a wise king, a great king, I was loyal to him. Samei and I, we could go over to his lines, join Ryn. Imagine his face and his joy, when we came to stand beside him.

Imagine it, she thought. Fighting beside both my children. How rare that is. What a glorious thing. A wash of red fire lit the sky, a gust of hot wind, death stink on it, hot metal, roast meat. Screaming. Shouting. Great beasts and grieving, dying men. Both her sons, together, beside her, screaming and dying, burning away, their skin and their bones melting away.

What all men long for, she thought. To see their sons dead.

The sky blazed green as water. Eralene's skin was cast in green. Soon, Lidae thought. The order to fight will come very soon. In the east where the dragons fought, the earth and the sky were torn away. A shriek. Filling the world. Grieving.

Such fury.

They saw it flying over them, high in the sky, twisting itself in pain as it flew. Its body was ripped open, its beautiful golden scales, the great strength of its limbs. Its head with its terrible eyes that a man must never look into, which were twin skies filled with stars and shadows the poets said. Ragged wounds ripped across the wonderous blossom of its wings. It threw back its head and vomited fire, flames dark and liquid, soiled with its dying pain. Its wings blazed up in fire like coloured silk burning. The treasures of a king's palace sacked and smashed and burned. A dark shape came rushing after it, claws groped out. It moved like birds. And the shadow was like a hawk. Writhing, shrieking, spiralling. On and on up through the night clouds. Plunged and bucked. Twisted. Teeth bared, fleeing. But the shadow caught it.

So small, the shadow creature. Lidae thought of men surging against the walls of a city. Tiny weak things flung against towers of stone. The dragon screamed in pain so vast the ground shook beneath her. A great explosion of white blazing flame.

A hot wind on her face. Rattle of rocks and trees. The tent canvass creaked in the wind. The smell of burning hair, singed cloth, hot wood, hot metal. Her armour was warm against her skin.

It came down to earth, far to the north of them, a sunset in the midnight dark.

Then gone. Nothing.

A long silence in the sky and in all the men watching. All that lives on the face of the earth stops a moment, grieves a moment, when a dragon dies, they say. A sigh of grief from the trees, from the stones of the hill they were camped upon. The moon and the stars, the clouds, all stricken with grief.

A dim rumble of green lights in the east where some strange sad beast was still fighting. A crack of lightning, a scream, a flicker growing dim. That battle too fading. Ending.

'The order will come now,' Lidae said. 'Any moment. We'll fight.' The night was very calm now. All the battle fury briefly spent. Who won? Who is winning?

She got up from the fire, went towards her own tent, and Samei stepped out of the darkness.

His face and hair were stained black, he smelled of smoke and scorched metal, like a pot boiling dry on the hearth. He had already been fighting. There was blood on his armour, on his hands and his face.

A hero, cast out of bronze and iron. A man. A stranger. Lidae thought: I can barely think that he's my son. He smelled of drink, too, over the heat smells.

His voice was angry: 'The dragon...' And exultation: 'I was fighting

the dragon! I was part of … We wounded it! I wounded it!' And pain:
'Seras is dead.'

Oh Samei. Little one. Little one. Baby one.

A rumble of green fire, in the east, far away. In its wake, the first traces
of the morning's gloaming. Any moment now, the trumpets would ring.
A long low howl rose now over the camp, very sad, almost frightened.
The cry of something lost, like a seabird calling. Lights in the sky, high
up almost hidden in the clouds. Lidae might have thought they were
stars.

'Why aren't you fighting already?' He shouted, 'I've been fighting
since sunset.'

Lidae said, 'Are we winning?'

'I don't know.' He stumbled, almost fell. 'You infantry … you should
be fighting.'

The plain where they would fight almost visible now against the
morning's gloaming. Tiny figures drifting, moving. They looked like
snow. In the north, a flash of white magefire.

'Samei—'

The trumpet rang the order.

Lidae leapt to her feet.

Samei stepped towards her, his face … She thought: he thought I was
leaping up to hug him. Comfort him.

'Samei…'

I have to go. The trumpets. All this long night, death raging around
me, over me, I have to go now, the trumpets, and there's no time, it's too
late. He'll die. I'll die. Ryn—

'Samei!' She threw her arms around him. Baby, baby, baby Samei
littlest one. 'Samei: Ryn is down there fighting. He's sworn to kill you,
Samei. Samei! Promise me, swear it—if you see him, if you fight him,
swear to me you won't kill him.'

The trumpets rang. Pale blue light in the east. All this long night, and
it's too late. The trumpets rang. She dropped her arms from around him.
Pushed his arms off her, pulled herself away. Almost shoved him away.
Grabbed up her sword. Deljan's voice: 'Lidae! Where are you?' Eralene's
voice: 'We're fighting. Now. Lidae.' The trumpets. A drum began to
beat. If he'd come a moment earlier … All night she'd been sitting here,
waiting.

The trumpets, voice calling, 'Lidae! Lidae!'

I love you, Samei.

It's all right to be afraid, littlest one.

He looked at his mother with great dark eyes. 'I know about Ryn, mother. if I see him … If I see him, mother, I'll kill him. I swear it. I'll kill him.'

Ryn loves you, Samei. Like I do. Like you love him.

Curse you, Samei. Rapist. Monster.

I hope Ryn kills you, if he finds you.

She ran from her son into battle.

Fifty

Rank upon rank of them. Long lines, soldiers armed and armoured, bronze helmets covering their faces, making them no longer men. Marching down all together shoulder to shoulder, keep the ranks, keep in time, the trumpet rings, the drum beats, they cease to think of themselves as men, as single beings, they are a line marching together to fight together, they do as the trumpets order them. Keep the line. Keep the soldier next to you from dying. The shame and the grief, if you are the one who breaks. Hard to remember, in the drumbeats and the trumpets, bronze-clad, staring straight ahead, hard to remember that the soldier beside you is a man, his name is Delin, he was crying in his tent, he was afraid, if he dies, he will be identified by his broken boot. The bronze is a wall between you and the world you lived in. You cannot hear him breathing. You cannot feel his eyes trying to see your face. You are carrying a spear, an ashwood spear, a magewood spear, a deathwood spear, a spear made of keep-safe, of north-tree, of soldier's-tree. You have drilled carrying the spear until your arms are aching, you are so used to its weight on you that you barely feel it, like a man does not feel the weight of his limbs. But you are so very aware of it, the weight of it, the smooth feel of the wood beneath your hand, a slight dent in the wood there, a slight shift in the balance as you walk downhill and bend your body so slightly back. Your sword is at your side, that, too, you are so used to, the weight of it on your hip, the feel of the swordbelt. Man-killer, life-stealer, iron-biting, death-in-iron, forged-wolf. It too feels different, you are more aware of it than you are of your breathing, hissing fast and frightened through your clenched teeth. You cannot remember your name, sometimes, in the line, pushing, struggling, feet slipping in the dust. You pant for breath, you grit your teeth, brace your body, all the muscles in your legs and your arms ache. You are not a man. Not a woman. You have no children, no lover, no parents, no friends.

You have your spear, and your sword, and the earth you stand on, the line of soldiers holding together, shoulder to shoulder, holding, holding. You cannot see them through the bronze of your helmet.

Why are you fighting? For your king? For glory?

You are not fighting for anything. You are fighting because you are fighting.

You birthed a child once. And when you were at the end of your labour, your body screaming, you've shat yourself, you're floating somewhere, lost in blind pain, no longer a part of yourself, if someone had said to you then, 'why are you struggling? What are you doing?' you would not have said that you were birthing a child, pushing a baby out of you into life. You were struggling because your body screamed that you had to struggle, because you could not stop it unless you fell dead.

It's like that, white and empty, and you don't remember it, like a dream you know you had but can't remember, when you fight. And you're never sure if it's the same for everyone there fighting. Sometimes you think it can't be. For those generals, those leaders, who say they know what's happening when they fight. Or those cowards who hang back, look for something, when they fight.

You think sometimes, in the last moments before the battle is joined, when you're waiting and the enemy are waiting so near you, and the sky is brilliant with fire overhead, 'Why am I doing this? What am I doing? Why don't I run?' You can't run. Like trying to run from the knowledge that you are mortal and will die one day. You thought it was impossible your child would ever been born, in the last days of your pregnancy, you could feel the child kick and move inside you, you had a cradle by your bed waiting, swaddling clothes, clout cloths, but when the village women said any day now, you'd have a baby in your arms, a living thing suckling at your breast—how could you believe them? Truly? You think, sometimes, in the last moments before battle is joined, that war is like that. You won't be dead. None of you will be dead. And the battle is a wall in your mind that you can't see across, to the time when you might be dead, and all those around you might be dead.

Your bronze helmet and your iron sword and your ashwood spear —in the last moments before the battle, these things are more real than you are, and more permanent.

Fifty-one

The soldiers stood to order behind the defences, waiting. There was frost too on their fine gleaming armour, the points of their spears crusted with it. Laughter in King Temyr's army: these fools, the queen in her naivety: they have marched all night in their armour, stood all day in the cold and then all night thinking the battle will come, while we have rested, eaten, warmed ourselves by our fires, readied ourselves to fight. Queen Elayne's soldiers have the better position by far, defensive, they squat on the road back to Illyrith and King Temyr must engage them—but they have stood all day and all night in armour, frozen, weary, waiting for King Temyr to assault them. A day and a night's wait and they are dug in solidly there, have thrown up ditches and palisades and horse-breaking, man-killing spikes. But they have stood all day and all night in armour in the cold, waiting, staring out into the night with the whispering running around, 'They're attacking! They're coming!'. But on the other hand— But we— But they—

Queen Elayne has the better position, uphill, well defended, with the marsh before her, the river to her flank. King Temyr's men are better rested, warmer, better fed. The ground is crusted with frost, the sky is heavy, a cold thin rain is falling, soaking its way into men's hair and bones.

A flock of birds, black on the dawn clouds. A column of smoke where the hills are burning. Dragon fire smouldering there. On one edge of Elayne's camp, they see as the sun rises slowly, there is black ash where something has been burned, a twist of shapeless metal, there is a smell of metal and ash and burned flesh. Something huge and terrible came down there, crushed the men standing waiting. Lidae thought of Samei fighting. Ryn, burned and dead.

The trumpets rang for them to stop their marching. They formed a long line standing shoulder to shoulder. The enemy before them, slightly above them, just out of bowshot reach. Lidae was three lines back from the front.

Bronze helmets watching them. Not seeing them. We see our deaths, they see their deaths. We see and they see only meat to kill. My companions beside me—I will not let them kill. King Durith fighting King Temyr, King Temyr fighting Queen Elayne ... years ago, when I was young, we fought to make Durith himself king. And years before that, before I was born, men fought and died for kings whose very names we have forgotten. We might switch sides in a heartbeat, if our commander choses. Turn on the men next to us, kill them or be killed by them. Waiting, waiting, with rain cold on our faces, the enemy's blind faces waiting back for us.

Lidae thought: I should be able to see Ryn. See Samei. Somewhere, off to her right, the Winged Blades would be posted in all honour in the van. Thousands of men in their rows, faceless, men of iron, uncountable as the waves of the sea: I will not meet Ryn or Samei. Samei won't meet him.

A trumpet, a single harsh note that called them to advance on the enemy. In perfect order they went forward, feet splashing in cold water, sticking in cold mud, keeping their formation over the rough ground, through gullies and stinking patches of bog. A drumbeat, a single lone drum, slowly, slowly, beating like a heart. Measuring the passage of their feet towards the enemy, keeping them from running. Spears lowered. Eyes narrowed. Teeth clenched.

The spell closes over her. Bright joy. The drum makes her shiver. The hairs on the back of her neck standing up, her blood pumping, racing. We fight for glory! For honour! We fight because killing is good!

She has to think that. Otherwise ... Every one of them, marching forward, spears held fixed at the enemy, they hold this in their hearts.

Children? Lovers? Parents? Justice? Coin? Bread?

Killing.

The last part was the worst, uphill, the slope was harder than it looked, the ground was loose earth, slippery with frost. Her feet slipped, holding the heavy spear straight and perfect. A deep ditch to scramble down and up again, freezing water splashing her legs. White magefire crackled overhead, shattering into the enemy ranks above waiting. Iron-men, standing waiting unflinching to meet their spears, three of them go down in front of her, collapse into nothing, the blast is strong enough to make her face flush hot, the smell is sickening. In silence the enemy ranks shift up, the gap is closed. Blind bronze faces wait.

A burst of magefire strikes their own lines. She can't see it, but she hears screams behind her, the same blast of heat on her back. She stumbles down and up another ditch. Men go down in the enemy ranks. Men go down in their ranks. She sees it this time out of the corner of her eyes, a flash of white and shrieks to her right. There are the stakes ahead of her, with the enemy in a solid mass behind them. Bronze spearpoints aimed at her throat. She is ready with her own spear. The sky begins to burn. A great thing of shadow is coming towards them on eagle's wings. Cursed thing. Magefire brings down a man so close she feels not heat but pain on her face. A neighing, like a horse, louder than a horse. The front ranks meet the stakes, push on them, their spears meet the enemy, the enemy spears meet them. A roar of fire at her back. The enemy's dragon. And she is trapped, third row back, between the enemy and the dragon's jaws.

Screams. They have a great magelord who will take the dragon. If she did not die last night. A great blast of heat and smoke, she can feel teeth and claws longer than her spear closing on her back. The lines behind her push forward, she pushes forward, up against the man in front of her whom she thinks dimly somewhere in the back of her mind might be someone she knows. Keep her spear held level. Brace herself. Move forward, pushing, crushing against the enemy line and the cruel stakes. The man beside her stumbled, rocked back with a hiss of breath. Flopped and fell sideways, blood at his throat. She pushed up to take his place, the spikes and the enemy right in front of her now, her spear caught and drove into enemy flesh. The line heaved itself, shifted: a stake loomed up right into her face. Almost lost her footing, jerking to avoid it, slipping in blood. A shout from the line, and a shout from the enemy. Hot harsh wind on the back of her neck.

Push. Push. Hold the line. Push. Her feet edge forward. Keep it going, keep working, keep the spear steady, keep the line, keep the line. Her face and her whole body are tight clenched. Eyes stare at her across the boundary, fix her face and for a moment her eyes and the enemy's eyes meet. Young eyes. Sad eyes. Wide and pale. She thrust with her spear, the line heaved and she heaved with it and the eyes vanished from her sight.

She felt herself go forward again, feet trampling over the dead. She almost slipped again. A stake loomed up in her face.

Howl, roar, shriek, in the line off to her left, a flash of light ringing in her head. Blind. Keep clenched, tight, pushing, holding. A great weight slammed into her back, throwing her forwards. Her spear slipping in her hands. The pressure pushed up against her to her left suddenly dropped off. A scream—not of pain but of triumph. A great rush of horses, so huge, like storm waves, came down shattering onto her. Flung up her spear, flung it out at the horsehead rushing towards her. Filling her eyes like a cloud covering the sun. The spear was ripped from her hands, shattered, she went reeling backwards into the man behind her, the ground sliding under her, hot fire wind roaring against the back of her neck. Roaring pain in her ears. She's hurt somewhere. The pressure of the line broke behind her, beside her. She almost fell as the pressure of it broke off. Groping to find the right way up, the right way forward. The sword was there at her hip, in her hand, lashing out already at the enemy. Fighting alone, pressing forward, the line breaking up into drifts and clumps of men struggling close up with their swords. A trumpet sounding urgent, rallying them. A great dizzying flash of white light, and an answering flash of blue. Her sword met the enemy, glanced off hard metal, bit into flesh.

A crash like thunder behind her. The earth shook. Horses' hooves, drumming down towards her. The front horse coming at her went down almost as it met her and crushed her beneath its hooves, horse and rider soaked red. The enemy line was dissolving into men running, hurling themselves at her with their swords out now, slipping and dancing on the boundary's edge. Her sword moved in her hand, whirled, cut, slashed, stabbed, an enemy's sword glanced off her armour, an enemy's sword struck at her left arm.

Across the boundary, her eyes met and held Ryn's.

Fifty-two

There was blood on him. He had lost his helmet. Blood in his beautiful shining golden hair, his perfect face. His fine armour—finer than her own, all bent and buckled with the weight of sword blades. Bloodied like it had been coloured red. A great cut hacked into his left arm.

Everything stopped around Lidae. The battle, the screaming, the heat of dragon fire. The red glass in the hilt of her sword winking, singing, *kill, come on, kill, you soldier, kill or be killed, you're a soldier, woman: fight, fight.* The sword hung loose in her hand, cold metal, as Lidae stared at her son.

He did not know her, in armour, her helmet over her face. Then he saw the sword, the red glass brilliant, and he looked at her and knew her. He recognised her, his mother, by the glass in her sword hilt.

I love you, love you, love you. My most beloved. In her heart, always, she has loved him more than Samei. Always. Why she fusses Samei so much, petties him, babies him, gives him things: because she will never love him as she loves Ryn. If she could go back to the time long ago when it was just her and Ryn … If she had to choose, between Samei and Ryn…

Ryn's mouth opened. He raised his sword; he lowered his sword. His eyes were fixed on her face.

A crash, the ground shook, the thunder of horses' hooves and of vast beating wings. Wavering, swimming in shadows, the battlefield came between them, Ryn turned, and he was fighting a man and she was fighting a man, and a shadow of great beating bloodied wings hung over them. She killed the man, because she was desperate. Lurching and stumbling on the battlefield thick with light and smoke.

She screamed in her own mother's voice, 'Ryn! Ryn!' There he was, further off from her, fighting a man in dark armour. Lidae ran towards him, her feet slipping in the wet rough mud. A ditch between them, choked up with corpses, the borderland between the living and dead.

A gout of dragon fire seared the churned mud, the bodies, the terrible strong stink of scalded meat, the spit and scent of meat. 'Ryn!'

Smoke and steam and hot wind in her eyes, blinding her, she rubbed ashes from her face. The ditch was burning. She could see Ryn through the flames. The earth shook, almost knocking her from her feet, a vast roar, screaming. Gods. Gods. The dragon had come down to land. She thought: we are losing. King Temyr is losing. The moment the soldiers think this, the battle is over and lost. 'Ryn!'

Soldiers, running past her, over the burning ditch, away from the dragon, on towards the enemy ground. Lidae ran, stumbled through the flames, fire-heat hissing on her face, scorching, hands clutching at her feet. *Help. Help. Save me.* Acol had died by fire. Ryn lying in the fire, in her house, she had thought he was dead. We always burn the dead.

The fighting was slackening. Temyr's troops fleeing or surrendering. A riderless horse came running past her. Running in mad circles round the battlefield. The dragon gave a great roar of furious triumph. A voice shouted, 'Queen Elayne! For Queen Elayne!'

The boat coming into Navikyre Fortress in the dark, in silence, bringing a message; forced marches, secrecy, lies, rumour, planning. For this moment, for Temyr to end up defeated. 'Ryn!'

He turned, stopped, stepped towards her. His sword bloody in his hand, his eyes huge.

It's over. You've won, you've beaten them, whatever it is your young queen wants you can do now. Queen Elayne is victorious: we can march in her army side-by-side, you and I, Ryn. Lidae dropped her sword. Fell on her knees before him. She pulled at her helmet, struggled to take it off. It was sticky with sweat and blood from a cut on her face she had not felt. Claggy with ash. She dropped it at his feet.

He said, 'Mother?' He was looking around the battlefield in astonishment. Knots of men still fighting, those that would fight until the end of the world, men standing leaning on their swords, panting, stumbling already trying to find someone. Talking a long drink from a waterskin. Lidae's own mouth curled dry as a stone at the thought. A hot dry roughness in her feet, her hands, her face.

Ryn said, 'Where's Samei?' He hesitated. Looked at his sword blade. 'Is Samei alive?'

She said, 'I don't know.' She tried to smile at him. 'I'm sure he is. He gets away unscathed from everything.' He fell out of the apple tree once, and he wasn't hurt, but the branch he'd been holding broke, came down after him, hit Ryn. Flood of warmth, remembering it.

Ryn said, 'Get up.' He didn't help her. Stood very awkwardly, holding his sword.

'Are you hurt?'

He shrugged. 'It's nothing.'

'Your face is bleeding. Your arm is bleeding.'

He said, 'We've been in a battle. Of course I'm hurt.' Tried to make it sound like a witty clever sarcastic boy thing to say to his mother. He shifted on his feet, awkwardly, looked around looking for something. His friends? Lidae thought: he's a grown man. He's embarrassed. Meeting his mother on the battlefield, and he hates me, he's so ashamed his friends will see him. Oh gods, she thought, does he have a slavewoman waiting in his tent? He looked so much like Samei, in his soiled armour. Then she thought, how stupid, it's Samei in his armour who looks like Ryn. Not quite as tall as Ryn, but he's still growing. Running carrying heavy weights in his bag, to make his shoulders wide as Ryn's. Half the reason Samei wants to be a soldier so much is to impress Ryn.

Trumpets sounded. Voices shouted, 'Queen Elayne! Victory to Queen Elayne!' On the battlefield a few men were still fighting. Men were cheering. Two men were embracing. A man was beginning to creep, already, over the bodies of the injured and dead.

This is not how a mother and son should meet, after two years apart, his army victorious. *My hero, my son, my most beloved, you are alive, you are victorious*, she should weep with joy, clutch him to her, shout to the world that he is safe. Her heart should sing songs of gold and wonder, light should burst in her eyes, the air should ring with bells and shouts of triumph. She stands staring at him in the mud, in the killing ground with his comrades' gore on her hands, and she cannot find words to speak across this great vast wall of pain and guilt. Fear of his hatred. That she might scream at him in shame and hate.

I love you so much, Ryn. Forgive me. Not begging, not pleading, just saying it.

I don't know what to do, she thought. How do I know what to do? I've walked through a wall of dragon fire, my sword smoking and glowing, my face blazing with heat. I've stood my ground while the sky grows black with shadows, they came down on me with claws and great bloodied teeth and I held the line, hacked away pointlessly at them. But Cythra the wise woman … she knew what to do with a child's grief.

Emmas would have known what to do, she thought. Or Cythra. Or Ayllis.

'What will happen now?' Ryn asked. He asked her like a child asking its mother, and Lidae felt herself going to weep. A thin line, a crack, a wall of fire between them, the killing ground beneath them splayed out.

'You've won, Ryn. Whatever Queen Elayne wants. I suppose Temyr and Prince Fiol must be dead.'

They were talking so stiffly, she thought. Like strangers. Hug him, hold him, sing his baby songs to him. Her body was hurting now she'd stopped fighting. A raw pain rising in her shoulder, all the muscles in her arms and her back aching, her hands and her knees burning with pain. She felt like she might vomit. Her body slowly unclenching itself from the fighting. Need to piss and shit and eat and drink. They had been fighting for hours, she thought, looking at the sky where the sun came thin through dust and smoke. Though it never felt like hours. Like moments. Like a lifetime. Hours, days, before she could remember how she was before the battle, go back to that. That's why it's so strained now, so odd, talking to Ryn. Nothing more, just battle feelings, shock.

'We should go to find Samei,' she said.

'We should, we— You're an enemy soldier … So's Samei.' The thought struck him suddenly, she saw it rush into his eyes. He hadn't realised. They hadn't meant it, she thought, Samei or Ryn, when they each swore to kill the other, didn't realise even now really that they might have fought, killed each other, that Samei might be dead. That this had been a battle, with death, with killing. Boys playing with sticks, shouting, violence, boy things. *Hate him, hate you, wish you were dead. Love you, love you, love you, love you.* Unreal and impossible to them and to anyone, all the battles they'd seen and fought in. Reached out together, crossed the boundary. Burying the bodies. The sound of a great wall crumbling. 'Queen Elayne wants to have peace, mother,' Ryn said. 'No more fighting.'

A voice shouted. A roar of wordless, senseless noise.

There was Samei, coming towards them.

Fifty-three

His face was raw. Burned up. He was bleeding. His armour had a shine to it. Gleaming, shimmering, rippling. Sunlight on water. A slick heaviness, like the metal was muscle and skin. Like Ryn, he had lost his helmet. Her careless children. His golden hair was red and his eyes were red. He shouted, 'Mother!' and he came running, crying, 'they're all dead, mother, all dead, all dead—' He stopped, eyes wide, when he saw Ryn.

They looked so alike, Ryn and Samei, in their armour. Looking at each other seeing themselves. *'You can't be Samei, no, surely not, you've got so tall, young man, I thought you must be Ryn; if it wasn't for that one standing beside you I'd say you were lying, that you must be Ryn.'* And the blood and the darkness rubbing out any differences. And their mother between them.

'Samei. Are you hurt?'

Of course he is hurt, she thought. Look at him. His face and his chest all opened up, burning. Been fighting worse than men. He swayed on his feet, stared around him half blinded. Teetered, almost fell. He held his sword out at Lidae.

'Get away from her!'

Lidae said, very quietly, 'Samei.'

'Get away! They're all dead! Everyone's dead!' His face was bleeding, the skin peeling off him. Shadows danced on his face, crawled around the bronze of his corselet. Burned and crushed and spat out by great beast things. His sword moved in his hand, jabbing out: he brandished it but his whole body was shaking. He shouted out, 'We've lost! King Temyr is dead! Seras is dead!'

He screamed in pain. Threw himself at Ryn.

Swords crashed. Grappling. They were shouting at first, cursing each other as they fought. Their swords moved slowly, moved round each other, circling, eyes meeting, not meeting, meeting. Hate poured out of them. Tiny weak pointless fragments of their lives that made them scream and weep. Lidae could laugh, seeing them fighting like this. They can't mean this. Their swords crashed again together, music of metal on metal, the horrible dry sound of iron dragging on iron and on bronze. A hiss from Ryn's lips. Stopped, looked at each other, eyes meeting. Ryn's sword came up. They closed quicker, harder, swords ringing, bodies pressed close. They were silent now. No more curses spat at each other. Focussed more and more on serious fighting. Their feet slithered in the red mud.

'Battle's over,' a voice shouted distantly. 'Battle's over. What are you two fighting for? Stop!'

Another voice, baffled: 'Battle's fought and won and lost. Order is to stop. Spare them.'

Another voice, wondering: 'They're brothers. Look at them.'

Soldiers looking between them, looking at Lidae. A circle formed, watching, soldiers dry and stained with blood. Two men fighting over a woman. Ryn and Samei were slithering, hacked and grappled together. Unaware of the men watching then. Ryn's sword caught Samei hard on the shoulder, and Lidae felt the impact, heard and felt the grind and rip of her son's bones beneath her son's blade. Samei staggered back, his feet slipped, Ryn was on him. A moan from the crowd. Samei lashed out, stabbed, slide away out of Ryn's reach. Froze, staring at Ryn their eyes meeting. They didn't speak, either of them. Gasped out a breath.

The crowd murmured. A wide circle around the two boys and their mother. No one dared to get close.

A ritual thing.

Almost a sacred thing.

Heavy silence. Ryn gasped for air, bent over, his sword hung in his hand. His right thigh was cut deep. Samei's eyes flicked from his brother's face to his brother's wound. Samei's left shoulder was a mass of blood. They looked new born, Lidae thought. The stink of their blood and her blood, the mud and sweat on them. Ryn grunted and struck out at Samei. Samei blocked it, struck back. Ryn's arm gleamed red.

The crowd was growing, a great circle, men came up at a run, winded like horses, to watch. 'Battle's over, what you doing?' 'Battle's over. Stop!' Each man would fall silent as he saw the two faces circling each other, felt the fear in the crowd. Look at Lidae, just once, and look quickly away from her. Hands moved in a warding gesture. Men blinked their eyes to wash them clean after they had seen her.

'Why doesn't she stop it?' a voice whispered. 'What are they fighting about? Does anyone know?' The crowd hissed, silencing the questions.

A raven called overhead.

A beat of wings, and a flash of shadow. A single black feather drifted down. It landed almost at Lidae's feet.

Ryn moved back. He was awkward, panting, his left arm was clutched at his side, holding his body just above his right hip. His left leg was bent under the weight of his wound there. Lidae thought: he's losing. Samei will kill him. Samei stepped forward as Ryn stepped back away from him.

Shout. Say something. Throw yourself between them. Ryn, my most beloved, I want Samei to kill you, Ryn, because I love you more than I love Samei, and I am so ashamed of that I have to want Samei to win. A single voice hissed even as she thought it: 'Why doesn't she stop it? Stop them?'

Shadows: the ravens gathered; an eagle, most accursed of all birds, spiralled overhead. On the edges of the circle now there were other shadows. Things watched drawn by the shedding of brothers' blood. The sun was setting now and the fires on the battlefield burned blue.

Ryn stepped back. Hs feet slid in the mud. He clutched at his side. Samei stepped towards him. Grunted. A blue light, very faint, flickered on Samei's blade. Their eyes were fixed on each other. Both were smiling.

Shout. Say something. Do something.

This is magery. Almost like that of a god.

Samei raised his sword. He shouted, and his sword came down, and Ryn blocked it. Ryn lunged forward, slipping in the mud, gasping in pain. Lidae felt the pain. Felt Samei's shock. Samei moved back, just a little, the two blades struck together, a shriek of iron. Music. The eagle screamed, the raven screamed. The crowd hissed and fell back to sacred silence. Ryn jabbed at Samei, Samei blocked it. Samei moved back, lunged forward, moved back. Their sword met. Samei thrust, Ryn blocked it. Samei pressed forward. Music of bronze and iron. Samei thrust, Ryn blocked it. Samei pressed forward. Samei thrust, Ryn blocked it.

Ryn's sword flashed up, and Samei gave a jerk. The sword fell from Samei's hand. He staggered, collapsed down.

Beat of wings.

Ryn! Ryn, my most beloved!

Every man watching was staring at her now. Mother who is watching one son kill the other. At the edges, shadow creatures watched her, snuffling at her shame and grief.

Ryn raised his sword.

She shouted, finally, her voice cracked, dry as stone: 'Ryn! Please! Stop! Ryn!'

Ryn did not look at her. But he lowered his sword.

The crowd hissed.

Ryn swayed on his feet. Looked down at his brother. Samei was hunched up, not looking. I remember once, Lidae thought, I remember a game they were playing, and Samei asked Ryn to tie a cloth around his neck like a halter, and Ryn couldn't get it undone, and they were both so frightened and I screamed at them and screamed at them, after I'd untied the cloth I smacked Ryn. That night I burned the cloth. Which was stupid.

Ryn took two steps back. Bent over, vomited in the red earth. Said something. Lidae couldn't hear what he said.

Samei got his feet, stumbling, slipped in his blood, got up. Took one step towards Ryn.

Samei had his sword in his hand again. He lunged at Ryn. Stabbed at Ryn.

Ryn blocked it. Shouted something.

Music of bronze and iron. Stink of bloodshed.

Ryn's sword flashed and Samei's sword flashed, and they met, clutching each other, embracing, and they drew apart, and their swords flashed, and they came together with a crash.

And a silence.

Ryn stood bent over, clutching his side, grunting. Sound like stones grinding in the waves of the beach. Smell of smoke. Smell of new green leaves and summer sunshine and the sweet, not quite pleasant smell of a child's hair. Sound of wing beats.

Samei lay in the red mud all crumpled up, twitching. His head moved, twice, tried to come up. His right arm jerked. As though he was fighting. He was holding his sword gripped very tight.

Then he was still.

Fifty-four

Ryn's sword blade glowed blue, very faintly. The great high magery of a man shedding his brother's blood.

Hands moved in warding gestures. Whisper of curse words and prayers, rippling across all the men watching. The shadows on the edges faded into darkness. Ryn looked at Lidae and his eyes were huge and very bright.

'He's hurt,' a voice cried in the crowd, as if this was a strange thing.

Still no one was looking at Lidae. She felt eyes flick towards her, hurry away. Close to wash the sight of her from them. The man nearest to her spat for luck on the ground, stepped away.

Ryn took a step backwards. A step forwards. Looked all around the circle of faces staring. He looked down at the sword and saw the fire there, licking at Samei's blood. He raised the sword like a hero. A few cheers from the crowd. Ragged. He lowered the sword. Looked down, finally, at Samei lying dead.

He might fall to his knees, scream, snatch up his brother's body in his arms, his blood mingling with his brother's blood, weep over it. *'My brother, my brother, my brother, my brother, I love you, love you, love.'* Scream with shame at what he had done. He might look at Lidae with the face she remembered from his childhood, *'I didn't mean to do it, it was an accident,'* which means somehow that he hasn't really done it and it could easily be mended, not if it wasn't meant. But that was usually Samei, she thought, who'd say that, not Ryn. Ryn would sit quietly watching Samei's tears, her anger, looking down at the broken thing that Samei would insist through his tears wasn't really broken.

He might look at her, Lidae, his mother. Say something.

There was a stirring in the crowd, people moving—reluctantly, fearfully, people moving. Feet slipped in the red mud, for they were standing, they remembered now, on the killing ground of a battlefield where a battle had just been won. A trumpet sounded, harsh and angry; the crowd parted, ebbed away like floodwater, muttering; a man's voice shouted out, 'What is happening here? Why are you here? The battle is won.'

A general and his retinue of soldiers, a great man, victorious, striding through the corpses of the killing ground, his armour bloodied and shining. The crest of his bronze helmet nodded as he walked, brilliant red, his cloak was red. Golden snakes twisted across his bronze forehead, curled their tails down his bronze face. The soldiers surrounding him carried long spears, their points clean of any blood. The trumpet that rang for him was made of silver, the trumpeter's helmet covered his face leaving only his red mouth and it was worked in silver-leaf. A huge man, thick and wide as a bull, huge shoulders, a heavy belly through his armour, his arms sagged with fat. Ryn looked what he was, beside him: a child. The crumpled thing that was Samei was like a child. All the men watching were afraid of him, stepping back drifting away not like water but like thin morning mist, until there were only a few men, and Lidae, and her sons, left.

'What is happening here?' The great general's voice was too thin for him. Dry, with an accent of the east somewhere, a little like she remembered Acol's accent.

'Nothing. Two boys, fighting, you know brothers, stupid boys fighting.' She, Lidae, waited for someone to say that, one of her sons or someone watching, 'There's the mother, there,' someone will say, pointing to her, 'Can't keep a hold of her children, useless woman, can't manage them.' The boys will get up, Samei crying. The general and his guards will look at her: *bad mother, useless woman.*

'A fight,' someone said. 'That one's dead.'

'He was on the other side,' someone said, 'so it doesn't matter. Wouldn't surrender, maybe. Gods know. But he's dead anyway.'

She thought: that's not true. Doesn't mean anything. Those words. Don't mean. Anything. It sounded as though the speaker was crunching on a mouthful of sand. She was hearing words in the nonsense.

The general waved his hands at his guards. 'Get the other one to the sick tents, then. And you, men, get off with you. Battle's won. The trumpets have sounded calling you back to camp. This is a battlefield. Fights all over the place.' A little flicker of golden light, a star falling, in the north even as the general spoke. The queen's dragon, flying off a star of victory over the battlefield. A great roar of voices and a bellow of drums and trumpets.

'And her?' someone said. The great general turned away without answering. What's a single bloody enemy footsoldier to me? The battle's ended and I've won. The great general was gone back into the killing ground, his feet stamping in human gore, walking across the borderland where men lay both dead and alive and dying, shifting irritably at the fastening of his beautiful red cloak. The sun was sinking in the west in fire, and his armour was lit up, blazing like a torch, his big soft arms scratching at his neck to loosen his helmet strap.

'You heard him,' a voice said. 'Get the living one to the sick tents. Come on.'

'Leave him,' his comrade said. A nice voice, sweet, with the accent of Raena and the desert. 'He's dying, I'd bet. Just leave him.'

'Got anything on him?' the first voice said. 'The dead one, I mean?'

'Fancy armour. Nice. Is that gold leaf there on the corselet? Wouldn't mind that.'

'Wait here, then. You, hold on to this dying one. General Gaethen says he gets to the sick tent, he gets to the sick tent. But hang on.'

The sweet voiced one and his friend bent over Samei's body, working at the armour straps, while the companion they had whistled up held Ryn. He was flopped over the man's shoulder, his head lolling. Lidae saw Emmas's body hanging over her shoulder when she dragged him to his pyre. The men rolled Samei over, his right arm crumpled under him, and she could almost believe he was dead. A man near them, lying in the red mud with his face all caved in, reached out a hand, called weakly for help in the queen's name, but they ignored him.

'Thought his sword had magefire on it,' the sweet voice said. 'Must have imagined it. Get that one off to the sick tents, then. If the general commanded it.'

Careful with the strap there ... looks in bad shape ... there!'

'He could have taken better care of it. What's he been fighting, the bloody dragon?'

'Thought the other one had a mage sword too. Our one. Must have been wrong.'

'All this fighting. Plays tricks with your eyes, sometimes, battle.'

'No, it really doesn't. You ever tried listening to the words coming out of your own mouth?'

Lidae watched them carry her living son away. She stood by the stripped body of her dead son.

He's not dead, she thought. Not dead. Neither of them are dead.

Fifty-five

'They've already been picked clean. No one here worth going over.'

'Always someone worth going over.'

'Not here, there's not.'

A pause, a clink of metal.

'Told you.'

'It's broken. Blade's snapped off, look.'

'But the hilt's fine. Could get the blade shortened.'

'There are broken blades snapped scattered around for miles. What use on this earth is a broken old knife?'

'Yes…' A sigh, a clink of metal being thrown down. 'What's this …?'

'Nothing.'

'This one's alive. Look.'

She's talking about Samei, Lidae thought. See? He's not dead.

'Now that's worth something. That sword there.'

'Except she's still alive. You.' The woman's voice was very cold. 'Get up, there.'

Yes. Lidae got to her feet. Her body was very stiff, her legs almost gave under her, she had to put out a hand, grab hold of Samei's body to keep herself from collapsing back onto him. He was very cold. Clutching him, she hadn't noticed how cold he had become.

Two women. Ragged looted finery, a bright yellow dress sewn with flowers, a green cloak, a copper necklet around a thick, white neck. Even on the corpse field they dressed in their fine things, so everyone knew they weren't soldiers. 'If they're still alive, the dead out there, it's nice to think, maybe, that they see something pretty, bright, colours, before they're dead. Maybe worse things I can think of, to see when you're dying, than silks and flowers.' Someone had said that. Acol, or Emmas, or Maerc.

'Is that a ruby in her sword?'

'Get up, you.'

Lidae stood looking. 'My son,' she said. 'He's dead.'

Roses, she thought. That was the flower embroidered on the woman's yellow dress.

'He's young,' the woman with the necklet said. 'And someone's already stripped him.'

Her friend looked down more gently, looked at Samei's burned face, looked away. 'Are you with the queen's army?' She gazed at Lidae with kindness. Even pity. Even sympathy, Lidae thought. Might think she understood something of what Lidae felt. That seemed a terrible thing. Though she, Lidae, she herself did not understand what it was she felt.

My sons are not dead. Neither of them. This is not my son, this dead thing here. My son will come striding up in his shining armour, and I'll embrace him.

A shiver from the first woman. Smell it in Lidae, or taste it, or see it like a great shining jewel around her neck. 'Leave her alone, Han. Come on. Don't talk to her.' A little frightened hiss.

But: 'Are you with the queen's army?' the woman, Han, said. Her eyes shifted, taking in the darkness of the battlefield. Victory fires were burning, over in the east, and the sky was lit up. A few torches moved in the twilight across the charnel ground, camp women, beggars, thieves, cut-throats—

Is there any difference?' she asks Acol: the camp women, the cold-eyed ones with their cruel faces, they look at her with such loathing she's almost afraid of them. But Acol says, 'Oh yes, the camp women are honest in what they are. What they're doing. Better to look at if you're dying, too.' And Lidae the poet of the sword nods, not understanding, and this thing Acol says about women who are not soldiers, she never understood it—camp women, beggars, thieves, cut-throats, scavengers, soldiers looking for a lost comrade, brother, lover, father, friend. A glitter of lights and fine armour, moving carefully over a great hummock of the dead, a voice shouted to drive off the crows; sent to look for some great noble, scrabble amongst the meat of two armies until they find him. Digging and turning the dead. In the morning Queen Elayne will order her men gathered for the pyre. Our men will lie unburned, unburied, and thus we cannot forget them. Though who can tell which body is which? Those that look like heroes, fair-faced, they must be Queen Elayne's. The victorious army will be drinking, dancing, tending its wounded—Ryn, Ryn, Ryn, be living, be well and sleeping with your slavewoman to tend you in the sick tents— the defeated are no longer and never were an army, prisoners, slaves, killed-to-keep-them-from-returning, killed-for-coin, fled. 'Are you with the queen's army? You must be, I think. Yes?'

Lidae said, 'My son and I, we fought for Queen Elayne, yes.' She groped for a name. 'General ... Gaethan. We fought under him.' *His name is Samei, he's a great hero, King Temyr's army made songs about him, have you heard the name? Your General Gaethan would have trembled to meet him. His beautiful young face that shone as he killed like a star falling, it is all burned and cut away now, so you won't recognise him.*

'That's good then,' the woman Han said. Lidae thought: you cannot imagine what has happened here to me. You're not even a soldier, you scavenge off soldiers' littering like a crow. I want no old-woman pity from you.

'I'm going back to the camp now. Seen enough here, got enough.' She swung a bag that hung from her arm. 'Not much to find and to take.' She said, 'Care to come with me? I could ... I could use a woman with a sword walking beside me, tonight, I should think. Be helping me.'

'My son—' She thought of Cythra. 'I won't leave my son.'

'Well...' The woman in yellow had walked on, was bent over something a little way away, gestured at Han to join her, mouthed 'come on'. 'If you're sure,' Han said. 'I'm sorry,' Han said. 'About your son.'

She thought of Gulius and Taim who had been kind to them in King Durith's camp so many years ago; Clews saying kindly, 'And now they're going to find you food and clothing and everything. A good tent.' And she thought suddenly of helping Cythra bury her sons, and feeling that was a good thing to do, the hope on Cythra's face when she asked to be allowed to help her, dragging the body of Niken-the-youngest, who was older than Samei was when he died, *'We can bury them together beneath the may trees.'*

Ryn is alive, she thought, and how must he feel, knowing he has killed Samei? I should go to him.

'You tried to get Samei first. You looked at me and then you went to Samei.'

'I thought you were dead, Ryn. But I knew Samei was alive.'

She looked down a long time at Samei's body. I will forget his face, she thought, like I forgot Emmas's face and Acol's, and my mother and father. I will remember the red cloak and the great crest on his helmet, his whoops as he ran with a stick raised like a sword, his sulking, furious, comic anger when I told him he was being naughty, but I will forget his face.

'Wait,' she called to Han. The woman turned back to her, it had not been a long time that she had been looking down at Samei's body, Han had taken perhaps five steps. 'I … I would like to come back to your camp with you,' Lidae said. 'Walk back with you.'

A smile of relief on Han's face. 'Are you wounded?' Han said. She held out a flask, 'Do you want a drink?'

'I … Thank you.' They walked side by side; the lights of the camp in the distance drew near, the sounds of laughter and song, the smell of woodsmoke and drink and sweat and horses, the stink of the latrine pits. A line of dancers wove its way towards them, faces flushed warm in the light of the torches they carried, singing and laughing. When they saw Han's bright dress, Lidae's armour and the sword she carried, they cheered.

Han said, 'My tent's over there. South of the main camp.' They went on without speaking for a little. The victory dancers swirled around them. Glossy ribbons of bronze. 'I can lend you a dress, if you want,' Han said.

'Thank you,' Lidae said. 'Where's the sick tent?'

'Over there.' The same direction they were walking in. 'Most of the women don't like to camp there, near it,' Han said. 'Scares them. Unlucky, you know? But I like it. Safe.' She said after a moment, 'But your son— Change your dress, have some wine, some bread,' Han said, 'before you go there.'

'Thank you.' All pretence that this was her army, these soldiers her companions, gone. Except I'll meet some of them soon, Lidae thought, from a few years ago, or from those few days with King Durith's army, or from King Durith's army long ago before Emmas and Samei and Ryn. And I'll smile, pretend I remember their name and cared whether they lived or died, and they'll smile pretending the same, my friend, my companion, you who were by me at the ships at Ander!

'Here,' said Han. 'My tent.' A little huddle of three or four women's dwellings, their tents just big enough to fit a man and a woman in together, if the man didn't sleep the night. The poorest of the camp women, desperate, camped here near the sick tents where most men will not go willingly, but the men who do come here are also desperate. Han had a gentle face, Lidae thought, no different to her own face or Cythra's face, she had seen women in fine silks, the men muttering how expensive they were, a month's pay for a few hours, who were no prettier than Han might once have been. Han's tent was rank with mildew, the canvas ragged and split.

Han lit a stump of candle. 'I share with Hayla, usually,' Han said, 'but she'll be off tonight, I expect.' She pulled a dress out of the bundle of things in her tent, held it out to Lidae. 'Here. Try this on. I think it will fit.' It was bright scarlet, very large, Lidae struggled awkwardly with her armour beneath it; it covered her like the huge loose dresses Cythra had given her to wear when she was eight months pregnant. It had a strong smell of mould to it, felt greasy on her clammy skin. But beneath the mould, the smell of women's sweat and bodies, Han's and whoever had owned the dress before her, and beneath that old sour-sweet perfume, long faded, perfumed oils for the skin and hair, a sweetwood chest lined with fragrant herbs. The tallow candle flickered, it had a heavy fatty smell to it, rancid, almost like a woman's unwashed cunt. The whole sad little tent smelled of women's living bodies, Lidae thought. A square of cloth hung over the tent entrance, too small to keep it closed against the damp winter cold, flowers and birds arching and dancing, dirty and frayed and torn but the flowers hung there still very bright. Honeysuckle, lilies, roses, the birds with green breasts and pink wings. The bed was a tattered blanket, beside it stood a box containing a glass bottle, a bead necklace, a wooden comb with strands of Han's hair caught in it like cobwebs, a single chipped bowl, a cup. A little posy of dried heather, old and crumbling half to dust, tied with string.

Lidae bent her head and screamed and wept and screamed and wept at her own grief and this stranger's brief unasked kindness.

Fifty-six

The camp was noisy with victory all night. The stub of candle guttered out, leaving the tent lit from distant campfires that threw patterns of light and shadow in the mildewed walls. Lidae lay on the floor of this strange woman's tent in the mud, curled into herself with her body tearing itself apart in grief with a pain like childbirth. The same desperate screaming in her body to push something out of itself. Her hands curled around her thighs where her old battle scar ran, around her shoulders that ached from the recent fighting. Her mouth still tasted of the battlefield. She buried her face in the red dress to breathe in the smell of stale perfume, other women's skin and sweat. She pressed the cloth against her mouth to choke her screaming. Beat her hands against her stomach and screamed again. Her screams faded at last to sobbing, because she was tired, too worn out from fighting and screaming, to scream any more. Men's cries drifted over from the sick tents. Ryn was there, Lidae thought, perhaps dying. Twice she got up, almost went towards him. Twice she fell down like a sick man herself, shaking.

'I hate you, Mother.'

'I want Samei to kill you, Ryn, because I love you more than I love Samei.'

When her screams had turned to sobs for long enough, Han said, 'You don't remember me, Lidae, do you?'

'Remember you?' In the dark in the tent she barely knew where she was. Somewhere outside time, outside the world, where she had stepped through her grief like a doorway. She was no longer herself. Back in Raena, crouched in the filth of her parents' bodies, seeing herself from a distance stumbling to her feet to join the army that had killed them.

'I'm Rena the healer's daughter,' Han said. 'Hana. Do you remember me?'

Hana was a child, Lidae thought. She had last seen Hana ... when?

Safe in King Temyr's camp, surely, settled, with a blanket and hunk of bread and a tent? And then Lidae had had her posting in the army, and Hana had been a young woman, sixteen, independent, almost grown… The boys had spoken about her sometimes. But all that was years ago. Rena and Hana and Salith Drylth were almost a dream.

Han said, 'I knew your sword first, I think. I remember it… I was frightened of it. Ryn showed it to Ayllis once. I remembered it. He waved it around and it terrified us. Is it Ryn who's dead?'

'Samei.' The word hurt in her mouth.

A pause. 'Samei. I hadn't thought … that he was old enough for war.'

Lidae said, 'You still remember their names? Samei and Ryn?'

A bitter laugh. 'Of course I remember their names.'

'Ryn is in the army here,' Lidae said after a while. Another silence, then Lidae said carefully, 'If you've been with the army … if you've been with the army a while … If I'd known you were… Or either of them had known… But I suppose, the army being so huge, so many men…'

Hana said in a flat voice, 'I've been with the army a while. But I don't suppose I would have recognised either of them. Or them me.' They both looked around the little dark stinking tent.

'Ayllis was here in the camp,' Lidae said. 'With Ryn. If we'd known, Hana, that you were with the army…'

Again, Hana said nothing.

'Ryn is in the sick tents,' Lidae said at last. 'He—' She drew back from it. She remembered Hana tending Ryn's wound, in the bright morning sunshine falling through the branches of a birch tree in the ruins of Salith Drylth, yellow buttercups crushed beneath him and springing up between them so that Hana had to push them away as she worked, birds singing overhead. Real birds, real flowers, a spring breeze. She thought, confused: I have sat here all night, mourning for my dead son, and in all that time my living son is so near here. Waiting for me to come to him.

She put the too-long sleeves of the dress to her face, breathed in the smell of women's sweat and stale perfume. 'Ryn hates me,' she said. 'He won't want me to come to him.' We'll meet, look at each other, he could be dying, what could I say? He could already be dead and cold.

'I'll go to find him,' Hana the healer's daughter said. She got up, very weary: Lidae realised she must have been sitting hunched for hours, exhausted, watching her grieving, when she could have scavenged more trinkets from the corpse field, made a few coins from the men out celebrating. She must still be young, Lidae thought, she was a girl in Salith Drylth, Rena wouldn't let her near Emmas when he was dying because she was too young. But she looks so old. I thought she was as old as I am. She was thin, the red dress must swallow her up. Her hair was ragged, her eyes had tired silver scar lines snaking around them.

'Do you .. do you have any children, Hana?'

'I had a son,' Hana said. 'I gave him away. I … I didn't want him to be a soldier. He would be nine now. I don't know where he is.' She put her hands to her stomach, as Lidae had, as Ayllis had. 'After that … I didn't want to have any more children.' She covered her face with her cloak, went out to the sick tents to look for Ryn.

Time passed. Lidae sat in the tent, waiting. So much time. Endless time. The night was so long. I wonder if they have taken Temyr alive, Lidae thought, or killed him? All this … it is always good to know what the outcome of it is. I wonder if Queen Elayne will be a good queen. Which of the generals in her army will fight her one day, and if he will succeed. Ayllis's child might be a soldier on one side or the other, she thought, by then. Durith, Temyr, Elayne … Lord Sabryyr, or that one today… Lord Gaethen. Lining up, all of them, to kill men so that they can end up dead. A gust of wind made the tent shake, flapped at the red dress, stirred up the smell of women's bodies, women's skin and sweat.

Outside the tent a man's voice called, and Hana's voice answered telling him to get away. Hana appeared in the tent entrance, the cloth with its flowers and birds tangled against her forehead.

'Come,' she said. 'Come and see Ryn.'

A shock ran through Lidae. She felt herself begin to shake. Waiting here longing and hoping, and he's alive, he hadn't refused to let me see him, he's alive and real. She got up. She had put on her sword-belt, over the red dress, she couldn't risk being without it, the sword hung awkwardly caught in the great folds of the dress. But the sword…

She said, 'Wait, Hana, just a moment,' carefully hid the sword beneath Hana's thin tattered blanket. I'll only be gone a little while, it will be safe there, because he won't see me, he'll spit in my face, I'll curse him and spit on him, I hope he is dying and already dead, he won't let me see him.

The camp was falling silent, the soldiers settling down for the night. But Hana had not been gone very long at all, she realised. She followed Hana, keeping close like a child, although she could hear and smell the sick tents ahead of them, as they came closer her legs were shaking under her, she thought: I have to run. I can't do this. He'll curse me. Turn his face from me. I had only one son and he is dead, this is his murderer. I have to run. The huge loose red dress flapped against her legs, fine silk that left her cold but so big it felt as though she was wearing something soaking wet.

'Just up ahead,' Hana said. They passed the first tent, dark and almost silent, the second, walked on with the tents behind them, walking uphill past a clump of pine trees.

'But where we going?' Lidae whispered, like a child, afraid. 'Where are we going Hana?'

They stopped before a large tent, cleaner and airier, a torch burning at the entrance. Hana pointed. 'In here.'

'Is he dying?'

'No. He's not dying.'

I wish, Lidae thought, that I had worn my sword. She clasped her hands together tightly as she stepped through the heavy leather doorcurtain. The air in the tent was warm, smoky, damp with steam, familiar. Several lamps burned: keep the men from having to sit in the dark, die in the dark. She remembered the constant light of a lamp burning from her own times in the sick tent, the lamp going out one night and some of them whimpering. In the centre of the tent a brazier was burning, giving off thick pale scented smoke. Lavender blossom and sulphur and juniper berries: cleansing, healing. Long strings of hagstones that hung on the inside of the doorcurtain clicked together as Lidae pushed past them. The place seemed very large and uncrowded, compared to her memories, the men lay on thick blankets with good thick blankets covering them. A woman in a dark gown was bent over a man propped upright, heavily bandaged; Lidae wasn't sure if he was shaking or if it was simply the flicker of the lamps.

Pale faces turned towards Lidae. Drank in the sight of two women in bright clothes.

'Here.' Hana led her to the farthest corner of the tent. Samei was lying awake, staring up at the canvas ceiling. She thought, from the way he was already looking towards her, that he had been waiting.

Ryn. Ryn was lying here awake. Samei was dead. But Ryn looked so small and so young.

She stood over him, and that felt wrong, she bent down crouched on her heels beside him, uncomfortably, as she had when he was a child, beside his bed. She was so afraid he would curse her. Turn his face away to the wall. From the corner of her eye she could see the man beside Ryn watching them, and then looking quickly away to smile at Hana's pretty dress and green cloak.

Ryn's left arm was heavily bandaged, his face was bruised, one eye gummed shut. Oh gods, she thought, he's lost his eye. His right eye. His forehead was smeared in a thick poultice that gleamed bloodily in the lamplight, a bird's skull and the twig-like bones of a bird's wing had been hung around his neck. Tiny and fragile. Old and well-used. His one whole eye blinked up at her. He coughed, as though he hadn't spoken for a long time.

'Did I kill him?'

'Yes.' It was not as hard to say it as she had thought it would be, now it came to it. Ryn closed his eye and sighed. Oh gods, Lidae thought, is he pleased that Samei is dead?

'You called to me,' he said. 'I heard you. When we were fighting.'

Did I? She had a very clear memory of begging them to tell her he was alive after he had been born. The silence before they told her that he was alive, the brief moment of time it takes a mouth to open, that had seemed endless. A very clear memory of Rena shouting helplessly at Samei still half-born to come on and live. But she couldn't remember the battle. Their faces, their swords, the certainty that one or two of them would die, and nothing beyond that.

'My left arm is a mess,' Ryn said. 'The arm, the shoulder. They don't think I'll have much use of it again.'

'And your eye?'

'It should open, they said. I'm lucky with my eyes, I suppose. You called to me,' he said again. He reached out and took her hand. She remembered him again and again pushing her away.

Why don't you listen, when will you ever just listen to me, Ryn?

'I'm tired,' he said. 'I lost a lot of blood, they said. Where's Ayllis?' His thoughts were all vague, as they often are after a great wound. The hagstones at the door rattled, the fire hissed and spat in a cloud of scented smoke as someone threw more herbs onto the brazier.

'I don't know,' Lidae said. It was worse, somehow, than telling him Samei was dead. *I left her alone as a prisoner in King Temyr's camp, Ryn, and now I expect she's dead. Someone else I couldn't keep safe.*

'I'm tired,' he said again. 'I couldn't sleep, waiting for you to come. A woman came round selling hatha, to ease the pain, help us sleep. But I had to wait until you came. Be awake.' He opened his one eye, squeezed her hand tightly. His hand that had killed Samei.

'I'll let you sleep, then, for a while. I'll come back soon. Get some sleep.' Lidae bent over him, kissed his bruised cheek. He let go of her hand reluctantly, his fingers tangled and holding on, stretched out around hers, like he had when he was a child, not wanting her to leave him to go to sleep.

Outside the tent Hana was waiting for her. She looked exhausted. Lidae remembered again that she had been awake all night with her, that all this had lost her a chance to make good coin. They walked a little way back towards Hana's tent. A great tiredness coming over Lidae, and the grief back tearing at her, huge and fanged.

'You didn't stay long,' said Han.

Lidae thought: bitch. Hateful cruel stinking bitch.

She said, 'He needs to sleep.' To be cruel, she said then, 'You should have been a healer in the sick tents, Hana.' Remembered Hana caring for Ryn beneath the new green-gold of beech trees and a great shame came up in her heart. Hana frowned, her eyes too bright. Lidae said, 'I can't thank you enough, Hana. For helping me. Finding him for me.' The thin shoulders shrugged.

Lidae looked around at the fires still burning in celebration, the distant figures of the men, the dark sky. And now...? Sit outside Ryn's tent? She stumbled, she was falling, the ground beneath her seemed to open up in a wound, the world was burned and black. She felt Hana's hand in her arm, distant like when she was sick with fever, or, no, it was like it was sometimes in battle, just before their spears first meet the enemy. Or ... like trying to look back at the moment of childbirth. Reeling, shivering from the absurdity of it. The impossibility of it. Ryn will get up from his sickbed, Samei will come up smiling, the three of us will walk off. In a few moments, Ryn and Samei will be bickering about something stupid.

'You can sleep in my tent, if you want,' Hana said. A pause, and Hana said hesitantly, 'Do you have any coin, Lidae? To buy bread and meat?'

A little, in the purse around her neck hanging inside the huge red dress. I was going to buy Samei a present, she thought. She took a deep long breath. Felt Hana's hand on her arm. Put her own hand where her sword would be hanging. I need the money for Ryn, she thought. But Hana's thin old grey face. She looks older than I do... It was so late it must almost be morning, but of course they found a sutler woman yawning and bleary-eyed but still selling the last dregs of hot spiced wine and roast meat. Sydela, her name was, very old and white-haired. She clicked her tongue when she saw their clothes: 'Been worked hard tonight, ladies? The meat might be a bit dry, mind, as it's been roasting since sunset.' Hana ate so fast she was almost choking on it. Couldn't eat much, because the meat was too rich. She made a thin noise, whimpering, as she ate.

Lidae thought of Samei's slave woman, who would be utterly alone and destitute now, clinging like Hana to the edge of living, picking over the soldiers' leavings. Thought of herself at sixteen, in Raena, and what would have become of her if King Durith and Maerc and Acol hadn't come.

They ate, and then Lidae should sleep, her eyes were aching, her body was raw with exhaustion. Dawn was coming, finally—one day and one night, she found herself thinking over and over, drumming in her head in time with their footsteps, one day and one night. The camp was stirring awake in the half-light, men's voices cutting through the air, a trumpet rang off somewhere, muted by distance, and then another much nearer, and voices groaned. Lidae started at the sound. I should get up, fall in for orders. 'Bastards,' Eralene had been muttering the other morning, 'bastards, it's like they don't want us to get any sleep.' I haven't even thought, Lidae realised, about Eralene or Deljan or any of them, the squad I've been fighting in now, if they're dead or prisoner or fled. They're probably here, most of them, footsoldiers in the Army of Illyrith. 'A queen! About time! Maybe we'll see some sense now,' Eralene will say.

A trumpet, a man's voice called out a filthy comment: she was jerked back into the real world, falling asleep on her feet, her mouth felt very dry, her face puffy with tiredness. She thought: Samei is dead. She was so tired. Was I talking aloud? she thought. Hana, Rena the healer's daughter, made a filthy comment back to the soldier, and Lidae thought: Hana can't know words like that. Rena would be disgusted. It was a damp cloudy morning, very dark, has the sun risen? Gods know. The red dress was damp and cold flapping around her legs. The man had been making the comment at her, she thought, from Hana's answer: how stupid, to be mistaken for a camp whore. When they got to the tent she felt a rush of fear, would her sword still be there waiting? She groped beneath the blanket, in the thin bed, it was missing and she was frightened and then her hand closed on it. The metal was so cold to her hand. She took it out and the red glass in the hilt looked black. She lay down beside Hana trying to keep from touching the woman's body. The tent was cold and damp like the dress. The wind blew through the ragged walls, the ill-fitting doorcurtain, the morning light poured in. I've slept in worse, Lidae thought. The tent smelled so strongly of women. Women's cunt, women's sweat, women's grief. When she closed her eyes, she saw Samei.

Being born. Dying. When she opened her eyes, she saw Ryn sitting in the sick tent. Pain tore at her heart and her stomach. She was so tired her eyes burned. She got up, her body racing now, her heart beating fast as if she was running. Hana was awake, she saw, but the woman did not say anything.

When she came back to the sick tent, they all knew what she was and what Ryn had done, and they would not speak to him.

'Get him out,' a woman said to her from her sick bed. 'Get him away from us, before he curses us.' They had heaped the brazier with sulphur, the tent reeked of it, made them all cough.

What? Lidae thought: every man here has killed someone's brother. Every man here has killed a mother's son.

Cursed. Lidae said: 'Curse them! What right have they got?'

'I can walk,' Ryn said. 'If you help me up.' He struggled, tried to pull himself up without using the left side of his body, bit his lip in pain. The bird bones around his neck rattled loud and dry. He struggled to take it off but Lidae said, 'Leave it,' and the woman called 'Leave it on,' from her sick bed. But— But— But when a man gets a shadow on him, Lidae thought, the rest of them stare at him, whisper, won't meet his eyes … and then he withers away, believes he's cursed, dies. There was a man once who lost five tent mates in one winter's campaigning, he took sick, died from nothing, no one would bury him.

'I can walk,' Ryn said. 'Just help me up then I can walk on my own.'

Lidae took his hand in hers to help him, the hand that had killed Samei; she heard them all gasp, all staring, and it felt, yes, it felt briefly like fire, like a spark landing on her skin. Like his hand was burning blue. Perhaps, if the tent had been darker, she would have seen his hand burning blue. She felt raw, the touch of their skin together was unpleasant, she wanted to drop his hand, push him away. All the people in the tent were staring. A voice behind her was muttering words to avert ill-luck. I held his hand before, she thought, and felt nothing but love. They had to walk slowly, Ryn leaning heavily against her; he was taller than she was, strongly built in his shoulders, the tent was low and crowded. So it was awkward. 'I can walk,' he said, loudly, but she had to hold him to stop him falling. The skirts of the red dress tangled against their legs. They had to step over the legs of a man stretched out sleeping, Ryn staggered and leaned hard against Lidae. His foot struck the man's leg beneath its blanket, the man was not asleep, swore at them.

Emmas, carrying Samei in his arms, new born, stepping across Ryn playing on the floor, Ryn's little hands, his fragile wooden toys, so close to Emmas' big heavy boots, and if Emmas slipped and trod on them he'd fall over, drop Samei, fall on both of them...

Outside the tent the air was very fresh. Ryn took a great mouthful of it. More colour came into his cheeks. He stood more upright. 'I can walk,' he said again. 'You don't have to help me.' Like he thought she was angry with him. He said roughly, 'Soldiers came this morning, under the command of someone there, said they'd throw me out. Cursed.' Ryn blinked, almost laughed. 'And that the tent for officers, cavalry, grand people, they all knew I shouldn't have been there anyway. But they said, all of them, even the man whose soldiers were there, they were, they said I could stay until you came for me. Eledae—the woman who shouted—she even gave me some of her wine and food. So don't be angry with them.'

'I'm not angry,' Lidae said.

So many things hung in the air between them, visible around them in a grey mist. His weight on her body was crushing her. All the weight of her rage and grief and shame before her sons. I tried, I tried so hard, Ryn, Samei, you can't understand what it was like trying to raise you through everything we suffered. What would you have said and done, Ryn? Samei? You think I don't wake every morning and remember all the ways I've failed you? You think I don't fall asleep at night swearing to myself that tomorrow it will be different? Every moment since I knew I was pregnant with you, Ryn. I remember when I was first pregnant with you, I was so frightened you'd die in my womb, that I'd do something, not do something, and you'd die of it. That you wouldn't feed, wouldn't crawl, wouldn't speak. And I was so afraid, Ryn, that you'd hate me for it. Poet of the sword, they all called me.

'He was going to kill me,' Ryn said. 'If I hadn't killed him, he would have killed me, even when I tried to end it without hurting him, I could see it in his face, he wouldn't stop, until he'd killed me or I'd killed him.'

Yes. I know. I saw it. His face and your face ... if I'd called to him as I called to you, he wouldn't have listened. Lidae said, 'We can find your tent, I expect.'

Ryn looked around the camp, pointed. 'That way, over there by those trees, you see that ridge? Just down from there.' A thin veil of rain making the trees Ryn pointed to look like they had been painted on a wall, the sky and the further hills beyond them nothing but grey. A flag somewhere between them and Ryn's tent, brilliant red. 'I can walk,' Ryn said.

'It's a long way,' Lidae said. 'The other side of the camp.' Ryn's breath came as a little hiss of pain. He leaned so heavily on her, then he would try to walk a little without support, biting his lips, then he would lean heavily on her until she was almost trying to carry him. His face was grey, ran with sweat. She could think, dimly, memories she'd tried to forget, of helping her father home when he was drunk, he'd cry sometimes, sad useless man, 'you deserve better than this, Lidae.' And of course she'd done this before, helped wounded men back from the battlefield, supported them to or from the sick tents.

'He was going to kill me,' Ryn said. 'If I hadn't killed him.'

'Yes. You're doing really well, Ryn,' she said. 'Keep going. Just keep going. Look how far we've got.' Ryn clenched his teeth, squeezed her arm. 'You're doing really well, Ryn. Really well. Just keep walking.'

There was a bustle of activity up on the ridge, men moving around, voices calling. A shout went up, triumphant. A faint smell of fresh cut wood drifted down. They're building the funeral pyres, Lidae thought. She squeezed Ryn's arm back, felt him press himself close to her. She was crying for Samei, and Ryn was crying.

You are alive, Ryn. That's all we need to say. Alive! You're alive, Ryn! One of my sons is dead, but one of my sons is alive and beside me, and I am looking at him, holding him. And that is a joy and a wonder to me.

Fifty-seven

Ryn's squad was camped up on the hill with trees behind them, facing south into the sun, the trees were bare and very black but as they got close there were flowers beneath the trees, tiny crocuses in pale purple, white, brilliant yellow, pressing up so very delicately through the mud. The tents were good-sized, new canvas, everything was ordered, neat, clean. They'd put pine branches down around the tents to walk on to keep the worst of the mud down. They were cooking soup over the fire in a big pot. Men leapt up when they saw Ryn, one of them called out joyfully. Two of them came hurrying to take Ryn from Lidae, help him into what must be his tent. 'I'll find Lycan, he thought you were dead, Ryn, he was out there looking for you…' Lidae found herself standing alone beside the bare trees. She thought: they think I'm a camp woman paid to help him. In a moment, one of them will probably come to pay me. Two in iron. Go and get yourself a scrap of bread to eat.

A voice called out, rejoicing, a woman throwing her arms around her, hugging her, 'Lidae! Gods!' Laughter: 'I almost didn't recognise you! If Ryn hadn't said it was you…'

The woman was trampling down all the crocus flowers. Lidae said, wondering, joyful, 'Ayllis?'

'You found him! You survived, and you found him! I was asking anyone, all last night and this morning. I was frightened. Someone said they'd seen his body. But I knew, I knew he wasn't dead. And I knew you'd survive, Lidae!'

Lidae said, very slowly, 'Yes.'

'Yes!' She was a girl. Child Ayllis, clapping her hands and dancing with delight at such fine good things. *Alive, alive, alive, alive, alive, little things, little things.* 'Oh gods, I'd almost given up hoping!' And her hands dropped. 'And … Samei?' She said, suddenly fearful, 'There was a story, someone said, about two brothers fighting, and their mother …. but they said they … they said they were both dead…'

Lidae thought: how can it not be carved into my faced? Carved into Ryn's face, his wounds, bloody marks of writing?

'I don't know. About Samei.' The lie was too huge, sat in her mouth too painful. She said at last, 'I think he must be dead.' She said, 'I know that he is dead.'

Ayllis opened her mouth. But Ayllis said nothing. They hugged each other very tightly. Two women who understood lies and grief and life.

'Come and sit down,' Ayllis said. 'You look exhausted. Are you injured?' Her eyes went wide. 'Your army lost.'

'And you? You were a prisoner in a cage in our camp.'

'Our soldiers came. I told them who I was.' She shrugged at Lidae, almost apologetic. 'My husband was a hero of Elayne's army. *"Poet of the sword, glorious, his name will live forever in song, I'm pregnant with his son."* She put her hands on her stomach over the baby. 'The blood-covered murderers flowing into your camp to rape and pillage were falling over themselves to help me, they tore the cage apart with their bare hands, almost, escorted me back to my tent. Almost sitting down on the battlefield to knit me booties. Ryn's captain let me stay here with them, until I can go back to Illyrith. Here's my tent, see? Come and rest.' She said loudly to the soldiers who were trying to pretend they weren't listening, 'This is Ryn's mother, you've gathered. She came here to find him.' A man smiled, he was hurrying over towards Ryn's tent but he stopped, came towards her smiling showing a great bruise on his face, clasped her hands. He was sweating and breathing hard, he must have just been running, is he … Lycan? Lidae thought, the man they said they'd fetch who'd be so happy to see Ryn?

'You brought him back to us!' Big scarred hands squeezed her fingers. 'He talks about you all the time. It's good, so good to meet you. He was so worried…' A frown, the kind youthful innocence replaced briefly with a soldier wondering: *you were on the enemy side, I think.* He clapped her hand again tighter. 'Well! Anyway. You must be frozen, in that … that dress. There's a spare cloak in my tent, I'll get it for you. Just wait until I've seen Ryn. Then I'll get it.' He was off into Ryn's tent, almost singing, with Lidae behind him. Ryn was lying huddled, his face grey and sweating. I should have forced him to stay there in the sick tents, Lidae thought, curse them, I should have told them… But Ryn's face almost lit up when he saw Lycan. The two boys clasped hands. Lidae stopped quietly outside, listening.

'You look worse than I do, Ryn!' And a pause, again a soldier thinking,

taking in the battlefield with tired knowing eyes, a pause, a laugh, loud
and false and casual, Lycan's voice careless and loud, 'Gods, Ryn, all
night I thought you were dead, looking everywhere, freezing my nads
off, and you're snoozing in the sick tent.'

Ryn's voice, all false too with trying, blankness to it, but with
something deeply real and happy beneath: 'Should have looked in the
sick tents, then, shouldn't you?' A flicker of a smile, briefly, in his voice
as he said, 'Dumb, you are,' and his mother knew, just knew, it was some
old joke between Lycan and Ryn.

Lycan, very loudly: 'Dumb I Am, he says, our fine soldier Got
Himself Wounded! I did look in the bloody sick tents, obviously.'

Ryn, his voice still false and trying to be normal, and so, so grateful
his friend was playing along: 'Just not the one I was in, obviously. But I
got the grand one, only the best, they gave me. Two of General Gaethan's
men personally escorted me there, made sure there was a bed for me.'

Lycan: 'Oh, well, I'd better get out now, hadn't I? Got-Himself-
Wounded is far too grand to mix with the likes of me.'

Lycan, in a different voice: 'I'm so glad you're not badly wounded,
Ryn.'

Lycan knew, Lidae thought then. But he was kind also.

The pyres burned that evening for the victorious dead. The Glorious
Army of Illyrith—so who the army had been that Lidae had fought for,
Lidae could no longer say. The traitor usurper King Temyr, may his name
be a curse word. Half the men here rejoicing must have fought under
him, there were faces here she recognised, men here she recognised from
her own ranks only a few days ago who everyone now knew had always
been in Queen Elayne's army. Lidae looked for her own squad, Eralene
and Deljan, the captain. The faces blurred, she couldn't remember what
they looked like to recognise them, found she was looking for Maerc and
Acol and Emmas, Cythra, Devid, even Myron and Taim and Gulius.

She saw Elayne once, from a distance, when the victorious queen rode
through the camp to greet her soldiers, thank them. She was tall, like her
father, her hair was dark, her skin very white. She was wearing armour,
her corselet was gilded, studded with rubies, her cloak was crimson and
gold- and silver-thread. She wore a crown of golden flowers. Her horse
was black, its hooves gilded, its trappings all gold and scarlet, worked
also with nodding golden flowers. An honour guard followed behind
her, and their armour and their helmets and their cloaks were all red
and their horses were red. The first of them carried the red banner of

Illyrith, but the rest that rode behind carried a banner of gold cloth that was the queen's own banner. She was young and fair and brilliant, the men cheered and cheered for her, clashed their swords and their spears, stamped their feet.

She had fought in the thick of the battle. Three times, she had led her horsemen in a charge against the cream of King Temyr's troops. In the second charge, her horse had been killed beneath her, a young cavalryman had dismounted in the thick of the fighting, bowed to her, given her his horse. He had been killed in the next moment, and she herself had avenged him. In the third charge, she had shouted to Prince Fiol to face her. They had fought together, a king's son and a king's daughter, she had killed him with a sword blow to his throat. Temyr had sent a great shadow beast against her, even that she had fought with, even after it had wounded her she had fought it, until at last a great god-bird shining as gold as her banner had come down to save her, destroyed the shadow-beast, carried her on its back to her tent. Temyr's last godbeasts had deserted him then, slunk away into the dark in shame, her gods and her dragon had leaped into the sky and made the sky burn gold for her, her dragon had cut down the ranks of the enemy without mercy. Temyr had been burned up in its fire. Clews, Lidae remember, had said that Temyr should have married her off to his son. But here she rode alone, a queen, magnificent in her victory that hung about her like a golden light. She herself might almost be a dragon, she was so beautiful, so glorious.

'She looks like you,' Ayllis said.

Lidae said, 'What?'

'That's how I always imagined you as a soldier,' said Ayllis. 'Mother used to talk about it. *"Lidae, she was a soldier, Ayllis, a warrior, when she was young, she wore bronze armour, she had a sword, a helmet … You know that silver cup of hers, you've seen it, yes, the one Emmas brings out to show people? She won that for herself, in a battle, and lots of other things, valuable beautiful things. She went to the great cities in the south, she's seen kings' palaces, temples, marble courtyards with crystal fountains."* When I was little, I thought your armour must have looked like that silver cup.'

'I—' Trumpets rang, musical as the crystal fountains that Lidae could see now clearly, remember, white marble, gilding, sometimes the water would be perfumed, or coloured red or green or black, sometimes, in the richest of the cities, the fountains would sparkle not with water but with strong sweet dark wine. And the trumpets rang now just as they had then in those cities, Ayllis gasped in excitement, the soldiers clashed their weapons and cheered. Queen Elayne drew her horse up before them, looked at them, her beautiful eyes met every eye that sought her, hungered for her to see them, know them. She drew her sword, its hilt was golden, there was of course a great ruby set in the hilt.

Lidae thought: I know what she will say. We all know. And we will cheer her, weep with joy, reach out to try to touch the hem of her cloak, men will stand in her horse's hoofprints and kiss the dirt, men will say, voices breaking, 'I was there, I heard her speak it, gods, I was there when she gave the order!'

'My people,' Queen Elayne cried out. Her voice was sweet and gentle, a fair young maiden's voice, it made Temyr's gruff man's voice, warrior's voice, seem very crude.

A time of war, of violence, all good government is overthrown, the fields are barren, the rivers poisoned, armies and warlords and warrior bands ranged across the world of Irlawe in fury, children have grown up knowing nothing but war and bloodshed. Women live in fear, staring at the horizon waiting for another warband to come down on them. Bear their assailants' children in shame and grief. Beggars, refugees, the poor, the starving, at the mercy of any man who can wield a sword. This, Queen Elayne swore to them, this horror she would end, she would make the world one empire of peace again, beneath a gentle loving queen. Good laws, justice: these things she would bring them, her people would never need to live in fear again. She herself had lived in fear, in hiding, poor and starving, waiting every day to be raped and knifed. Peace, she would bring them! Prosperity! Peace! Only for peace had she led them against the traitor Temyr, may his name be spoken only as a curse. They must march south, against the false queen of Eralath and her monstrous sons; they must march east where the islands had betrayed them, set up a demon's child as their king. And when they had defeated these threatening evils, when all of Irlawe bowed to her justice, her mercy, and then the great Empire of Illyrith would have peace and prosperity such as they had never before dreamed of. And the pale winter sunlight fell like a cloak on her sword and her crown and her long dark hair, and, oh, she was beautiful and wonderful.

At dusk they burned the bodies of their fallen. Mighty pyres, the flames rising so high they looked like a city wall, or the tree trunks of a forest. The greatest of them, on which the heroes of Elayne's army lay, was lit not by human hand but by the queen's dragon, ancient, its scales red and black, its wings laced with battle scars. It had fought in every battle for the crown of Illyrith since the Empire was founded, gods, monsters, wonders, princes, heroes, had all fallen before it. It had killed many of its own kind. They sat in its shadow, frozen, the shadow of its wings like a curse screamed at them. I have never seen anything as beautiful as a dragon, Lidae thought. After it had lit the pyre into a column of gold it came down to landing; silhouetted against the flames, the Army of Illyrith watched as the dragon knelt at Queen Elayne's feet.

Ayllis said, later: I suppose … at the beginning, when she first rose up against Temyr, she did mean it, that all she wanted for Illyrith was an end to the endless fighting, to bring peace.

Ryn said, later: I suppose … if she knows that the false queen of Eralath will attack us, if we don't attack first … if she knows that this new King of the Islands is a danger to us, which I'm sure, if she says it, he is…

Lidae thought, later: I suppose I did look a bit like that, when I was young, yes.

Fifty-eight

'Mother couldn't understand it,' said Ayllis. 'Why you stayed in Salith Drylith. *"It's a good place for the boys,"* Father would say. *"Emmas is making good work of that farm, they'll be better off than us soon enough."* But Mother, she'd shake her head ... And I'd think, listening to Mother: she was like ... like that, and she came here to live? I thought: she's been in battle, she's seen temples and courtyards and palaces—I thought, when I was little, that you'd, that you'd lived in temples and palaces... And here you were, mother would say, amazed, living in Salith Drylth like a common thing.'

The bonfire outside the tent crackled, a gust of wind blew the doorcurtain and they saw the flames licking up blue. Men's voices cheered. Among them, Lidae could hear Ryn's.

'Cythra talked about me?' Like that? Like .... wondering? Like .... she was envious? Like ... she thought...?

Ayllis looked astonished. 'She talked about you all the time. She...' Pause. Wing beats, distant. Silver trumpets, and the smell of fire, and men singing. A roar of laughter. A cold wind. 'She thought you must despise her, sometimes, you know? For how little her life was. So envied you so much. *"I did everything my parents told me, and then at fifteen I got married to your father, the first man I'd ... and I had my children, and that's it. I'd never been further than Karke, and that barely more than twice."* That's what she'd say. *"And look at Lidae, all she's done, all she knows—she saw the king once, in Thalden. Listen to her talking about the places she's seen, the things she's done. She chose her husband, from all the men she'd met, and only when she was ready. I had sons almost full grown, before she even decided to get married at all. Four children and I'm worn out and dying at forty, and I piss myself when I cough... And then when your father died, I was nothing and had nothing..."* That's what she'd say. *"She fought off the men who came to kill her children,"* she'd say of you. *"I hid in fear, and let my sons die for me, but she fought them off, saved her children's lives." "I'm sorry,"* she'd say, *"Dylas. Marn. Niken. I'm so sorry I couldn't be more like Lidae."*

'*"Be free, like Lidae, Ayllis,"* she'd say. That was the last thing she said to me when she was dying. *"Be free and strong, and chose your life, Ayllis. Like Lidae."*'

Lidae thought stupidly: I slept in a temple once. After we'd sacked it. Its floor was solid gold and its walls were made of gold and pearl and ivory, it was so big and so high you could have fitted in all of Karke. It was the coldest hardest most uncomfortable place I've ever slept in. And I slept in a palace once, it belonged to a princess, her ancestors had been kings once, they said. She was very old, blind, deaf, senile, she was pushed around by a serving boy in a wheeled chair carved of dragon bones. The serving boy wore nothing but a golden loincloth and a diamond collar. The princess wore a gown of white fur even in the summer heat.

All that time, thinking Cythra despised her for her failure. Be more like Cythra, Lidae! Try, come on! Tomorrow it will, it must, be better. Lying awake in the dark, listening to the boys' breathing, wanting to cry with shame, with pity for them that they are my sons and not Cythra's boys who had such a good mother to raise them. Tomorrow it will be different, tomorrow I'll do better, I promise.

I don't know, I don't know what to do, tell me what to do, Cythra. Help me be more like you are. Your good gentle life, that never hurt anyone in the world. A house, children, the smell of new-baked bread … all that's best in life.

Outside the tent, she heard the men dancing, a whistle playing a fast tune, very badly, hands clapping out a beat.

'And look at me,' said Ayllis. 'Pregnant, widowed … I have a bag of coin because my husband was a richer man than my father. When a man with a sword came at me in your camp, I survived because I could shout my husband's name. *"Spare me, spare me, my husband was Eliades the man-slaying hero!"* I knew when I married him that he was likely to die in battle. Maybe I wouldn't have married him, if I'd thought he'd live to be a hundred and never leave my side.'

I can still go back, Lidae thought.

Ayllis said, 'I shouldn't say that. I'm sorry.'

Another pause, awkward silence, Ayllis's hands on her stomach. Lidae said, to say something, 'It seems to finally be quietening down out there.'

'Or else someone broke Lycan's flute. I don't … I don't blame you, Lidae.'

Blame me?

'For mother's death. If you thought I did.'

'I—'

I don't know.

'Father wanted to be a soldier when he was young, before he married Mother. You wouldn't know, but he was so desperate to be a soldier, he even saved up coin to buy armour and a sword. Mother told me about it after he died, said she thought it made him happy to be going off to war finally after all. He used to talk about it sometimes, Mother said, when they were first married, even after Dylas was born, talk about men he heard of who went off soldiering. Wistfully, she said. And then after the boys died that night, and he…

'Going to be a soldier was the only thing he could do, after that, Mother said. So she … she didn't blame you for that either, Lidae. If you thought she did.'

Being a soldier is an escape from things. A solution to things.

We didn't really have any other choices.

I like being a soldier. I suppose I assumed Devid did.

Everyone did.

I don't know.

I never thought about it. About Devid.

Ayllis said, 'Ryn and Samei would have been killed in Salith Drylth, like all the others, if you hadn't fought to protect them. They would have been killed that night in the woods, or at the River Nimenest, or they would have ended up trailing along as camp followers behind the army, child whores, beggars, thieves, or as refugees starving on the roads driven out of every town they came to. If you hadn't done what you did. They both knew that, Lidae. Mother told that to Samei. I told that to Ryn.'

Fifty-nine

And the battle is over. And Ryn's battle is done. His left arm was ruined. 'Just about able to wipe my bum, give it a few months and a lot of practise.' He blushed with horror when he realised his mother had heard him. Coughed and gasped. Even in all that has happened, Lidae thought.

Ayllis said, 'Doesn't he care? He's not even upset. Look at him.'

He thinks about it every moment. He'll never stop thinking about it. Never forgive himself. Over and over, he thinks of the sword coming down, he can't remember the sword-stroke, not really, but he sees something, his brother looks smaller, weaker, terrified, begging him, and he thinks: if I'd just … a little to the left … a little higher … or stepped back, or …. Next time, he thinks, over and over, when it happens for real, if I just… Or he thinks: he would have killed me, he was going to kill me, really kill me, he wouldn't have spared me, if I hadn't killed him. And in the false memory his brother is a monster like a dragon. A child's memory of his brother raging at him. A child's memory, she thought, thinking of her own childhood, of himself raging at his brother. His shame at those memories. So he laughs, he fools around with his friends, he brags about his injuries, he doesn't have a care in the world, his friends pretend they don't know. He won't speak to me. I can't speak to him.

'I can stay on, in the army, I can use my right arm still, hold a sword, look.'

She heard Lycan say, 'I don't know, Ryn…'

'I'll be fine. Trust me.'

And Lycan's voice, firm, loving, understanding everything: 'Bugger off back to Illyrith, rebuild your farmhouse there, buy a cow, plant your plum tree, you're finished in the army, you dumb.'

Ayllis would go with him. 'Strictly, actually, he'll go with me.' Her hero husband, bright and brilliant, man-slaying Eliades, what he'd been a hero for, it turned out, was dying. 'Run away, you fools,' he'd shouted to his companions, 'just bloody run.' But he'd been rewarded in death with a purse of gold and the status of hero. Thus she had the coin to take back to Illyrith, set up house.

Lidae went to Hana's tent, where the smell of women's bodies was so strong. Hana wasn't there, the other woman her friend was, regarded Lidae with suspicion.

'I'll wait,' Lidae said. The woman was afraid, she thought, that she had come to take Hana away. She waited a long time, and Hana's friend watched her all the time. The worst, the cruellest of the camp women. Gods, she thought, I should kneel down to beg her forgiveness. But she would look back at me, curl her lips in revulsion, *All that was done to me by you soldiers, and you say you're sorry?'* Like Ryn saying he's sorry for killing Samei, me saying I'm sorry for not stopping him. Hana's friend had a ragged cloak that she was mending, muttering a charm against the cold under her breath, sucking her fingers between stitches to keep them working. Lidae stood by the tent shifting her weight from foot to foot, her knees aching, her back aching, her hands getting horribly raw and puffed up. It was damp, almost raining, freezing cold to the bones but not quite cold enough for frost. Her feet squelched in the mud. She searched the ground all about for signs of spring flowers, snowdrops or crocuses. The sick tents and the soldiers' tents were lost in the damp, thin ghostly shadowy things. A woman in the next tent hummed to herself, as if she was happy, and then Lidae thought, of course she can be happy.

'Good, neat stitches, and that's almost done', Hana's friend said, delighted.

When Hana returned she was very tired. Her hair was beaded with damp, the hem of her green cloak was sodden with mud. A brilliant flash of colour in the grey, her green cloak, the polished copper around her neck.

'I've got your dress to return to you, Hana.' She'd found someone to wash it, make some attempt to dry it. Hana took it wordlessly. The red silk swelled over her thin cracked raw hands. Bundled up in her arms she seemed to be holding something beautiful.

'How's Ryn?'

'Ryn is … well. Recovering.'

Hana smiled. 'That's good. I was worried, the stuff they put on his wound, from the smell it had ashes in it, I wouldn't have used it, not on a wound like that.' She frowned, looked away. 'Not that I know anything about healing, now. I'm glad Ryn is recovering. Thank you for bringing the dress back, Lidae. And for the food the other night.'

'Hana, wait.'

'Yes?'

'Ryn and Ayllis are going back to Illyrith. To settle there. Rebuild the farm at Salith Drylth.' Lidae said awkwardly, 'Would you go with them?'

A very long silence now. Hana's friend put down her sewing. Lidae had thought that Hana would cry out, laugh, hug her. Thank her. But I'm thinking of her as a child, she thought. Hana's friend had such an expression of contempt on her face: *You think that you owe her something, because you chose to kill people, rather than to live like this?* A long silence, and then without speaking Hana got her things together, her comb, her necklace, her bowl, her cup, the dusty crumbling heather sprig. Folded them in the red dress.

She didn't speak the whole time they walked back to Ayllis's tent. The damp turned into rain, soaking them both. At the tents some of Ryn's squad were sitting around a fire with their cloaks over their heads, playing dice; they stared at Hana, one of them whistled, one of them made a warding sign with his hand. She looked back at them fiercely. Lidae shivered to think of her walking a battlefield in the dark to scavenge from the dead. How brave she is. How brave she was.

When Ayllis came to greet Hana, the two girls did not recognise each other, hesitated because they must both know who the other was but couldn't recognise the face. They did not hug each other, shout out in joyous greeting as old friends. Hana flinched, drew back from Ayllis, clutched her bundle until the red fabric was squeezed tight against her body. Ayllis was pale, shocked. Ryn came out of his tent, bent over from his wounds. Hana wouldn't embrace Ayllis, who had been her closest friend, but she hugged Ryn.

Hana turning her nose up at the idiocy of little boys, although she'd always been soft on Samei because she'd been so grown up when he was born that she'd looked at his baby sweetness like the women did…

If she'd only been a few years younger, thought Lidae, back at the beginning, at the Nimenest.

'You're pregnant,' Hana said to Ayllis.

Ayllis said, 'You know about these things, don't you, Hana? Could I ask you?' She was not speaking as one childhood friend to another, nor as a hero's widow to the lowest of the camp women. A grown woman asking another woman for help and advice.

'I'm not a healer,' Hana said. 'I've forgotten it all, that's gone.' But then she was asking questions, how far along was Ayllis, could she feel it move yet, any sickness, pain anywhere? It's been a long time, she said, I need to remember, are you sure, squeezing her bundle, the showy gaudy red dress, are you sure you trust me? Let me remember. Her voice mimicking exactly her mother's, she sounded very alive suddenly. 'I can look at your wounds, too, Ryn,' she said, 'what did they use on them, is the pain lessening? Any fever? Heat in the wounds? No? That's good.' A warmth had come into her. She touched Ryn's arm gently, concentrating.

Ayllis had found a cart for Ryn to travel in, others who were going back to Illyrith, wounded soldiers, another young widow, soldiers from Durith's army who wanted to go home to forget everything. Elayne was sending men back north to secure her position, they could travel in the baggage all the way to Karke. Ryn and Ayllis and Hana would leave the next morning at first light.

Lidae looked for Clews, also.

He was dead. He must be dead. Most of the captains from Temyr's army had been killed in battle, one had fled, two had surrendered and been executed, two had surrendered and sworn loyalty to Queen Elayne. Lord Sabryyr had surrendered very early on in the battle, sworn loyalty. Lidae remembered the boat coming in in the dark, at Navikyre Fortress, and wondered. Secrets and conspiracies, whispers, betrayals, Clews's grief. If Lord Sabryyr had done more than just surrender, had refused to send us into battle or ordered us all to put down our swords or to change sides… These great powerful men. She walked to the place where the heads of Temyr's dead captains were displayed: Clews was not there but then he was not important enough to be there. He is out there on the battlefield, she thought, with Samei. As a sign of reconciliation, Elayne had ordered that the enemy dead be burned the next evening, accorded full honours. This should make Lidae glad, that Samei would be burned and she could forget him. It is mad drivel, she thought, that once he is burned I can forget him. Who first made up this rubbish? How did I believe it? She thought of all those who had died and thought, I never believed it, none of us do.

Or some of them do believe it. The camp women don't believe it, she thought suddenly, the women like Hana, the hollowed-eyed ones in the streets of a fallen city, trailing after the army begging for a scrap of bread: they remember every death. But some of the soldiers believe it, I believed it once, because we have to.

Tears came up again in her eyes for Ryn and Samei. She felt herself again falling, teetering on the edge of a great chasm opening up. I shall lie down with the dead, my comrades, let them burn me alive with Samei. When I was a child, I hid myself in my family's corpses, piled them over me, buried myself in them. Everything since then, everything I've done, I've been… She was on her knees in the earth, sobbing, tearing at her hair, rubbing her face with soil. 'Ryn. Samei. Ryn.' I wish I'd died at Raena, I wish I'd never lived. Look at this, this farce of my life. All I've ever loved in the world, and I've lost you both. 'I'm sorry,' she cried, 'I'm sorry. I tried so hard to protect you, but everything I did was wrong.'

A warm weight on her shoulder. She shook it off, thinking she was imagining it. Clews said, 'Lidae. Stop. Please. I…' His voice shrank very small. 'I can't bear to hear you.'

You shouldn't be alive! I was looking to find your head here on a stake! Her hand went for her sword. Kill him! He was an old, old man, she saw, who was eating his own heart out in grief for Samei whom he had loved as if he were his own son.

They sat together in the mud and grieved, Lidae's head pressed against Clews' chest. She cursed Ryn, cursed herself, cursed Samei for refusing to stop fighting. 'Ryn was going to stop it, yield to him, and he attacked him, refused to let Ryn stop fighting, he wanted to kill Ryn he really truly wanted to kill him. Curse him. Curse him. He was my son,' she screamed, 'and I let Ryn kill him.' She screamed out all her rage and shame and guilt and hate for her sons into Clews' chest.

Finally after a long time she stopped crying. Her face was disgusting, soaked in snot and tears and spittle, gummed to Clews' shirt. 'I'm sorry. Gods.'

'It doesn't matter. It's just a shirt. I did try,' he said, 'to persuade Lord Sabryyr to keep most of the men back from the fighting. Believe me, I did. But Elayne wanted victory in battle. She had to prove herself worthy to her soldiers. Queen by right of her sword arm. She insisted Lord Sabryyr send you all in to fight.'

Lidae said blankly, 'You betrayed her father. Killed her father.'

Clews sighed. 'I was a very small insignificant part in her father's death. Elayne and her advisors … they know what I did. But they know I am more useful to them alive than dead.'

Lidae thought: that's it?

That's all it is?

'In twenty years' time, or thirty years, or ten, or one … Elayne will be grey and tired. The southern cities will still chafe against our rule. We'll still be fighting the false Queen of Eralath and her sons.' He shook his head. 'Go home with Ryn, Lidae.'

She thought: I have no home. Everywhere I've felt safe, you've betrayed it for the sake of one king or another king. She said, 'This is my home, Clews. The army.' Still now saying that made her feel proud. She put her hand on her sword. The red glass in the hilt felt warm against her skin. 'We both love soldiering. I'll go south,' she said, 'with Queen Elayne.'

'Lidae,' Clews said, 'Go home, Lidae. Please. Go back with Ryn.'

She thought: the one thing I've ever been good at is soldiering. The one thing I've ever enjoyed doing is soldiering. I'm soaked in blood up to my eyeballs. Go home, sit by the fire, milk the cow, mind Ayllis's baby? A grandmother, Clews, is that how you see me?

'Why don't you go home, Clews? A farm in Illyrith, a man, a life of peace?'

'No!' His face was burning red. He said, angrier than she'd ever heard him, 'I'm not suggesting it, Lidae. I'm ordering you. As a captain in Queen Elayne's army. Go home to Illyrith.'

'Ordering me? You, are ordering me?'

He said, more gently, 'I'll have them find Samei's body, burn it separately, you can take his ashes back with you to Salith Drylth.'

Sixty

It was heavy going, through the mud, the cart jolting and sticking, Ryn grimacing in pain; it got colder and the mud crusted over with ice, slippery under foot where the columns in front of them hadn't churned it knee-deep. Why guarding the baggage train was the worst job in the world and to be avoided in any way possible, even if doing it did mean you got to march nearer your children. Ryn rode in the cart; Ayllis sat beside Ryn sometimes, Lidae insisted, even if Hana said there was no need. Then another wounded soldier joined him, who'd found the walking too much in the mud and the cold, his first battle as a boy Ryn's age had been against King Durith, he shook his head in confusion. His right arm was heavily bandaged, he walked with a limp, he had an old scar where his left eye once was. Sometimes he sang in a clear, fine voice, gentle songs from Illyrith, a girl lying on the grass beneath an oak tree, two friends out hunting geese in the marshes with the sun warm on their backs. If the wind wasn't blowing too cold, Ayllis would join in.

They went through empty grasslands, rolling green hills empty of people, they would see the tracks of wolves and deer, dark shapes running, far off in the vastness; the sky was blue with high, thin traces of cloud that were luminous even in the daylight, like lanterns, a shadow would fall on them and they would look up, pointing, to see a huge eagle high above them. The air had a crystalline smell to it, utterly pure. One day Lidae found that, like the goose hunters, she could almost feel the sun's warmth on her skin. Ahead of them, splendid on the horizon, rose the Emnelenethkyr, the Empty Peaks. They joined the miners' road that led through the mountains, bringing tin and copper and quicksilver and pinewood south, and the going was quicker. A good road, stone, well-kept, scored with wheels tracks. The horse almost trotted along. The first night in the mountains it snowed, they lost two days but the second morning the sky was pink, the strange high clouds burned too bright to look at, and Lidae was certain the weather was turning to spring. They set off with the snow crunching under the horse's hooves and the cart-wheels sticking, light dancing off white mountains, every branch glittering with silver like bells. After that the warmth came quickly, the snow rushed away before them singing, wet feathery snow lumps came scudding down leaving the mountainsides dark and ragged. Lidae looked for snowdrops and crocuses and even starflowers on the sheltered banks by the roadside. Began to see them.

Ryn did not talk to her. She walked beside the cart-horse, tried not to see him. She could feel him behind her, a weight in the back of her head, sometimes it was almost as if she was carrying him. He would talk to his fellow soldier about little daily things, the cart-horse, the country they passed through, birds, animals, a long-running unresolvable debate on the state of the cart's left rear wheel that he was certain was going to break. Around Ayllis he was hunched, hidden into himself, he would talk to her crudely, or sometimes as if she was much younger than him. Around Hana he was frightened. He had not recognised her. Did not recognise her. It confused him too much, Ayllis thought, she herself was frightened, she said, trying to make sense of Hana now and her memory of Hana as her older, wiser, tougher friend. To Ryn, Ayllis pointed out, Hana must have been a woman grown; the last time Ryn had seen her, she had been treating his wound, caring for him.

'But I couldn't leave her,' Lidae said. 'What was I supposed to do? Leave her as she was?'

'No, of course not. Of course she had to come back with us.' Ayllis sounded like Cythra. It was difficult talking to her and seeing Cythra and Ayllis-the-child, both at once. Lidae, too, tried to keep herself from talking to Hana, being too near her. Those raw old-woman fingers, tending Ryn's wounds once beneath the birch trees. And Hana herself avoided talking to anyone, looked ahead of her in silence, strained. Lidae thought: perhaps I should have left her, forgotten about her. Then one night she woke and heard the two women talking, it had started as something worrying Ayllis about the baby, now in-between Hana checking and reassuring they were talking as two women together, who might be sisters or close friends.

No one spoke Samei's name. Lidae found herself repeating it over and over in her head, SameiSameiSameiSameiSamei until it was nonsense. It was with them like another person, sometimes it was almost visible, a shadow-shape sitting in the cart beside Ryn. The words always in their mouths. The soldiers they followed, the people around them: they must all know, they must see Samei sitting there beside Ryn. Ayllis called Ryn 'your son' when she spoke to Lidae, as if she couldn't help but dare herself to say it.

I can't ever forgive him, Lidae thought. He won't ever forgive himself. He won't ever forgive me. And the cart-horse's hooves on the wet stones of the road beat out SameiSameiSameiSameiSamei in her head. She touched her sword, thought sometimes that if they were attacked by robbers, or by a wolf, she could use her sword, fight to defend them all, the only one who could. How proud she had been, she thought, when she had been the only one able to defend them. If I had to kill a bandit, here, now, to save them... But they were following a long column of soldiers, they were safe. We can't go on like this forever, Lidae thought, we can't live together, work a farm, sit down together to eat. *'The byre needs cleaning out, Ryn, can you manage that, with the ruined arm your brother gave you when you killed him?' 'I should think so, Mother, I hate you, if I killed him it was because he almost killed me, I hate myself for it you know that, I wish he'd killed me, and I blame you, Mother, and you blame yourself, I can clean out the byre tomorrow, yes.'* And Samei sitting in the corner, almost visible, faceless and shapeless like a bloodclot, he looked like Ryn and when I think of him now I see Ryn's face. I remember his thin little body when he was little, his skinny flailing legs that I wanted to grab up to kiss, the sleek smallness of him compared to Ryn. But I can't remember his face properly. When I think about him, I see Ryn.

I loved Ryn more than Samei, she thought. Always. Sometimes in the night, unable to sleep, her back and her knees and her shoulder aching, she would think, like an abyss: what if it had been the other way round? If Samei had killed Ryn? What then? And sometimes she thought, in dim anger: what if Emmas had been alive when the soldiers first came to Salith Drylth, and it had been him who fought to defend them?

The road ran low through river valleys, sheltered from the north winds. They turned through a narrow pass, steep green sides all rock and grass and moss, a crag that might be a grey watchman's face; a meadow fell before them, spring flowers in spring sunshine sprawling away as deep as soft thick blankets, yellow and red and blue and white and pink. The road plunged into it, leaves and flowers knee-high, waist-high. Two years ago, one year ago, Lidae thought, Samei would have whooped with delight, thrown himself into it hidden, swum in pink and white and blue and green. 'Fruit and cream,' Samei would have described it. 'Sweet wine and thick honey and spiced apple cakes.' She picked a single flower, a pale blue-purple, fading to white at the petal tips. A tiny black beetle crawled drowsily on the pollen at its centre. Too early to come out, she thought, a cold wind will come. A long loud call, clumsy and joyful, she looked up and the wild geese were flying over the meadow, on into the mountains, going back north to Illyrith for the summer to breed. Soon the swifts and the swallows would follow them.

And like the birds, they came one wet grey morning to the Nimenest where the King's Bridge had been rebuilt, smaller and thinner and plainer. Traces of dragon fire were visible in a blackened dead tree trunk, shattered clear as a spear point at its top, blackened twisted boulders that had melted and cooled like the slag from a metalworks. But plants had grown up again, a tangle of slender young birch trees furzed now with gold-green leaf-buds, willowherb in green banks, nettles, brambles with a few wizened dried fruits; the stones of the bridge were losing their raw new-cut edges, sinking into the landscape around them in a crust of lichen and moss. And the woods and the marshes of Illyrith beyond the river, the wheat fields stubbled green, the high hills. The thin beckoning line of the sea. On the edge of the eastern marshes, looking down onto dark rot-scented water, buried in dark reeds that hissed in the wind, Lidae saw the swallows. The drift of them in the air turning, murmuring.

Ayllis's belly was swollen now, she rode in the cart, grumbled at how hard the cart was to sleep in. The old ex-soldier left them to go west to Thalden where his father had once kept a tavern. Hana hummed the songs he had sung. Ryn's wounds were mending, he walked for hours at a time, practised stretching and moving his left arm. But he grew more and more silent, his face haunted. Stared off ahead of them.

And then one wet grey afternoon they came at last to the ruins of Salith Drylth.

Blackened stones all tumbled. Blackened timbers. Gaping empty windows, the roof fallen, the doorway dark and yawning. The apple tree in the garden, last year's fruit in the grass at its foot. The may tree, readying itself to blossom. The long low view across soft turf to the clifftop and the sea.

A long, long time, Lidae stood in the ruins of the farmhouse. Everything was overgrown with brambles. Weeds and wild grass as high as her knees. She pushed her way through, fighting, through to the door. She had to use her sword, absurdly, to cut the brambles back. Her hands were scratched. The door was hanging open, the wood blackened by the fire, she thought that she could smell the smoke. It had half come off its hinges. She went through it, trying not to shudder. It felt like walking beneath the horse head. She closed her eyes and she was walking out through the gates of Raena as a soldier. Walking into the house with Emmas, pregnant with Ryn, and she had thought that she could still go back to something else. The long table was burned into a heap of ashes. The cookpot was overturned in the hearth, green with verdigris. Sherds of broken pottery crunched under her feet.

There. Just there, Ryn had lain sprawled, he's dead, he's dead, she'd thought.

'You shouted for Samei first. You didn't shout for me.'

'I had to shout one name first, Ryn.'

There, she had stood in the doorway to the sleeping place, sword in hand, trying and failing to defend her children. She said, very quietly, to the shadow in the doorway, the shadow sprawled in the floor, the shadow at the hearth with its bright hair and its bright eyes smiling at her, 'I told you not to run. Why didn't you listen?' The bed she had slept in with Emmas was burned to ashes like the table. The looted coverlet burned. She saw the coverlet so clearly, the pattern of silver flowers, the red silk, the water stain, obscene like a semen stain, the tear she had crudely mended. She saw herself at eighteen looting it. She saw herself in bed with Emmas. She saw herself from very far away, red and screaming, giving birth to Ryn.

'Come on, push now, Lidae, push.' 'I can't push. I can't push. I can't push.' 'You can bloody push, Lidae.' 'He's dead. Isn't he? Dead.' 'He's not dead, he's a big bouncing baby boy, Lidae.'

The bed the boys had slept in was burned to ashes. The bed Samei had hidden under, refused to come out from even as the house was burning.

Why don't you listen? Why don't you ever listen to me?'

Something crunched beneath her foot. She bent down. A long lump of bone. She picked it up, turned it over, rubbed it with her sleeve. A little man, carved out of a bone, perhaps a cow's shin bone from the size of it. Very worn, its face chipped so that its nose was missing, and one eye seemed to squint. It had never been well carved to begin with. 'You can't give that to him,' she'd said to Emmas. 'You just can't.' She'd been afraid he'd laugh at it or be insulted by it. 'Silly old Samei,' Ryn had said, when Samei had hugged it the first moment he saw it. His best thing, Rov.

War is a terrible thing. But, she thought, the freedom war gave me … that is not a terrible thing. I had a far better life, she thought, than would have been possible in Raena, if my parents … if my parents had lived. Freedom, coin—which means freedom—little to fear—which for a woman also means freedom. And endless countless numbers of people had died, for almost nothing, and she herself had killed many of them. And Hana, and Samei's slave woman, and so many others: they had a far worse life.

She thought, almost laughing: my children wouldn't have been soldiers, and they might both be alive now, but then they might never have been born at all or they might both have starved in the street. I've done terrible things, but I've also been free and happy and strong. These two things of her life, both true things, even as they were unreconcilable things. And I tried all my life to protect my children, I poured myself out in guilt and shame trying to protect them, but I don't know whether I protected them, or I failed them.

Rov. It means 'peace' in the old rune language, Rena had once told her, and she'd never asked whether Samei knew that somehow in some strange magical child's way. Assumed he didn't. A baby sound, before he could speak properly, that meant something that only he understood.

She thought: there's no answer. There never was, never will be.

She dropped the doll back down into the ashes. Brushed ash and stone over it. She went back outside to join the others. Ryn took a step towards her. Flinched as she put her arms around him. She flinched as she put her arms around him.

At dusk, with the swallows flying low, the gulls calling, Lidae buried her sword beneath the may tree. The red glass winked at her as she pushed the earth down over it. At dawn, in the dew with the sea-wind blowing salt in their faces, she and Ryn buried Samei's ashes. Her knees and her back and her shoulder ached, her knees cracked as she knelt, she heard Ryn hiss with pain as she helped him up and he helped her up. They scattered the first yellow buttercups over the grave. The air smelled of wet grass and seaweed and apples. A grey sunshine of spring with the sky a nothing colour, cloud-scudded.

'We can rebuild the house,' Ryn said. 'Can't we? Mother?'

She said after a moment, 'I hope so.'

A soldier and a mother and a woman, living.

Acknowledgements

Yet again, so many people made this book possible.

Francesca at Luna Press is an inspiring publisher and a wonderful human being. I'm extremely proud to be published by her.

Shona Kinsella, my editor, had to deal with deliberately missed comas, accidentally missed commas, passages where I'd collapsed sobbing with exhaustion after a day home-schooling, and passages that Microsoft Word had decided were written in Arabic. That the book is readable at all is largely down to her abilities.

Stas Borodin created the most amazing cover. Stas's art never ceases to astonish and inspire me. A warrior woman in mum jeans! Just: yes!

Ian Drury, my agent, had faith in the book despite it not <quite> meeting his brief as a mainstream commercial blockbuster.

Adrian Collins at *Grimdark Magazine* gave me exposure and support from the beginning. Words can't convey the debt I owe Adrian and the GdM team.

Sammy K Smith, Steve Poore and Michael R Fletcher loved the book as an early manuscript, which helped a lot at a pretty dark time in my life.

Authors whom I admire and am proud to say I can call friends: Adrian Tchaikovsky, Allen Stroud, Steven Erikson, Michael R Fletcher (so good I thanked him twice!), Anne Lyle, Mark Lawrence, Peter McLean, Luke Scull, Jo Hall, Juliet McKenna, Tasha Suri, E M Faulds, Sam Hawke, Graham Austin King and Alicia Wanstall-Burke.

Quint Von Canon, artistic genius who draws things I haven't even written yet. Tom Clews and Rosa Watkinson, who are far better people than I somehow ended up writing them. James Allen Razor—thinking about you and Stacey. Team Grimbold Books, not at all grim in person but very bold indeed. Alex Khlopenko at Three Crows Magazine. Womble. Matt at the *Broken Binding*, seller of the most beautiful books known to humanity. Nick and the team at *Flame Tree Press*. Shawn Speakman at *Grimoak Press*. Alistair and Chloe at *Books on the Hill*. Everyone at the British Fantasy Society. Everyone at BristolCon.

And last but most importantly, the friends and family who give me support, encouragement, and a shoulder to cry on: Nick, Peter and

Ginnie, Karen Fishwick, Judith Katz, Kate Byers, Kate Dalton, Julian Barker, Charlotte Bond, Naomi Scott, Jo Gibson. I couldn't have survived these last years without you.